Jan Vivian

Payment Deferred

A stolen bequest divides a family until an eventful reunion.

by

Jan Vivian

authorHOUSE®

AuthorHouse™ UK Ltd.
500 Avebury Boulevard
Central Milton Keynes, MK9 2BE
www.authorhouse.co.uk
Phone: 08001974150

First published by AuthorHouse 7/24/2007

ISBN: 978-1-4343-1178-8 (sc)

Printed in the United States of America
Bloomington, Indiana

This book is printed on acid-free paper.

Author's Note

Events in this story involving the main characters are fictional. Anna Elisabeth and Henri were the names given to my maternal grandparents; for me, it added context to the story. Crooked Tree Water (Krom Boomsloot) is in the centre of Amsterdam, close to The Damrak. The warehouse where Anna Elisabeth spent some years of her youth still exists but these former working canal-side properties have become luxury homes or offices. The Kahn family in New York, and any associations I have made with a family in Amsterdam, are entirely of my own creation.

Maria, my mother – and the only survivor of eight children born to Anna Elisabeth & Henri – is 94. I dedicate this story to her with my love and thanks for telling me of the city of her birth and her recall of rides on the dray horses used in the conduct of a busy concern.

My associations with Amsterdam and The Netherlands run deep. New York is a city I have visited many times. So, I felt compelled to write out an idea that came to me some time ago.

Jan Vivian - Autumn 2006

1
New York

John Albert Kahn knew of the power that money could bestow, the influence to be exerted by a carefully spent dollar, the return in years to come after a judicious investment, the pleasures to be bought and the silence a regular payment could yield. It helped with the mundane exchanges that passed between people day, night and day again, but these were of no importance now, he had risen above the street.

He was an urbane and charming man of fifty-five, still handsome and impeccably dressed; it was just as Pa would have expected of him. A tailored, dark blue, single-breasted suit of the finest cloth was complemented by a cream cut away collared shirt, the cuffs neatly pressed and just protruding from the jacket's sleeves. John's thinning blonde hair with its streaks of grey was swept straight back to reveal a broad forehead and lent distinction to a high-cheeked face; under a strong square chin were the first traces of a jowl. Thick untrimmed eyebrows framed grey green eyes and a thin nose was turned slightly to the right, as if a blow had been administered at birth to disturb the symmetry of his features. A thin upper lip had a protruding, fleshier companion.

At six foot two John Kahn looked fit, gilded by the soft tan of someone who spent as much of his precious free time as he could muster outside, at the Long Island beach house, when a holiday off a West Indian island on his family's yacht was impossible.

"Decided yet on the tie you're going to wear?" Marie Christine studied her husband closely as she smoothed the jacket over his broad shoulders, the tailoring a perfect fit on his strong physique.

"Hm?"

"Enough," she whispered conceding, but only for an instant, to the caress of roving hands.

"No…you help me decide," John answered before turning to the racks where rows of ties were meticulously arranged.

"Pick one with lots of colour, not just blues and reds; the election's over, so appeal to your wider constituency."

She had yet to dress and fussed over him wearing only a towelling dressing gown, a thin chain and pendant still at her throat. Earlier, she had rewarded him with one of her *"afternoon specials"*, an event that happened only too rarely now but which she knew, and heard from him, John enjoyed.

He faced her once more, holding out the chosen tie and closing the door on the cavernous walk-in closets that lined their joint dressing area. It lay between the high-ceilinged, over-furnished bedroom and the marble-floored bathroom. A mirror fronted secret door led into a small cedar-wood lined steam room and solarium.

John raised his eyebrows in enquiry searching for her nodded approval. He said nothing, rehearsing the text of a prepared speech he was to give before a press conference convened to mark his election victory. Success did not come sweeter than this and he regarded the moment as the culmination of nearly one hundred years of endeavour by his family, the marshalling of resources through good and bad times, and the attention of his lawyers to any potential obstacles.

Marie had been his wife for thirty years, a union made not in heaven but by two families with only one goal, the pursuit of power and influence through wealth. The Hudsons could trace their family to the early days of the Revolution and before, to the British Isles. The émigré Kahn's fled to New York in 1876, the young man and wife, his father's nurse, arriving by steamer from France and settling into a small apartment to start a new life, in commerce and property, any contact with their previous existence all but severed. The Hudsons acquired their status through notable marriages, the acceptance of positions on committees that supervised the growth of the city, and in banking. The Kahn's owed their beginnings on new soil to trade and service, then a cold-eyed determination to profit from their new beginning, a genesis in a hitherto promised land they had only heard of or read about.

Frederick Albert Kahn bought and sold property, invested funds in the import of fruits and spices and picked up on the life he had left behind in Amsterdam following the death of his father. He and his wife Margaretha lived modestly, deferring any enjoyment from their growing prosperity until 1880 when their son, Henry Albert, was born. Frederick had seen the improvements that transport brought to urban life; during his trans-Atlantic voyage he had marvelled at the transformation shipping had undergone following the introduction of the propeller; for him steam driven paddles were from another age. Together the family began to invest in property, buying where they thought the growth in metropolitan areas would provide the buildings to accommodate the inflow of migrants from Europe and beyond.

These investments represented only half of the wealth that they brought with them; it underpinned what they considered to be their family's security. The remainder was speculatively placed in manufacturing businesses and the proceeds carefully reinvested in buildings that yielded an income and a roof for their own expanding interests. But Frederick never forgot the trade he had learnt at school and when returns from his non-property interests dipped he would revert to what he knew best, his food and spices business. People had to eat and the expanding city population meant varied tastes and palettes had to be catered for.

"Not bad, for a fourth generation Kahn." John said, with a satisfied look at his reflection in the mirror. "We almost lost it in the Depression, but Opa always planned for the *'rainy day'*, he spread the risk, even put his assets into gold, and hung in there. Thank God for that! We survived." He pushed the knot of his tie emphatically tight against the collar button.

"With a little help and understanding from...who?" Marie smiled.

She knew the history, the close knit mercantile elite looking after themselves. The two families were only ever associated through business but she had come to know John over the family's summer breaks on Long Island, at their beach house in the late 1960's, a few short years before the draft took him to Vietnam.

"Okay, sweetheart, we couldn't have done it without all of you. *I couldn't* have done it without you beside me." He held her, she smelt of scented soap and a lingering perfume; he undid her robe and stroked the skin of her back; Marie relaxed against him.

"Remember how it can be?" she answered giving him an affectionate kiss before pulling away once more and moved to arrange her own outfit for the evening. A smart figure-hugging two-piece from a boutique on Madison Avenue, in grey with a black velvet collar, was her preferred choice. Black court shoes and the sleekest pair of stockings would complement the ensemble.

John watched her, seated in a chair facing the dressing area; the naked figure he saw posing provocatively in front of the mirror still sought his touch. In profile Marie was tall, her thick blonde hair cut short to the nape of her neck and revealing the slightest lines on her throat. A voluptuous body retained a mannered elegance and nimble movement, just as John remembered from their early days; but the years had given Marie a fleshier sensuality that still made him seek her touch and frenzied clasp. Her body showed only a few of the ravages that bearing and nursing three daughters had wrought upon it. They had been born within four years, in an unfulfilled and frenzied quest for a male heir. She had come close to death following complications with her last born, Dayle, and they had accepted their lot.

Marie saw him staring, his lips parted and he moved his tongue slowly over them. He did it to tease her, to let her know how he felt. *'Yes, you still want me'*, she thought smiling at him in the mirror; you can still make the breath catch in my throat when we are joined, but it was not always like that. She dressed more slowly; she had kept him with her that afternoon like in the early days of their marriage when nothing and no one could interrupt them. She never ceased in her efforts to keep him with her, emotionally and physically.

"Still beautiful, like the girl in slacks and chequered blouse with the sun in your hair".

He stood by her now, his large hands on her shoulders, looking at the black silk underwear so stark against the pale skin. Only her hands had a darker colouring, aged, but still with their slender fingers and neatly varnished nails.

"We've come a long way since seventy two" she replied, letting him kiss her neck but holding his hands.

Marie stared at him and John relaxed his embrace, moving to lean against the wall watching silently as Marie stepped into her skirt and buttoned the jacket, adjusting the fit against her breasts, the cut like a waiter's jacket, longer, and tapered gently at the front, down onto her belly. She moved to the ornate dressing table and put on his engagement ring, given before he left for South East Asia, and the wedding band, a reworked idea from her grand mother's bequest, some of the gold melted into the making of John's ring. It was wedlock, as she had always intended her life to be with him, through good and bad times.

Their marriage had survived; she had kept him in spite of the occasional wounding betrayal. She also knew of the secret that drove him in pursuit of a political career, forged out of the business that he had inherited as the eldest son and which he ran as a CEO and the family holding the controlling shares.

"You're my darling wife, the one who has helped me get this far, channelled the Kahn's ambition and the Hudson's influence."

"Yes," she brushed her hair with busy, almost rough strokes and feeling anxious for him. Ambition was what made John attractive, powerful, but its realisation made her withdraw, into herself. There was so much that he had come to do without her; the Kahn's had a history and from tonight, as in years before, she could only help him with what was in the public domain.

"I still love you, Marie." He took her hand as they walked to the bedroom door, for the last private moments before an evening in the full glare of the media.

"I know – but are you *in love* with me?" She felt his grip tighten only for an instant.

Marie didn't know how the evening would end, if he would return with her or whether Henry, their private and the company's lawyer, would take him away for meetings or some other celebratory diversion. John carried a small leather bag, with a few toiletry items, a clean shirt like he had on now and a brighter tie; anything could happen and John was always one-step ahead, always prepared it seemed. He kept himself mentally and physically sharp, a legacy from his military service away that had never quite deserted him.

"Mervellosa!"

"Gracias, una noche muy importante," Marie answered smiling brightly.

Imperatrice, the Empress, the family's Latino housekeeper for as long as the Kahn's had been married welcomed them, her excited exclamation echoing around the vaulted, marble floored hallway. She stood at the foot of the stairway that led in a graceful arc from the bedroom suites above onto the duplex apartment's gracious reception area below. With her staff of three she ran the household with an assured authority that had been acquired over the years and begun as an awkward teenager in the Hudson family home and continued under Marie's critical gaze.

It had become a partnership, based upon the instinctive acknowledgement of how John expected his home to be managed; it remained a mistress and servant association, but subtle nuances changed their dealings with each other on essential domestic issues into one of kinship that went beyond accepted practice. Boundaries were never crossed but experience and suffering had forged a bond, the heat of Marie's long convalescence being a pivotal moment. Imperatrice had long ago given up any hope of having children but the affection she felt for Marie encompassed Dayle a sickly daughter, John and Marie's third child. She had helped to nurse the frail bundle as if it were her own flesh and blood. Servants had come, and gone, but The Empress and her husband, Manuel, had been compensated for their loyalty. They had the use of a service flat within the condominium block that the Kahn's owned in Park Avenue.

Their duplex apartment, huge even by New York's standards for excess, was kept spotlessly clean. The marble or waxed hardwood floors were polished, the family pictures feather dusted; the drapes were perfectly hung and vacuumed, the metal-ware and silver buffed, the glasses and mirrors in the wet bar sparkled, and the furniture kept in a state of faultless presentation. Nothing was out of its place, the whole maintained as if in a permanent state of readiness for a society magazine to descend upon them, uninvited. It displayed order and control; it was a sun-filled haven of stability. On the terraces, only the potted palm trees, the ferns and neatly trimmed shrubs could show any dissent, fluttering their foliage in the frequent gusting winds.

"Que linda, senora!" She clapped her hands to emphasise her point and raised them to her mouth as if in supplication, or thanks. "Good evening, Mr John."

He gave "Treece', as he liked to call her, a polite acknowledgement and strode purposefully into the living area where he hoped his closest friend and adviser, Henry Lascelles-Brown, or Elbee, would be waiting. Marie turned to allow time for sharing a moment of another important day in the family's history. They were from opposite ends of the social spectrum but there existed a bond of common humanity that Marie never failed to recognise. She had pinned a small jewelled brooch to her lapel and Imperatrice came to her.

"You make a beautiful couple. I still see love between you, not just '*big time*', not just '*business*', all '*show*'." She spoke directly, her almond eyes moving from Marie's as she adjusted the pin, like a nanny preparing her charge before she set off for school. "Mr John will need you now, more than ever."

Marie gave a soft, almost disbelieving, laugh but she nodded, studying her reflection in the hall mirror. Treece could have her moment's latitude.

"No, it's true senora! I see it, like last time, when he come back from the war. He needs you, someone soft but with a strong inner spirit, to help him when things get difficile…tough." She lapsed into her native tongue once more. "Traye lo tranquilidad…you bring him some peace."

"Bueno." Marie smiled, indicating that their conversation was over but that she had gained from the support and encouragement Treece offered.

"I will come to let you know the car has arrived, senora." Manuel would not be driving them. John's own man had been charged with that task.

Marie found John in his study, behind the large leather inlaid desk, with Henry lounging, one leg over the shiny arm of the antiqued brown leather chair and a tumbler of whisky in his hand. He rose out of politeness to her, a habit that had never deserted him in spite of the many years they had known each other.

"Hail to the chief and his lady," he said raising his glass in salute to them.

"One step at a time, Henry," she answered laughing and letting him kiss her cheek. He was a smart operator, a lawyer who enforced the contracts for the Kahn business empire now focussed upon pharmaceuticals and electronics. He was also the guardian of their private life and property interests.

"I wouldn't be paying his extortionate fees if he wasn't ahead of the game or his early warning system began to fail," John said, smiling, as he looked over the rim of his glasses at them. He riffled through papers Henry had brought with him.

"It's all done, I've signed them for you." He put his glasses back in his breast pocket, behind the silk handkerchief, looking younger again.

"Ever watchful," Henry answered equably taking a sip of his drink.

"And if you continue to be so you won't get me on your tail, harassing you. The election was just too close to call."

"Down to the last magazine clip?" Elbee smiled.

"Yeah, a good analogy…we've done that too, eh buddy?" They exchanged glances.

"You got elected," Marie said, standing by John. "You now have to convince the voters, and doubters, that the choice that has been made is a good one, over the time you've been given."

John held up a hand to her and she clasped it.

"See how lucky I am?" he said looking at Henry.

Henry nodded, but remained on the subject.

"You seem surprised to have won it, John. But, I'm telling you, an individual, a guy who is single-minded in his pursuit of the goals he has set is what the city needs right now."

"And they've got him," Marie said.

"Right, they have," Henry said as he stood up and took the papers; and put them into his attache' case. He was a stocky man with grey hair, cut short and a curly fringe hung loosely onto his forehead, as it may have done on a Roman senator. It lent classical distinction to an otherwise ordinary face.

They had met during preliminary training at the Marine Corps base in North Carolina, as twenty-year old draftees, neither choosing student deferment. Without delay they were learning the quick-fire drills, how to identify *'the enemy'* amongst the black pyjama clad Puerto Rican draftees role-playing as peasants in the mock Vietnamese village, and they learnt self-preservation. Their company studied methods on how to avoid the booby traps that could skewer a man with the thinnest piece of sprung wood, and never to accept favours that just might create an obligation or relationship – unless, they learnt later, it suited them only.

Then, to 'Nam, where the experience scarred them, changed young, self confident boys into hollow eyed, sunken cheeked men led by officers not much older than themselves. They were frightened beyond imagining by an unseen enemy, reliant upon each other to get through, colour and race of little consequence when they looked out for each other and their company. John developed a recklessness that bordered on indifference for his own life, but he led by force of character and a happy fatalism that some mistook as a drug induced bravado. Elbee and his men lived to see the truth, he simply saw it as his duty and made the best of the mess his country had got itself into. In the field he cut the men no slack; out of the line he made allowances for his fellow's weaknesses. He had them too.

John kept his betrothal in another world, beyond a vast ocean, and lost himself in excess, coming to crave the body of any doe-eyed girl that they might meet in the bars when on a period of *'R and R'*. Henry developed cunning, hoarding whatever resource necessary to make their existence bearable in a beautiful, decaying and fetid hell-hole where death could be delivered with almost primeval simplicity that no amount of technological power could prevent. Unlike his "best" friend he had become defensive, sought no trouble, but in the fire-fights stayed close, like a guardian. John returned with decorations for bravery, *'sheer lunacy'* Elbee had told Marie, and he with an armoury of experience, to protect a friendship that they told each other would last a lifetime.

John came home to Marie's arms, and a flower-strewn bed, with a tortured mind and yet with the clearest insight into the force for good, and evil, that his country's power could exert. He had learnt to be faithful to himself, the men around him a cloak, but knowing that each of them had confronted their own nemesis and had laughed at the miraculous escapes from bullet, bomb and disembowelling bamboo stake.

Marie had delivered three daughters, conceived in the fevered aftermath of his homecoming when creating life supplanted the babbled ravings that so often punctuated his sleep, in recall of taking life. She would cry as she held him, raw and subdued by the frenzy that bordered upon violence that accompanied his taking of her. She was reduced, at times, to being no more than a receptacle for the outpouring of anguish at his changed circumstances and return once more to an ordered world. Yet for her their frenetic reunions served as way-marks on the search to rediscover the carefree and passionate boy she had fallen in love with. Only, he had returned as a man with a soul in need of her healing, restorative touch.

As she watched the two men talking she understood what Treece had meant. Staying so close to John, loving and tending him, her inner strength and commitment had restored her life's one true man. Their daughters grew up in a loving home and as the horrors in his mind receded so he built up the business with his father, including government contracts, giving and preserving life with one hand and developing the means to take it with another. The early companies, 'Kahn Pharmaceuticals' and 'Kahn Electricals Inc.' grew out of the legacy left by Frederick Albert to his son, then on to John's father, William Albert. Their pictures were neatly displayed on the wall opposite his desk, all of them reinforcing the business mantra handed down, one half to speculate and exposed to the market, the other as security for the family to be held in property – the best once acquired was rarely to be sold.

Now the primary business was medicines and beauty products. John had changed the name, and the ethos of the businesses that now traded under the banner of KahnPulcriMed Inc. They developed, tested, patented and sold their products under that name and ran a nation-wide chain of stores, in prime locations. Everyone was treated with the respect they felt due to them as a customer of PulcriMed; the shortened name was friendlier, it told folks what they could find in the stores and expect from highly trained staff.

John was perplexed that the family's earlier ethos had been so rigidly adhered to until he read papers handed over upon his own father's death. John then understood; his eyes were opened to his great grandfather's beginnings on US soil. He had disliked being the middleman – he sought to produce and sell the goods he was dealing in unless it was the business of foodstuffs, fruits and spices which he left to others. He looked on this as steady cash, unremarkable but necessary. The real goal was the control and manipulation of ideas for profit, and this lay behind all his later business ventures. He had but one business aspiration, the guardianship of patents and manufacturing rights that would ensure a near monopoly in the products that ended up on his pharmacy shelves or in government aid packages.

"C'mon? Let's go and meet the people, all of our people."

John said it with renewed energy and in accord with what Marie had advised him to do. Meeting the press was to be only the start, he hoped, of a busy evening.

2
Amsterdam
It Is A Warm Afternoon Eighteen Months Earlier

Edith Dekker sipped on a hot coffee. The city's noise and bustle swirled about the narrow street flanking the canal; plain trees at the water's edge offered dappled shade onto the pavement where she sat. A meeting had been arranged with a distant cousin. Edith could not remember, exactly, when she had last seen Gerard Kahn but the most vivid memory was of a family reunion fifteen years ago – the day she had first met him. The photograph of them together showed a tall, gangling, good looking athletic youth with rather too long sandy coloured hair, the image spoiled by the heavy glasses he had to wear that made the soft grey green eyes stare too intently. But Edith remembered a strong and attractive spirit, Gerard's deep intelligence and his inquisitive mind. He was a kindred soul and she had need of him now.

"What's keeping you?" she said softly and tapped the cover of a fake leather bound folder. As if on cue her mobile rang.

"Hey, Edith? I'm late…by a few minutes, sorry!" Gerard was jovial, as she remembered him. The years fell away.

"Twenty minutes! It's not a *'few minutes!'*" she laughed. "I forgive you… but it'll cost you a drink."

"I'm nearby, really."

"At least you're still coming to meet me; no distractions or work to prevent you staying a while, I hope?"

"No. It'll be great to see you again. I won't be long."

"I'm outside, on the terrace. I'll look out for you," she said relieved that Gerard had not called to cancel their meeting. He was gone.

The café was in a favourite part of Amsterdam, at the heart of what was still called the Old City. Yet she knew of earlier changes to the city's character and had witnessed some of the transformation during her own lifetime, but none of this mattered now. The area retained the deepest family connections, for her they were associations to a past that had been awakened by her mother Helene Katherina a woman of inspiring loyalty. Edith was never left in any doubt; she too had Kahn ancestry and the tale of the family's past mattered. The blood-line may have been thinned by marriages over the generations but a silver thread was woven through her lineage back to another Helene, one who died in eighteen seventy six and to her only surviving daughter, Anna Elisabeth, a niece to Frederick Albert Kahn.

Edith was removed from her ancestor by three generations but she had studied the family history, traced the links back to the merchant family who had settled in the centre of her home city as émigrés, some from Alsace Lorraine, others from a region that was now Poland, from Koningsberg. The threads may have been weakened by the passing of the years, but the papers and photographs that she had so carefully assembled and duplicated for safe keeping fostered a deep sense of pride. The thick card on which the pictured family gatherings were mounted brought the personalities back to life and put flesh on the stories and images. She could hold the late nineteenth century in her hands and looking down the street on either side of the café imagined a slower paced world, before the city by the water was cut off from its historic life's source.

Gerard saw Edith before she noticed him walking towards the café's entrance. He had left his bicycle tied to a railing around the corner. She looked startled at being caught so unawares and clutched at a folder as though it contained all of her prized possessions. He smiled and then laughed with pleasure.

"Hey!"

"Gerard!" She removed the fashionable sunglasses and met his gaze.

"How are you, cousin?" He kissed her cheeks, three times. "It has been too long, far too long" he said in his relaxed manner and pulled at a chair, waiting for Edith before sitting down. "You look very well." Gerard stretched out his long legs and lounged back in the rattan seat but his eyes rested on her.

Yes, he had remembered correctly; she had attentive blue eyes. But the mass of blonde curls had gone, to be replaced by a neater cut that left her hair softly turned out at the neck, and with a haphazard parting that made it fall on either side of her oval face. The navy blue sleeveless dress with a modest v-neck accentuated a slender attractively formed figure.

"Thanks. It has been a long time," she said and held a hand out to him. Gerard took it. He remembered their intense conversations during one sunny reunion. "You haven't changed so much, outwardly anyway – so far as I can tell," she said.

Edith was an enigma to him. Her pictures showed an attractive, even beautiful woman of thirty-four whom he assumed would have a lover or partner. Instead, he heard only that she kept herself aloof from such entanglements and devoted time to her profession, as an Accountant in a specialised field. She investigated fraud and malpractice but worked as an independent, freelance consultant. Her activities mirrored his own work but he had studied Economics and turned to journalism to enliven what might otherwise have been a mundane existence.

"What can I get for you?" the waitress asked.

"Mine's a beer...and for you?" Gerard turned to Edith. "I owe you a drink for my late arrival."

"The same," Edith smiled.

"You've moved on from student dress," he said when they were alone again and looked approvingly at her. "As you can see, I'm stuck in a fashion limbo." He rubbed at his chin, the stubble growth was already apparent but it had been an early start to his day at De Telegraaf where he could wear the jeans and open-necked shirt he arrived in, a soft suede jacket lending scant formality to his appearance. "I'm sorry to be so casually dressed."

"Don't worry," she answered with a note of approval. "I had an image of you from the last time we met. This is like a uniform to me, a more conventional approach to the day, which you don't have. I also remember that of you."

There was the hint of finding this attractive in him. His lightly tanned, square jawed face was unlined and she studied him closely from behind the darkened lenses of her sunglasses. His hair was an unruly, curly unkempt sandy coloured mop that grew down over his collar and was not in the fashion of the day. He looked like a mature student trying to catch up with a time that had long-since passed.

"Are you going to clutch that folder of yours so tightly all the time we are together?" he joked but fell silent as the waitress came with their drinks.

"What?" Edith replied and looked down at her hands. "No…No!" The folder was placed on her side of the table but one hand rested close-by still touching it. Gerard observed this and smiled.

"Here's to meeting again." He touched her glass with his and began to drink quickly, noisily, sliding the foam from his lips with the edge of a thumb and licked off the residue. "Sorry, I'm parched after racing to get here."

"Be yourself." Edith stared across the canal over to the beautifully gabled houses that were also reflected in the water. "I'm glad that you've been able to set aside some time to meet me – there's lots to talk about, and to show you."

"I was persuaded of its' importance to you, Edith. Besides, why shouldn't we meet up, anyway?" They ordered lunch, both taking some meat filled croquettes with a salad and extra beers. Gerard asked after her family, his voice light and convivial and they relaxed. The breeze wafted through the trees and sunlight fell on them then left the terrace in shade. It was a perfect afternoon now.

"They're fine but quite unaware that I am meeting you."

"Mine too. Why should that be?" he asked fixing her with an inquisitive stare for the first time as they took a deeper interest in each other and forsook any reticence.

"The reasons may be in here, in this folder I can't let go of. But first tell me about what you've done since we last met. I've kept a few cuttings of articles that you've written. I have watched your progress, from afar."

"Sh, you'll embarrass me," he winked and gave Edith a smile.

He was often told that he had retained a physical presence, kept hold of his youthful vigour and enthusiasm that the women in his life seemed to find attractive; his impaired vision offered an unlikely advantage over his peers at De Telegraaf newspaper. His colleagues could only wonder how he managed it, winning the hearts of so many with a look of the intense grey green eyes behind the heavy lenses. The very modern frames gave him the aura of a deeply academic man and lent his appearance a seriousness that he reserved only for the right occasion. There was something anarchic in his laughter, in his whole demeanour that stemmed from his studious and contemplative nature. He showed apparent respect for obvious and not self-proclaimed authority but a rebellious streak invariably led him down the path of enquiry. *Underneath every stone there lurked…something?* It was a favourite means to explain his inquisitiveness and lapses in respect.

"I don't know where to start," he said. "You may have discovered from the contents of my work that people are never quite what they seem."

Some saw his attitude as cynicism, a deep mistrust of the human psyche but to him it was merely the quickest of observations on what he discerned as a shallow front to an outwardly worthy person.

Edith watched as Gerard pushed his hair back over a high forehead. She had seen pictures of him with a pony tail but the locations he filed his reports from had usually been exotic and overseas; so, she had made allowances. It was a less rebellious image she saw now yet she knew it was there, under the surface. Reading his work left you with the impression that a careful choice of words could so easily be reinterpreted to paint an altogether different picture. Presumably he had now achieved a level of seniority that carried with it certain standards of behaviour.

"From what I have read you think few deserve true respect just a certain level of tolerance?"

"I *try* to find the best qualities in my subjects, all of the time."

"I remember that about you too, there is no malice in what you write merely acute observation…and a way with words." She gave a knowing laugh.

"Don't embarrass me, I didn't know I had such a fan in my family."

"Am I family? Do you think with the long absences or separations we can describe our relationship in those terms?"

"Sure! In spite of the passage of time and having been away a great deal; I haven't had the opportunities to keep in touch with everyone…I've even lived abroad, in New York."

"Have you?" Edith sat up.

"Hey, steady on!" he laughed in response to her grip on his arm.

"I didn't know that, I thought you had gone on an assignment and come back…just a quick visit, nothing more."

"What *have* you got in there?" he said, attempting to take the folder. "Is it the contents that makes you so jumpy?"

She stared back at him, seemingly distracted. "What? Oh, no, it's not that," she quickly corrected. "I'll tell you all about it later, after we've eaten."

At the age of thirty four he had achieved a position that was founded upon his investigative skills, a dogged persistence to find the truth and an incisive mind that those who first met him could only guess at or glimpsed in the keen focus of his eyes upon them. The special glasses he often wore spared him the extreme fatigue experienced during the research phase of a story; transferring the notes to the page and drafting the text of an article caused the least trouble. To Monique, his current live-in-live-out girlfriend – she couldn't decide and the peripatetic arrangement suited him - the bifocal glasses detracted from his good looks, the strong set of his mouth. She told him people would pay more attention to his eyes than be engaged by the even toothed smile he could give and his hearty laugh in response to a joke. More often it was in reaction to the ignorance he saw in people of everyday realities in the political and business world that the modern media either glossed over or left unreported. It became a duty to comment upon and expose what he found.

"To get back to your question…I don't give up easily, I stick to the task and explore every source for material." He believed himself to be a tenacious journalist, not given to flamboyance or a quick assessment. He could be blunt to the point of rudeness but his upbringing often made him regret such bad manners.

"I know of or have seen the work that has gone into what you have written."

"I loathe the deadlines I have to meet, most of the time. I loathe them with a passion that others reserve for football, a national obsession that I do not share," he said with a derisive laugh. He was physically active, drove rarely and instead cycled, walked or jogged everyday. Existing on little sleep was a way of life he had discovered early and he possessed prodigious stamina. "They tell me I am a driven man, to the point of obsession about some things." He shrugged. "I have a fear of failing at what I love to do, probably like you and everyone else in this city."

"It's motivation enough for me," Edith answered.

"It was a great surprise when you called me…two weeks ago. Are you going to tell me about the project or will I have to work hard to find out? You got me interested…intrigued even, and there's a family connection."

"Possibly, but we'll have to check it out, Gerard." She looked across the narrow space between them and met his gaze upon her.

"I didn't know there were any secrets," he said evenly. "Your voice…the way you hint at things, you sounded so sure."

"Oh yes, but I'll let you know more after that." Edith pointed to the waitress as she came up to them with their lunch tray.

"Well, I guess I'll have to carry on talking and bore you into telling me something more."

"That's fine by me."

Gerard laughed. "Tease, and I'll have to pay for lunch as well I suppose?"

"I may share that much with you."

"Very well, for what it may be worth later. As far as I have understood the history, my father's family, the Kahns moved to Rotterdam, where they live to this day, in nineteen thirty nine. Why I don't know as they had most of their business interests here. Even while I was studying at the university, when I first met you, I felt more at home here in Amsterdam. I knew we had associations with the place and the harbour." Gerard stopped talking as Edith produced one photograph, kept loose at the back of her folder and gave it to him. "What have you got there?"

"It's a picture, of the warehouses the Kahns had, not far from here, in the late nineteenth century," she answered precisely.

"Where did you get it?"

"Later," she smiled. "I'll tell you all about it…later."

"Look, we can play this game, or twenty questions if you want, but I haven't got all afternoon to prolong it. There are gaps in my knowledge and I know that a space has been carefully but not obviously maintained between two sides of the family. I know nothing of the origins."

"Really?"

"Yes, really," he said with a soft note of irritation. "Snippets of news come over the wires to me from home occasionally, gossip if you like, but I'm too busy to dig too deeply into it all. Modern life is dysfunctional, why should our family be so very different?"

"No reason at all, you're right. Only I think there is something now that will change that view."

"Really?"

"Yes, in my opinion," she laughed softly and glanced sideways at him. *"Yes, really."*

"You know what my interest are…global trade and issues on the periphery of international dealings, the powerlessness of weaker developing countries to withstand the influence of larger economies. There is the tyranny of an all-powerful state and how it deals with it's own citizens…I've got enough there to be getting on with and to research and think about." He fell silent and ate his meal.

Edith had finished and now regarded him over her beer glass. "Our lunch will be worth your trouble, I promise."

The irony of his position on world politics was not lost on him; he was based in the home of the Dutch East Indies Company. He knew of slavery and the trade in people and of the colonies his country had maintained, but what had all that to do with their family? There were plenty of current controversies in the world to inspire the analytical invectives that he wove with his deft use of language into articles for the newspaper. He never spoke directly of his political leanings, his articles commented acidly on all sides of the political argument if the need arose. Instinctively, he was for the individual, the underdog, but the pervading thread in his work was the harsh realism encountered in the world as he travelled. It remained unfiltered from his perceptive vision and he seemed quite unafraid to express an opinion; he did so to stimulate debate, or sometimes the heated exchanges that could appear in the correspondence columns of his 'paper.

Retractions or apologies for what had been written had never been sought of him. He had yet to endure the contortions of getting out of a fix like that. He now had a reputation that won his editor's forgiveness if a deadline stretched out or he took up more column space than had been originally allotted to him. A personal following had been established, both at the newspaper and from the occasional magazine articles that he wrote or put his name to as a 'contributor'.

"Have you visited my web-site?"

"Yes. You explain your opinion on globalisation issues very well."

"I get too many hits to reply to all of them…that's if they leave any message."

"It's a reflection of the following you have built up."

"It includes you?"

"Yes, but that goes back to the reunion."

"I had no idea." He took his glasses from the breast pocket of his jacket and Edith gasped, putting a hand to her mouth as Gerard put them on. "What is it?" he said looking at her now with eyes greatly magnified.

"I'm sorry," she whispered, "I'm so sorry." She looked away only to return to him knowing that his eyes had not strayed from her.

"I still need these. I can't function properly without them, I'm sorry to say. At least that hasn't changed about me one little bit. Do I frighten you, or put you off that much?" He said it breezily making light of her reaction and gave her a winning smile. "I can take an honest opinion…from you at least."

"No…no." She held out a hand to him again. Gerard felt compelled to take it. "I simply thought it was a temporary phase you had to endure." She faltered. "I'm so ashamed to have reacted in that way." She even blushed.

"Forget it," he squeezed Edith's hand. "Really…forget it."

"Yeah…"

"Edith, listen? I wear them as little as I have to which, as you can imagine in my work, is most of the time…even now, here." He smiled and she seemed to have been won over to the idea of his personality being quite altered in the wearing of them. He was not about to wreck a reunion by wearing his glasses if he could avoid it but the folder held such interest for him that he squeezed her hand tightly once more.

Edith read the sign. "My turn to speak, Ger."

"I'll just get comfortable," he smiled then lay back in his chair with his eyes closed. "You were saying?"

3

"What I am going to show you are photographs, family groups and individuals." She prodded him with a folder, laughing. "Pay attention."

"I'll try." Only now did he notice that there was a slimmer volume beneath the one she held out, with its green fake leather binding.

"They have been collected from my family and in particular my mother who maintains an interest that is passed down, from woman to woman; she knows why."

"And in there, what have you got?"

"The purpose of my meeting with you...the whole reason for me seeing you."

"Not because it's just me?" he teased.

"I thought of no one else who could help me." She stared unblinking at him and Gerard took off his glasses. "And...yes, I wanted to see you again... this simply gave me an added reason for doing so."

He asked a straightforward question. "What is at stake here?"

"Nothing...and then, maybe everything."

"Don't talk in riddles."

"Look at the first album, I'll tell you a story. You may have heard it..."

"May I interrupt with a question?"

"No...or not many. Now, take the book."

Each photo that Edith carried in the first folio to be shown to him had been carefully annotated on the back by a past relative; the names were neatly written in blue ink; alongside them were the dates of birth and marriages. Poignantly, many recorded an early death from the illness often visited on large families, from tuberculosis and even cholera. The city was not always the healthiest place to live; in spite of the cold and bracing winds off the Zuider Zee that its' hardy inhabitants sought, the construction of the city's main railway station affected the route of an invigorating walk along a harbour wall.

Many of the names Edith had seen neatly written on the photos were adopted by following generations; their use perpetuated a family tradition.

Gerard began to study the earlier pictures; one, of a strikingly handsome woman, in a high collared close fitting dress held his attention.

"You will see the name Helene crop up, many times," Edith said softly then left him to continue until he came to a family tree, written out by Edith on light blue paper. "I will tell you now what I know...of the history."

She had prepared for the meeting and Gerard signalled his attention to her as he sat back in his chair again.

"Helene is also my middle name. It had been given to my mother and grandmother before her, but not to Anna Elisabeth, Helene Katherina's daughter. Her mother lived so the circumstances did not merit its use; besides, her father Peter Gierritz had asked his only daughter of one thing, a promise solemnly tendered by one so young and following the death of her own mother. One day, Peter asked, if she too were blessed with a daughter she would christen her with a name that also included that of Helene. It would be in memory of a woman tragically taken from the family."

"How?" Gerard asked.

"Some fever," she replied and held her fingers to his lips. "Let me speak... the christening name served another purpose. It brought to mind that Anna's inheritance from her mother, Helene Katherina Kahn had been taken, and her father duped by a brother in law...a certain Frederick Albert Kahn."

"What?" Gerard slammed shut the book. "What? How can you possibly know that?"

"Letters and word of mouth...between women, on my side of the family," Edith said evenly and she saw that no one paid them the least attention, in spite of Gerard's exclamation. "I have them," she said calmly before adding, "and, be careful with my book! Gerard...please?"

"Ja...ja! Okay." Gerard thrust his glasses back on **and** reopened the folio.

"Frederick, Helene's brother no less, had absconded with Helene's share of their father's bequest...it was a tough time for the family. Helene's father died shortly after Helene's own death. Frederick's father, we can only guess...was heartbroken at her loss to him. There was a lot to deal with...to cope with, and a heart-broken Peter, Helene's husband felt unable to prove the wrong done to his daughter and twin sons...or, we can only guess, pursue Frederick. He was too proud, a respected business man and yet taken in so easily. He felt deeply ashamed at confessing to being duped. For the boys he would provide. In time, he would find them work in the family business...they were importers and sold foods and spices, from their warehouses on Crooked Tree Water off the Dam...it's not so far from here."

"I know."

"For Anna a dowry had been lost and with it any realistic hope of a well connected marriage. And so, she lived with two aged aunts and cared for them. Peter soon re-married; he overcame somehow...in spite of the times, any softly spoken criticism of the haste in which he re-ordered his life. Most understood his decision but few knew that his new wife lost to infant illnesses the daughters *she* longed for. Anna Elisabeth remembered only too well the wounding remarks spoken under her stepmother's breath who was jealous of her. *Why had Anna survived to torment and remind her of her own loss...the death of her infant girls?"*

"How do you know all this?"

"Mothers and daughters care more for family history, we hoard things or keep things safe so that memories survive...we make sure they don't get lost."

"Or get thrown away by unsympathetic men."

"Well...that's another way of looking at it."

"Go on," Gerard sat back again, he had seen enough of the pictures; instead he looked at Edith who sighed deeply.

"It had happened so long ago. The family...some of them anyway, recovered from the deceit and unhappiness." She took the album and opened it at a page that had a group portrait, stiffly posed, the ladies seated with their men behind them, faces held up to the camera and with only the hint of a smile; it was more often a smirk. "Look at this, look at the richness and texture of the clothes conveyed by the photographs! It is a testimony, their expressions provide evidence, that they had to get on with things."

"But, who are they?"

"Who are they?" Edith repeated, staring at him in surprise. "Do you mean that...that you've never seen these before?"

"No, never." He looked again with renewed attention at the pictures. "No, I'm sure of it. If they were ever shown to me I have forgotten...completely."

"But...they're Kahns! Ger, look *that's* Frederick Albert." Edith touched his arm as if to confirm the shock she felt on hearing his admission.

He shook his head; the picture meant nothing to him; no memories existed of sitting with his own parents to go through a family photo gallery; it never featured in his life, at least not to review pictures so far back in time.

"And all the other pictures?"

"Gierritz's – my great grandparents, your great uncles and aunts from more than one hundred years ago." She looked closely at him. He gave not the slightest flicker of recognition that he knew any of them or that he recognised a picture. It was unbelievable; there was nothing in his manner that suggested any connection with the people gathered in the portraits.

"I've got some questions to ask later" was all he could say. "Go on, tell me more."

"Anna was undaunted by the life she had to lead, Helene had inscribed each of her children's Bibles with a personal message. For her it simply said, *'When you are disheartened or ill at ease think of them your riches soon could please'.*" Edith showed him a copy of the page. She had read the words many times and held the Bible that was a prized possession of her mother's, the now soft leather cover was torn, tattered and scuffed, but the words were clear and unmistakable.

"I see you've written out some of the history," he said. Putting on his glasses he sat silently to read. "May I have a coffee?" he asked without looking up.

"Yes…in a minute," she replied, momentarily distracted. The waitress was nowhere to be seen. "You'll have to wait." Edith pressed on.

"Anna divided her time between her father's home and that of her aunts. Anna showed resourcefulness, laughter was on her lips and in her personality, there was strength in her young and slender body. She earned a small living running a day school for children of merchants in the area of Crooked Tree Water. Some even came from the wealthier families on the Damrak, by the Palace or the homes along the canals that girdled the old city. The high ceilings and solid floors, the interest prompted in young minds on the origins of the foods and spices from all over the world made her school in the high gabled warehouse a haven for knowledge and a source of mirth, music and games.

Her accomplishments knew no bounds in the small circle of families that grew to know the deftness of touch and affection for her young charges. Only, none of this prepared her for the love she found with Henri a skilled silver smith and glass-worker, in crystal, who had been retained by Peter to make an anniversary gift for Anna's step mother. He was studious and blessed with a creative talent in his hands and eyes that made Anna watch silently. Chaperoned by a friend she would be permitted to observe him at work in the small atelier he shared with a partner; the commissions from Peter helped to set the fledgling business on a flight that offered modest prosperity.

'God given' – those were the words Henri used to refer to his talent. He taught Anna about religion and theosophy although the boundaries were never so distinct and the coloured drawings he pored over were small works of incomprehensible art. They married in eighteen ninety-eight, Anna's twenty fifth birthday and with the passing of the years Anna forgave the wrong done to her and the twin brothers who lived and worked nearby. Henri instilled the strongest belief in the virtues of doing so but she never *forgot* and could not refrain from wondering what might have become of her, and Henri, had some financial security been available. Competition from Japan was already making inroads into the viability of the silver smith businesses in the city. Revenge was not in her nature but she cultivated the belief in her children that wrongs had to be righted, not out of vengeance but as a consequence of a deepening sense of equity between human beings."

Gerard looked up when the waitress arrived to take their order and cleared away the remnants of the lunch.

20

"It's a compelling story, and one I have been totally ignorant of." He caught Edith looking at him. "You have brought the story to life."

"I've rehearsed it," she said honestly. "There's not much more to the first part," Edith went on. "Shall I tell you about it or do you want to read?"

"I am enjoying the way you tell it, but let me see what you've written first." Gerard turned again to the neat script. "Explain it in your own way, I'll want you to do that," he said without looking up, "in a moment?"

She continued in spite of him.

"Until her dying breath in nineteen sixty eight, just four years before my birth, she held onto the belief that a wrongdoer should be relieved of the burden he carried or in some way to be absolved for a misdemeanour. She could not explain whether this extended to reconciliation between the parties to the wrong."

She fell silent and watched Gerard read; her mind followed the threads of the story.

Peter Gierritz never forgave himself for the lapse in his usually watchful character. Edith had read that much in some of the letters her mother kept in a letterbox that had once rested on his desk. The deep blue ink stains had been lovingly polished into the light brown wood with its gleaming surfaces. Peter had suspected no duplicity in his brother in law, Frederick. There had always been a concerned expression on his face when they met, a solicitous word for the family even if he too grieved for the loss of his father. The offer of taking care of the inheritance that the children would be the beneficiaries of was seen as well intentioned and would assist Peter in his own time of grief and caring for a family of infants.

"He had taken the receipt for the funds handed over to Frederick, that much Peter's letters indicated, but it was the last time the two of them were to meet. The receipt disappeared into a lawyer's Deed box for the Gierritz family...that's all I know...never to be looked on again or found ...so the story went. By the time Peter's suspicions were aroused Frederick had disappeared with his mistress. They were on a steamer from France to America he heard later but the obstacles to pursuit or recovery of the funds were too great. He believed all too briefly that Frederick might yet do the honourable thing, treat the money as a means to start a new life...and pay it back when he could."

"But he didn't?"

Edith shook her head. "No, he disappeared without a further word being written to the family left behind and robbed in Amsterdam."

"What then?"

"Anna's father turned his attention to matters closer to his hearth. There was the question of finding a new wife to care for him and more importantly to tend the needs of his surviving children. Helene had borne him eight, amazingly…but only three outlived her."

"What happened," he asked, "to the wicked uncle?"

"He didn't disappear as many hoped, or thought that he had…only no one can say if any record of letters or telegrams from much later still exist. To all intents, from my side of the family, the man simply vanished. Your side of the family would really know the answer to that."

"Well, I've never heard any of it; if my father has anything of record he would have told me…or shown it to me, surely?" Gerard shifted in his chair. All that he could remember of older family photographs were those of his immediate ancestors, of his own father's bloodline. Absent, he thought, were pictures of the kind that Edith had just shown him. "Have you asked to see me in order that you can fill the gaps in your narrative?"

Edith parted her lips and gave a small smile.

"In a way…whatever your family has in store might help. But there's a much bigger picture to draw out, and one that I need you for, cousin. There are certain issues that I can not get out of my mind, clues to the personalities that may become involved and that I have assembled in the other folder. Take a close…a *very close* look at those now."

4

"How do you know so much? The detail suggests it is a story fed with mother's milk, at the breast." Gerard spoke as he thumbed through the stiff pages, the photographs covered by a thin film to avoid soiling them; they were all copies, he could tell from their grainy texture.

"Not quite," Edith answered.

"Well then, someone must be perpetuating a grudge, and after all this time…it's unhealthy, destructive even."

"If it dominated lives that would certainly be true; but, history is all around you, in these streets and the buildings, in the canals you cycle over or pass; it is buried in the mud, in the canals all around us." Edith pointed to the reflections on the water, the buildings a crinkled outline on the surface with a blue backdrop. "In this case it is an episode in our family history that re-surfaces every time you look at a photograph…or hear someone speak of a family member, however remote."

"We don't."

"I remember, and we still have them on the wall, pictures of the family, groups that you were told about…who they were…it was a tapestry woven by my mother of people she knew, was told about or vaguely remembered. It has all remained with me."

"To this day," Gerard smiled, but he dropped his voice. "And, are these recollections so frequent that a wound, or a sore, has to be continually picked at rather than allowed to heal over?"

"No!"

"Then why this interest, after so many years? A distant event, with no record? Dare I say it…it's obsessive even?" He looked at her. Edith had spoken without rancour but he sensed that she wished to move on. He held out his hand. "I'd better look at '*Volume Two*', the one you clutch so tightly."

"Soon, look at this first." Out of her handbag she gave him a newspaper cutting from the 'New York Times'. The headline was in the 'paper's distinctive typeset:

JOHN KAHN for Mayor?

Gerard shrugged his broad shoulders. The writing of the article wasn't bad; he had spent enough time there to get accustomed to their quirky journalistic style. He had even made his own attempts at copying the use of language, the turn of phrase, and even the choice of the vernacular in his own articles. But, his following looked to him for his own voice, the incisive investigation, the exposure of waste or excess; they found human frailty laid bare often enough in his prose, whether the subject's pockets were full or holed and emptied.

"So, his name's Kahn," he said mischievously. "You only need to travel… what? 100 kilometres east of here…a short Panzer drive, in fact, and you'll find Kahn's are quite common."

Edith smiled but she was not put off.

"It also happens to be your name. I didn't ask to see you to discuss ethnicity or the place of birth of the Kahn's." The smile had for the moment gone, to be replaced with a very direct stare of her beautiful eyes.

"Ja, okay…bad joke."

He turned the pages quickly, to gather an idea of the predominant theme, the thread that joined the photographs together. It was more like a scrapbook than a montage of pictures; there were short articles and hand-written notes amongst them, all anecdotal in her attempt to set out a story. But Edith had made the collection evolve into something more and Gerard turned back to the earliest pages before setting the book down on the table.

"I'll tell you what I see, after a quick scan."

"I had hoped you would take more time; let me order some more drinks, a coffee maybe?"

23

"Yes, fine, please." He did not smile and sat back and tapped the fingers of his hands together. Let Edith explain her motives, he thought. "Leave it, thanks...I don't really need another drink...so, tell me, what am I missing? What do you see?"

She took the press cutting and returned the folded paper to her neat, discreet blue leather handbag. For the photo albums she had brought a briefcase with gold fastenings, her name on a tooled leather tag fixed to the handle. Gerard observed, taking in all the hints at an ordered mind so delightfully encased.

"I don't want to lose anything," she remarked, catching his studied glances and smiling. "It has taken me a long time to get this far, and to collect all the items you have seen."

"You're marvellous! I could use you as a research assistant, only you have a much better paid job."

"Yes, but depending on how events or meetings unfold I may give it all up, for a while."

"What? For these cuttings?"

"Don't be so hasty, you mean?"

"Uh...huh!" His earlier look of disbelief had turned to one of interest.

"Let me explain," she said drawing her chair closer. To his eyes Edith was a slender beauty with an inquisitive nature and a sparkling intelligence, perhaps with a fertile imagination that did not complement these attributes he recognised. "The pictures tell only part of a story, not an obvious one but a tale that may not be so far fetched...and...it may yet yield dividends."

"Is it a story that is solidly grounded, based on fact or is it embroidered or fashioned by a wish to only see what...."

Edith interrupted. "To see what I wish to see? No, it's not that." She flicked at her hair and opened the album as she gave her emphatic reply. "Now, don't interrupt me!"

Gerard held his hands up in mock surrender. "Promise."

Her finger pointed at a picture he had not come to.

"Who's that?" The story was to be retold, in her own particular way.

"Don't be angry with me."

"I'm not," Gerard answered on a mobile phone, held tight against his ear, as he pedalled through the traffic on his way back to the office. "Not now, and in any case, I wasn't angry...not with you."

"That's good." She sounded relieved. "Just keep an open mind, and please stay in touch," Edith asked.

"Ja...okay." He had taken her home and mobile 'phone numbers and stored them with a distinctive speed-dial code.

"It's nothing personal, don't misunderstand my motives or leave with that impression." His angry stare as she recounted elements of the story had indicated the effect her revelations were having upon him.

"You've left me with more questions than answers, Edith. There's a lot to think about, and, come to terms with."

"Okay...I accept that. You'll get answers next time...see you very soon, I hope?"

"Yes, bye! Gotta go!" He negotiated an awkward traffic junction and struggled to put the 'phone back in his pocket.

His mind churned over the remarks she had made and at the recall of the faces he had seen, so formal in the posed photographs with the painted, scenic backdrops. He could not dismiss so easily the clever associations she had brought to mind; their placement in the small folio had a logic for which he gave Edith credit. Granted, she had ordered the images to provoke one conclusion but Gerard allowed her a concession; it took little effort to see that however they were arranged the casual viewer of the faded records would turn back, then forward, scroll through the memories they conveyed and draw a similar conclusion. In spite of their relationship, a distant one, he had to remain objective but Edith had an answer for every question and met his interrogating tone with a soft smile before she replied.

A reasonable doubt remained, that John, the candidate, and Frederick Albert Kahn were related. The mayoral hopeful could be a distant cousin. Edith was right; it would be interesting to check it out, for a number of compelling reasons, both personal and professional. A story lay in there, from whichever vantage point you cared to stand and survey the panorama of history.

The features editor had sent him several e-mails demanding a meeting; as he gathered up the first drafts of a piece on the sales of patented medicines to Third World countries his mind turned to the avenues of enquiry opening up; he thought of the strands to Edith's story.

"I've got more than one reason to see her again," he recounted, taking the treads of the stairs to the floor above two-at-a-time. A text message had been sent; he had decided to help Edith and to satisfy his own curiosity about an untold 'family' story.

5

'T Hof had been a family home since the nineteen thirties, in a district to the north of The Hague, sheltered from the North Sea by a wide expanse of forested dunes. Inland, farmsteads could be found, the grazing land divided into small parcels separated by tree-lined ditches and home to a wide variety of fowl and wading birds. Heron, accustomed to the presence of humans were commonplace and continued undisturbed in their measured search for fish beneath the algae drifts upon the water. Despite modern development, and the interruption of views to a distant steeple across the polderland, the area clung tenaciously to its character and was much-loved by Gerard's parents.

The mornings of early autumn were best, when wreaths of mist rose from the damp fields shrouding livestock as they grazed, like hummocks in a swirling grey cloud. An early shift-worker's motor-bicycle would shatter the stillness, the illusion of tranquility dispelled until the soft spoken 'morning' of a passing cyclist restored the pace of a human world, of sinew and flesh, not combustion and crazed metal.

He arrived from Amsterdam by train and as usual walked along the lanes he had frequented in his childhood; some were now choked with cars. The neighbourhood was still, wooded and held the unmistakable feeling of wealth; the trees had been no more than saplings in his youth but in many places now closed off vistas and put in the shade his former playgrounds.

The Kahn's had chosen the house for its convenience and architectural style. The situation was handy for their business interests, in both Amsterdam and Rotterdam. If isolation was required T'Hof offered it, set behind the high and imposing entry gates with their small hand-crafted red brick-pillars. The property benefited from a long and narrow driveway with paddocks to each side; cows lazed in the long grass; the whole offered a diversion from every-day cares providing a calming pastoral scene. Close your eyes and you could almost feel its rural seclusion; but the noise and bustle, the concrete mantle with its steel framed office and business complexes were all too near.

The influence of corporate status building was imprinted on his landscape, but Gerard acknowledged that it brought prosperity even if it was at the expense of what he, unfashionably, held to be the essence of his country's character. Ruisdael and Avercamp's scenery had long been buried by the bulldozer's scrape. The windmills looked incongruous, but the mind's eye could still conjure up a different world; what had been so familiar was now compressed for the easier pursuit of commerce and service. The western seaboard of his country was being assaulted, it seemed almost daily, by new projects that widened the gulf between a romanticised genteel past and the brash inflexibility of the future. The pervasive influence of another culture and style of building, the acquisitive maw of another world was everywhere or had to be replicated.

"Is this what globalisation has to offer?" he thought as he strode to the family home; it was a horrible phrase yet he could not deny the boundless come-and-go of trade, an amorphous aggregate of human existence. The small and weak *had* to work with their larger brethren, it presaged improvement, so

they were told, for the weak. He saw little evidence to reassure him; he had looked hard, so hard it had made his eyes, ears and brain hurt from the pain of denial; he had rejected the new mantra – membership of a global village would reduce tensions, increase wealth and well-being.

"Yeah...right!" She hadn't spelt it out, he would hear of it soon enough, but Edith was opening up the door to another investigation that had at its centre the same tenets of modern business that he had so often dissected in his articles. Only now there was a new twist – it could involve a member of the family. It was too good to be true.

The trail had to start, somewhere.

"Jesus...the stolen inheritance! Not that fairy tale again! It comes around every few years, like an asteroid visible only at certain times." Gerard's father looked first at him and then with a shrug of his shoulders to his mother. They were all gathered on the terrace, at the rear of the house, the orange awning had been folded away.

"So, you *know*?" He saw his brother, Willem, shake his head. "How come I, or we, never came to hear about it?"

"So we didn't know, so what?" He found his brother's phlegmatic reply irritating; he did not possess the same spirit of enquiry or curiosity.

"Yes, so what?" His mother took Willem's side, but he now surmised for different reasons.

"Because..."

"It's been years," his father interrupted. "Here's your beer. Who's put you up to this?"

Gerard looked at the walls of the house, illuminated by shafts of late afternoon sunlight through the trees. It seemed a pity to wreck the calm of a peaceful evening so soon.

"Edith...Edith Dekker."

"That old maid?" His mother laughed.

"She's a beautiful and intelligent woman, and is certainly not an *old maid.*"

"From what I hear there's no man in her life...or her bed...never has been."

"An avenging virgin, no less."

"Will!" His mother could not suppress a smile.

"It must be some time since you went with one?" Will persisted with his efforts to bait him.

"Your jokes aren't funny!" Gerard hissed. These attempts to needle each other had never been elevated beyond the language and tone they had used as youngsters. "None of you is in a position to comment, seeing as the two sides of the family never seem to want to meet, or circle each other when they do."

"Hey…calm down!" his father said, placing his hand on Gerard's shoulder.

Gerard looked at them all in turn. "Just what in hell has her personal life…or choices, for that matter…what has any of that got to do with the question I've asked? I asked you about a specific incident in the family, and I don't really care how long ago it was supposed to have happened! It would be interesting just to know if there's anything to the story I've been told, that's all."

"It is just that, a story." His mother's tone attempted to take the heat out of the moment; she had decided to settle him. "When did you see her?"

"Two days ago, we had lunch…I went through some albums, family photographs Edith had brought with her; they were pictures of a family I have never seen, or you have kept well-hidden from me."

"Nonsense," he heard softly.

Gerard stared across at his father who sat in the wicker chair swilling his drink round in the glass beer mug he held in his big hand. He could not conceal the accusing tone in his voice.

"Which one is it? We've got rid of any reminders of them, those ancestors from the eighteen seventy's *or*, have they been kept out of sight? God knows why, if it's so *long ago*…and doesn't much *matter*, now…and, most important of all, it never happened?"

"She's really got to you, this Edith," Willem smiled in the way he had of provoking further discussion.

"'*This Edith*'…is a cousin. Okay…a distant one, but still, she is a cousin."

"Right."

"She's interested in a family split, in the background to it."

"Hasn't she got anything better to interest her, or someone?" Willem continued to look directly at him. "Oh no, I forgot…she's different, in that way."

Gerard fixed his younger brother with a stare, removing his heavy glasses as he did so. He could know more than he was admitting to or he was merely perpetuating a habit from their childhood when they teased each other. It had become friendly badinage as they grew older, only now they were reverting to a bad habit; there was the added spice that a girl was involved.

"I'll get my things. We seem to be unable to talk of this, let alone get to the real story without demolishing one woman's reputation."

"Calm down," his father told him in a voice that held the authoritative tone he knew of old. "You've only just arrived."

"No! I don't think I can *calm down*. Edith's interested in the story; neither of us wants to be a party to perpetuating an argument from so long ago, unless we allow it to; distant events aren't going to affect how *we* are with each other."

"Why now?" Willem asked with affected boredom as he lounged back in his chair "Why bring this all up *now*?"

It was a good question, and he had no intention of disclosing the wider context of his enquiry. If this response to the simple enquiry 'did it happen?' was any guide the main point at issue would soon be buried by the direction his enquiries were beginning to take him and Edith. There was a compact between them that he had no wish to put at risk. His parents, and Willem, had made no connection with recent news; it was in all likelihood too remote for them to even contemplate.

Good. It was how he wanted to keep it.

"She's wants to find out more, and she's got me at it too, now!" Gerard forced a laugh.

"It's all hearsay. There's no evidence at all, so what is she doing dragging it all up for...and now? Can it be just for a new found interest in family history or is it to satisfy some other unhelpful curiosity? It's enough to know something may, or may not have happened." His mother's voice held that reassuringly calm tone that he knew of old but Gerard was not taken in.

"You *know*, or were told of it! If the events were to be forgotten why pass the news, any news of it, down over the generations? Simply forget, let the story wither and die with the last carriers of it."

"Who's put her up to it, that's what I want to know? And why call you, out of the blue and then only to discuss the story, for that's all it is?"

"I told you!" Gerard called out to his father's receding figure and rose to follow but his mother's restraining hand was on his arm. "Where's he going?" he muttered.

"Wait, Ger. I think your father has gone to his study."

"What? To avoid any further discussion?"

"No, whatever happened...it's buried history...maybe it should remain so; he's got some papers that may help."

"Papers? Papers on what?"

"On this issue you've seen fit to resurrect." His father spoke softly as he stood behind Gerard and held out to him a small packet, tied with faded red lint. "They're letters from great uncle Freddie, from America. They're dated eighteen eighty, look...there's no address except '*New York State*'. Here, see for yourself...go on, read them."

Gerard had not expected such assurance in his father's offer nor how quickly the letters had been produced.

"What do they say?"

"They are greetings, comments on how he and Margaretha, his wife, are settled in a new home. It's everyday conversational stuff, just telling people how he and his wife are."

"I know who she is, Edith told me of her."

"How they've settled, what has happened to them since they left Amsterdam…that's all they've got to say."

'*The truth, and nothing but the truth*'? Gerard wondered.

"Take them Gerard, you will see how foolish Edith's proposition really is."

"Sure of that?"

He unfastened the bindings, breaking with trembling fingers the sealing wax that had been melted over the knot so carefully; none had spilt onto the old and faded envelopes. Would these prove how big a mistake Edith was making, shoot down her theory and wider aspirations? He held the letters to his nose; they smelt of camphor.

"Against any weevil or moths feeding on them," his father said, still looking at him. "Go on, take a look. There's nothing to it, to her story." He stood by his wife and rested his hand on the back of her chair. "Shall I get you another beer?"

"Ja…go on." Gerard walked onto the lawns and opened the first letter, addressed to a house in a street close to Crooked Tree Water, Amsterdam.

6

"You've brought the albums again, I hope?"

"Of course, you left me in no doubt that I should," Edith laughed.

"I visited my parents, yesterday. This is the result."

Gerard handed her two copies of the letters. It had been a disaster if his visit was to be seen as a family reunion. His parents remained perplexed by the motives for his enquiry. '*Whose side are you on*'? they had all but asked him. An impossible question to answer in itself; he had not seen the issue as one of taking sides, more of taking a position on what was right and wrong, ignore for a moment the span of history. It had been the dredging up of old enmities, rumours of an event that puzzled and upset his parents. Will was as argumentative as ever; the years had not quelled any habit of jousting with his brother; he could tilt at his reputation within the confines of family.

"How did they receive your request for information?"

"With disbelief." He stared out over the water. They sat in the sun, then dappled shade, at the very same table as a few days before. "Never mind. All will be revealed in due course."

"Do you have regrets, that I ever called you?"

"No, I don't know why we never kept in touch before," he smiled at her and held out his hand. She took it slowly. "I won't let that happen again."

"What?" she released her grip on his big hand.

"Years, going by." Gerard looked again at the houses across the canal. "Crooked Tree Water, this city...New York...the Kahn's? It concerns us both, but it will not come between us."

"What do these say? Should I read them now?"

"They are what I suspected, and hoped that they would not say. They give no hint of what happened. At least they show he made some contact...it fills a gap in your story, or corrects a mistake I read when we first met." His mind had been turned to putting the jigsaw pieces together, as they discovered them. He already knew there would be many components to the whole picture.

"Oh," she let her voice fall in disappointment. "Still, you're not likely to confess to something so mean-spirited are you?"

"No." He thought of the emotions that had spread through him before he read the letters. "I hoped, just for a minute, that we, the Kahn's, could salvage something from what had happened."

"I can't get into the head of a man who would do such a thing – to his own niece and nephews, especially after all they had gone through. What type of person would he have been?"

"A desperate one, or a conniving and cunning, even ruthless businessman. Or, it could have been on account of a woman...she may have put him up to it."

"Someone with few scruples, or morals."

"Don't think they weren't capable of it even with their regular attendance at church."

"Well, for the moment I can only guess at the motives."

"We may never know for certain..."

"No, but we can at least try to find out."

"Theft...that's clean and simple; it's easier to understand for us, here and now. Why bother yourself with a wider or more complicated motive?"

"Because I want to get it right!"

"Is that what you get from your work? Certainty and no room for any doubt?"

"No, but it's worth aiming for," Edith said sharply. She relaxed again. "You said something about the woman?"

31

"The nurse? What was her name, my great, great aunt?" he paused for effect. "Margaretha?"

Edith smiled and tapped his arm. "So, you were paying me some attention."

"Oh, I was then and I *am now*, believe me."

"Well, what of her? What about Margaretha?"

"She had been little more than a servant, but she had ambitions, maybe lust for Freddie and his money; or, could it have been the power to affect a change?"

"In her circumstances at least; she had nothing to lose, whereas Frederick?"

Gerard thought of the man; he had over the past few days seen for the first time photos of a distant relative; he had really tried to dredge up any memory of hearing the name even mentioned – Frederick Albert Kahn. Now, his pretty cousin was leading him onto a chase through history that would end in God knows where. The scraps of background detail were on first sight next to useless, but he had started off assignments on less. Edith's enthusiasm was infectious only where did she think her enquiries or quest for the truth would lead them?

"Freddie may have seen no future for himself, or a lesser and diminished life here by comparison to what the risks had to offer. And, he had a woman… someone he was willing to take risks for." Gerard had seen no pictures of her. They were in an archive across the water, prized perhaps by another Kahn family of whom they all knew nothing

"He would not be alone…"

"No, and there was an ocean in between…"

"Between him and justice?"

"Yes."

"Agree to help me Ger? Help me find out all there is to know."

"I think I already have," he smiled. "I think I have agreed, but I want to widen the scope of any enquiry…and, I can be paid while I do so. Who knows, Edi? There could yet be a broader horizon than the one you and I are going to look at."

"But you don't know everything…where I am coming from on this."

"No, but you will tell me in your own time."

Edith smiled at his understanding. "Yes."

"We can only do so much here in Holland; the time will come when we will have to take our enquiry to the USA…the real answers may lie there, if we could ever get at them."

"Into the Wolf's Lair…." she replied in a soft voice.

"Yes," he smiled, "dramatically put, but if that is how you see it, I won't argue."

"No, I will have to moderate what I say. I must not allow emotions to take hold completely or any case for *follow up action* will seem less credible."

"And what is this follow up action you have in mind?" Edith sipped on her beer and fell into thought. "Okay, another time?" he went on. "Like I said, I had hoped that seeing the letters would help me salvage something of the Kahn reputation, but I'll have to wait a while longer."

"Maybe we still can, not as you imagine it, but restore something all the same to each side."

"Mama told me not to be Atlas, not to carry the cares of the world, as I saw them, on my shoulders."

"I've read your articles and I can see that you haven't always kept to her hopes for you."

"I've de-personalised them, I've pushed what I really cared for away; I put them in a room that I could lock the door on and find a life outside, with someone."

"Have you found that life outside, with someone?" Edith looked at her hands as she spoke then at him.

"Of a sort, but it's not seamless." He had two beers lined up before him and drank in large gulps from the first glass. "I'm in a relationship, but I live alone. Too many events keep crowding in. It's all very well having this "room", but the door bursts open – by itself!" He laughed.

"You know there are things to deal with, out there? They gnaw at you until there's nothing else for it but to get in there…tinkering at the margins is no good?"

"Precisely!" He admired her smart outfit; it was elegant but she was not overdressed. The cut of the black trousers and the figure hugging white blouse complemented her slender figure, gave a hint of a full cleavage, the eye drawn tantalisingly by the silver large linked necklace that hung at her throat. The red jacket was the finishing touch.

"You're beautiful," he said in a matter-of-fact tone of voice. "Is there…?"

"No," she waved a hand in dismissal "No."

"Sorry, I guess it's none of my business." "He did not mean what he said.

"Really?" she smiled.

"Well…I've told you a bit of myself."

"Let's just say I want it to be special."

"And until then?"

She laughed. "Ger! I've told you all I am going to say on the subject." Edith touched his arm. "Thanks for telling me, for the compliment."

"Okay." He thought for a moment. "About our meetings? Can we discuss motives? What have you discovered and what can I add that makes this whole project, if I can call it that, so urgent and of such importance?"

"You've been to New York, you have worked there."

"Ye...yes." He gave an expressive shrug of his shoulders.

"There's a mayoral election soon?"

"It's a fairly open race as I remember it, or read of the candidates and their platform."

"Who are the candidates?"

Gerard stared at her and a deep laugh rose to his lips. "There's a man called Kahn who has put himself forward as a candidate. Edith! We've already had all this."

"Ding? Ding?" Edith smiled.

"Yes, I know! Why do I get the feeling the dings are going to become a deafening peal of bells?"

"Because when I get back, and after you have read the notes in that album, just pages up to number ten, I'll explain."

"Where are you going? We're having lunch aren't we?"

"Yes. I'm going up to that bridge, then back again." She pushed back her hair and he watched it fall with a soft bounce on each side of her face. Edith saw his eyes soften as he took off the glasses. He was transformed and no longer disfigured by the lenses. She remembered the handsome young man with whom she had spent, it seemed, hours talking of art and politics; she had forgotten that he was a cousin and felt gladdened by the thought that theirs was a distant, a very distant family relationship.

"Don't be long."

"I won't be. There's no means to interrupt your study if I am not here, but I will soon be back. As you say, we've had too long between our meetings." She felt the breath catch in her throat and flushed at the open expression of pleasure to be with him.

"Right, more photos and papers. Then you and I can talk?"

"Yes, as long as you have time. I've given in an assignment today. I have the rest of the afternoon off. After you've read those papers I will explain everything and hope that I can persuade you to help in effecting a change."

There was blight on the family history that he had heard of too. It had not been spelt out in the manner she had come to know of the story but an opportunity could be exploited; she was convinced of it. She turned only once to look back at him; his eyes were on her, the glasses removed. He was special; she saw him differently. Circumstances had so far kept her from expressing

34

any attraction, but he had expressed his own, by the un-scripted compliment. Her *'singledom'* had inspired comment in her own family. If she could be with him anything could yet happen for her; she would not have long to wait.

The earlier folios had given Gerard an insight into the story; what she would now have to tell would convince him to commit to the enterprise. The rest would take care of itself.

7

"What did you say the outcome was of your trip home?" Edith asked as she came up to him.

"I didn't say but you have the letters." He put down the album and stood up to help her with the chair next to him. "Sit by me, sit really close."

"Anything along the line of *'let sleeping dogs lie'* as the British would say it?" Edith moved so that she could sit near him yet watch Gerard closely.

"Something like that. What I had to ask met with disapproval."

"I read the letters, at the bridge, they're of little or no help as you said, but then Frederick would brazen it out from the comfort of his new home and with three thousand miles of ocean in between him and justice." Gerard turned at the sharp tone of bitterness in her voice.

"Don't get emotional about it, not yet."

"Easy to say, from…"

"From my family, or *Kahn* perspective?"

"I didn't mean it to sound like that."

He sat back and saw the unmoving stare of her eyes; it would be easy to permit the quest for knowledge to dominate everything but he was absorbed in her.

"Not entirely fair, but I'll allow you that. So, as you can read between the lines in the letters, no one tried to look for him. The tone is all wrong, if you're trying to draw some comfort from them. They're newsy, if they ever wrote in such a down-to-earth way in the eighteen eighties."

"How could they begin to look for him?"

"Steady," his hand rested on her arm, the soft fabric of the sleeve gathered at the cuff by a small pearl link. He was inclined to familiarity but there was no objection. "I'm only sounding off, bouncing ideas around and seeking answers."

"Right…you're not eating very much, and the meal's very good." Gerard let his hand fall, back to the table.

"We'll have to make this place our special rendezvous, won't we?" His attention was on her and Edith flicked a glance at him.

"Yes," she knew his meaning.

"Before you tell me your plan or motives here's my initial contribution, the lynchpin of the whole thing, at least as a start."

"And it is?" she said impatiently.

"The receipt for the money. The *'piece of paper'* that started it all." He took a mouthful of food but seemed bored with the idea of eating and pushed the plate away from him, almost to the far edge of the table. "Without it we are going nowhere."

"I'm thinking about that."

"Good! Your family's lawyers, aunts and uncles, those that are paid up members of the cause should help you, assist *us* to find a record. Without that all we have is our meetings."

"A cause?" She thought of it. "Yes, maybe that sums my idea up perfectly; a cause celebre perhaps, by the end."

"How so?"

"Can't you guess?"

"Revenge or deferred judgement?" He sat back in the chair and clutched the beer glass to his chest and spoke as the ideas came to mind. "Let's not forget the small obstacles…the Statute of Limitations perhaps?….American and Dutch Laws? Proof, or the weight of evidence, and who really suffers now?" He nodded in condescension. *"Little things* like that."

Edith smiled. "Defeatist!" She nodded as her lips pursed in thought.

"Cheer up! You've got me, the realist. Don't worry! I can see something in all of this only we have to observe the niceties."

"Such as libel, and our families?"

"To name a couple."

"Any others?"

"Uh huh! The *'who cares?'* after all this time. There's another, a natural reaction… the *'so what?'* factor! I got that with my brother yesterday!" He put on his reading glasses and opened the album. "And then there is the 'does it really matter now?' response that you will get when you confront them with your story."

"But there will be more, lots more to make them think." Edith stretched out her hand. "Take those off for me?"

"Scary aren't they," he smiled. "I'm pretty useless without them, at reading anyway." He placed the metal frames on the table. "There, with my own eyes now, *'all the better to see you with'*…I'm no longer the big, bad wolf."

Edith laughed.

"I like you more without them, that's true."

"Well, that's something at least."

"Anything else worrying you?"

36

"That whatever you have to tell me of your motives, it won't come between us?"

"We'll both swear to it."

"I know! Swear, then kiss on it." He held out his hand and stood up. "Ger!"

"No, it was your idea." He pulled her gently to her feet. "Nothing will divide us and no-one will separate us."

"Are you sure...no-one? I heard you tell of someone outside the room you lock your troubles away in." She stood awkwardly against her chair. Those nearby looked up then carried on their conversations.

"I'm certain of it. No-one."

"Nothing will divide us; no-one will separate us." Edith laughed then moaned softly taken by surprise; he kissed her cheeks and offered the briefest touch of his lips to her mouth. It was all too public and spontaneous.

"Ger," she whispered placing her free hand to his chest, but not in restraint.

"It's okay, isn't it? I thought *'how appropriate'*."

"I haven't told you the plan or the motivation behind it."

"I think I can guess, or form a hazy outline...but, tell me anyway."

8

Hans Blokman was not a man to be trifled with. Whatever your reputation might be on the outside he took all of you, drained every last drop of creative or investigative skill from the writer's pen. Physically he could be intimidating; he was a tall man and far too thin; a penchant for small cigars did little for his health and made his voice sound like a gravel bed. His eyes stared out from under bushy brows, greying now in spite of his age; he was in his late forties and had commanded the financial desk of the 'paper for five years, a time Gerard had used to forge his own reputation. He might sniff out the stories and get the instinctive idea, the essence of the subject onto the page but Hans had a large stock of blue pencils. It helped having a skin so thick that he rarely felt the barbs that could be spat out if a correspondent thought his or her work had been emasculated. He liked to see hard copy, none of this electronic version nonsense; he had to *feel* the words *on paper*.

Gerard at first felt a grudging respect, then affinity for the quality of work he sought. In a fit of honest self-criticism he often laid his draft and Hans's corrected version side-by-side. He owed some of his reputation to Hans and his eye for the small adjustment, a single word that he introduced or its placement, elsewhere in the text. He possessed none of the formal education that Gerard had enjoyed. *'Just experience, boy'* was all he said when Gerard came to him with a cutting of his finished work and thanked him; he was not too proud to acknowledge Hans's touch.

"So, why the urgency? What's news?" Hans asked in a slight wheeze.

"The strap-line is *'Money buys Power'*.

Hans pulled a face. "Not one of your better efforts...girl trouble is it? Mind off the game, or at it too much?"

Monique, an air-hostess, was the latest on a list of conquests only she had succeeded where others had failed, taming his restlessness and the quest for a new fix. The chase was no longer necessary, she beguiled him; the novelty of the experience did not wane; absence only made them eager to renew their steamy bundling.

"No. I accept it's not brilliant. The story behind it may explain, and we can always think of another soon enough."

"You got that bit right!" Hans scrabbled in the drawers of his desk. "Ah! Knew I still had some...you buggers want to hide them from me." He chewed the end off a small cigar and, out of habit and with practised ease, spat the off-cut into the bin. "Well?"

"I've sketched an outline, a hypothesis if you like; before you read it let me say that what I propose is an investigation, not directly concerning the name you read here but of companies like the ones he controls; it has a wider corporate and international context."

"Leave the paper...just spell it out for me."

"My name's Kahn," he smiled.

"Now I know it must be a girl, you're not thinking straight! Shit man! I know who you are!"

"I may be related to John Kahn...the mayoral hopeful," he said after a pause. "New York?"

"Thanks, I haven't read a paper for a while you understand," Hans made as if he would play the game then thought better of it. "Are you sure?"

"No, but I have information, pictures and some letters."

"Look, I'm sorry...what has a little genealogy got to do with this paper, even if you do work for it, occasionally?" He laughed. Gerard wouldn't be wasting his time for nothing. "Check it out! Try the Internet, I hear it's quite useful."

Hans drew on the small cigar; the air-conditioning was turned up, full on in fact only the 'no smoking' policy did not have Hans as it's most committed adherent. He made exception to the rules; he re-wrote them. It was Gerard's turn for sarcasm.

"Thanks for the tip...I'll have to try it sometime."

"Piss, or get off the pot. What's the story here?"

"I've checked him out, some immigration sites, that sort of thing, read a bio of him but it doesn't all fit together with other bits of background. I think there is a family link, but that is not the interest. It's corporate, it's the businesses he controls and the spread of influence he has already."

"He'll have to give that all up if he gets elected, and a lot can happen between now and then. Some kiss-and-tell story, a few drugs, a cushy number to avoid national service - Vietnam, say?"

"He's been in action, he has the medals and a nation's grateful thanks to prove it."

"Just a thought, in a cynical hack's mind." Hans looked for a convenient place to drop the small amount of ash his smoke produced. The floor was handy.

"He won't have to give it all up, not completely, just the day-to-day control. He'll get to keep any money; his shares will be put in some vehicle that gets it past scrutiny; his family will have the influence, only he will be moving on a different level."

"Still, it's nice to have something to fall back on."

"Quite."

"So? So what?"

"Here's the good part, the political line. One of his key policy objectives is corporate governance, how the City does its business, how it behaves. You know? Honesty and Integrity."

"Very laudable, only we hear it all the time and we're still surprised when it gets unstuck. So it's good behaviour within his borders, but outside... anything goes?"

"Not as simple as that," Gerard smiled, "not if you want to keep the regulators sweet and off your back. They can be like a train wreck to your aspirations, to presidential hopes, may be?"

"Let him be mayor first!"

"Yeah, okay."

"So, what are you proposing, an inside job to expose him?"

"No, not that...or not yet. It's too early to say." Gerard held up his hand to prevent further interruption, but Hans was getting restless. "What I haven't told you is that the whole empire, the whole Kahn business over there was funded from the beginning...by stolen money."

"How the hell do you come by that!" Hans spluttered and began to cough.

"Here, have some water." Hans waved him to continue.

"Later, how do you know?"

"Research, a bit scratchy at the moment."

"Yours?"

"No, a useful source. She sought me out and told me a tale I didn't believe at first…about that family and all that. Kahn's…you can picture it?"

"Sure," he said expansively. "Pretty is she?"

"Yes, but that has nothing to do with it."

"Sure," Hans leered this time. "Go on."

"I think it has legs," he laughed as Hans pulled a face, "the story will run…" They both laughed at the clichés. "But, I don't want to make the whole investigation too obvious. I see the viewpoint as a look out onto a multinational business world, corporate strategy and effects on globalisation, again; there's pharmaceuticals involved this time, there's a new Third World drugs angle, patents, that sort of thing." He was thinking on his feet. I'll have to remember that, Edith has no idea where this could all lead to…or what the ending might be.

"Why that?"

"A guy like him, anyone with his influence…if he got to the top, I mean the very top…he controls us, you and me. It's what the word 'superpower' means. What a man in his position decides affects us all; it has either beneficial or dire, deathly consequences." Hans sat back, the chair leaning over so far that Gerard thought Hans would topple over. His silence could not be endured.

"It's nothing to do with revenge or the settlement of a past slight," Gerard felt compelled to continue. "There's a story to tell but with wider implications."

"Ha!" the snort accompanying the wave of one hand was dismissive. "Ulterior motives, but highly principled ones? Is that what you're asking me to believe…and not just me? Those who read your column too, it seems, have to believe this is about higher things, a moral principle is at stake or at issue…is that it?"

"And why not?" He regretted the remark before it had fully passed his lips. He'd not pursued in any detail the true motives behind Ediths' little crusade. What exactly were the intentions behind the words encouraging his involvement? He'd heard Edith speak of the Kahn's wealth; he had known as much from his own work at the 'paper; so what was she, or her family, really after?

"You'll get too involved with the personal details…you'll lose sight of the main picture." Hans spoke then adjusted his weight so that the seat sprang back upright, for effect. "I'm not sure yet that I understand what the primary motivation is here. Are you pursuing the *man?* Or is it the *man and the money* the family's made? Or all of it allied to what *he has done* with the wealth the company generates?"

"I'm working on it, the detail has to be filled in from the story's outline," Gerard replied. Once again Hans had brought him down to earth with a few choice questions. It hadn't happened for some time; but then, he had clearly not felt so distracted…by the story or the messenger.

"See that you do."

"Give me *some* credit!" Gerard snorted.

"You won't be able to prove it." It was like a punch from the blind side. Hans seemed so certain he sat back annoyingly in his chair and taunted him, rolled the cigar between his fingers, waiting for the case to be made.

"It'll be difficult…"

"And expensive…in your time and at my cost…at this newspaper's cost."

"Is that a *'no'* then? Do I forget it?"

"I didn't say that," Hans replied with forced patience. "Did you hear me say that?"

"No."

"Right. Investigate the lead this pretty girl…who you're not going to climb onto…has for you. Give me a synopsis or the product, say in three days? How about that?"

"Yeah, fine." He had a pretty good idea where he wanted to start.

"Tie it in with *real* life…what's out there today."

"Count on it."

"And Ger? See to Monique. You're distracted."

9

"Hello! Hello, my treasure! I'm back."

Monique's brittle voice sounded very close, only he noted the catch as she uttered the endearment, the choice of the word entirely of her devising and reserved for him alone. From her lips the greeting held the prospect of a tender reunion. 'Darling' was too easy, a common phrase that slipped over the tongue like honey, and its taste soon diffused. On the other hand, 'Treasure' was like molasses, strong and with a lingering after-taste; he couldn't so easily forget her.

"It's been too long, Moni! Come over, be quick!"

The mobile was wedged in the crook of shoulder and neck as he saved the notes that had been occupying him, cross referenced to a database especially created. Edith had been a lovely interlude. Soon, he would hold his lover's slender but firm and oh-so-curvy figure; then, he would *'see to her'*. Hans and his choice of words!

"I'll make it up to you, I promise." Her words soon faded.

"Oh Oh!"

"You can handle it."

"What are you waiting for then? Wash away your trip here?"

"Ger?" He heard again the catch in her throat. "I'm waiting for nothing and no-one. Say half an hour, the traffic's all but gone."

"I'll prepare your welcome."

"As only you can," she whispered. "Bye!"

The apartment at East Dock had cost a fortune. Glossily advertised and hyped as a new neighbourhood he had seen it as a sound investment; he would sell up in a year or two and buy a period property in the Old City, in an area he had long set his heart on. Now, he enjoyed the view over the darkening skyline, the roofs silhouetted against the orange pink glow of the setting sun; house and streetlights shimmered on the water. Nights were never truly dark and winter offered the only opportunity to study the starry heavens in the cold evening air, seated on his small balcony.

Star-dust of a different kind, all too tangible, was on her way to meet him.

To many, Monique was perfect. She was an unblemished specimen of almost glacial beauty, pale skinned with a shock of wispy curls to the loose strands of diaphanous blonde hair. Her loose-limbed feline slinkiness hid a vital energy that sparkled in her vivid green eyes with their faint brown circlet to the pupils. Some believed that Monique worked on her appearance in order to maintain the artifice of the catwalk – figure, make up, hair and above all her smooth skin. But no, it was God-given – he could testify to that. A few essential oils and moisturisers that he was only too willing to smooth and caress over her skin were the only supplements to maintain her beauty.

It had not escaped the attention of the airline; the lifestyle of a flight attendant suited Moni perfectly and she often featured in the advertisements, playing at roles that had no association with her day-to-day existence. But her image portrayed all that her employers sought. Exploitative? Maybe it was, but the financial rewards seemed to compensate. She also stirred imagination, the quickening of pulse and the occasional and unwelcome grope of hands.

Monique told him, and he believed. After all, he had met her in much the same way, he even admitted much later that 'perhaps' there was a lustful impulse behind his own initial suit, but she hadn't seen it that way. Following their first date the lingering eye contact they had exchanged on the flight to New York had confirmed what they had both seen in each other.

Therein lay the trouble. The fine cheekbones, the near flawless skin of her face – only marked by two, of the smallest, brown flecks that intrigued him by her lip and nose – drew attention to the softly pouting lips, invited a closer look at her exquisite features and the attentive gaze of her eyes. They contrasted acutely with his bespectacled stare, a glance that perturbed Edith and wrought the initial cry of dismay. Moni had been diplomatic, asked considerately how she could be of help during the flight and their routine exchange of words had prompted him to autograph a piece he had written for that day's edition of the paper. There was even a flattering picture of him by the strap line and attribution. He had torn it out, oh-so carefully.

"You must receive hundreds of these," he said disarmingly, "but, if you're staying over for a few days – may I see you?"

He had taken off his glasses, after he had spoken. She could make her decision armed with the before-after glimpse of him. He was direct; she could just as quickly give a 'yes' or a 'no'. Either way, it was all he would need to hear.

"If I say 'yes' – will you write about it afterwards?"

She looked down at the fragment of paper his fingers pushed across the shining aluminium work-surface of the galley. The artificial lighting failed to diminish her brilliant smile in response to the soft laugh that escaped from him – it was a beam of acknowledgement between them. His face was transformed and he had known he was in there. Moni's doubts about this *'trier'* evaporated, he saw it in those lovely eyes.

"Oh no – as you can see it's not a society paper. I'm heading for Seattle after a couple of days in New York, with a local correspondent."

"Not the easiest of reads, I suppose?" Moni studied the text for a moment and he had the opportunity to look at her fine hair, tied back but with delicious loose strands to break the formality of the uniform.

"No, I guess not. But, it's a memento, of our meeting."

"Or, an invitation to another?"

"I'd be happy if you saw it like that, yes."

"I'll see."

He almost blew it. "Look, I've written my number on it...back home as well, just in case?"

"Let me think about it? And....no, I don't encourage any ideas of leaving me notes."

She had made an exception in his case...years ago. An open relationship had evolved, a commitment not limited or defined by the sharing of his apartment. He took one last look at the pictures of the Kahn's from the 1880's and set about tidying up the place.

The open plan living area with its harbour views was lined to one wall with a floor to ceiling white wood book-case that resembled library shelving, crammed with esoteric books on art and history. The symmetry was broken

43

to accommodate urns collected on trips to Africa and carefully transported home, candle holders and an illuminated glass case.

In the middle of the wooden floor large sofas were arranged in an 'L' shape, with a bleached pine table set before them. The high ceiling permitted a tall palm to occupy one corner, softening the geometrical sharpness of the room. Modern art prints provided the only decoration to the smooth texture of the walls.

The apartment was home, not a venue for temporary and furtive liaisons. Moni's carefree voice and laughter filled the rooms bequeathing a legacy that ensured he could never regard his space, or refuge from the pressures of deadlines and long hours, as a bachelor pad. The deal was that each retained their own space, in spite of the physical intensity they felt for each other; only he had conceded without much debate to stylistic changes to his surroundings. It had become too easy to fall into the seductive habit of inviting Moni to spend her time with him. Affectionate hugs accompanied the realisation that he should accept her idea for an almost seamless transition between the intimate atmosphere of the bedrooms to the spacious glory of the living room.

Cohesion, the sense of an outside world – the views, the light and sounds if he chose – meeting the cloistered refuge of his home was the end result of their collaboration. They travelled for their work, absences were common place, but the innocence of rediscovering each other in his home was the touching and tantalising prelude to their intercourse. They seemed inseparable; he should articulate his commitment to their partnership; love had never meant dependency or possessiveness, it was not a word that crossed the lips too often, but their reunions usually communicated just those sentiments.

Candles on a tiered stand were lit and he dimmed the lights; in the flickering gloom he pressed the taper to the wicks of other candles on the hallway sideboard, one Kahn hand-me-down. The passageway to the master bedroom suite had been panelled with salvaged timber from an old barge and the warmth of reflected light from the polished surfaces contrasted with the living room.

He sought to bring a relaxing stillness to the rooms, the scent from the candles inducing an instantaneous feeling of calm; the floating candles for her bath would be attended to later, after a hurried shave, strip wash and change of clothes. The buzzer sounded in Moni's tell-tale announcement of her arrival in the lift lobby.

"Hey! Beautiful lady, looking for me?" Gerard lounged against the doorframe, his dishevelled hair flopping over his face.

"Yes!" the wheels rattled on the wooden landing floor before the bag scraped to a halt. Moni had dropped it by his feet and hugged him. "Oh yes!" She planted quick kisses on his face and held onto him so tightly, her arms locked behind his neck, that he had to take hold.

"Wow! What next?" he mumbled through their kisses. "You okay?" he leant back. She looked exhausted and eyes misty with tears stared up at him.

"Yes, I am now. Just hold me...hold me tight, please?"

"No excuse is necessary, lievert." Moni shook against him. Work took its toll but he had never known her to return to his embrace quite so agitated. She rose against him and clasped his neck once more.

"No...no excuses. I wanted to get back to you."

Moni was lifted into his arms like a rag doll and as he cradled her, the travel bag was kicked across the floor into the hall way. Her head flopped against his shoulder and he felt lips press his skin and suck gently on his ear lobe.

"Still," he said gently. "I'll run a bath for you...everything else, anything, is for later."

"Love me."

"I do, you know I do."

"Truly, madly...deeply?" she said. He nodded, offering his mouth for a simple habitual kiss, reaffirming their companionship. Her lips trembled. "Say it..."

"Ja!" he said in that quizzical tone that at any other time Moni said she loved about him. By nature he found a rational explanation for everything and occasionally teased her with his carefully argued reply. Without exception it was always an affirmative answer that he gave. Only now, the response reduced her to a flood of tears, her characteristic poise shattered.

"Ger!"

"What is it? Okay, a bad joke...but, what is it?"

"For me, once...all three, treasure," she said, brushing his ear with her lips.

He stood very still, sensed only the gentlest sway as he tightened his embrace on Moni's trembling frame. So, the lifestyle, the stop-overs and the occasional party away, their *'open'* relationship had finally taken her from him.

"Only...'madly'...'deeply' now?" He turned his face slowly towards her.

"I did a stupid thing," she spluttered. He felt numbed by her confession sensing that Monique had become another person, without the slightest warning from her previous behaviour.

"I'm not the handsomest guy in the world just the luckiest, for a while anyway." Even now he tried to make a joke, while his mind began to imagine her extended trip, the modelling assignment for an American advertising campaign and promotional literature.

"I don't call you treasure, my treasure, for nothing!" she sobbed giving up any pretence to help him carry her. Moni fell back onto the bed they so often shared.

"Still…sh." His fingers brushed her lips as he bent over her. "I'll call you when it's ready." His face was set in a mask,

Moni lay in her uniform, arms clenched to her breast and listened to the roar of the taps, turning her head from side to side taking in her familiar surroundings.

"Ger! Come to me, please?" she called out. The rush of water moderated. "Talk to me…Ger?" Her voice softened on seeing him framed in the doorway, silhouetted by the soft flicker of candlelight. "What do you see now?"

He stood watching her silently but raised his hands then dropped them to his sides.

"I can't answer that. I can only feel right now." On her face he saw fear.

"And?" she said staring up at him. The room was cool but Ger removed his shirt and lay down. Skin on skin; even now he sought that form of exultant communion between them.

"So," the voice erupted from a hollowed part of him, out of the depths in a quick exhalation of breath, expelled in resignation. Moni lay still, her face turned to him and he began to unbutton her dress. "Let me see you?"

"Yes." Her fingers brushed the short hairs on his breastbone but he paid no attention, slipping away to turn off the taps. The lights dimmed, a match flared then died.

"So?" It felt like another was speaking on his behalf in a distant voice. He lay back on the pillows, his arms behind his head, looking only briefly at her.

"So…we went on somewhere after the shoot….I got high…I drank too much." She forced the words out. "It all got a bit woozy….out of hand."

She knelt over him now, like an animal on all fours. It had become a debauch for the other girls; they laughed it off as something that had just '*happened*', a stop-over to remember. Only, she could not remember seeing much of them.

The reflex of desire was strong but the longer he delayed his reply the more she would be inclined to reveal. "So…?"

"So….it was different…it didn't mean anything…it was quick." Her soft hands gripped his sides expecting some reaction but still he waited his breathing slow. "So...I couldn't stop it....and....I couldn't keep it from you."

"Let me see you," he said at last stung by the choice of words, pushing her off him, considerately but certain of his purpose. Moni tensed at the touch of his fingers on her belly, over the thin triangle of fabric then between her thighs.

"Ger!"

He held up a hand to silence her, clenching shut his eyes. "There's a mark on you."

"More, unseen," she whispered.

"Oh yes," he murmured in reply. His mind was filled with images, of them, doing something 'different'. Her words of how 'meaningless' the liaison may have been would have their own corrosive effect. He could think of no way to blot them out. "Come, I'll bring you a drink, relax in the bath. I'll...I'll look after you."

"Fuck it!" he said in English. What a useful phrase that could so often be. Moni's wash bag slipped from his wet fingers spilling its contents onto the ceramic tiled floor, including a red topped white pill tube. "That's all I need!" he growled.

"What?"

He held it up, turning it so that she could read the label.

"This!" The tube hit the water and bobbed in the suds. The label was clearly printed. 'KPM Tranx" He could make out that much.

Moni watched him as he juggled the tube in his hands then slid gracefully, like a sleek skinned reptile, into the water over the sloping end of the bath. The candles flickered then hissed, spluttered back to life as Ger arranged them on the shelf then joined her.

"I don't understand."

"No...it doesn't matter. What are they for?" She made a feeble attempt to snatch at the tube. Tranquilisers were not her usual remedy.

"They kept me going..."

"At what?" He kicked out at the tube; water splashed onto the floor as she made another lunge for it. The tube bobbed merrily, like a storm tossed buoy, the red top peeking out from the soapy waves their struggle had created. Ger's hands slid over her body.

"Not what you think! It was a...mistake," she responded. "Got that! Mmm?" She moaned; his mouth covered her lips in a kiss so intense that she twisted against him to prolong the first sign of a loving welcome, nestling into his unexpected embrace and reaching up to his face."So! You won't complain if I check out what's in there?" he said harshly . The little tube held a motive for him now, beyond family.

Their unequal struggle resumed but soon subsided as their skins touched and slid, their eyes closed, mouths meeting in soft kisses but Moni's eyes strayed, to the surface of the water and that damned tube. He stared at her through their kisses. Was there more to them than she could admit?

"Got it! I'll tell you!" Moni growled. "We've been open about everything before." She threw the canister into the basin. The label would stay in tact.

"How I want to help you," he said as their lips scarcely touched. "'Open' doesn't have the meaning we thought...I intended it to have. Not at all, not for me." He pressed his tongue between her lips and moved across them slowly without surrendering to a full kiss. "A matter only of degree...but truly...madly...deeply."

"Lievert," she kissed back, 'treasure' had fallen from her vocabulary. "I was possessed."

"I don't want the details...just tell me? Were you safe...when you played, away?"

His words were like a thunderclap. Moni stiffened.

"What?" she yelped. "What? Oh God!...Yes!...Yes, I was!" Her voice echoed in the room as if to reinforce the memory that Ger's words now brought to mind. Her eyes widened in sudden anguish, staring, then she turned away. "Oh God, yes!"

Moni could no longer escape his clutches; large hands held her and Gerard wrapped his legs about her waist. She settled against him.

"How can you be so sure...if he gave you those pills and mixed them with a drink or two?"

If it had been that quick, that easy and 'different' from his attentions... 'he' may not have wanted to take a chance. And yet, an unconfined hit...or two...why torture myself with such thoughts of her...*fucking* with someone else...an unconfined hit was not to be missed. A piece of 'easy ass' is how he remembered hearing of it from the photographers the paper used, when boasting of models and girls they sometimes picked up.

"I...I...I made sure! Everything, you...and me, it still mattered."

"Even then?" he called out, burying his face against her throat and clasping her so tight. He felt her nod.

Monique had beauty and class, and he even dared to admit, at least to himself, that she had a permanent place in his life. For all he knew, or had been told, she could have spent time with a man who saw her through very unconventional eyes; she was a lustful alternative that had readily conceded to his advances once inhibition's chains, and her fidelity to another, had been loosened.

A name lodged in his memory. KahnPulcriMed, KPM, would have a treatment, you could bet on it, for any of the consequences her liaison might bring upon her. But, did they have a pill or two for him? What treatment was there to dispel the tortured imagery of her lustily, energetically and noisily joined to someone else...while her 'lievert', her treasure, was so far away?

Moni's mobile beeped, fell silent, then it sounded once again. The caller could be anyone and yet he felt in the grip of a jealous and possessive paranoia, wishing to disassociate the woman with him now from the consensual acts that he thought of as particular to *their* relationship only. As for Monique? She ignored the persistent intrusions.

It was hard, very hard and he had it covered. Moni understood; he had finally *'seen to her'*. An open relationship had come to mean something so very different.

"Jesus!" Gerard jumped up startled.

"No, only me," Moni chuckled, happier now that she had renewed a cloying intimacy. She bent to kiss his shoulders and brushed his skin with her breasts. "Why are you away from me now? What are you doing?"

"Secondary research, off the internet. I didn't want to disturb you while I tossed and turned."

"I always know when you're not there, beside me..." The remark hung in the air.

"Ja," he said softly; the anger and destructive passion for the moment had been put aside. "I've got a deadline for submitting a synopsis of an article...maybe more. I can't afford to miss it."

"Was it all work during my absence?"

"Not entirely...I met Edith, a distant cousin for lunch. The one I told you had called me after so many years of silence, fifteen years to be exact...so long after a family reunion." He turned to look then beckoned to her. "You remember?" His hand stroked the back of her thighs.

"Vaguely. What I do know is that you said she was attractive."

"And?"

"Nothing..."

"Look at this," he pushed back the chair. Moni sat on his lap, gloriously naked.

"What?" she giggled, groping down.

"Later. No, look at this. It's a photo, of my great, great uncles and aunts from the 1880's. Edith found it. I've never seen it before."

"You met over that?"

"Yes...and to talk. It has come to have greater significance for me."

"What of them, these ancestors of yours?"

"Most are in heaven, one is in hell."

"Like we have been through?"

"Tell me which it is going to be between us," he said in a softened voice, "and tell me soon?"

That slip of newsprint with an invitation for them to meet, given to Monique so long ago it seemed now, on a flight to New York, had been direct. The situation now required nothing less, in spite of their passionate exchanges and the intrusive calls to her unanswered mobile phone that set him thinking of her seduction from him once more.

He kissed shut her eyes and tasted the salty tears. An email had been sent, before Moni had woken.

"Edi – I'm with you all the way. We need to find a lawyer, the lawyer! We need to, have to, find all the papers, the paper! You set it up. I will research the 'other' side. Can we meet, v.soon? I'll send you the outline of an article...or a series of articles that I intend to write." Your new found friend, Ger.

10

To:HansB@detelegraaf.nl
<u>**Subject**</u>: **Outline – Money buys Power**

'Hey! It's late, or early, depending upon what you have been up to. Wrote these ideas out as they occurred to me. Discuss over the next few days?' Gerard.

A rich man tells a poor one, "I'm here to help you." The answer may, if honestly recorded and printable, come as no surprise. Take a representative of a rich country, in the G8 say, conferring with his opposite from a poor and emerging country and diplomatic speak will, at the conclusion of a sumptuous conference, describe loud voices and finger pointing (all of it behind closed doors) as a full and frank discussion. The resulting stalemate can have one, of many, consequences – death for thousands.

So it is with aspiring politicians. I had to look it up, refer to the ideas of the Enlightenment in Europe. The thoughts of Locke and Rousseau, to name but two philosophers of the age – 'no government was possible without the consent of the people'. Only, in the eighteenth century, consent was given by a small influential group of people. Is that so very different to the world order today, in spite of the 'United Nations'? Self-advancement on the backs of others would be too cynical, too honest, too damaging to the confessor.

Instead, the hapless electorate, (or the majority who vote and who are persuaded by the millions thrown at them over a short campaign to win hearts and minds), are confronted by a well-funded publicity machine. The money devoted to that electoral process would tackle the deprivation faced by just such an emerging country's government seated at the table. Denial of basic rights, or change, can be achieved by various means – usually by force or the lack of money.

To what end? Four boys once crooned 'Money Can't buy me Love' – well, it can; for a minute, a day, however long it takes to cast a vote. For others it buys friction of short duration – excuse the 'ions'. They're molecules, energy that is dissipated quickly to achieve some goal, or satisfaction. Short-lived unless a source of truly sustainable power, belief in the inherent good of an enterprise, maintains progress. The exercise of will, or the lack off it, pervades both.

The trick is to overcome the sentiment expressed in another line of the lyrics; it goes something like "What I've got I'll give to you". You know, it happens so often that you feel embarrassed to comment upon the innocent belief it holds; in exchange for what I trade with you I will receive something at least of equal benefit in return. Only, disquiet at the fakery of (the one-sided) trade returns to confront you, like a wayward boomerang. Put another way, 'all take and no give'.

Money buys power, in all its guises. You can conceal intent; retain copyright to essential medicines to cure common ills – common in those countries that beg for relief but have a wall to climb to reach it. Wealth buys silence, or represses discussion and dissent; it buys companies who may work to a different code of social (world) responsibility, or who have been assiduously undermined by price controls. The wealth of some hinders the true pursuit of ethical trade by others that neither exploits nor costs lives that are perilously short already. Worse still, it can heap indignity on those that die from malnutrition and disease, or from the absence of infrastructure, however primitive, that can effectively dispense the aid the recipients require.

And what, you may ask, has this to do with well-heeled political aspirants? It depends where the money they dispense to seek a vote is gathered.

From **true supporters,** or believers taken in by the evangelical zeal of the protagonist? Okay

⊠*From the **party faithful?** There are some on the bandwagon and confidantes expect a job and advancement out of it – if the protagonist is elected. Reluctantly – okay.*

☒*From business* – venal and I have my doubts. They expect a favour in return – how does their business plan and the ethics of government meet? I would argue – not okay.

☒*My own money?* There's nothing like paying for your own beliefs, hoping that you can persuade by force of argument that you have a cause worth following. If you lose, tough – no one else lost his shirt for your ambitions. So – definitely okay.

☒And then there's **someone else's money** – taken from those who never knew you and were (possibly) condemned to a harder life had you not taken their savings, or inheritance. The use of that is – UNFORGIVEABLE.

"What were you doing sending me mail at 3 am? Sleeping alone?" Hans was on a fishing expedition.

"No, but something has come up that has crystallised my initial thoughts." Gerard felt tired but not for lack of sleep.

"You're on a high...cuhuhhuh." Hans coughed raucously taking the unlit cigar from his mouth. "The ideas are there, in what you have written...only they don't make up a coherent picture. Work on it some more."

"I am, but I can only do so much from here."

"You want me to send you over there?"

"In time."

"Get Nico Brant our local guy with the contacts...he can do it."

"No, not a good idea – at this stage," Ger suggested as he saw Hans flap the two pages of text he had printed out, remembering too late that he had not asked for an electronic version. "Let me give them something to work on?"

"If Nico does it the leg work's still cheaper, and impartial."

Ger digested the remark for a moment, tapping his lips. "Since when did I stop being objective about any thing?"

"Since now! The outline screams out at me. What's happened....or *not* happened?" Hans was infuriating, so perceptive – or had he made it all too obvious how he felt following Moni's disclosures. The calls to her mobile suggested a different story from the one that he had been told of.

"Nothing...I can't handle. I'll get over it. I will do what I am paid for, and you will get your expanded version."

"Good." Hans sat observing him with the chair tilted back at an impossible angle. It seemed a game to him making his staff think, or hope, he'd tip over, fulfilling a wish or a bet that one day he would and earn someone a pay out.

"As we speak it's a wide-ranging investigation, as I have outlined. The detail, the specific theme...the one I spoke about, in your office? That comes later. That's when it becomes personal, but the wider perspective continues to apply."

"I'll be the judge of that. The 'paper can't allow its correspondents to work at settling old scores...and this one's *ancient,* you can almost feel the dust on it!"

"Human interest, linked to a wider business and social context? I'd say they were reasons enough for you to keep an open mind."

"Sure Gerard. Only your relation, if that's what he turns out to be, is the focus of all this."

"Right now it's of local interest...what if he got elected?" He had reviewed all the counter arguments in his head during his run that morning, just as he had done with Edith. The *'so what, it was so long ago'* counter-blast seemed to predominate. He said out loud the thoughts that now came to mind as Hans quizzed him. "What if he did a good job and went all the way, beyond Mayor, what then?"

"It would be another story for you...and what a story."

"No, there wouldn't be a story for a guy with that baggage..."

"Don't count on it," Hans interrupted, "the Gary Hart effect only worked once if I remember right...and Clinton? He was already elected when the other stories broke and the counter offensive began."

"Okay, I hear you. There still remains the broader issue to consider like the public face and what lies behind it. In that sense I don't need to personalise it at all. You could even apply it to business figureheads...look what happened to a few at the EU when fraud was uncovered."

"Those that went...they moved on, quietly. There was a pension to console them..."

"Sure, I'm only making the point, behind the mask...what? Another human being with all the frailties that you and I have."

"At least they don't have their cigars hidden!" Hans once again had run out of stock, the cigar had been chewed to a pulp. He pulled at the drawers of his desk. "Go on, but not much longer?"

"The investigation may turn out that we can open a few eyes and show the wider implications of what he may be involved in."

"He?"

"Yes, he – Kahn! Or any man like him."

"There you go, personal again."

"Christ! Hans. I'm interested in the type of guy who comes from a background that may have at the core a streak of dishonesty that, however long ago, gave an advantage that should have been shared out. Who knows what can be raked up, or raked over." He smiled; it was beginning to sound pious. "Ideals? If you're going to peddle them we may as well know if they can be supported by actions?"

"Idealism! I'm glad there's at least one who still believes in them on the 'paper amongst us cynical and bruised hacks," Hans laughed.

"So?"

"So, work on it. I'm only giving you stick to see how strong your conviction is, to see if you will carry it through." He paused but Hans received no answer. "Listen carefully – twin track the personal angle with the wider perspective. I've thought over what you said a few days ago, before Monique messed you up."

"She hasn't."

"This is me you're talking to."

"Ja...okay, okay!"

"The guy who has the power over there, he influences and affects all of us. We may as well see if a much wider constituency should have a small, distant voice in what goes on?" Hans threw the printed sheets over the desk at him. "Work on it some more. In the meantime...let's get on with the present jobs in hand, hm?"

"Thanks."

"One last thing...ever seen the film, *"The Mouse that Roared"*?"

"No...never heard of it."

"Check it out. Fiction may become fact."

That was three days ago; it seemed longer.

He had lived through what he took to be long hours tracking down interviews and belting out proofs for the City desk reporting on the financial markets. The indices of the Beurs, the equivalent of the Dow Jones and the FTSE 100 ran in a ticker tape along the foot of the PC's screen. The endless flow of figures was distracting, more irritating than the e-mails that popped up to interrupt his concentration. But what remained of his attention was all over the place, a jigsaw of ragged thoughts, and, worse still, images. They merged to become a pornographic, an erotic, wet dream; only he was too awake, too involved and not too phlegmatic after all.

He cared and found out that he had 'loved' her, *'whatever that means'* he'd once heard someone say, the cynic. He had been a lucky man too with a beautiful companion. But in me, he thought, there had been no ambivalence, no alternative was being sought much less discreetly available, no one different to lose sight of the company and faithful pleasure - back home.

'What a jerk I've been!' he thought. Moni should have been told, open in fact meant closed; the door, the arms and legs, the moist bucking haven shut to all but him. Never mind the pills and alcohol, the spirit fuelled chain-breaker that left them now on two sides of a divide he had never even

considered in the same breath that wafted the air between them when they were close, so close that they felt as one.

Sure, the magazines, the streets, the clubs and bars were full of look-a-likes, more enhanced in figure, voluptuous and somewhere, someone in time would grow susceptible to his interest. But they weren't Monique, and she wasn't the girl – there was an age difference, don't you forget that – of his memory, the carefully sculpted image that after all distracted him from reality. They led separate lives, shared hectic moments in between the things normal couples do, but they returned to their own places.

It was a dysfunctional relationship and the chink of light, a breach in a defence – yes damn it, a matrimonial one – gave another, *him* over there, an opportunity to exploit. Would a little band have signalled that they were truly – madly – deeply one body, the necessary seam that bound them together?

I need time. Once, we had so much more; now it seems like we're on the road to losing everything between us. He sat in the sunshine and waited for another, but unsullied, beauty.

11

"Hey! Edi! Over here!" They met at the usual table but Ger gripped her hand with vigour, kissed her cheeks with the full press of his lips, not the air-kiss or lighter brush of skin that passed for a greeting.

"I saw you, don't worry!" she laughed with a flick of her head that transformed her blonde hair to a sun-kissed halo for an instant. His hand detained her and seconds passed before they sat down. "You look tired..." The note of concern drifted away.

"Not on account of my assignment, or you..."

"Want to tell me about it?"

"I...," he toyed with the idea. "No...it'll be okay. The outside world, the one we spoke of last time...it came in and took what I had."

Her lovely eyes rested on him; he had changed his mind. Edith's world, so he thought, would not encompass what he knew of another's. He opened a canvas bag, with it's smaller pockets concealed by the flap, and held out the tube; the pills still rattled. Moni had taken what she needed, transferred them to another; he kept two as samples for analysis – so, she might miss them. "Look what I have managed to obtain!" He smiled now; they were on track at last.

"Where did you get this?"

"My outside world brought it...lucky for us." He forced another smile.

"Really?"

"No," he sat with shoulders hunched looking out over the water. "Fortunate is a better word. Happily even, for us."

"I understand now, what you meant by your mail – *'with you all the way'*.

"I *really meant* it," he growled. Edi's hand touched his arm.

Skin-on-skin, it always worked even at this simple uncomplicated level. Two people sharing a thought, forging another link. He had kissed Monique good-bye, not for good they said, but it felt like it. Her tears had been those of loss, the insistent calls to her mobile 'phone the removal of his take on proceedings. He had told her that if something new, different and an alternative had been awakened then she should follow the impulse; he could not detain her. *'We'll meet as friends'* he had said in a rare moment of banality. The telling of her story had wounded him; but, it was the faint love bite on her thigh, the sign of wanton intimacy that provoked deeper outrage. It was so male, so possessive, so unexpected. It was a tag, a proprietary claim; it seemed irrelevant how quick or how easy the squelch may have been; the sight of it on her fair skin brought discord.

Moni had been honest, she could not hide that from him; she had been brave, he loved her for that; the mark had been a sign, that she had thought and finally given herself to someone *else*.

"Ger?" The voice was different, softly modulated. It held nothing of the brittle vitality he had grown accustomed to.

"Yes?" he said absent-mindedly.

"I'm here, Ger." Edith didn't quite know why she did it, then. Her fingers touched his face.

He sighed with a sense of melancholy. Pull your self together!

"And I'm glad for that." He acknowledged her touch. "This measly little tube," he said brightening, "has fanned the small flame of interest that you ignited." Before she could react he kissed the tips of her fingers. Edith looked about her and pulled her hand out of his loosened grip. "Look…this is a piece, an outline that I submitted to my Editor. Don't show it to anyone else…promise me that, please?"

He had removed the two pages from his bag the text amended to add cohesion to some of the arguments or strands of thought Hans had faulted.

Edith took the pages without a glance. She had started the day especially early, to make time so that nothing would be rushed with Gerard. He was the focus of attention now; he wore a dark blue suit, a cream soft collared shirt – no tie but then she was already prepared for his relaxed approach to dress. Only now, he had made an effort and she had to smile; it was a little ray that he basked in as their eyes met. Their paths had up to then run parallel to each other; now they touched.

"I've got this for you," she said evenly in spite of the touch of skin as he took the pages from her. "Pictures, to give you some context, a valuable…and I'd say…telling insight."

12
At The Kahn Family Beach House On Long Island

"Where's that girl? Where's Dayle?" Marie asked looking at her daughters in turn. "That girl needs a spanking, just like when she was a kid!"

She laughed, fussing over them all, the photographers were set up and they now had to wait. Her youngest was still a handful; she'd been to College, made her folks proud and made her own luck. Maybe Dayle was blessed; she had earned a trial period at one of the City's main media houses; it had been her reward for putting her mind to any job she secured. It gave experience, of life and people she had to mix with. She drew attention to herself, but the bad girl image was a con, Marie knew she *just* loved to rebel against family orthodoxy.

"I'd offer to do it…but business would suffer."

Flip Forsell spoke under his breath, close to the ear of his photographer. They exchanged a sly laugh, soto voce. The girl in cropped slacks and cotton sleeveless blouse, her blonde unruly tresses framing an all too worldly face had been checked earlier, walking barefoot through the grass of the compound to the Kahn's beach house on the south fork of Long Island, off the Montauk Highway.

'Grade A' nooky for some lucky guy' they had said to each other.

"Just like her to keep us all waiting."

Her eldest sister drew on a cigarette and blew the smoke with practised nonchalance up towards the ceiling. Smartly dressed with immaculate make-up and hair she was clearly well acquainted with the society photograph routine. Fakery certainly, but the image was what mattered here.

The two from Forsell Promotion paid little attention to her opinion, they knew where their preference for picture taking lay. It wasn't in the stage-managed ritual that provided the easy dollars that kept the business respectable in the eyes of customers. Careful networking with Kahn contacts had finally delivered work that could be syndicated and promoted the name. Magazine shoots, models and the ritzy bitchy lives that sold clothes, cars and attitude were more their thing. And then, there was the bottom drawer work, the discreet delivery service of audio-visual material that turned the most bespoke tailored clientele into pestering texters and dialers. The cash, and that was the only way to deal in that trade, rolled in. Not too many deals were struck or had to be done. The players willing to join didn't just call you. They were hand-picked, drawn in at first by offers of a contract after a 'meeting', a drink or two in 'glam' surroundings, and a discussion considered all the options.

For this anniversary shoot both FP and a society magazine were the only snappers. The glossy would take the pictures to grace the cover of the next issue – inside, sycophantic words on the sociable minimalist house, the expensive clothes, the furniture, the lifestyle, the future and the known past. It was the Kahn's at home, en famille; the prose would be gushing, fawning and routinely everyday, hairdresser's chair or manicurist salon reading. FP's shots sold the man with his family about him to the voting public – tailored to confirm a suitable choice for the influential, restrained for those that did not read the airy garbage that cost three bucks and put a hole in your bag. No, FP would put John Kahn where the real voter would read it, better still for them see the party political machine in action for them.

The sunny afternoon shoot, in the understated family room with the windows flung open to the Atlantic air, was the top-drawer session. The real man, at work, was scheduled for a couple of days; that was the start of a bid to win the campaign for the hearts and minds of the ordinary citizen. Someone had to do it and eye-candy in the shape of Dayle Kahn offered distraction enough. There had been nothing docile or youthful in the girl's unflinching stare, no petulance in the pout of her gently parted lips when he greeted her, acknowledging that in the short time she had been at a competitor company he had already heard of her, professionally.

Her name alone brought invitations to parties, promotions for a new range at a fashion house, and – he couldn't grip this – art galleries, but the Met had a show on Goddesses and there had been a few imitations then. Only in rare cases did the high maintenance women and rich partners that he associated with frequent such events. Instead they hung out at functions were new money, business and media types spent their time, mingling with edge of mainstream musicians and the mayhem that brought excess, as a participant or recorder.

Dayle was becoming adept at personal appearances and she enjoyed her entrance now, still barefoot but in a floating swirling floral print dress that screamed '*look at me!*' Attention seeking was one thing she did not, after all, have to work too hard at. The overall tan, the tied back hair with the floral band, and the look she now gave John said it all.

"Jeez!" was all the photographer had to whisper. Flip heard the digital camera hum twice, as shots were taken, from the hip.

"D'ya get that?" Flip's mouth barely moved.

It made his wick twitch just looking at the girl who's eroticism lay in the break with convention all around her, in his perception of the *'possible'* that lay in her eyes, of lowering herself and enjoying the experience. Dayle fascinated him; he had taken his predilections for such women, or girls, further and made money from it. Not simply from the more prosaic photo sessions for clothes stores, corporate advertising or flyers but the freakier option that lay in the intimacy of home – his bedroom – and a concealed camera or two.

"Yeah…a few on her own before she took hold of Jack's arm."

They were images to be stored away, in ambition's catalogue, Flip thought. You can never tell when they might be useful. They were the lascivious thoughts of a carefully packaged and well-dressed man whom Elbee relied on; product and the ambitions of John had brought them together.

"Glad you could make it honey," a cultured voice sang out, waspish in discomfiting her sister.

"Place our sis by the sofa, and cover them legs gal!" another piped up. "Better still, kneel down."

It was a small chorus of good-humoured malcontent from older siblings. Dayle merely tossed back her hair with an imperious finger twitch and twisted to stare up at John. He murmured something and she smiled, posing all the time, her dress tightened against her voluptuous form.

"It's hot and we're at the beach house. So, what's the rush to be a Park Avenue grande-dame?" She gave Marie an apologetic smile. "The time may yet come…for me and all that."

"I got that too, the body beautiful," the photographer murmured. "I'll crop the rest of them out of it…take only the best."

"Keep on snapping," Flip said pretending to make an adjustment to the tripod, brought for effect rather than out of necessity. He moved towards the group. "Nothing too formal for us, please? It's a shot of a family brought together for the weekend…it's a break from routine. We can use the shoeless weekender too!" The glossy could take its turn.

They all laughed, except Dayle.

"Stop movin' around!" Jay, that was the guy's name, called out. Pretty as a bird, and self-obsessed, just like his boss. "Hold still, this one pose!"

"Let them see I'll vote for him." Dayle spoke out looking up at her father. "We do as we please, it's our home," she whispered to him and winked.

"Still!"

"Whatever you have in the camera…Flip, it's copyrighted," she said directly. Her sisters turned to look up at her. The slow practised eye scan as Flip re-arranged the pose was intrusive. "Isn't that so Elbee?"

"What are you saying? That we should tell them what they can use?" He stood by the photographers, arms folded with an occasional twitch to adjust his slim framed glasses.

"Well, we don't know what camera-boy has taken, now do we?" She gave him a short stare before she looked again at Flip. "I guess you can check it out, as the family's legal counsel?" She turned to Elbee once more.

"That's my girl," John laughed. "Competition for you Flip, she's learning fast."

"Any new product?" Elbee shot Flip the question as they stood by the front door of the house. He acknowledged the wave of the magazine's correspondent as she drove past them on the crunching gravel, a few grains flew up in the dust. The shoot was over. Dayle had made her point but did not follow through.

"In the trunk of the car. I don't know what was in that tube your client's company makes but it was more than steaming."

"Oh?"

"Nothing quick, just those pills and a few drinks…and it all became very easy after that." Flip arched his eyebrows and chuckled as he remembered the night with those stewardesses. "Yeah, more like a one long pleasure cruise."

"You'll get the usual pay out…what about delivery?" Sometimes he had to deal direct. Middlemen were safer, a defensive shield, but there was an element of self-interest in doing things this way, for both of them.

"Now. Got your laptop, in its bag?"

Elbee nodded.

"Meet you in five minutes, in the hall," Flip said.

"Right…" Elbee answered slowly and shifted his weight. "After this we cool it for a while, everything on the level, no calls or talk about product. We keep working but for the man himself and the campaign."

"No diversions…no new activity at all, along the way?"

"Hell no! That's history, we did most of that as kids, in 'Nam, big time!" Elbee laughed. "Wild oats and all that stuff." John did his own thing now; they weren't in each other's debt like then, recreational wanderings on their minds wherever it could be found.

"You said," Flip said and left him to wait.

He had heard a few anecdotes, the tales of derring-do in and out of the jungle. It had been more like *'fucking blind crazy dog antics'*. He remembered nearly all the words that Elbee had used on the one occasion they had a drink and talked of their 'client'. Out of the Huey and away, with a few trusted and hardened colleagues, Elbee had been one of them, though looking at him now he had to wonder how he'd kept up. John Kahn was still in shape and he could imagine that he had endured the hardship with his men, as a non-com…but not as much as some.

"So?" Elbee wanted the transaction over with as Flip came up to him with a small, neatly wrapped package.

"Feast your eyes!"

"Sure." Elbee flicked him a glance and made to leave.

"Any sense in a trip down to DC? Arlington, maybe?"

"No. We…John did that for the 'New Yorker'. There'd been too many names on the marble walls but John had spent his time looking for those of guys they'd known.

"Oh, yeah." Useful promotion for FP had been missed.

"Flip, you'll get your chance. Only, get me the takes from today, the rest will follow over the weeks." Elbee turned to walk over to his car. "Guess I'll have something to unwind with later?"

"Got an hour or so?"

Flip laughed out the words. She had been hot, taken as a lucky hit, but the corporate customer was too big to mess around with copies. Elbee would get one; he would keep the other, in a safe. Repetitions were now strictly off the record and for him, just pleasure steaming, and nothing close to work.

"I wasn't fooling, being clever with that man," Dayle rolled her eyes. "That guy…Flip!" She looked at her father evenly. "What a name! Know much about him?"

"Elbee introduced us, said he was good with the type of folks I need to appeal to. He's had him checked out."

John studied his daughter's face. She had Marie's hair just as he remembered it when she was younger; the girl also possessed the same vitality but not the style in high society that he had fallen in love with. Marie had confidence and a carefully nurtured class. Times had changed and Dayle, by comparison, was simply up to the minute in attitude and fashion. Reflectively he touched her face; it was a shame she had something of his fleshy nose that spoilt the oval symmetry and cheekbones.

"Dad?" she looked at him fondly.

"We're not looking at flash money and apartments up in the clouds…with no understanding of how it is on the street when things are tight."

"When did you last connect with that?" She gave him a hug; there were few moments to be truly alone together. "I didn't like the camera guy either, by the way."

"I'm in touch through my work, darling," he smiled softly, "my special, unrecognised work. As for 'camera-boy'…I heard that much from you."

"He was at it…snapping. The pair of them were up to something… snapping mostly me, when we weren't close."

"You're a beautiful young woman, different from your sisters, that's what caught their eye."

"Sorry," she said shaking her head. "I didn't like either of them, they seemed to be coming on to me." She shuddered.

"Darling, they don't stand a chance…they'd have to get past me first." He nudged her shoulder and they laughed.

His youngest had caused him heartache, from the earliest days of her life. She was never quite his *'little girl'*; she fought, how she struggled for her right to be amongst them, and with him. He sensed her importance from the earliest hours then days, hearing in the ear splitting cries and halting breaths that each day should never be taken as *'easy'*. Now, she took her life as it came and tried to make something of her own; he felt protective but had no say in what she did. Dayle never called on him except for his attention; her allowance was barely touched, Marie had told him. Her sisters settled into privilege and were manipulative on account of the security it gave – he and his wealth gave them. They were through one marriage already, the pair of them. The 'glam fest' as he called it, the parties, produced too many distractions. But Dayle watched and listened; her bitchy riposte at the shoot was typical; if really pushed she could be goaded into less than lady-like remarks. But, when they were alone she was his girl and they could speak of commonplace things. Her eyes were still, untroubled but contemplative.

"I can take care of them…don't go worrying about that."

A distant rumble of thunder broke the stillness of the warm evening and made them turn, a shroud of misty cloud and the grey white slant of rain could be made out behind them, far enough away not to force a premature return to the house. The Atlantic stretched out before them. John sat down on the sand, buried then wriggled his toes, filled his large hands and watched the grains run through his fingers like an hour glass.

"Right."

"What do *you* know of 'FP', Flip's outfit? What a name for a man!" She bubbled with relaxed laughter and held onto his arm.

"You always were my *'questioning'* daughter," he smiled. "They're fashion and reportage photographers, develop promotional audio –visual material, that kind of thing. Elbee persuaded me that we should try a more street-wise outfit." He studied his daughter with sideways glances. She had his full lips, possessed too much of his wide nose to make her open face outstandingly pretty but the fresh skinned, almost raw complexion and sun bleached hair with its ragged parting gave her the appeal that many men craved to be seen with. "Something tells me there's more to what you're thinking...you gonna share that inside track?"

"No...just take care, and...watch Elbee as well."

"Huh?" He was amazed, then laughed. "Why...the guy's been to hell and back with me! Next to Mom, Elbee's the one I can trust...the most."

"And me."

"Sure, only with him it is all wrapped up in business and this mayoral thing."

"Thing?" Dayle let go of his hand. "Thing? You're going for office, one of the biggest...in the US, maybe in the World. Show that you *want* to do it...show *why* you want to stand for office...you do, don't you?" She knelt before him, "Otherwise you're fooling...with a lot of people who expect more of you and all the other candidates...wackos some of them...but they believe in what they're trying to do, they have some sincerity in their intentions, I hope." Flip Forsell wasn't going to sell sincerity that quickly.

"Sure, I want to do it...there's a dynamic all of its own in there." She heard the steely edge to his voice as he stared out over the water. "We...our ancestors came from way out over there." He pointed and she clung to his strong forearm, his finger barely moved. "They chose this place to settle into a new life...to get it would be the peak...bar one." His hands cupped her face. "I've got things to attend to next week...business and family things that you needn't worry yourself about. Just take care...of *you*."

"Promise me *you* will...watch out for those two especially that Flip, he's too smooth in that tan suit and fancy striped shirt...with surfer boy, only I don't think he's been near a board."

"Wanna be on my team?" John pulled on her hands. "Come on, the squall is going to hit soon." The breeze had risen to a gusting wind heralding the approach of the rain.

"I am on your team...only, I'd be more use as someone on the outside looking in." She threw her arms about his neck and kissed him. "Let's just say I hear things, and.....see things. The suit's just cover, he wears other more hip gear...that helps him blend in with the more *usual* company he keeps."

"Said as though he were low-life."

"No, not quite. You've given his career...his business, a boost. I think you need a team from our world to do the complete job."

"I thought you weren't part of *'our world'*, Mom's and mine?"

"Dad," she said softly, "I love you...I owe you everything."

"Almost..."

"Yeah, almost everything to you both. I'm not cloning material, easily moulded or manipulated." She knew exactly the type of guy Flip was. Mom had told her Dad was wild, great fun when they met...he had gone and returned. She hadn't been used, simply treated as an object. "The guy's come from nowhere," she said speaking out her thoughts; a stranger had entered their lives and she already felt he was far too close to make it feel comfortable. The media world was tightly knit and descriptions of him didn't come anywhere near to the man her father needed if he was to fulfil his ambition.

The first spots of rain began to fall.

"Race you back?" he said pulling on her hand but his grip also meant '*no way*', just keep me company for these last few moments.

"Okay!" She ran flat-footed and he slowed his own pace. The clouds above them burst, the rain stabbing in gentle pinpricks then increasing in tempo until they held up their arms in useless protection.

"Come on girl! Show me what you can do!" John ran ahead, turning to look at her and slipped flat-arsed, slithering like a snake, his track a silvery mark in the flashes of light on the coarse turf. The trees and shrubs were bent over, rustling furiously as noisy accompaniment to the swirling wind. "Whoaaah!"

"That'll teach you!" Dayle shrieked as much in pain as enjoyment from their short-lived experience. She bent down to him as a veil of thin clothes now stuck to her skin, outlining every curve. "Another scrubbing job for Treece on them pants of yours!" She laughed joyfully and splashed the water on the rough grass.

"C'mon girl? Race ya again!" He lunged off once more with Dayle close at his heels.

"I've got a better idea, Pops!" She grabbed his hand as they slowed to a stop near the house. Dayle held out her hands and waited.

"Dance? You mean dance, in this?" He began to hum, then sang out the words as they took a few swirling slippery steps. "Can't hear you!"

"We're singing…we're dancin'…we're slippin…" she sang tunefully but to the accompaniment of the noisome wind and rumbles of thunder.

"We're a prancin'…we're a slippin' in thuuhhh?"

"In the RAAAIINNN!" they chorused.

They didn't care anymore how the rain hit them and finally leant against each other gasping and laughing like kids as they sheltered in the portico, watching the gutters overflow; it was like standing behind a wall of water as the storm rumbled and flashed overhead. There was no sign that any of the others were in the least bit interested in them.

"I'll handle it all," he yelled in his baritone voice. "I'll do what's needed, don't you fret, darling." She just about heard him in the echoing chamber.

"Okay," she nodded slicking back her hair and looking very youthful. "That was fun!" Great fun, for a while, she thought.

Her Dad had enough to contend with, in the shape of Henry Lascelles-Brown. He was danger, of a different kind though, an enigma if he was to act as her father's communications and advocacy advisor. Mom had shushed her idle thoughts, expressed during one of the weekly visits to the apartment and re-acquaintance with Park Avenue living. They went back a long way, blah, blah, blah. It was a mutual life support system with Elbee around to take care of trouble or to see to it that intrusions went away. So, why admit someone like Flip Forsell into the circle? He was even travelling down to the facility in Virginia, and a visit to Williamsburg in the morning; he would be there to glimpse, at first hand, their way of life as they were taken in the expensively hired executive jet from East Hampton to Newport News.

She knew there was *'family'* down there, only, they never met and Dad rarely mentioned them.

13

"Family, associations and relationships. They keep all of us and bind human kind together."

John said it to himself as he pulled the skin of his face taught. Shaving was a good time to think, to look at yourself and to ask yourself *'are you doing it right'*?

The conclusion soon came that family only concerned *his* immediate blood relatives and the loving wife who still lay asleep in the bedroom behind him. Family also existed in another state but they were *'just'* people with whom business was transacted. There was no unity of spirit or affection. These remote, even cold and perfunctory dealings with 'family' was so alien to his real nature. It created a barrier but that was how his father had bequeathed a link to the past. It seemed more like the shackles of history, a bequest and one that he continued to pay for. A wrong had been committed that could not be made good or righted, however much he thought of it and how to do so. The unwanted burden was a cross that he would gladly cast to one side. Necessity then, way back, had become for him, now, an unnatural habit.

Elbee took care of the everyday details just as the law firm had done, long after the hope filled early years of Frederick and Margaretha had been left behind. Service in 'Nam, and a few quiet words, had seen his buddy placed in a legal practice where his guile could be relied upon. The family personalities were known only by reputation, or from grainy and fading photographs, from a few tattered letters and fusty legal documents with their almost indecipherable script, from affidavits and meticulously witnessed scrolls of thick paper. None of this 'history' seemed to belong in a family as he wished to know of it, but he played his part in this complex grouping or intricate web.

Apart from him, and in certain circumstances Elbee, no one asleep in the beach-house around him had anything to do with that side of the 'family'; they barely knew any of the names, he was certain of it.

Hold up a photograph and a name could not be put to any of them. They only knew the figureheads from long ago, faces peering out from an oil painting on the wall of his den, in the city apartment that was miles away.

Virginia was home for the Koehlers, a branch of the family that had gone its own way, led by Margaretha into their own wilderness and separated from Frederick. She had been the loyal wife until scandal tore them apart. Reconciliation had been forsaken and her name had been changed...to that of her own family, back in Europe. A child was expected, conceived by a beauty, Frederick's new mistress, whose reputation was sullied. It was news beyond enduring after all that Margaretha had renounced. She had forsaken everything and crossed an ocean to be with her own man; only Frederick forsook her and callously disregarded the sacrifices she had made to be with him.

She too had been a mistress, once. The mistress, the nurse, the woman who married a wealthy Amsterdammer had fled before, carrying a secret. Margaretha had learnt from a wise man; she knew that secrets could be traded. Frederick had taught her well. But, one secret remained hidden, for the eyes of only those in an immediate circle of confidantes, and there were very few...it had to remain that way.

"Pa told me that much, I worked the rest out for myself." John splashed his face and removed the remaining shaving lather. "Another day of give and take...in the family way."

Margaretha's secret became a chip in the game that she had come to recognise as life in a far off continent where all of Europe's dispossessed, new beginners and starry-eyed hopefuls turned to. The language was foreign to her ears, yet others were all too recognisable. But, why live so far from your own kith-and-kin and listen to a polyglot of languages when you could do so in a society and culture so comfortingly familiar? Because of Frederick. She had given it all up for the love of one man and he had betrayed her.

John glanced at his watch, stainless steel and gold on his lightly tanned wrist. Thirty minutes until the car came, then a day of business and family. For any other sane human being the two would be distinct; for him they melded into one, inextricably. The sting had been taken out of the hurt, the wound cauterised over the years, but the legacy remained to be spoken of across a table, confined to formal handshakes and polite conversation. If any emotion surfaced the mind overcame the impulse of the senses. There would be no reaching out to touch; absent was the offering of a kiss to recognise a family or blood tie; the acknowledgement of a common heritage remained unspoken even if the origins of a new dynasty lay far away over the sea.

He was a member of a wider world; technology was of no consequence, insignificant, cold and dispassionate in the meeting of minds that perpetuated a divide they were no part of, merely the inheritors and uncomfortable perpetuators. The story had been woven into their lifes' tapestry; it could not be unravelled, the threads were woven in too tight; they were too brightly coloured by experience over the years to be rewoven into a looser open weave that spelt renewal and a relinquishing of the past.

"I am...me!" He spoke it out clearly at his reflection in the mirror. The words echoed in the small room, bounced off the walls and returned, harshly modulated by hard tiled surfaces. "I am...*who?*"

A man perpetuating a guilty secret? No, a man with a mission to accomplish, a man to reduce or eliminate risks, to go prepared and armed with forceful arguments. It was not a life-or-death struggle, a combat by force of arms. Yet, the endeavour he had embarked upon involved intellect and perceptions of those from a very different world that he moved in. He had dealt with the likes of the VC, those zealots he had killed, from afar, or face-to-face, the ones whose agonised expressions stuck in his mind to that day. He remembered only too clearly the look that drilled into him from lifeless staring half-closed eyes and a half smile on the brown lips.

'You took my body, my life...but not my mind'.

Now the roles and the expectations were reversed. The electorate he was soon to meet had to be won over in a very different contest but he saw it as a fight all the same.

Dayle, that lovely daughter of mine! Her words remained with him.

Argument had failed with the Koehlers; right had been on their side; it was not openly expressed but he always came to trade and, to strike a bargain once more that maintained a fragile status quo.

Fragility was not a character trait that he saw too much of in himself. Never give another the advantage over you. It had been drilled into him, saved his life and brought him venal pleasure in the arms of countless whores during his tours of duty and on R & R. Elbee had been his saviour then and he could think of it no differently now. The Koehlers remained family; you could stretch the word to breaking point, no elasticity left in the band, but it held, just. It was all he could hope for. He hated it, even the thought of the shabby start, the inheritance that became the family endeavour, *his* family's enterprise in the United States of America.

Dad had whispered it all to him, in the days before he passed on. Everything he did in 'Nam had been worth it. He'd justified his actions then as one more correction, a reason for being a Kahn living in America, fighting and maybe dying for the country his family had taken to and made their fortunes in. The start didn't matter so much now; by his reckoning he and his forebears had expunged much of the legacy by their own deeds. PulcriMed had made good in abundance the hurt of betrayal left by Frederick on Margaretha and with the proceeds of money so secretively taken and invested over the years.

Only...only the mind could never quite be free of it.

He had no doubts of the importance that had been attached to the bequest, for the business, for the family asleep around him, and to his aspirations.

'Guilt' was not a feeling that he felt, too often.

"Hi," a sleepy voice said. Marie put her arms about him, and groped for the flesh that had pleasured her. "So many men...in just one body."

"Uh...huh," he smiled and winked at her.

"Not so fast," she said against the skin of his back.

"Gotta go...I really have" He had finished shaving and almost dragged her, for she clung to him in a sleepy torpor, to the shower cubicle. "You joining me in here?" He only half smiled before Marie covered his mouth in a deep kiss.

"Wherever you are lover..."

"I am with you."

"Yes." She had spoken and written the simple statement countless times, from the very first excited breathless calls when they had met to her long letters when he was overseas. They had been teenage lovers tempted but, unusually for the permissive times, indifferent to the attractions of anyone else. "Come back soon?"

"Yeah..." He had a lazy, laconic way of speaking that could often border on the complacent side of indifference. He always returned, even after activity elsewhere and with someone else. "You're still the best....the only one for me."

She had lost a best friend on account of him. Retaliatory flings were an idea, the preliminary engagements had been tried but penetrative sex never followed her own attempts at escape from wounding betrayals of what she saw as wedlock. She was at one with him, 'of one flesh', you might say. Sharing or giving herself to anyone else meant the rejection of all that she had been brought up to believe. Different certainly; her classmates and girlfriends who became women at the same time as her seemed to know how to carry on. But, they were through several marriage partners already, got the houses and cars, whatever, and moved on. Now it was lifestyle management, shopping, good times and personal trainers, programmes to exercise all body parts.

"And you're still my man."

She worked very hard to ignore these diversions. Promiscuous indifference passed her by. Denial made her times with John all the more potent. He knew it, called out to her that it was so…and, she felt it from him. She still believed in *'them'*, even if the whispers sometimes came to her, or the evidence told her otherwise. Without her, John would be just another businessman, with other hopes and dreams, and a partner that spelt out loser, untrustworthy, a man with few or no principles. She knew John was none of those things. John still cared and needed her; yes, it lay deep down within her one and only man.

There hadn't been anyone else for a long time, but then a partner found out long after the activity ceased and the innuendo and muted sympathetic laughter – maybe the jostling for a replacement - began. These preceded the calls to do lunch or a fashion show. For many nothing settled fractured egos and a broken heart more than the maxing out of an account with your favourite fashion house, a statement handbag or two, or a pair of dying-to-get boots.

To hear some of her more indiscreet friends, one-to-one over a cocktail, in flagrante' had a whole new meaning when a masseur had his hands on you to tease out the hurt and resentment. The oils soothed, you didn't feel so bad and the door could be locked or wedged to increase the sense of discovery. You couldn't help yourself slip-sliding to temporary oblivion. He'd almost taken you there already, your mind and his probing flesh did the rest. After that, you found a new place to work out and bubble away the hours.

"How do I look?" He was dressed in a dark blue suit and cream shirt, his favourite mix, and a sober striped tie. "Better than when I arrive after a flight?"

"You've still got it all, John." She kissed him and relaxed in the caress of his hands over her back and buttocks. "Love you…come back and love me."

"Wherever you are, lover…" he smiled.

"I am with you."

John had it all, thirty years and she never really looked to anyone else, any male, for consolation. And, he'd become serious and devoted to a whole new project, to service but of a very different kind. Their marriage made a whole lot of sense again; forget all the doubting moments that surfaced when he was away from her. They both had real family names to wonder at. It could yet count for a heck of a lot – for everything.

14

"I trust you implicitly, buddy."

John spoke quietly as he stood by Elbee, near the car that had taken them to the airport, waiting for Flip to appear from his hotel. Even before Dayle's remarks he had decided that the beach-house was not open to all-comers.

She had clearly arrived at the same conclusion but via an altogether different route. He riffled through the papers in his attache' case, checking once more that due allowance had been made to deal with a family matter before the facility visit aimed at raising the bar on a performance target. Then, a flight to Newark and a dinner date.

"And I you," Elbee said in reassurance. "These annual meetings get to you I know, but it's one hell of a lot simpler than it was before."

"Take your word on that; it couldn't be worse in my book. Should've settled the whole goddamn business decades ago. Now we have to make provision for all kinds of things....in case someone leaks the story or someone noses around....or butts in." Like this guy walking towards them. "Here's Flip and the camera man."

"Camera boy..." Elbee smiled and turned.

"Right," John acknowledged their wave. "It's good to have Dayle around in that circle. We can check out other talent, source people we can use or tap for any help when we need it."

"Flip? He's okay."

"Let's keep an open mind and our eyes open...that's all I'm saying."

"Right."

The car took them to a Gulfstream IV on hire for the day, the cost shared with an associate company, the executives staying over. John made certain there were no free rides, each subsidiary accounted for its own expenses. Luxuries like these would have to be scaled back in the coming months even though they made for a long but productive day.

"You guys okay with the itinerary when we get to Newport News? John and I have some business away to attend to." Elbee clutched his own copy of the programme, mailed to him by Cassie his PA. She provided personal activity for him; he was nothing but up front about that to John. Whatever else they spoke of he invariably answered John's questioning look when his roving eye settled on someone of interest. She was not the usual pneumatic sort he went for and found on the party circuit, but his indiscretions had been tamed. On any other business trip she would be with him.

"We're going to be quick, keep to the timetable real close...so, you won't be kept waiting and I get through the day's business. Right?" John stared briefly at Flip and nodded in a way to suggest there would be no discussion.

"Elbee's given me the programme...we'll fit in John."

"Good. Then let's go...let's get started."

The neighbourhood gave the property a settled appearance, its place in the tended landscape assured. The trees along the street gave full shade, a defining contrast to the sun-picked tiles of the roof that they brushed in the breeze. The not so perfect lines of the boarded walls lent the building a sense of place it could only have acquired through the passage of time. The grassed front garden with its neatly clipped hedges gave formality in contrast to the yard that they knew had been laid out behind the house; in the past it had been a comfortable and no doubt noisy home.

Now as they stepped from the car John could hear the screech of children's voices at play; the sounds were carried on the wind; here, it was family of a different sort, youngsters associated by handicap and a denial of all that he could take for granted.

"Wait here, please?" John said to the driver.

"We gonna get through this, quickly?" Elbee asked with ill-concealed tedium as they walked up the path.

"Yep…as long as it takes, and no more."

John was relaxed. He saw possibilities in every new day; sure, these meetings were never easy but he always looked to the positive, even out of situations that were not of his making and today, this was one of them. There was always an opportunity to be exploited; he had no plan in his head but you never could tell exactly what would come at you. Flexibility in response was nothing new.

"Okay."

"I'm not going to worry myself on this. Anna Beth is doing a valuable service…for all the folks around here, and for us, and the IRS knows it too." He smiled, persuasively. "C'mon, the coffee's good."

"I hate weak links…I want to close everything down or keep out what may hurt or bite you." Elbee fiddled with his thinly framed glasses.

"Copy that. The money's not the real issue, not deep down. They still like to think they have some influence in what we do or how we manage the business. The Kahn's built that from nothing, years after the break up of the marriage…it's an embarrassment I could do without." They stood in the middle of the path talking, half way between the sidewalk and the front steps leading onto the porch. "We manage the threat just as we've always done."

"For too long," Elbee interrupted, "for years."

"C'mon, Elbee?" John jerked his head in the direction of the house. "Let's put you out of your misery. You never know, we may even get a drink out of it, to congratulate ourselves on a deal."

Anna Beth Koehler-Denton ran the school that lay in a quiet suburb of the town. From the roadside, the colonial style property appeared to be just a house with a neatly tended and colourful front garden. The paved yard was out at the back and the only clues to its other purpose lay in the industrial grade fence enclosing it and keeping the kids from straying out of sight. The classroom block was separated from the house, its timber-clad walls and large picture windows topped by an asymmetrical roof that gave the structure some anarchic architectural style, a distinctive feature for visitors to remark upon.

In all, it offered an unassuming front for a charity that had been established by the Koehlers in the 1920's. It had been the brainchild of John's grandfather; there was nothing obvious or predictable about it as a vehicle for buying silence; from that viewpoint it was just as Elbee liked it. To his God-less and cynical heart a foundation that served both good and evil, however distant now, was the ideal. Donations lent greater authenticity and a respectable nuance to the real purpose. The work of the school and Anna Beth's devotion to undertaking public and private service drew praise; besides, benefaction looked good in company statements and press hand-outs. It seemed a 'win-win' arrangement for everyone.

"Good day, gentlemen," the receptionist said lightly, her confident eyes taking in the visitors. She'd observed them through the glass set into the heavy front door. "D'you have a pleasant flight?"

"Fine, thank you."

"You probably know we're here to see Mrs Koehler?" Elbee cut through the pleasantries and John restrained him with a click of his tongue.

"The property looks very fine, how has the year been? It's all spruced up, new coat of paint and all...I noticed." John smiled and appeared totally at ease.

"Had it done for the Board of Education visit a month or so back. We're going to do some expanding."

"Oh?"

"Yeah...so I hear others talkin'...you understan' me, sir?"

"Sure I do," John spoke reassuringly. "And the kids? Are they all happy.... as far as you hear others talking?"

"They sure are," the voice sounded shocked. "Mrs Koehler has a fine place, folks ask about it all the time." She picked up the house 'phone and announced the guests.

"I'll wait," John said as they came away from her.

There would be a pointed delay so he sat on a high backed, very polished bench; he took in once more the pictures on the walls; they had been explained to him the last time they called. It was a routine to be followed, a prelude to the meetings they always had with Anna Beth. She told them it gave *'context'*. Anna Beth had pointed out Margaretha's as one of the finer portraits, during an earlier visit.

"I hope the lady doesn't play this out too long," Elbee observed quietly. "We know the story well enough...no more reprises."

"Sure." John rested easily and with a soft clap of his hands, as if to confirm that he had come to a decision he went on, "Go get them camera guys over here, this'll be more valuable than a few snaps at the plant later."

"I wouldn't advise it." Elbee stared at him. "We're in Virginia…they'll ask why not do the same at a place in New York." He thought some more. "No sense in advertising the place's existence and your connections with it."

"Not *mine*…the business."

"Don't see there's a difference…I still don't advise it. Think it through John? There's no tellin' where the pictures may end up."

"This is family and business….if Flip's outfit is so good then we can use today, we can agree what is said, can't we?"

"Sure, we can spell it out. But, you lose control."

"Right…I've heard you. Now, please? Go and make the call." He turned to the receptionist. "So…how's Anna Beth?"

"You'll find out now. Come this way please?" Her eyes moved on. "He coming too?" she asked pointedly.

"Yes…I've asked him to bring our photographer over. I'll let Anna Beth know."

"She don't like surprises."

"I'll make it easy for her, I promise." John noted the sign of protectiveness in the young woman. Money and some publicity would overcome the shock, he felt sure of it.

Anna Beth Koehler-Denton was a striking woman, fair skinned and with a shock of blonde tinted hair that lent dignity to a kindly face. The fleshy features showed every soft furrow and line gathered over an interesting life of seventy years. The visitors knew of her shrewdness but the age softened eyes still held humour; they could sparkle, the creases by them deepening in concert with those on each side of her straight mouth. The lips were confidently coloured, no concession given to the passing of the years. An elegant yet simple collar-less navy blue outfit with its long sleeves held a vital spirit. A knotted primrose scarf gave a flash of colour; it was worn no doubt to demonstrate her contempt at the very idea that the spirit of youth should fade with the passage of time. She had been widowed for fifteen years; her life's work now rested in giving opportunity to children less fortunate than she, or one of the men now before her. A small starred brooch twinkled; fake or not, the stones glittered like diamonds on her breast.

"You messin' with me, John boy?" The matriarchal eyes flickered then rested upon him and her lips parted in a grin.

"No ma'am," he smiled back. She was an endearing old bird though she took you for what she could.

"You're nothing but polite," she said, disconcertingly heavy on the 'po'. "You should go into politics."

John stuck out a foot towards Elbee's leg. No need, there wasn't a twitch of a reaction, they'd learnt it all. Stay silent, don't make a sound, wait for the other side to talk or make a move. Less you said the less it would be held against you.

"I've got my parents to thank…family."

"How many you got?" It was always the same, these opening exchanges.

"Three, just like last time. It's nothing but fun now." He winked and after a moment's pause she gave a cultured laugh, soft and appreciative.

"Now I know you're messing with me!" Anna Beth sat upright in her chair. "There's family and then there's business only here we join them up. True?"

"Wish it were otherwise, but yes…it's true."

"So, what have you got for me to chew on?"

"Same as last time, nothing's changed."

"No business, if it's any good, doesn't do '*change*'"

"That's true," he had to agree with her.

"Why then…come here and tell me '*same as last time*'? She gave her voice a mimicking inflection.

John sat silently and made a few notes, doodles on the leather bound note pad that he carried. He wrote down the names of his children, then Marie; he drew a pair of feet with another pair inverted between them When they put their minds and bodies to it they were so good together. 'Change', that was okay for showing what you really had and took for granted, most times. Marie gave context to his life; the rest, the occasional extra activity was simply fooling around.

"Hm?" he replied almost humming.

"We've got plans, just like in your business…the one that grew so long ago from next to nothing."

"Others made more of it," Elbee interrupted.

Anna Beth continued as if she hadn't heard him. "My school has plans."

"And what are those…plans?" The doodling stopped and John looked again at Anna Beth. He wasn't going to take too long over this; the receptionist had already sown the seeds for his own solution.

"Building, out over in the yard, at the back…on the field we bought as an investment back in eighty six not long before your Pa passed away. He talked straight…no humming and hahing like some love-sick boy…none of these cold airy silences, like you two."

"We're just products of a different time, we've known other things. Deep down I still carry his torch."

"Speak then…what's on your mind?"

"Doin' the best for both of us, and …keeping the IRS sweet. Planned giving with the maximum tax efficiency…treat what we do as a donation maybe…see that we get it treated as a business expense or the like." John wrote it down then looked up to Elbee.

He nodded. "Just keeping the family in touch."

"Sweet you mean," Anna Beth responded but without any malice. "We've got a good school here…Ma's work with her second husband."

"And you can be proud of what you've achieved after her." John smiled. "You're doing fine, I can see that. So, a helping hand would I guess be welcome in the project…somethin' you can touch or feel. Make of the work an asset worth more than just cash, somethin' that won't run through your fingers."

"What else?" She twisted the rings on her left hand, each one in turn; gold bands from the middle finger to her pinky.

"A bit of publicity. I've brought a cameraman with me, just in case you agreed."

"Where? Is he snooping around?" Mary-Beth spoke over her shoulder as she went to the window in slow steady steps.

"No, take it easy. I've sent for them…but wanted your agreement first, before we set up anything." The idea was forming to include some of the kids with him and Anna Beth out in the yard.

"You've had it figured out, all along?"

"No ma'am. It came to me in the hall, when I was looking at Margaretha's picture."

"Fine portrait of a fine woman."

"We ain't losing sight of anything Anna Beth, just keeping some perspective…keeping a hold of things."

"The hold on things is a split between what was once family."

"Yes, long ago in the sense that you mean. I'm sorry for that."

"How sorry?"

"Not as in 'bleeding heart' sorry," Elbee muttered loud enough for her to hear. "Not so's we keep dripping on about it, over something from so long ago."

"And we were getting along just fine till you butted in, mister!" Anna Beth flicked her be-ringed fingers at him.

"He just means we treat, I treat the whole thing between us as 'legacy', we just help each other out where we can?" John soothed. "There's no bad blood between you and me…just legacy."

"Legacy," Anna Beth murmured. "Hers was to be cast aside while others…" Her voice drifted away. It revived. "But she was strong. Margaretha just got on with things…she rebuilt her life."

"And she wasn't left nickel and dime poor," Elbee butted in. For once he was irritated by the routine exchanges.

"No, just on the outside looking in, never enjoying what became of him…on account of her."

"Okay…," John began but she cut him short.

"Not okay! She missed out on what he achieved, the new family, your forebears John! He almost started off a dynasty on the wrong side of the blanket." John's stare hardened.

"Frederick never forgot the debt, not quite! I have to do something with it too, now, here with you, even now."

"So?"

"I made you an offer."

"No value attached to it."

"You mean how much?" John spread out his hands then pointed them at her raising his eyebrows in enquiry.

"Yes…name it…your price."

"No. You tell me what the bulding's worth to you and we'll figure out how to fix it."

"About one mill…"

"What!" Elbee exploded.

"Hm," John sat back and thought, looking only briefly to his friend. "On top of everything else you get, and I give…that's a very high price…a great deal for something neither of us was around to witness."

"But I had to live with it, the *'legacy'* as you called it."

"We both have to…it's getting the measure right." John made his reply sound thoughtful.

Anna Beth appeared to be pleased with herself. She had shocked them both. "Others, far away had to do much the same…I guess." She finished with an almost girlish sigh.

"Maybe the time's come to put an end to this?" John smiled at her upon the expression of a wish.

"We'll see on that."

John scribbled some figures and a sentence in capital letters and held it out for Elbee to read. As he waited for him John thought it over. Frederick had picked his spot for her but Margaretha had gone her own way, paid off by annual inducements to buy silence and discretion. No-one from the outside came looking for them; Margaretha's name change had been subtle and of help to Frederick and his new family; the death of his first-born made the tracks still harder to pick up. It broke Margaretha's heart until she found new hope, new love and a new world family out of it with another.

Only, there was no sense in being made to feel the past should be ignored. Even he, John Kahn, could call in favours given.

"She was provided for," Elbee said without looking up. John was willing to consider a more generous concession.

"Except for one thing…" Anna Beth answered him.

John sighed for the first time. "Anna Beth…we won't get anywhere going over all that, it's history."

"Living history, else why are you here?" Her eyes became very still and the lips pressed together.

Because your silence matters a whole lot right now, he thought. "Oh, family reasons…and I wanted to see you."

"Hah!" A hollow laugh greeted his remarks but she saw the smile on John's face and burst out in her own deeper laughter. "You want something, it's the same every year."

"And you don't?" He sat impassively again but Anna Beth was not so pushy now and looked at him. "A man could die of thirst here…any chance of a drink, please?"

"Go on! You've only just arrived."

"Seems longer…"

"What's it to be then?"

"To drink?" John smiled.

"Later…maybe. When we've got something to drink to," she winked. "Now, stop messin' with me."

""I'll agree to the money…for a *two* year deal. That's it, *no more*. If needed we spread it to keep the Revenue off our backs and to make it work for you too. I also get a few pictures with you and the kids outside…call it a memento."

Anna Beth smiled. "Fetch me that 'phone Mr Elbee, please?"

"Yes ma'am."

"They're not just any kids, John."

"No, and that's why I can go for this deal." He'd use it as a test for Flip to make the most of. There would be no pretty girl to impress or get his hands on.

15
Amsterdam

"It's hard to believe it…looking at this picture, that they're family, our relations in the New World." Only the New World was being exported, along with its attitudes, dress and influence. "Where'd you get it?" Gerard took off his glasses; there was no sense in spooking her.

"On the Internet," Edith gave him a small smile in acknowledgement of his concern for her. "I'm not bothered by them now."

"That's a relief."

"Yes…yes it is."

"You've been busy…"

"Yeah…in quieter moments when I was away. An interest in the news of John Kahn became an obsession…there, I've admitted it." Edith only just managed to smile now as she recalled all that she had been through. "The web's wonderful…you can obtain a great deal of genealogical and biographical detail on people…the Americans have a society devoted to it all. Then, there's tax records and other stuff to get a look at…to dig into…if you're minded to be involved."

"I'm impressed…nothing more or less. Dealing with census and tax list information is not the most exciting work to do…"

"But necessary…it got me, or us, where we are now. I have no doubts that John Kahn is a distant cousin…far removed from all of us here, but that doesn't change the blood ties."

"It's okay," Gerard soothed, "I can't help it, or wonder…why a woman like you…beautiful, should devote so much time to all of this…there are other distractions, or people to know and be with."

"Yeah…but for me it was a case of being particular."

She had not looked at him when the words had been spoken but Edith did so now.

"And that is how I am too," he smiled and held a hand out to her.

"I've got a folder with all that I've learnt of the man and his family…the obsession to learn about him is over. I'm through with all that, looking at births, marriages and deaths…where they migrated or moved to, when they proudly claimed to be 'American'. I even learnt when they discarded the Dutch connections and treated them as an episode of a past life. I learnt of land ownership…and that they did very well. The original stake went some way to making them what they…those Kahns over there, became."

"And who they are now?"

"It helped…I'm not going to deny that they had the business brains to make a life…how they just got on with their new life. They made the most of it at the expense of others, their family…here in Amsterdam. I laid it all out, the dates and the detail of their progress. I then looked and saw what the family here went through, how they made good after the setback. You don't see it just in money, or in terms of possessions…you see it also in altered lives, or an opportunity denied."

"Edith…Edith." He could only stare in sympathy at how obsessed, or overcome, Edith had been by the story and the effort to piece the few snippets of information together. He got up from his chair and leant over her, placing his arm about her shoulders. "Come on cousin…we move on and see what we can now make of it all."

"I'm your distant cousin…far removed, Ger. It is how I will continue to see us." She turned to the picture book once more. "Look…"

The family shot was clear, of beautiful women on parade with a practised sense of dress and style; he could only imagine what they were really like, their characters and how they behaved towards each other. Loving and supportive as he knew of his own close family and that he could pick up on with Edith, or was it competitive on account of an almost poisonous sibling rivalry?

Gerard replaced his glasses and gulped at the beer. An attractive blonde, with much of her father's features to see on her face paid no attention to the camera; instead she beamed at John Kahn; she played the doting daughter, maybe it was exactly the image they had sought. They alone appeared natural in the carefully composed picture. Intentional or not, the magazine had broken with a tradition and shown the family as he imagined the reality would be, on the day. John enjoyed Dayle's company; by the look of her she was rebellious and maybe behaved like a spitfire on a long leash when crossed. How could he know just from the picture he dwelt upon? His imagination began to run away. The readers would make their own judgement, just like him.

"Do you find them interesting?" Edith leant closer and studied the picture.

"Yes, very and strangely compelling." John Kahn was casually dressed in tan trousers and an open necked shirt, not the preppy fashion that the beach house setting might have required. It was the informal breaking of the rules that he saw and compared to the wondrously dressed and fleshy beauty of Marie Christine, the voluptuous but managed form of the dutiful wife. The others were 'A' list high life members, like their mother. "They could almost be like us," he said in a thoughtful whisper.

"Give or take half a billion dollars!"

"Much…much more!" He studied the second picture, altogether different in style and intended audience, far removed from the glossy. "And who might these two guys be with our man…sorry, our possible distant cousin? Hm…Henry Lascelles-Brown, legal counsel. I guess John can't move very far without one of those can he? And what about this one?"

"PR…his media man." She watched his finger stab the paper.

"What's he for, and why in the picture?" Gerard gave her a puzzled look. The idea should be to promote the main subject, the candidate to be.

"To show who is on the team…that he's part of it. He's a media man, corporate promotion…image building, I guess John's brought him in." She saw the look of concentration and now a new mannerism; his index finger pressed the glasses to his face indenting the skin above his nose, between the blonde and darker hairs of his eyebrows.

"Not so hard…Gerard," she said softly. "Please, don't press so hard."

There, her hand was again on his arm in mute restraint. He looked up but his eyes had a stare; for a moment she felt as if he could not see her, or he stared right through her.

"The man is out of place…he confuses the message. The caption says facility visit…to PulcriMed. I wonder? Have they got a place there, in Williamsburg?"

"You can't make that connection. In any case I've found out something else…something altogether different."

"Oh, can't I?" he said flatly then regretted his change of tone. Edith pouted, pursing her lips in reproach.

"It could be anywhere."

"Why him in shot?"

"Free publicity! I saw them here, from five thousand '*klicks*' away." She raised her eyes in mock exasperation. "I could have downloaded a couple of others, this one put them all together…it's easier for reference and for storing away."

"I was just thinking out loud, that's all…don't mind how I spoke to you just now. I don't mean it. I don't bite…I simply tell it the way it is, or how it appears to me, anyway."

"I know…it's what I liked about you the first times we met."

He gave Edith a soft smile then looked again at the caption, lifting the beer glass to his lips as he read it. 'FP Inc'. They were sure to have a web site, only a *finger click* away.

16

"The second picture? It's one of several I found on a current affairs web site. This one," Edith held it out for him to examine. "I discovered this one… taken at the same time only there's a clue with it. I think an important piece in the puzzle has come to light, saved me, us, a lot of searching around."

Gerard pressed his glasses. "Can't make out the writing very well…"

"Don't," she put her hand to his arm once more. "I'll read it out."

"No…thanks, I'm not that bad," he said tersely. "Don't be so concerned."

"I…I am."

He read the caption:

'New York Mayoral hopeful, John Kahn, called in at the Memorial School today, making a special detour from his planned visits to company plants in Virginia. School owner Anna Beth Koehler-Denton is pictured here with the candidate and some of the handicapped and disadvantaged kids that she seeks to help lead a better life.'

"Why Virginia? It must be a couple of hours flying time away."

"Factory visits are one thing…read this." Edith's slender fingers sorted through a small bundle of papers. "Look…"

"You've been busy." He counted up the print out, ten pages or so of downloaded documents.

"You should know me by now…it's a distraction. I followed an impulse." She yawned behind an elegantly placed hand. "Sorry."

"It's all right, I know the feeling. Working long into the night?"

"And the morning…I was hooked and it went on far too late."

"Why is there no-one else, at home?"

"I've told you…in any case you're an alternative to all that."

"Thanks," he smiled doubtfully, "I'm not sure what it means."

"Stop prying and you may find out."

"Spend time with me, at a weekend…forget this for a few hours."

"We'd only end up talking about it…I've found another clue."

"Not if I can help it. Is that a '*no*' then?"

"Do you always jump to conclusions?" He looked back at her as if to *say 'and what do you take me for?'*.

"No." he lied, a small one. With women he made his mind up pretty damn quick. "Say at least you'll think about it."

"I'll think about it." She smiled radiantly then laughed. This time his look said 'you've decided already'.

"When you have," he said in a deadpan voice, "will you let me know?"

"Ger!"

"About this picture, the woman in it, Anna Beth Koehler-Denton...you've checked her out I suppose, when you were sleepless...here in Amsterdam?"

She looked at him. "Yes."

"Well?" His hands made a beckoning, 'give it to me' movement.

"What is the origin of the name 'Koehler'?"

"German..."

"I found dozens of them, but I started with passenger lists, ships that arrived in New York...about the time Frederick disappeared. Frederick should've married in France, before they set sail."

"You stayed up for that?"

"Yes. It became compelling...clicking on various genealogy web sites."

"I'll take your word for it."

"I found what was needed...that might be of help to us." She sought Gerard's approval; instead, his easy acceptance of her search results was disconcerting.

He held out a hand to soften his teasing of her.

"Ger, we have to get on."

"Edith, spend time with me, forget it all for a while, please? I want to go out on a date with you."

"Soon...maybe."

"You playing hard to get? And you're so beautiful!" He put his hand on hers as it rested on the table; she took it away slowly. Edith hadn't looked at him, only the smallest pout of her lips gave any sign that she was moved by his attention.

"Later, leave it now...please Gerard."

"Okay."

"I discovered that several Frederick Kahns arrived in New York about the same time; I've made a list and will have to check them all out somehow."

"You'll need help," he said. The seat was not so comfortable as he lounged back, raising his face to the sun for a moment and ran the fingers of both hands through his hair; he would let it grow again. A new assignment was forming, the ideas still shadowy, shapeless even in the whole, but the predominant theme was becoming clearer. He needed another distraction to fill the remaining hours. "Spend time with me?"

"There you go again!"

"Yes," he laughed, "and there you go saying 'no'."

"I'm not!" she said in a sudden outburst.

"That's what I thought." He held his hand out to her and as she slid hers into it he closed his fingers. "Help me...and I'll help you to stay away from this compulsion you've discovered, sleep deprivation and all over a man...a man across the water."

"Ger..."

"It's okay, you don't have to explain anything in your life. Just be company for me...I'm lucky to have met you again, I know that now." The feeling of restraint was something new, or a habit that had fallen into disuse. His mobile phone vibrated in his pocket and the screen, when he produced the contraption, showed the office number. "Got to go, sorry...sorry to have been so pushy." The chair scraped on the cobbles of the terrace. He noticed another stored number on the screen and suppressed a sigh.

"Ger?" Edith instinctively straightened the collar of his jacket as he made to leave. "See you soon?"

"Yes, and next time we meet as friends, not as cousins?" She nodded as he kssed her cheeks, "We need to find that receipt don't we?"

"Who's distracted now?" she smiled.

"Ja, okay," he said engagingly. "The lawyers...we *just* need one name...of Pierre's lawyer...that's all."

"I may have some news of that too next time." Her hand rested on his arm and gave it a squeeze.

"Saturday?"

"Yes, not too long." She had only three days to wait.

One call had passed unnoticed as they talked. The message had been from Monique; separation had become too much to handle; travel, living out of a suitcase and whatever else was getting to her. She would wait up for him, and the rest? Well...

Her warmth and scent filled the bed. *Her* skin was pressed close up against him; *her* fingers, mouth and soft breath had elicited every response. 'We'll get through these times' she had whispered to him and for a while he had dared to believe. The soft skin had held him, drawn his gliding flesh to her and finally they had lost themselves in each other.

Only for him there was an emotional 'disconnect', and yet...and yet, they could still perform together, God knows how, as if no one else existed for them.

Only, the protective measures he now took leant their frictions a mechanical pre-emptive outcome, no longer did he feel the spontaneity of the fleshy sharing of juices.

Only, in his mind and imagination there was now a barrier to moving on...forgiving would be easier than forgetting how the loss of her had come about.

Only a few days and the analysis of the tablets he had found would be made known; the outcome was either 'PulcriMed Tranx' in the dock or with a clear sky before it.

He listened to the rise and fall of her soft breath; it would be a gradual process, accepting that they were letting go of what they gave and shared with each other. He held her slender body and struggled to be free of the thoughts that came crowding in. However hard he tried, the advice of an Australian reporter – it could've been an American – had never worked for him; as they surveyed prospects at a party he'd been advised with a beery breath *'to find'em, fuck em, forget em'*.

Whatever others might think of him, sharing pleasure had to have some meaning, casual frictions were a thing of the past. He was beginning to understand the very unfashionable mind-set of Edith; experimenting with emotions, breaches of trust, deception, using others or treating them as objects had no place in her life.

His embrace tightened; realism and ideals jousted for supremacy as Monique stirred at the renewal of his touch.

"Hope he treats you kindly." His whispered words caressed Monique's skin.

"You do," she whispered back and drew his hand to her breasts.

Monique had left him again, two days ago. No plans were made for their future, or how dysfunctional lives could again be ordered now that she had found the impulse to stray, even once.

The station was busy at mid-morning but most of the weekenders had only one thing on their minds, a day at the beach. Lucky for them, the noisy crowd was headed in the opposite direction and as their train sped eastwards they each gave silent thanks. They were travelling away from the car-driver's self-inflicted mayhem. Soon they would be near Utrecht; the occasional rocking movement bumped them together in the narrow seat and Gerard put his arm through Edith's and held her hand. He gave a phlegmatic shrug of the shoulders and a disarming smile to meet her look.

"Just holding your hand," he said.

"Kahn and Dekker," she replied.

"That's right, at least for today."

She squeezed his hand. "Good idea, us getting out into open spaces."

"I haven't been there for so long…it's time…with this sunshine it'll be perfect…space, trees, sky and works of art. All of it in one magical location."

"I'm relying on you to make it so." Edith stretched out her legs as he had done under the vacant seat before them. The plans had been changed, the idea of a trip away sold over the 'phone the night before, just the two of them and no outside interruptions. She had asked what to wear; had she to dress down for the occasion? 'Surprise me', he had told her and she laughed now as his words came to mind.

"What?"

"You said 'surprise me' when I asked what I should wear…you've done the same."

"Shocked you? Dressed down still more than usual? Is that what you mean?"

"No," her grip tightened once more in laughing admonishment of the thought. "No, I guessed right and see now that we're more in tune than before."

"You're a smart lady, in every way that counts. Don't change."

He was dressed in faded blue jeans, and not the *stressed* variety she found so awful. His smile acknowledged her observation that she had found reason to comment on the unpredictability of his wardrobe. The polo shirt fitted tight against his firmly muscled arms and her first sighting of him that morning had again confirmed the picture she carried of Gerard, a big attractive man whose company she again sought. A small haversack was on the seat opposite them containing a light sweater, a camera, a notebook and pens. 'I never go anywhere without them in case an idea pops up that I can use in an article…or our little project' he had told her.

"I've got it right for once?" she smiled when he had kissed her in greeting. "I won't embarrass you by being over dressed?"

"No, it's perfect." Edith looked wonderful, 'beautiful' as he now had the habit of telling her. It sounded too matter-of-fact, the holding of her hand too youthful, too innocent, but, they each seemed to take this simple act of communion as normal. The white sleeveless blouse and cropped light blue jeans, the neat white sandals with a small bow, all of it was a delicious contrast to the suits or formal business dress he had seen before. A thin band held her hair and the sunglasses gave her style.

They sat and watched the flat scenery, the pylons that crossed the landscape, the distant steeples and the windmills by the water, the neat fields and tree lined margins. The countryside and large cloudless skies were opening up, no more the claustrophobic mesh that they lived in.

"Found him," she whispered. "Our lawyer man."

"Sh!" His fingers pressed Edith's lips. "Remember, we agreed?"

"Yes." She nodded but moved his hand and gripped the wrist. "Get the other business out of the way," she smiled. "A week on Thursday. It's a long wait, too long, but it's the best he could do, it's the earliest he could see us."

"Us?"

"Yes…us!" She poked him and laughed before resting against his shoulder. "Tease!" she added looking up at him.

"I just wanted to be sure."

The wooded landscape and manicured grounds set off the gallery and pavilions perfectly, the tall trees that towered over the buildings lent majesty, the supremacy of nature as he saw it.

"There!" he gripped her hand. "What do you think of that?"

The taxi had driven slowly over the long approach road, past the measured pedalling of the cyclists, a tourist bus and the parked cars. The dunes with their stands of spruce, silver birch and larch, tufts of ground covering heather all gave the view a primeval appearance. They knew the landscape was managed but the human imprint was not overbearing; ignore the road that took them just for a moment, they smiled. It all felt so unspoilt.

"We can imagine can't we?" Edith said as they passed through the large wooden gates by the entrance toll house.

The modern buildings of the Kroller-Muller museum were set in the ancient landscape; they almost believed that it had been dropped in amongst the trees and a small lake in order to house an art collection and sculptures. Outside, man's observant eye and artful mind had created objects to draw a wondering gaze; the variety of sculpted shapes, colours and textures captured the imagination. The observer was provoked from the outset by industrial art. An enormous red 'K' girder sculpture greeted the visitors on the approach path to the main entrance. Opposite, two small glazed kiosks, 'phone booths Gerard said provocatively, had been placed at the edge of the Beech tree's canopy.

"Clever…an optical illusion" he said and they stopped. The mirrored sides reflected the lawns and woodland all around, them; they had to see themselves as part of the space.

Industry and art, hard and soft materials shaped by man's ingenuity, all had been combined to present a vision of the world. In the larger rooms sculptures lay or stood, plinths had been dispensed with and as they passed through the galleries the changing views of the works altered perceptions, just at the artist intended.

"Confronts all that you feel or see…doesn't it?" Edith paused by a series of wooden boxes each with one angled sheet between the sides.

"The light from up there, from the windows and the woodland beyond… the shape of the room…it's all supposed to make you deny the place of the sculptor, the artist, in its conception." He studied it dubiously.

"Hm?"

"It had to visit the place again, seek confirmation of what I like or don't approve of."

"The atmosphere, surely that makes the art as much as the work itself?"

"I associate more with the human hand and the brain in the outcome of the endeavour, in the finished work. I don't receive any feelings of a human dimension in any of this."

"It's there…you have to learn to see it."

He thumbed through the pages of the guide book; helpful explanations aplenty, but he could not associate with it. "I'll feel differently when I'm outside."

"It's written in the book, let me find an interpretation on the pages you've skipped over." Edith bent to study them as he held the thin publication; he hadn't noticed the freckles before and he let his gaze rest upon her face.

"I've certainly skimmed it," he said still looking at her. "You mean the separation of man and nature in these works?"

"Yes…so you have read it?" She laughed softly but Gerard stared back.

"I don't really need to be reminded of it, we experience the split all around us in town. That's why I thought to ask you here and breathe a different air." He walked on and Edith felt the guide book slip from his grasp and into her hand.

"Do you regret coming now?" she asked drawing near to him and holding his arm.

"No, not at all. It's supposed to make you think. What I am feeling is nothing new…we can see it all again later. 'Arte Povera' they call it, I read that too."

They leant against each other in silence. Only the soft tread of other visitors and hushed voices, almost reverential, intruded on them.

"Did you notice anything in the photos of the other Koehler's?"

"No," he said looking at her. "I thought we agreed not to mention them today?"

"You've become very solemn, introverted….are your thoughts elsewhere?"

"You're right. Come on…break the spell."

"You're not diverted by being here…or with me?"

"On the contrary, I am." In a touch of intimacy he brushed strands of hair from the side of her face. "Come…let's go back and find our Vincent van

Gogh? I'd like to see his version of sunshine on a canvas." He put a renewed lightness of tone in his voice.

"More understandable?" she said when they halted again, after only a few paces.

"More human, the man and his life."

"Yes."

"I saw a reproduction, behind the family grouping…in the photo of a few days ago."

"Flowers…on the wall of a sunny beach house."

"Flowers in a blue vase," he said, pronouncing '*vase*' as an American might do so. The work was on display in the gallery dedicated to Vincent. "We've got to see the original, make the experience real and our association with it."

"We can't escape them can we…not even here?" She looked into his eyes. She found him to be a handsome man, with or without the glasses; she couldn't ignore the effect he had on her, the redoubled intensity of his stare that could hold her.

"No, but we're gonna try," he smiled. "And, I'm gonna make out I'm with a beautiful lady who's not my cousin."

"Distant cousin," she corrected brightly.

"So, you won't mind?" He drew close and kissed her, a brush of his lips on her mouth.

"Ger!" she flushed and broke free.

"It's not the first time I've done it."

"It's only a kiss," she said looking up at him.

"Exactly, it's precisely what I would say."

"Exactly…that's why I said it." She pulled on his hand now and smiled. "Say it again later…Vincent van Gogh, now?"

Later, they stood in an open air gallery, a creation within the landscape; the walls were the stands of trees all about them, the floor the tended grass, the ceiling was limitless blue sky. The natural envelope was reflected in the water upon which a lightweight sculpture floated in complete silence.

"It's by..?" she smiled at him over the edge of the guidebook.

"Marta Pan," he smiled back raising his eyebrows in turn. "See! I have paid some attention to the pages." Pay Edith all the attention he could had been his intent, once they were outside and he saw the sun in her hair and they could talk more freely, unrestrained by any protocol that went with being in a gallery. The exuberance of youth could not be stilled in a group of art students who sat about sketching a chosen work, squatting or sitting cross-legged on the floor, notepads on their knees enthused by the artwork but still bubbling with conversation and soft laughter.

"Good…I'll keep testing you, just to make sure you behave."

They marvelled at the contrivance that drifted, moved by the smallest waft of the air through the trees, only they could not sense it; the artwork's lightness on the water alone indicated that it behaved under the influence of a natural force.

"Damn!" Gerard started then fumbled in his jeans pocket. "Sorry, what a stupid thing to have done, leaving my mobile on." He looked at the screen, shielding it with his hand from the sun. "May I take this one call?"

"Yes…be quick!" she mouthed with a delightful pout of her lips. Edith walked on only a pace or two before she stopped, to observe the sculpture from a new position against a changed backdrop; she stared at him.

"Mam?"

"I've been trying to reach you for a couple of days, don't you ever check your messages?"

"Distracted, I've been distracted…I can only say sorry. What is it?"

"Nothing much," she said huffily, "just calling to see how you are."

"I'm fine…just busy, that's all. Everyone else…how are they?"

"Same as you *fine'*…a bit more talkative. Are you at home?"

"No."

"Well…where then?"

"I'm at an art museum…in the grounds, studying works of art, sculptures, the collection of a shipping magnate, his legacy and that of his wife. Can you guess where?"

"Kroller-Muller?"

"That's the one."

"On your own? It's not Monique's thing at all."

"No, I'm not with her…and, I'm not alone."

"Gerard, do I have to drag it all out of you, every last bit of conversation? You're not usually so secretive."

"No," he laughed and beckoned to Edith to come by him but she shook her head and pointed in the direction she would take. "Wait for me?" he called out.

"What's going on?" He put the 'phone to his ear again.

"Not as much as before…we're splitting up." His direct reply prompted an intake of breath.

"I can't believe it! Why?" She asked him sharply. A bond of friendship and keeping him in a way that passed as order for them had been established. Monique made him ring more frequently and it had felt a small concession to make.

"It's not the time or the place, Mam."

"You didn't waste any time finding someone else. Was it your fault?"

"No," he said keeping the irritation from his voice. "She found someone else, or something else more attractive."

"Oh!" she paused as she thought of it. "Oh." She still made it sound as though he was at fault.

"Yes, blame me for not asking her…for failing to make a more permanent arrangement."

"You're not the type and I guess she got fed up waiting." So that's that? His relationship with Monique was settled.

"Don't be so sure…you don't know me that well. I've changed."

"Really?" The tone was incredulous "You haven't changed *that* much! Anyway, the older you get the less likely it's going to happen."

"Well…you may yet be in for a surprise."

"Who are you out with? Who's shoulder are you crying on?"

Handy these little red phone buttons, technical glitches at the press of a finger.

"We got cut off," he said. "Damn it!"

"Don't know what happened there," his mother said pointedly. "I was saying…"

"I'm with Edith…a day out, away from the hustle and bustle of Amsterdam, a taste of different air."

"Reason for the reunion just the same…just as it was last time?"

"No…just two cousins seeing each other."

"You don't need her." The tone was cold and unforgiving and he looked over to Edith. The repercussions of his last visit home seem to have lingered.

"Au contraire, it means a great deal. Is there anything else, otherwise we can talk some other time when it's more convenient?"

"Gerard, there's nothing more to the story, forget it. Edith's just mischief making. I'm surprised you haven't seen through it all yet."

"Love to Papa…I'll call you soon…and, thanks."

"Ger?"

"I really must go, bye!"

He felt down and a fool for having left his 'phone on, the revival in his spirits following the leisurely stroll past the Impressionist paintings in the collection had evaporated, momentarily. Edith had read out the notes to the pictures whenever they stopped; he had listened to the soft voice and relaxed in her company again. Now, she retraced her steps and stood close to him. He allowed his eyes to scan her figure and he mouthed *'beautiful'*.

"Take care, both of you," he had heard his mother say the last time they had been together. On hearing it he had been unsure what she really meant by the remark.

"Okay? Edith asked him as he put his arm about her shoulder. The tone had been unmistakable, the message equally clear. Leave the whole enterprise where it belonged, in the past; but the undertone had conveyed another message, Edith was trouble.

"Not the 'phone call, but you, yes. Can't we see that lawyer any sooner?"

"No, Ger," she pressed her fingers to his lips. "People asking where you were...who you were with?"

"Yes...I told them I was with you, yes...I said I was with you." He kissed her fingers. "Come on, there's still time to enjoy the rest of the gardens, forget it all for now."

"One family split is enough." A delicate stroke of her hand on the inside of his arm made him stop.

"I'll forget you even said that. I intend our times together to be worth every minute. We're shadow boxing, let's get in close?" They walked on through the glades with their arms about each other.

"It's just a hug," she said.

"It's only a hug," he replied, "just now."

"The story won't get in the way, will it?"

"No...not if I have anything to say about it. Others may think differently."

"But...but we won't care about them, will we Gerard?"

17

"Nico Brant can get all the information you need, hard copy if necessary, the rest he can email to you." Hans' gravelly voice grilled him as they sat by his desk. "Don't let this personal *'crusade'* get in the way of your job here, get me?" The smile also held a gentle warning.

"I've already been in touch with him," Gerard answered forcefully, "And, it's not a *'crusade'*...and it won't get in the way of the day job."

"Glad to hear it," Hans pointed to Gerard with the soggy butt end of his favourite cigar. "From where I'm sitting you don't seem to be in the best of shape."

"It'll pass."

"That's women for you."

"Where would we be without them, eh Hans?"

The screen threw an eerie light into the room. Nico's mail contained the attachments that he had sought, information on KahnPulcriMed Inc. the parent company. They gradually came up on the screen, seemingly endless pages of financial data, notes and a few pictures. He could work late into the night analysing the consolidated accounts. KPM Inc was a big player and studying the pharmaceuticals industry would bring him back into line, as Hans had ordered.

Hours had to be filled somehow and his fitness regime did not provide all the distraction he needed. The day out with Edith had been pleasurable, mildly flirtatious and uncomplicated. She knew that exorcising Monique from his mind would take more than a few hours of them together. The photographs were still on his desk, them skiing together, the villa holiday in Greece, the impulse trip to Africa and the Botswana safari. She looked stunning leaning out of the window of the Jeep, a bright smile transforming her open face; he leant against the battered and muddy wing close by, smiling but his eyes watchful.

The tanned gamin features would be a temptation for many; she had succumbed to one overture to share moments away from him. His reaction was to be so old-fashioned, behaviour he thought so contrary in a still young man. Forget it, he said to himself as he turned to the task displayed on the screen, but the arguments kept buzzing around his head like flies.

There had been no complacency, the reunions between them after even the shortest of absences always felt fresh, like a new date or the discovery of someone who made a vital difference. He had always spoken of how 'lucky' he felt; she had replied that good fortune played only a small part; it had been the moment of their initial meeting. Everything else had been the affirmation of the first spark of desire for them to be together. Now, the illusion of togetherness lay in pieces; the unusual and the different had been enough to seduce Monique from him.

It affected his work, his attitude. He was almost feeling sorry for himself – yeah, that was part of the problem. Get on with life, get on with Edith, write the column on the challenges that she had brought to him and the connection with the Kahn's; get *onto* her – find someone new and different. Why not try both extremes of the pleasure that women could bring? He knew worldliness and rampant technique with one, opening another's eyes to the joys of skin-on-skin offered an erotic challenge. Who or what was Edith waiting for? Idealism left you lonely, out on the edge; realism left you to take what was on offer; face the guilt and confront cherished ideals later, or never. Depended on how you were made and these so very different women made him think of it.

You had to face realism and idealism everyday, you woke and thought of strategies to get through the hours. Is that how John Albert Kahn lived his life and conducted his business? What had driven Monique to do it? Did Edith deny herself any earthier pleasures, the touch of another or the experience of profound intimacy until a dream could be fulfilled? Many would say *'take what's on offer now, but live with your eyes open'*; yeah, that was it, be conscious of all that faced you and find the solution to any moral dilemma from within. The cynical voice within him said *'whom can you trust anyway, but yourself?'*.

If Monique had popped a pill, pepped up the quick and different easy moment, the spurting clammy spells, then now in her detoxed state she would have time enough to reflect. There would be times enough when she could think it all over just like he did. She had been seduced from him for a few minutes; she had exchanged those climactic moments with another for the years with him, four years to be exact. Had it been worth it? She would never tell him and he could not forget.

His jokey airy tone had to be rediscovered and in Edith's company he felt fine, even upbeat. She offered a counterpoint and restored balance to his spirits. He would have to stop sharing his time; casual frictions with Monique confronted the emotional and intellectual commitment that he understood lay within Edith's soul and which he realised he would seek himself.

"Silly question at this time of night…but, are you still working?" He sent Edith an e-mail.

Ping! The reply was very quick. "Yes, or rather I woke up and switched on. So I'm not the only obsessive one?"

"Couldn't sleep either…I have financial info on KahnPulcriMed Inc, or KPM…it's shorter! Our local man got the stuff for me and I'll start to analyse it all."

"Want me to help? I know what to look for."

"Not at the end of a computer link…not without the sight, sound or touch of you. I need the company."

"Now?"

"That's a thought…it's only been a hug before."

"Behave!"

"Oh, all right. We need to see that lawyer; it's no good poring over all this data if it's just a dream."

"It isn't."

"I know…only I'm not sure!"

"Schizophrenic too?"

"Too? What else am I? I think the word you need is 'and'."

"Lonely…and don't be so clever."

"Just a phase…it'll pass."

"Hope so, I'd like to help but I'm leaving for Brussels in the morning for a few days. I'll keep in touch."

"Prefer to hear your voice."

"Then ring me." He pressed a speed dial number on the mobile.

"Hey! Quick enough for you?"

"Didn't mean now!" she laughed.

"Bye then!"

"Wait! Gerard!"

"Yes?"

"Stay there! Talk, I want to hear your voice too. The article or outline you showed me?"

"What of it?"

"Will you write it?"

"Not in so many words; the approach will be different and the argument not so direct...not aimed at an individual. I'll have to de-personalise it."

"*'Money buys Power.* Do you believe it?" she asked.

"Buys influence, opens doors, buys you paintings, gets you into places where others can only stand outside of and look in."

"Like us and the magazine pictures?"

"Yes, doesn't make them bad people though...or at least not until we find something that shows a different picture, or tells a different story. That's what I've got to look into with the accounts I've been sent"

"It may not seem obvious; creativity is not the preserve of artists alone. I can help...I can work on it with you."

"We're in it together, at least at our level the family is drawn together."

"You said we were going to forget the cousin thing."

"I am." He thought of the couple in the picture taken at the museum, outside in the sunshine.

"*We* are."

"I know, *we* are."

"We are going to forget all that, I mean." Her voice was gentle but he had heard the hint of an impassioned plea before. Distant relations can have an affair; they might yet figure it all out. He heard a soft yawn.

"I won't detain you much longer, Edith. I'll send you the picture we had taken of us together."

"And?"

"It's fine...very shapely...the statue in the background I mean."

"Of course," she gave a soft appreciative laugh.

He found the image and attached it to his e-mail. The picture captured the brightness of her smile, brought to mind Edith's soft spoken manner; it also revealed in the touch of her hand and body language her closeness; there was no space between them and her face was turned towards him. He knew in the moments while the picture was being composed of her affection; he also knew that she would not commit to it totally, something held her back. Perhaps she had seen the turmoil that his mother's words had provoked, all too briefly…or the recurring thoughts of Monique.

"Do you want the 'Flowers in the Vase' too?"

"It may be the nearest I'll get to the owner of the reproduction."

"You never know…lawyer man may yet help us."

"Mother says he's only got packets and packets of letters, not much else."

"We've got to start somewhere…the pictures are coming to you now." The labelled digital images, 'VincentvG' and 'Us' flew away. They looked good together and he felt disconcerted by the thought that there was no family likeness between them at all, but then why should there be? So, what if they did get together?

"Ger?"

"What do you think of 'Us'?" The clock at the bottom of the screen said 2:30. "Edith, look at the time! I'd better let you go, or you'll be wrecked for your trip."

"Us are going to make something of all this…and the family." He admired Edith's spirit.

"Hope so; we can't lose this much sleep and not get a result."

"Either way?"

"Yes Edith, we'll get something out of the *'Us'* part."

"See you soon?" she yawned then gave a sigh. "Sorry, time to go."

"Yes…night. Take care and keep in touch? No matter how late?"

"Yes…and you do the same, promise?"

"Promise. Next time, I'll see you at the lawyer's office…then we'll start to fly."

"Soon…we'll make it soon, Gerard."

18

A silk scarf of silver grey, patterned with a white check, encased the instrument. The open deed box had revealed masses of buff envelopes neatly tied together with faded red lint, all of them marked in copper-plate script of Indian ink. Beneath these had been concealed other more personal items. Even after so many had passed on and surviving relatives had considered the contents, it seemed likely that they had been forgotten.

"Who does this belong to?" Gerard held up the violin like a new-born child in swaddling clothes.

"Pierre...it used to be Pierre's. It hasn't seen the light of day in years, as you can tell."

The lawyer observed them both. He found the telephone call requesting a meeting remarkable and mystifying. No one had laid a claim to any of the historic documents and instead paid for his firm to keep them securely, and in a dry environment; that was a trick in itself with the propensity for some deed rooms to flood, or absorb damp. Expensive de-humidifiers had been installed and the atmosphere now had a dry, chilled taste.

"Then why keep it, so well wrapped up amongst all these papers?" Edith saw that Gerard wore his tell-tale frown of concentration.

"Unwrap it," he said quickly, with no room for dissent.

"Ger?"

"Give it to me!" He glanced at them both. "Why here, with all this dry dusty stuff and not with his own children...and their children?" Edith handed the instrument to him. "It's what I would do."

"An unwanted family heirloom...but they haven't the heart to part with it, so they keep it here." She looked at him intently.

"Did you know it was here? Did your mother know?"

"She never mentioned it," Edith whispered. "My God."

The cloth was held together by a ribbon which once opened revealed the rich patina of the violin's wood; the strings were intact but useless and hung loosely against the neck. Gerard turned the instrument over then studied it from every angle, his eyes wide and disconcertingly large behind the heavy lenses of his glasses.

"Well? Mr Kahn?"

"Gerard." He didn't take his eyes from the violin, and ran his fingers over the sound box.

"Yes...Gerard. Well, are you satisfied? Is your curiosity satisfied?"

"No." Gerard ran his fingernails over all the rounded edges, then with the tips of his fingers in painstaking strokes, like a deadened caress. "Nothing... there's nothing here." He shook the instrument. "Nothing."

"Nothing," the lawyer almost sighed; it seemed in equal measured disappointment. "Ah well, it is just an unclaimed or forgotten possession. If you wish it can be left here; it's hardly in the way."

"And the case? Shall I examine the case?" Edith's voice had lost its earlier expectant tone and she now lifted the lid with its soiled lining still intact; a residue of dust from the strings covered the baize surface. "Anything in there?" she asked as Gerard examined the canvas sleeve with the tattered leather trimmings to the seams. She gave him a smile; he was so painstaking in his search.

"No...nothing here either." He dropped the sleeve onto the table. "Damn it!" He spoke for them both and they looked at each other. "Why here? Why leave it here?"

He leant across the table and pulled the case towards him; the black mock crocodile hide was worn away exposing the wooden base underneath, close to the snap fastenings that secured the two halves. The lining of ecclesiastical purple velvet still fitted snugly, with the bow neatly tucked into a slot especially fashioned in the tapered lid. At the opposite end a compartment containing packets of horse-hair strings for the bow, a purple carton box for the wax, its lid torn, could still be found.

"Untouched, for a hundred years or more?" Edith fingered the packets and tried to keep her hands from shaking. Would the search come to nought? They had spent two hours going through each envelope, considered many old letters that she would collect after consultation with others on her side of the family. It was a barren set of everyday papers, not the evidence she had spent so long searching for.

Gerard continued with his finger tip search, feeling for any possible weakness in the lining. He had taken so much on trust, carried along by her enthusiasm but he gave no sign that he now believed they would have any success. Still he muttered on.

"It being here...unclaimed...it's simply strange...it must be here, for a *reason?*"

"Or you want there to be one...only it isn't there, whatever it is you're looking for, this piece of paper." Edith's confidence wavered.

"It's not any piece of paper...it has divided a family."

"It's not there," Edith said, "we've looked everywhere." The words fell from her lips with a despondent sigh.

"Really? Really?" Ger almost shouted and snapped his fingers demandingly. "Scissors! Quick! Scissors...something flat, a letter opener...ANYTHING!" He held out his hand to her. "Come here Edi. Come over here!" He'd never shortened her name before and she shot him a glance. "Edi!"

She sat down beside him and he took her hand. "Touch...touch, here." He spoke so softly.

"The...the lining's loosened," she whispered anxious now of what it might portend. "Be careful." She handed him a flat bladed knife.

Gerard gave a snort of triumph. "Ha!...HA!"

The material came away and a piece of notepaper came to view. It was a perfect match, the sheet was seen to be in Pierre's favourite colour, blue. Even the texture was the same. There could be no doubt.

"My God…Ger!" Edith cried out and put her arms about his neck, kissing him quickly. "At last…at last! Something powerful!"

"Yes," he smiled. "Do you mean this?" he said through barely parted lips and holding out the folded note, "or, what you've just done?"

"That of course." She turned to look at the lawyer and as she did so her fingers brushed over Ger's neck. "Both," she whispered.

"May I see *exactly* what you have discovered in there?" The lawyer smiled recognising that he was one too many in the room just then.

Gerard unfolded the paper slowly, saw the neat handwriting that was unmistakably Pierre's. "Yes, please take some copies…say three. Make one copy for each of us. The original stays here. No one, I mean *no-one* must know of this." He looked first at Edith then the lawyer. "Clear?"

"Yes." Her eyes stung with the first prick of tears.

"Understood. I will certify what we have discovered today, and have it witnessed." The lawyer smiled at his clients then pushed the speaker 'phone number. "Francine? Come down to the Deed Room for a moment, please?"

Edith and Gerard sat beside each other and stared at the words. The writing, all swirls and tails, overdone and out of its time filled the page. It bore two signatures and had been completed by two business-men, related by marriage, right here in Amsterdam, in 1876. Gerard offered Edith his handkerchief, but she took his hand instead and gripped it.

I, FREDERICK ALBERT KAHN, of Dwelling 6, Crooked Tree Water, Amsterdam acknowledge receipt on this day 15th April 1876 the sum of FL. 5,000 from PIERRE GIERRITZ being the funds of my niece Anna Elisabeth, my nephews Johannes Albert and Albert Frederick, the funds to be held by me and placed in the Amsterdam Bank to the order of PIERRE GIERRITZ, account holder, such sum being the said Anna Elisabeth, Johannes Albert and Albert Frederick's inheritance from Anna Elisabeth Gierritz (mother) deceased.

Signed by me FREDERICK ALBERT KAHN on this day 15th April 1876 in the presence of PIERRE GIERRITZ (father to the afore-mentioned children).

"It's no longer a story, a distant memory of a family split, it has become a tale reborn," Gerard said. Edith nodded and looked back at him with tear filled eyes.

"I don't know why it has come to matter so much to me," she sniffed, "that I should feel so…that I should feel this way." The tears ran freely now.

"Sh…you don't mean that. I've seen and known for weeks how absorbed you are in all this, to the exclusion of everything and everyone else." He held his handkerchief out to her. "Come? As someone said not so very long ago, *'it's not the beginning of the end, but the end of the beginning'.*"

"I forgive you your moments of doubt." Edith took the handkerchief this time. "Did you get the quote right?" She still managed to tease him, arching her eyebrows enquiringly.

"Sh! Let's just say the doubts have been dispelled, okay?" He took the handkerchief from her. "We can make progress; we have a keystone in the window looking out onto a life that continues to affect us, or parts of the family, to this day."

"Lives we know nothing of, or it feels like next to nothing, of them over there."

"We've seen some photos, have a few leads. We can find out and be involved, together."

"And…Monique? What about her?"

"We…we both lead separate lives now; we have done so for a few weeks." It was easier to talk of it as though the relationship was finally, irrevocably, irretrievably over.

"I'm…I'm sorry for you."

"Yeah…well, that's how it goes." He made it sound like a routine event he'd lived through. "We've found the paper. That makes me feel a whole lot better. I don't need to feel that it was entirely wishful thinking that they were so methodical then…down to the smallest details, even amongst our own family."

"It was a small fortune in those days."

"A very good start in life…for a new life."

"A start that ended up with multi-million dollar businesses, a beach house…and a mansion no doubt, in New York." They had seen the pictures. A seed had grown into a tree that bore a rich fruit.

The door burst open. "There! Take your copies," the lawyer said. "I'll put this, the receipt, where we can retrieve it, with Pierre's papers. It won't be hidden this time!" He smiled then a louder laugh. "Who'd have thought it…to hide the paper away, in there?"

"The family was musical, Pierre was an outstanding musician."

"You never said, Edith."

"No. Other more important work got in the way. Now," she said turning to the lawyer, "please let me see you put away the receipt." Sandwiched between two sheets of thin copy paper the letter was again placed in the deed box, in a large stencilled envelope. "Good. Now, Ger and I have some thinking to do."

"We may need to retain you on certain family matters." Gerard saw Edith nod then smile as she turned to him. They were at one now. Somerveld de

99

Witt, of Prinsengracht, Amsterdam would be asked at some point to represent just them.

"What may I ask is involved with this quest...that I'm happy to see has meant so much to you both?"

The Deed box had remained unopened, unclaimed for years, it had been moved from one secure store to another. At such times when the issue of the papers being returned to the family had been raised, Edith's mother, and her mother before, had instructed and paid for the firm to retain them all. They never asked to see any of the contents of the boxes, merely confirmation, twice yearly, that all was well with their family archive. Now, the livid interest of a granddaughter and distant cousin aroused his curiosity.

"We're looking at our joint family's history," Edith remarked with uncanny perception of his thoughts. "I don't want to lose anything now." She stood up and looked down at Gerard. "Ready?"

"Sure. I'm ready."

When they had stepped off the stone steps that led to the lawyer's polished front door Edith embraced him. Her voice held the thrill of a renewed sense of purpose.

"It means everything to me, finding that piece of paper. Everything! And I did it with you!"

He heard not for the first time the word 'project' as she whispered happily against his ear, then let go. He thought more of their efforts as a joint endeavour; he was going to be in Edith's company a lot more and that would be the diversion he so badly needed.

Edith's energetic pursuit of background information, the shining of a light into every corner of his family had only produced half of the tale. The receipt was a Gierritz or Dekker record; he would have to try to find a counterpart record, but such an admission would have found no place amongst the Kahn papers. Eliciting information from his parents and uncommunicative uncles and aunts had been useless. It was a closed book to them and his pursuit of '*facts*' only brought him into conflict with those he had previously enjoyed good relations, albeit distant ones, at a remove. Now, he was picking at the very sore that he had once told Edith should be left alone to heal over. Only it had a compelling dynamic, it drew him in too.

Edith clutched his arm as they walked along the cobbled pavement. She was overcome by the import of the discovery and he knew that she would devote all her energy in the single-minded pursuit of what she saw as the truth. The receipt, the recording of an event was only the start.

"We've got the pictures to urge us on, we have some names; I haven't been idle in spite of work...and everything else." He stopped and they faced each other, people walked round them. "What now?"

"Buy me a drink?" She smoothed his jacket.

"Yes, good idea. I need one."

"I need two or three!" she laughed, lifting her face.

"Come on, I know a place, not far from here." He took her arm and they held hands. "A joint endeavour. As I said, '*with you all the way'*."

"I'm glad. I realise that I can't do this without you now."

The café had a floating terrace, nothing more elaborate than a decked over barge, a picket fence along its edge to the canal; flower boxes had been arranged along the rails. He would have to return to work and be at his desk late into the evening but prolonging his stay in Edith's company was all he could think of. She draped her jacket over the back of the rattan chair and sat down, resting her elbows on the table, fingers loosely folded as she stared at him over the short distance between them.

"You won't have to do this alone." He smiled then gave a soft laugh. "What do you think the lawyer thought of us and what we were up to?" The thought entered his mind that he knew exactly what he would like to be up to right then. "The project has the power to consume everyone."

"We can't let that happen!" Her hand shot across the table and gripped his fingers. "It's just the two of us! We can call upon others but this can not become widespread knowledge...us finding the receipt...what we're already checking out."

"Who gave you this?" He nodded and twisted a thin gold band on the ring finger of Edith's right hand. It seemed to be an eternity ring, two diamonds with a ruby set between them.

"Oma, it was Anna Elisabeth's long before that."

"So she had beautiful slender fingers? Just like you."

"Ger."

"I just want to hold your hand, that's all." He let go. "The power will lie in keeping the secret, the element of surprise, is that what you meant earlier?"

"That's exactly what I meant." The tips of their fingers touched across the stiff green linen. "See? I knew you were the right one...to help me." Her eyelids fluttered; there seemed to be no artifice in her action but he was captivated.

It felt strange, the little touches they gave to each other. Would it be so wrong if he entered a relationship with her, a physical union that would be more than a fling to rid himself of the emptiness Monique's absence caused? Edith was exploring the possibilities too; her eyes seemed to express her feelings; they had done from their first meeting; he could recall her attraction to him at the reunion.

"I'm not a controversialist setting off arguments for the hell of it, and certainly not within the family...unless there's a wrong to be confronted. I may laugh at what I see or learn about the subject of an article, but for the most part I merely comment. If people reading my work choose to argue about the details of what I've written or been provoked to write of, fine, let them be. I don't express those views with the intention of changing the world or even a small part of it."

"Don't you? You can influence opinions." She smiled at him. "Where did that little speech come from by the way?"

"I've had the time to think...and what we've found today may change another's world." He waved his hand casually. "It may lead to nothing more."

"We'll see. Something changed today."

"Hm...only in a small way, in barely perceptible ways, Edith." He thought it over. "The Portuguese have a word so much more expressive of what the expression of an idea or thought may provoke...it's 'opiniaou'." They laughed as he gave the word due expression. "Pain from thoughts...there's some truth in that."

"You helped me change some of mine a long time ago. There was no pain, just the clash of ideals and realism." He listened and gave a soft smile in acknowledgement. They would have to meet some time and discover a different unity, that of bodies as well as minds.

"Opinions," he said clearing his mind of other intrusive thoughts, "in a small way, give a nuance to the words that are used, that is all." He thought of Hans and his blue pencils, and how long it would be before the office rang to ask where he was. "Come on, we'd better order something. I have to get back and catch up." He pulled a face. "It'll be a late night."

"Meet up with me again, over the weekend?" Edith said softly. "Put all the pieces of the jig-saw, what we have so far, put it all together?"

"I'll call you, come over to my place?"

"No, come over to mine," she laughed. "Is it a deal?"

"Meet your folks too?"

"Not especially, but it's an idea, we can go over and mend some fences so to speak, but not for long...there's so much else to be involved with."

"Okay." He beckoned to the waiter. "I'll still have to call you, to say that I've caught up with everything and what I have checked out during our separation."

"No more of those, for a while anyway."

102

"No." They parted and sat back in their chairs, smiling. "I'm not a helmsman changing the course of his boat by bold tacking manoeuvres, that's all too visible. No, there's nothing so dramatic in what I do."

"Whereas, Mr John Kahn?"

"Yes, he's something else. What about you, Edith?" She tilted her head slightly, waiting. "You want to influence events, or at least attempt to."

19

The tram line in 'Old South' passed the end of her street and terminated in the shaded square by the Olympic Stadium, half-a-kilometre further on. The Rijksmuseum had been on his route as he travelled through the familiar tree-lined avenues of the Old City and the inner suburbs. He felt at home amongst the tenement-like buildings and street names associated with painters and composers, the painters tripped off the tongue more easily – Titian, van Eijck, Vermeer and van Goyen; Richard Wagner was the only musical genius he could recall from the city-plan he had consulted from time-to-time. The buildings held an understated grandeur within their interiors that he was unable to emulate in his own apartment. His heart, his very soul maybe, might lie in the midst of these old buildings but pragmatism and a lack of real money had led him to invest where he now lived and where, until recently, a dysfunctional but passionate life with Monique had been enjoyed.

How neat it all is he noticed; the pavements had to have been re-laid; they were too level, too new in appearance and without a trace of the disfiguring works by cable companies and others to connect, re-connect more like, the neighbourhood. His feet could tread without being fouled; dogs were made to crap in the gutter or so the neat signs beseeched their owners, only cars were parked to inconvenience them.

He clutched the large spray of red roses and smaller complementary white blooms and fern-like foliage to bulk up the bouquet. So much colour, and sentiment, for the price of a few euros; even now, two or three years on he still reckoned these daily exchanges in Guilders; it kept you grounded in a more real world he was used to telling his work colleagues. There wasn't a uniformity of view on the single currency, thank God.

So, here he was, in Edith's neighbourhood walking purposefully towards the Vondelpark, with the intention of working on some background, to compare notes. But, he'd left his papers behind, deliberately. He carried most of it in his head, the salient details; her pretty face wouldn't make him forget those. The rest was froth, or padding; the essence of what he had found was uncontroversial. Tell her the truth he thought as he turned the corner of *the* street where Edith lived; he was early. Simply say, '*I'm here to see you';* the rest of it was just an excuse, a plausible enough reason for not being alone. He'd thought of her all the while she had been in Brussels; her image had vied with that of Monique, but she hadn't been in touch for over a week now; the bindings, the informal threads were unravelling.

He listened to Edith's soft voice, imagined the laugh and smile on her lightly made up lips, recalled easily the colouring of her eyes made so appealing by the absence of all the gunk that women often settled on their eyelids. Maybe he simply didn't notice the detail enough; there was much to admire in her that needed no glasses to improve the vision of loveliness.

Kiss her! God how I want to really kiss her! Gasping, noisy and deliciously wet, suck her lips and tongue and forget *everyone* else. That's what he thought of as he almost stumbled on the first step that led up to the front door of the building. He pressed the buzzer, twice in short bursts; '*let me...see you,'* he murmured in unison with each press of his finger.

The intercom distorted the answering voice.

"Hallo! It's me!" he said cheerily and thinking, 'I won't have long to wait now'.

"Hallo! Who's '*me*'?"

"Me!" he said again; come to hear it better and without the anticipatory keenness to see her maybe the voice was not Edith's after all. "Uhm…it's me, Gerard." He checked the name by the buzzer. I got it right, first time, he told himself.

"Oh, Gerard," said a voice with teasing laughter in it. "It's Aunt Katherina."

"Hallo! to you then," he laughed. "I forgot the password." His aunt chuckled.

"Do we let him in?" he heard her say. "You're in luck, and I'm not staying."

"I'm very fortunate in many ways," he replied before the door release clicked and he pushed into the lobby. The lift rose slowly, in a stately glide to the top floor where he was met by both of them.

"Gerard!" His aunt held him and thumped on his shoulders as she planted firm kisses to his cheeks. Her eyes studied him for a moment while she clutched his arms. "Still the full mop of student hair…nothing changes." She fingered the leads to his portable CD player's headphones. "Beatnik!" They had to laugh; he hadn't been called that in years.

"Nothing changes, at least on the outside, no," he smiled at her. "Sorry."

"Don't apologise, you've remained yourself."

He'd have to take her word for it as his eyes rested on Edith.

"Hey!" The kisses were restrained, forget the careful plans he had made on his way. "These are for you, and," he pulled a single rose free, "here's one for you, aunt."

"What are you listening to?" Edith asked.

"Pieds-en-l'air" by Warlock. "Moody, even romantic."

Edith shook her head, "Don't know it."

"Neither did I, but the CD came with a magazine " He smiled at her as he took the player out of his jacket pocket and laid all the pieces on a chair. "Listen to it later."

"So?" his aunt began, and studied him with a smile teasing her greying lips, "another reunion? I've heard from Edith that there have been a few recently."

Such coyness in the pretty woman he thought as he smiled at her. "Yes, there have been."

This was no spotty adolescent on the stoop waiting to take the family's darling out for a night of, what? Sex, drugs and rock-and-roll? He could try it again. The more prosaic day-trip to the art museum had been the highlight so far, so he wasn't about to charge around the shop knocking the merchandise off the shelves. Edith shut the door behind him.

"Come on, we're not staying out here." She flicked a glance at her mother before looking at him. He surprised her, again; she was dressed in smart casual clothes this time and as they stood alone she stroked his arm. "Glad you found it."

"I know where aunt Katherina lives…I worked the rest out from there."

He looked around the inviting hallway towards a brightly lit, sun filled sitting room, the tall windows thrown open onto the small balcony. Curtains hung to the floor from turned antiqued metal poles, held in place at the door's edge by matching tie backs. Moulded plaster work cornicing and high, painted skirting boards framed the rooms, all of them decorated in the softest yellow. Antique furniture, painted ornate mirrors and a tall armoire made this small time capsule a haven of quiet. Edith's love of plants was obvious, but in the room only a large Boston Fern stood on a short stone column by the ornate fireplace.

"Okay?" Edith led him slowly so that he could take in every detail and see how she lived.

"Beautiful, and not just your home." He took hold of her hand and kissed the fingers. They winked at each other and laughed.

"Just holding your hand!" It was said almost in unison.

Katherina had disappeared into the kitchen. "Coffee you two?" she called out.

"Yeah fine...yes please!" he said and they followed the sound of clinking cups and spoons. Edith took a vase from under the sink and put his flowers in the water, she would attend to the details later.

"So, what do you think? It's been a Dekker home for over seventy years. It's Edith's now."

"Lucky, lucky girl." He smiled at them both in turn. "Keep it in the family and avoid the tax?"

"Something like that, if you get it done soon enough. Edith looked after her grandmother...she lived here while she did so. The title deeds were signed over to her long before Oma died. Edith earned it, for her kindness."

"Okay mother, Ger doesn't want to hear all the details."

"Go on, please," he said out of politeness. "I haven't had much from the Kahn's....a picture or two, and a cupboard, that's about it." He made it sound light-hearted and of little consequence. Whatever had occurred so long ago Edith's family had pulled itself up.

"Nothing else?" Katherina stared at him. "I heard that you've both been piecing together some family history."

"Yes," he said taking the coffee that he was offered, "we're not getting very far though, are we Edi?" Her mother shot Edith a glance at the choice of name. "But, maybe today will change all that."

"Go through." Katherina seemed to be in temporary charge of them and Edith gave a wan smile; 'humour her' it seemed to say. The bright living room was in open plan, furnished with modern sofas and period pieces; there was nothing incongruous in the mix of styles, wood predominated, complemented by soft colourful fabrics.

He went out onto the balcony alone but it wasn't long before Edith's touch roused him.

"Missed you. I'm glad you could come over after all...you rang me so late last night."

"I worked through...snatched a few hours sleep before I came out."

"When is publication day?"

"Monday's edition." He leant against the sun-warmed brickwork and felt luxuriously tired in the glow. "This feels like a home..." Her fingers brushed his arm and he opened his eyes. But, Edith had gone.

"Watch out Edith. If you're not careful you'll make him fall in love with you!" She whispered while Gerard was still out of the room. "I'd forgotten how handsome, and strong he looks. And....no glasses!" She hissed out the last words as if it spelt doom. "He can't take his eyes off you, in case you haven't noticed?"

"It would make up for a few lost years...." Edith began but let her answer trail away. Instead she gave her mother a silencing stare but it was ignored.

"The stain will always be there, Edith. Then and now, so many years later."

"We'll see. I'm not, and I know Gerard is not going to live by the fall-out from that old story. It's in the past. But, as you have told me over and over, it's far from forgotten."

So, the feud or schism was perpetuated by default, at the behest of both sides of the family. She had never quite heard her mother express it so clearly. She understood Gerard's reaction to his mother's call. It would be left to the 'kids' to sort it out, if any of them were interested or bothered enough. Life went on some would say so why meddle?

"I'm going. See you again soon I hope Gerard," Katherina said it around the door opening. He sat slumped in the chair. "Gerard?"

He stirred with the small shove of Katherina's fingers to his shoulder.

"I'm...I'm sorry," he said drowsily and stood up. "You haven't forgotten your rose, have you?" He kissed her cheeks before his aunt waved the stem and gave him a broad smile.

"You're very pretty when you wear those," he said admiring the thin rimmed glasses she wore, photo sensitive lenses that were now a soft mauve tint. They sat at each end of a short and narrow table on her cramped balcony that served as a small and scented garden. It was filled with glazed and earthenware pots.

"And, when I don't?"

"You're quite beautiful."

She had taken of her tan jacket, and the figure hugging cream ribbed t'shirt highlighted every curve and the gentle swell of her stomach. The matching slacks hugged her slender legs and leather sandals complemented the grace of her feet and lightness of step. It seemed as though he noticed something new and entrancing about her every time they were together.

"C'mon, concentrate. What have you brought?"

"Flowers, you saw me."

"Nothing else?"

"Up here...wild imaginings," he pointed to his head as he fished for his glasses. "Oh! And I also found this short piece about the company."

For a group of companies with its reach confined to one hemisphere the results of Kahn PulcriMed Inc. can not fail to impress the harshest of its critics, amongst

107

them groups campaigning for the easing of patent rights held on core, but dated, HIV/Aids products.

The increasing challenges of R & D productivity that leads to the discovery and testing of new products have been met and, as industry experts confirm, imaginatively overcome. The CEO, John Kahn, calls this corporate attitude 'Right Treatment'. He sees clinical development projects as a continuing core activity and devotes a substantial dollar investment to ensuring the company's future is founded on the pipeline of new medicines. DeNovo, the anti tissue rejection drug, is one of the lead projects for a company priding itself on beauty and health.

Critics, again, point to the jealously guarded patents and even product line extensions being at odds with the core philosophy of 'Right Treatment'. They say the company can only claim such a moral stance if it releases medicines to the market, the Third World market, in a different way. By that they mean taking products out of patent controls and making them available to those most in need of them. There's talk of partnering, between suppliers, health authorities and patients but critics say it's just talk; there's little evidence to show a real lead in changing attitudes. Too much is at stake.

As the CEO, John Kahn has motivated, or as some say he's driven, his loyal staff to improve turnover by 5%; it stands at some $15 billion for the current fiscal year. The growth has come from the increase in dedicated retail outlets, nation wide in the US and Canada, the devotion of dedicated sales teams in key pharmaceutical products and this last trading year the launch, exceeding expectations, of beauty products under the banner, 'You Deserve It'.

John Kahn, the CEO with political ambitions, told a selected gathering of Wall Street analysts: "We start every year full of noble intent and my team and individuals throughout the company see to it that we deliver on expectations, for the business and for our customers in the improvement of health, beauty and the development of medicines to meet the ever-changing challenges of the modern world and way of life."

"Not bad," Edith told him as the article was flicked across the table, "and that's just from the pharmaceuticals business. There's nothing about the consumer electronics or property interests."

"In family trusts…we can't get at them or information about them. Most of those investments are in the Kahn name and rented back to the business. Personal wealth of John Kahn…are you ready for this?" He looked at her and waved another piece of paper. "A mere seven hundred and fifty four million…and five cents."

"Three quarters of a billion dollars," she smiled ruefully. "I stops you lying awake at night worrying about the rent."

"That's what I thought when I read it. A lot of the wealth is inherited but the guy has obviously made his own way and increased the wealth due to him and his immediate family"

"Unbelievable, and just from that initial stake."

"And brains, skill admirably deployed to make the most of things during the Depression…a heck of a lot of hard work and…some heartache along the way, no doubt. The pictures and the story tell us something, but not all of it…not by a long way."

"Yes, but…all the same."

"Look Edith, it's not going to be easy…not a single part of it."

"You don't have to tell me!"

"Sh…." he held out his hand to her. "Still now, I'm merely painting in the background."

"Yes."

"Then there are his three daughters. Two are divorced and play at being socialites; they're hangers-on and don't seem to be any trouble. And then, there's the youngest, the one we both recognised as the feisty one, the girl who breaks the mould."

"Dayle. You noticed all of that, from a few pictures?"

"Yes I did," he replied smiling and pushed a picture of the young woman across the table towards Edith. "I found this too. To me she's Dayle, the wild…or wilder one of the girls." He thought a moment. "She's in media, in fashion public relations or the like. I'm not clear what that really means but I'll find out from our local man, when Hans gets off my back…after Monday."

"Hans?"

"My editor." He unbuttoned his shirt and sat back in the sunshine. "Dayle looks the sharpest of them all, she's smart and yet she wants to live up to her wild side. I saw that much in the family snap, how she was dressed, no make up and her hair all blown about…she must know all the routines and yet she does just as she wants." He opened his eyes and turned in his seat to face her. "How am I doing?"

"Fine, I'll get my other notes…although you seem to have it all stored away in your head already and made your assessment." She eased out of her chair and as Edith drew level he took her hand then just as quickly let it fall from his grasp.

"It's not going to be all work, is it…promise me?" he asked.

"Yes, promise. I won't be long."

It was now or never. He stood up and putting a weight on the papers already laid out on the table followed after only a moment's further thought.

"Edith?"

"Hm?" she was half-turned towards him.

"Let me hold you?" he whispered pressing his lips provocatively close, then touching her ear. "Let me hold you in more than just a simple embrace or a hug?"

She did not resist and took hold of his hands, laid so lightly against her belly; their warmth suffused her skin through the thin fabric. "Yes, hold me...more as a..."

"More as a lover might?" She nodded in reply and stared at him before meeting his soft kisses.

"Whatever else others may think, or wish to prolong...nothing will come between us, will it?"

"No...no," she whispered in hoarser breaths. She parted her lips and felt the sliding kiss and press of his tongue then lips on her mouth, teasing, insistent, imploring her to respond. "Is it madness to continue with this?"

"Edith..." He kissed the soft hair at her temples and inhaled her scent. "In your own time...a great deal has happened and without us rushing into anything."

"Just...just hold me." She held his hands and permitted only the briefest of caresses before she rested against him.

"Edith..."

She gave a soft gasp and turned to meet his deeper kisses. "Soon...soon," she said at last, "when you are ready...here?" She put her fingers to his head then kissed his eyes. "See me...as I want *you* to see me, soon."

"Yeah...soon."

"Very soon...I know how it will be." Edith took up some papers drawing back her hair with an elegant sweep of her free hand as she did so.

"I...I couldn't resist you any longer...the e-mails and calls to each other can't continue with out some expression of a deeper wish."

"No, it is how I hoped it would be for us...one day." She smiled at him and moved her head in response to the gentle caress of his hand to her neck and throat. "I've...I've not been single out of some perverse pleasure...or some other preference; I'm not in denial just for the *fun* of it." Her eyes were moist with tears.

"Hey? What is it?"

"You took me by surprise...but it's okay," she smiled.

"Tell me, when you're ready...." He pressed his lips to her hair and Edith leant against him; finally, as she moved away her hand slipped from his grasp.

"People have talked, or speculated no doubt. I know of it." She stared at him again as they sat in the sunshine.

"Yes," he confessed, and met her gaze upon him unwaveringly.

"You? Even you heard?" He nodded.

"Only a few weeks ago…it caused quite a disagreement." Even then he had protected her reputation. "I…I didn't believe any of it. I know you, or have come to know that you have certain beliefs, or feelings. Order has to be established."

Edith slid her hand across the small space between them. "So good, that's what you are to me." Her lips trembled.

"Tell me later," he answered in a voice full of concern. "We're together again…it's a beginning."

"I…I…I was attacked some time ago." She pulled on his hand, to make him look up at her. "Gerard?"

"Yes?" He felt numbed. "You mean, raped?" His grip tightened on her slim fingers as he uttered the harshest of words.

"Yes…when I was an exchange student, not long after we were together at the reunion, when I first really talked to you and felt something awaken in me about you."

They stared across the gap between them.

"Is…is that why we never met again?" he asked.

"Possibly…I don't know. You never called me, and in any case I thought the word must have got out."

"Edi," he whispered, "no…no…it was nothing like that." He stood up and went to her. "Come, let me hold you…a big special hug." He embraced her quivering frame, remembered the rash of thoughts that had entered his mind when he had last seen Monique and compared them. "I never heard a word said about it, or of you."

"That's a relief," she spluttered. He must know of the reasons for her clumsiness some time. "I was worried that we'd never meet again, or that I couldn't persuade you about our little project."

"Why did we wait…so long?"

She shrugged her shoulders. "You had others in your life."

"Have I made a difference to you now?"

"Yes…oh yes!" She looked up at him with eyes moistened by tears. "Yes, I was afraid my idealism…"

"Would clash," he smiled, "with my realism?"

"Yes!" she clung to his neck. "How did you know I would be thinking that?" she whispered and pressed her lips to his ear. In response he shivered, and felt a surge of longing for her.

"Because, fortunately…and, by some trick, I have come to know you. Maybe we are kindred spirits and can draw from each other's well?" He kissed her lips gently but Edith drew his head to her.

"Love me," she whispered. "Show me? Help me to feel how it should really be between two people?"

The tenderness and considerate attention, the gradual awakening of deeper longings could only be found with him. She had fallen in love with Gerard at the reunion, held on to the words he had used and remembered the expressive hands that seemed to confirm in the softest touch an understanding of what they sought from one another. Then – nothing, she knew only emptiness. She never saw him again, until one university reunion much later; she only heard of him from time to time as life changed and she thought Gerard was lost to her. By then no one else seemed to matter.

Yet, the caress of his hands had awakened all of her suppressed feelings for him. The man with the rebellious student streak held her now, resonated with all of her passion and released her inhibitions. He had been so deliberate, so patient and finally so responsive in spite of her faltering touch. Acquaintance with every part of him, the fan of warm breath and touch on her skin held the thrill of innocence and discovery. His hands had guided her over his strong limbs and body, coaxed his flesh to a firmness that with another once before had meant subjugation, possession, enforced gratification, and ultimately indifference – she had counted for nothing then.

But now, she had known vaulting unity, her body joined to a man who's mind she had lived to know from his writing; she had fumbled and almost cried, flushed with embarrassment at her lack of experience. Yet, Gerard had kissed her, hushed her lips with gentle words and told of the beginning of a new life.

His eyes so often disfigured by lenses were softened by a deepening affection. She felt drawn to him; she had seen in the flicker of his long lashes in the heat of their final union the stirring of a different response; she had aroused this in him, a man with worldlier knowledge. He had made love to her, shown no arrogance or conceit only respect for her and what the moment held for them both, together, and singly. Gerard's bulk, his ample gliding flesh within her had the power to subdue but by his gentle words and measured touch he had brought her to him and become as one with him.

"So different, so wonderful...I need you," he whispered as they embraced, all of her body in contact with him. She lay with her cheek pressed to his chest, her belly, her thighs and feet weighing warmly against him. His firm flesh still pressed her skin and she felt deliriously spent; she thought of nothing else than to doze with him.

"Only you," she murmured in reply. "I needed only you to make me complete again."

"Still frightened to love?" He never thought he'd ever utter such concerns with a woman but then she had, until recently, been an enigma, a mystery to him.

"No." She slid over him and looked into his face. "You were kind and gentle, loving as I knew you would be." Her lips closed his eyes, breathed onto his lips but did not cover his mouth as she had done to stifle her cries of pleasure. "You brought me back to reality…to how it could be."

"Skin-on-skin?"

"Yesss…." she sighed languorously. Her breasts swept across his chest in a lazy teasing sweep of flesh and he moved to caress once more.

"You've learnt what pleases me," he smiled, "already."

"This?" she repeated the tantalising moment.

"You know very well!"

In time he'd show her everything; only now, in her bed on this warm afternoon it was enough to have exorcised a part of Monique's clamping hold on him. Gentleness now could be elevated to the frantic and extended couplings he had so often enjoyed. This was no short-term tryst, a fling or experiment in how to reduce the purest soul to the more common denominator that in some circles passed for liberation.

"Will you be distracted?" she asked softly.

"No."

"Are you sure?"

"No." He held her face. "I don't take advantage and what we have shared is too important to allow others to break up, or destroy." His kiss silenced her immediate reply.

"Oh Ger," her lips trembled against his cheek.

"Forgive me…I am not completely free except in a physical sense but time with you will take that too…into my past." He moved her onto the crumpled sheets.

Sunlight still came into her bedroom from the fan-light set high up on the wall and as he gazed upon Edith's outstretched body he felt utter contentment. He had left no mark of possession on her! Only a rosy glow flushed her firm breasts that had been teased by his lips until gasping responses had drawn him by encouraging hands on his hips to enter. The outcome could have been so different, the taking of her the self obsessed severance of all links with his previous amour; but he felt nothing else than concern for her fragile memory of another, a selfish brutish man.

"I've lost all shame!" she laughed and held her hands up to him, seeing the lazy desiring sweep of his eyes over her naked skin.

He had learnt of a sense of renewal that they could offer each other; flirtation had become passionate fulfilment.

"You're beautiful…and we're a couple now." He spoke softly as his lips pressed her belly. Moving slowly his tongue entered the flaxen haired cleft of skin between her thighs.

"We are now," she whispered. "Ger!"

"I'll love you gently...I promise."

And they had done so. She looked radiant.

"You've let go some of the demons that lived in you," he spoke to her as she prepared the simplest of meals moving her slender feet over the bare boarded floor. A thin chemise covered her nakedness. Shortened altar candles on cast metal bases burned at each end of the scrubbed wooden table that occupied the centre of the kitchen. A five-armed metal chandelier with candle shaped low intensity lights hung from the ceiling, casting a glow into the room.

"Some, not all." She bent to offer him a kiss and took the wineglass that he had held out to her. "That will take a while longer, but I will have you by me...won't I?"

"Yes...what are they, the demons that remain?" The meal of grilled fish and a large salad had been laid out before them. "Can you tell me?" Once more his hand reached out to her and single-handed they picked at their food, unable to let go and drinking too much from the start.

She bit her lip and looked away. "There was a legacy...from what happened to me," Edith said dully.

"Do you provide, for him or her?"

"No, my predicament didn't go that far. There was a termination...I was 'lucky'...the result of my behaviour was not so fortunate and paid the price, you could say, for my selfish behaviour."

"Edith, talk sense," he said softly.

"Had it coming to me, obviously. The man, an executive at the placement I was at must have thought so and...I shouldn't have punished the result of that." Her face had lost its gentle smile and now she stared at him. "You asked me..." Edith shrugged as he heard the tremor in her voice.

"Don't, please don't. Let me help to set you free of those memories and experience...share different moments with me."

She took his hand and brushed it against her cheek and kissed the palm. "Yes, I want to share many more moments like...like this afternoon."

"Look ahead, one day at a time and share as many of those with me as you can?"

"Yes, I have that...but how many rape victims who do bear children in much poorer countries can say the same?" Once more she had lost the lightness in her voice. "Rape is trauma enough; the kids die from malnutrition, or times of neglect due to the absence of their mothers. Once stigmatised by that event the mothers are considered worthless, the sell themselves just to live."

114

"Or they get HIV/Aids" he mused over the thoughts then shook himself. "Grr! Enough! Enough lovely lady! Leave it now, just for a while, please? I feel great because of you, let me see you again as you were earlier."

"Take this off?" she smiled.

"If you like," he reached for her and Edith leant away, laughing at last. "Who's to know?"

"I'm safe with you," she said. Her fingers tapped her lips and he leant across the table to kiss her. "So many are used, abused and enslaved when there could be some help for them, if we weren't so greedy and protective of what we have."

"And here I was thinking I've made love with a beautiful woman and we can be at ease with one another...with no intrusive thoughts to distract us."

"And here I am wanting to put the world to rights, you mean?"

"Something like that...now, SH!" He didn't remonstrate, his lips gave a pout as if to acknowledge the expression of her concerns.

"We got distracted this afternoon," she persisted, "and I still want to talk...of other things."

"I'm not complaining. I started it all." He gripped her hand tighter. "So? When is it to be?"

"Soon," Edith looked pensive. "I was lucky, no after effects except what you now know of and have helped me with. Companies like KPM Inc., the pharma-cartels as some call them...now they can make a difference to those less fortunate."

"It's the theme of my article, lievert."

"Am I that?"

"I'd like you to be, give it time." He poured out some more wine and drank on it. "If I'm not careful I'll have to sleep here, and that would never do."

"The neighbours would wonder why the change in preferences."

"What do they know, silly? They never see you."

"We all talk to each other, left right and up or down" She waved her arms and relaxed with a soft laugh. "Like this, see?"

"That's better...the real you again."

"You get my point though?"

"Just what do I have to do...to you, to take your mind off all that?"

"Be with me when you can and help me sort out our distant relation in some way."

"I can't do anything about patent rights and TRIPS."

"TRIPS? What's that?"

"Read my article."

"I will, but you can tell me, while I've got you here in the flesh." She got up and came over to his side of the table. "Move your chair over," she said and wafted her hand imperiously. The chair scraped on the floor and Edith straddled his legs. "Concentrate and tell me now."

"Very easy you probably think," he laughed. The skin on her thighs was smooth and soft under his fingers.

"I'll make it *easy* for you," she whispered. "Hold me again." She rubbed her cheek on his bare shoulder, then lay against him.

"Better," his hands moved under the thin chemise.

"It'll take me a while to get used to this," she breathed against his throat. "I've hidden my real feelings for too long to let it all go in a few hours."

"No one knows the truth, Edi." He remembered a sunny evening at the house in The Hague and the disparaging remarks spoken about her. Reality had come violently to Edith shattering her imagined ideal of a loving embrace in a respecting relationship between two people.

"They still talked," she whispered.

"Sh..." Languid strokes silenced her but for no time at all.

"Can you stay with me and hold me all night?"

"Not this time, no." He kissed the soft hair by her temples, pressed his lips to her ear. "I'll stay as long as I can...to finish what we were distracted from."

"That and only that?"

"No, but work before pleasure."

"Realism against our ideal?" she chuckled softly nibbling his throat.

"You said it."

"But I want everything of you now, lievert," Edith replied.

20

"I've changed the column, worked on it through the day, I left it to make sure I had written what I wanted to say, then I came back to it once more. What have you done to me?"

"Not as much as you have for me," Edith said. "Are you very tired?" Her voice had a contented listlessness about it.

"Not that it would show."

"Well...my mother called in," she laughed. "It was very difficult to hide how I felt from her!"

"To my eyes you're beautiful, but then you've heard it from me before. Part of you is in my work now...you'll see, tomorrow."

"All of you is with me now, Gerard."

Charity – Help Or Power Play?

A Personal View on Business – by 'The Owl' (Gerard Kahn©)

'Reality, realism, despotism – for millions in the poorer countries of the world, Africa say, it is a short and brutish life, helped on its way by the oppression of your own kind, or by the distant hand or weight of process imposed by others much, much more fortunate. I had dinner with a beautiful woman recently and we spoke of this, and that – I never could (and she never mentioned it, bless her) speak of the banalities that dominate some of the printed media. The 'I've got it all but want still more' stories; greed and excess have become a branded commodity, like so much else today. It helps the gross national product – gross it may well be to some. But, we live in a more caring world don't we? Globalisation is a good thing in the long run – so, why is so much protected by tariffs, laws and attitude? Imperialism isn't quite dead yet or have I got that wrong too?

Money buys power. There! I've got one cliché out on the page. Possession of it can be subtly exercised or it can be overt. On the one hand, it hints at help and dribbles into the hands of agencies and is distributed over a weakened infrastructure. Or, it is more physical – a militia man's boot in the crotch, on your neck, or pennies thrown beside a naked or dishevelled form after pleasure has been taken. The recipients count for next to nothing, just another pawn in a bigger game, a global game. I have to admire the distributing agencies – they're defenceless, and hold their hands out like the poor people they come to serve.

Cynical? Sorry, it probably is. Do I believe it? I try not to. In everyone I look for the better side, the caress rather than the blow – spoken or real. My lovely dinner companion made me think --yes I love beauty and brains; image is only skin deep. She sees that in me. What I want you, one(!) of you to think of is 'motives'; what lies behind it all? Why does one group of human beings behave in a venal, acquisitive, cruel or sadistic manner towards another? I'm not going to complicate the issue by throwing religion into the brew as well – not yet.

My date's comfortably off, educated and she's attractive – she also made me think outside the comfort zone, as I like to do. That is also why I will see her again…and again. Why? Because I need to be confronted with reality not just a picture of it. Repetition brings it all home – like HIV/Aids. Not the subject of a date, but like I said she made me think as well as look. Repetition might make you act rather than just listen. Someone has to tell you what is really going on, tell it louder each time and then, who knows? Beauty in the human form and mind (before this date I went to Kroller-Muller Museum with the lady) in all its guises, male and female, should be enjoyed. It should also be allowed to live. Treat it with respect, no – treat it with an open hand. Better still – treat it with the medicines we have at our disposal. Above all you might think by now, treat them in their homeland, and do it quickly. Globalisation means without borders – the killer disease can be in your neighbourhood in next to no time. See then how quickly the treatment trucks arrive.

The soldier, employer, anyone enforcing someone else's will takes the woman or girl, infects her and forgets them just as quickly, oblivious to the plight that is left behind – disease, stigma, death. It's only one disease, of many, and it's a killer and spread by both sexes. There are others that we in richer countries can help to alleviate only barriers exist to protect other interests: R & D costs, development expenditure in billions, shareholder value, the majority shareholder's interests. Then, there's the research-for-profit companies protecting global patent rights while others try to find generic alternatives that can be afforded.

Money buys knowledge of ideas and products others might use to live by, if they can pay the price, or they can offer something in exchange. It's a barter system, only the trade is human life. Well, that's how I see it.

My lovely dinner date cheered up; thankfully, help is at hand or on its way – it's called TRIPS a forum or an offshoot of the WTO. It's a set of rules, Trade Related Intellectual Property Rights. They have yet to be fully implemented, but it's a start. And yet (cynical me again) I came back to realism and in my friend's case her delightful idealism, or vision of Utopia.

"Why, I thought teach poorer countries the art of negotiating the means to break the hold of pharmaceutical companies – some call them cartels; you judge for yourself – when what they really want is help, dare I say it 'human charity'? My friend's ideals tell her it's one human being holding out a hand like the Good Samaritan; my realism (or cynicism, and in time I will receive her help with that) tells me 'nothing for something in exchange'. Otherwise, I see you but I'll walk by on the other side of the street.

There! I knew religion and belief in human kindness would surface, somehow. So, what's my line here? It is called Global Ethics. A world-renowned business should become an admired company for all the right reasons. To those of you in charge, my dinner companion and I would say 'Be a mensch' and mean it, consistently. Globalism, commercialism, protectionism – someone can argue a case for any 'ism'. If you had to vote for the CEO of a company, would the Good Samaritan or the Patent Holder get your vote and how would you feel?'

"I've read it!" Edith said rather too breathlessly. "You darling man!"

"And?"

"Who was your dinner date with all those ideals...a Utopian view of things?"

"A figure of speech...but I saw that too in the woman I spent a day with recently. I also recognised it a long time ago, only I left her."

"But you're back," she whispered. "Misplaced ideals do you think?"

"Oh no. You read what I had to say on the matter. I'll probably get a flood of mail saying I'm the fantasist…it'll never be like that…get real man! You know the sort of thing."

"You can still comment, or express an opinion! That's what it said, a personal view…you articulate what others might think but can only say in private."

"Or don't put into practice?"

"Exactly…just image."

"Would you vote for our distant cousin?"

"Depends on what he truly believes in. Like you said, the figures we looked at don't tell us very much. We need to look at the photos, get the clues from there."

"Start with Anna Beth," he told her.

"Why?"

"Lievert…look at the notes to the accounts. Why pay a relative to run a charity?"

"Cynic!" Edith laughed, but her voice softened. "Come to me soon?"

"No distractions, remember?"

"No," she said slowly. "Work and play…I think you can manage that."

"Oh yes, soon Edi. I'll call you." He had to clear another hurdle in his mind, the connection he kept making between Monique and the tube of pills. "Anna Beth, her scholl charity and PulcriMed…I'll be looking at them all, and John boy. I mustn't forget him. He started us off on all this."

"And I am very happy to have done so…to have called you and to ask, '*help me.*'"

21

New York

The I-pad showed a full diary; his attention was drawn to a preliminary meeting with an oversight committee later that day. It was to be a beauty contest of mayoral candidate hopefuls. Before then he faced a daunting schedule dealing with company matters, too many interruptions to detain him in the small but fully equipped apartment ten floors below the Director's office suite. It was his very private work den and, best of all, where he had re-ignited a special flame.

Joey Clarke drew vaulting responses by the clamp of erotically smooth legs and her exquisite timing. Technique was everything and stamina a commodity he seemed to have in abundance. The lady had become more than a panting diversion to enjoy when he was in town.

John dealt with private work, writing out before the first meeting a brief history of the family, a *'bio'* on the Kahn's from the earliest days. He had to show the committee his association with the boroughs, what he could bring to the party; what difference would he make in running the city and dealing with the multitude of interest groups? This was no breakfast meeting at the Hoffman House Hotel and others, like grandpa Frederick used to attend in the early days. Even then, with citizenship in his pocket he could still be thought of as an 'alien', a new arrival on American shores. By the 1890's he had made good; he had amassed a great deal of money but acceptance into the nearly blue-blood circles of the City or the new society of men and women took a little longer.

That called for breeding and social pedigree. It may have been denied to his face but behind his back his peers checked him out.

One woman had caught Frederick's eye and John picked up a picture of them together; it lay on the desk before him. Johanna Meyers emerged from the society Frederick and Margaretha had been admitted to, those who like them had gained a foothold and then worked their way up. She was unmarried, lissome and far from the bosomy well dressed women that made so many contemporaries stray. Johanna possessed refinement, a beautiful porcelain white skin, and lacked the outspoken social stature that so often alienated Frederick and his wife. Frederick was captivated, ensnared by a woman who recognised the man for her and the fulfilment of cherished ambitions and finally, after their value to each other had been fully explored, did they concede. That he was married did not seem to be a hindrance to their union.

"I can't tell them all of that!" John chuckled, remembering how Pa had recounted to him the details; the evocative picture was laid to one side. Like him now, it was of no consequence that Frederick came from a well-to-do family in Europe; he had to reinvent himself and adjust to new surroundings and overcome the distrust his accent provoked in some. But Frederick's handsome features, the humorous twinkle in his eyes and the oh-so-neat moustache with its' waxed points gave the man something that won women's hearts. John knew that much from his father's stories and the few letters full of bitter words following Margaretha's rejection. She poured it all out onto the page; Frederick, the man of so many gifts and yet the possessor of a stony heart, so feckless and ultimately so deceitful.

"That's what made you fly," John said as he scribbled on the lined pad of paper; a few dates, what the charitable gifts had been to hospitals and schools, the family's association with business and the community. He was his type of man; okay, so he had abandoned a wife, a doting woman, who sacrificed so much and stood by him through the early years.

"I don't go for all that," John mused. "Frederick had to make his way. He had committed two sins but he made amends…and stayed true to his family after that time." He scribbled some more even though it seemed unlikely he'd need to go into the detail. They would be looking at him, John Kahn.

"Yeah! Even I have strayed from the path, occasionally, not so often like in 'Nam, and rarely now."

He convinced himself of the story. Frederick travelled on business, or so Margaretha thought; it was often no further than across the sprawling city; what others might enjoy over breakfast at a swank hotel he partook with some society lady. *'He had come, after an extended journey…over the sheets'.* One lady had complimented him; his own father had passed on the anecdote. Johanna put an end to those wanderings and Margaretha made him pay for his mistake.

"What will they say about me?" John wondered.

Marie had stuck by him, he loved her, often felt in love with only her, but 'Nam had changed so much in him; it often seemed that the long view of life and a relationship had been taken, forever. Everything was transient, but not for Marie. She was spectacular in her understanding, and her love did not deserve his complacency. He could not say the same of himself; Marie wanted it all. At least his diversions hadn't attracted any scandal or attention to compare with Frederick's.

He had been the aspiring blue blood only he had his feet at the bottom of a seemingly long ladder. Too many occupied the topmost rungs and he finally concluded that he lacked the pretensions needed to climb that high. In one sense he knew his place; others could keep the highest perch. Instead, Frederick acquired, by whatever means, the wealth he had taken a grubby risk for – the one that really mattered, that initial enhanced stake.

"Which I'm still paying out for," he scribbled faster. Not all of it would be typed up; he'd have to pick out what he would dictate to his PA, Kelly. He'd found her looking at his pictures one day, those on the shelves of his office, of him in combat fatigues with his helmet on, in the field somewhere with *'Marie'* stencilled on the canvas cover, torn but all too real. He was filthy and had the all too familiar haunted look on his face following arduous combat; relief at having survived was there for all to see; the droop of a cigarette in a corner of his mouth fooled no one. The M16 rifle, hung so casually by its sling against his side, seemed a needless prop.

Then, there was no previous war to liken his days with, and far too many since. World War Two had been different, principle was at stake…and the saving of a race…he wondered at the real truth and altruism that may have lain behind all that killing. In 'Nam he'd kept quiet about any doubts and left the decision of the dodgers to hole up in Europe, or elsewhere, as their business. He'd gotten the call and stuck to what he was assigned to do, prepared at times to recklessly face down the enemy or die in the attempt. Elbee never saw it his way and the guy's refusal to take it all saved them both. At the time, it was hard to figure out just why in hell they had been sent out there…but the women helped him out, soothed and jerked him off through the darker times of his tours.

"Marine Corps?" Kelly had asked.

"No!" he laughed. Others had made the same mistake on reading the faded letters.

"Oh?"

"That's my lady," he said pointing to the only woman who kept him, "my wife…she stuck by me through those times"

He'd put that in the bio; he'd massage their story somehow. Joey kept him too, in all her quirky, sinewy but not marriage breaking ways. 'Family' was what he had and would keep, but there had to be, still had to be, the occasional diversion.

"Marie?"

"Yes, my wife," he told Kelly, "Marie Christine". Yes, she the girl with flowers in her hair and kissing him without restraint at the airbase, the garland of flowers around his neck and the prospect of ensuing heat, the unconfined passion at his homecoming. Joy on his safe return was ecstatically, shamelessly and hopefully proclaimed.

"I'm a city dweller, just like Dad, and Frederick…" he muttered to himself.

From the beginning there had been no wish to tie up capital in the boondocks, in a patch of dirt somewhere out in New Jersey. Owning mansions and cottages passed him by. He had only one desire, apart from bedding Johanna and that was to make his fortune and his businesses impregnable, as far as that was in his gift. Everything else was down to lawyers, or private detectives; he listened to gossip, not tittle tattle, and took out of it the hard news that could be used to his advantage. He could dig the dirt if it secured advantage in a business deal, close off options until he had his quarry where it suited him, with no exit route and a lower price from him alone, Frederick Kahn. Safely remarried he could even use others' indiscretions, who was being covered, where and how often. It helped to be well informed and one step ahead. He learnt the skills quickly, on his own, in another continent and unfettered by family and convention. Risks had been taken but there was never any real gain without the jeopardy of a gamble.

Intelligence on competitors and rivals brought him into pharmaceuticals in a bigger way than when, with Margaretha, interest in the coal fields of Virginia were first being shown. His father had told him how it went. Drop a gentle hint that his intended business victim may have been seen in a lady's company…or was it your wife? Maybe I mistook myself?' It had been a phrase handed down, a mis-translation of a Dutch saying. The hint, the possibility of a draining divorce settlement was often enough to secure favourable terms for a deal.

And so it went; the businesses grew because they listened and learnt, attended meetings to develop a network of contacts, kept in touch with their markets, and analysed trends. The practice continued relentlessly until they could be fully integrated into their adopted community; there was nothing remarkable in that. It was prohibited for aliens to deal in shares and property, so Frederick used intermediaries and held minority stakes in businesses and property, traded up or took advantage – of people. He was methodical, analysed risks but he was impatient to get a hold and move on, but he could never quite escape his conscience. Money and the welcoming arms of Johanna helped refocus his attention, away from Europe. That was in the past.

"I wish," John said loudly, "if only that were so."

"Mr John?" A youthful nasal voice registered.

"Yeah?" engrossed in thought he failed to hear Kelly enter the room. His watch read 8am. Josephine Clarke would soon be on her way to his office for a meeting that included Elbee.

"Sorry to startle you…good morning," she smiled. "I have some papers I need you to check through then sign…before your 8.30."

"Okay. I don't know what I'd do if you left us…if you left me." He took the sheets of paper that she held out to him. Kelly was more than his personal assistant. Graduating with a business degree helped and he recognised talent. Kelly could sit in on some meetings and afterwards express an opinion on the subjects discussed.

"Don't think I'll be doin' that, Mr John." She brushed away loose strands of her short red hair. The caramel coloured dress might be a size too tight but she made an effort to be immaculately presented; she moved with an easy grace that made the fabric of her dress rustle on her petite body with its cup cake sized breasts. That was a change, the dress would soon fit again.

"Your son okay?"

"Yes, thank you. He's with his grandparents…they'll take over if I don't watch out…he won't come home for the spoiling he gets." She smiled again brightly, too much gums and teeth perhaps, but her face lit up.

"When you need to, work from there. We can get you connected…you won't be lost to me…it'll be like you're still in the next room!"

He laughed; she brightened the start to the day even more. The kid had been unexpected, the result of a holiday romance, then an affair and finally the nightmare of rejection. She told him all of this quite candidly, 'you've got daughters so you'll understand'; that's what she said, he remembered, almost verbatim. She had also said he'd been very understanding; she even asked if she would come back when things were settled; he hadn't been too angry, more frustrated at losing a good helper. At the time business had been tough. I guess after that…what the pictures of you up there with Marie show is that none of this *'work shit,'* as she so graphically said it, came close to being difficult.

"Thanks. Anna Beth's sent back the papers. I've checked them, so Elbee can take them to his office, once you've signed. The IRS stuff needs closer scrutiny; that's his bag…or Joey's?"

"Surely not?" he teased. "You've done your work on them too?"

"Don't know it all, but I'm learning all the time," she drawled. "That's why I'm staying. There's more to do here than I could find on the 'outside'."

"Well, try this out…decipher my notes if you can. Voice recognition is not for me or I'd have dictated it for you to clean up. I've got a mayoral selection meeting tonight…I have to impress some new folks…I have to come over all *sparkling* if I'm to even get to first base."

"Take pity on the competition…you'll walk it…if you don't mind me saying so." Her confidence was a tonic, in spite of his mood.

"Not so sure…just yet."

He was too well connected, too rich, too immersed in widely spread business interests, far from the city for him to have a wide appeal; it could all come down to a more parochial outlook. Joey told him that experience of wide horizons was a bonus; he could work with that and the knowledge would count in his favour. Doubts surfaced in quieter moments then were quickly dispelled. He cared; it wasn't all about business and making money. How much did you really need? New challenges would make him buzz; the more off beam and away from his usual tracks the better. A male heir eluded him, the business interest could not be handed on like Dad and Grandpa had done, with that bothersome hitch and all. Dayle had spark but she was a pretty, young woman and rarely set foot in the building. The gutsy determination would help her succeed – until now there had been no problem; the Anna Beth moments, annual reunions if you went that far, were the secret legacy that he inherited. Men didn't always make the best of it – intellectual muscle could be brought in, or bought. The price was too high and the dilution of the company ethos not to be countenanced. The business had to stay in the family; the means had to be found for him to let go, while he was Mayor – if he got that far.

Sure, I'll get that far…just keep on repeating it.

"Here everyone seems to be on the same team. Women *and* men," Kelly said pointedly. "We get the chance to shine."

"You make it sound like philanthropy." With her he could talk of anything.

Joey? In the end the pillow talk had a number on it; by then he was past caring, too much; when they were hot she'd almost pull it off him. *'Then where will I be?'* he'd ask her. *'There ain't a place your tongue's not been, you'll find a way to please me.'* That was no lawyer speaking, and they consulted regularly. She grew rich from the business her firm earned for their undivided attention to Kahn Inc., when it counted. She never tired of him, in spite of the 'no-through road' to a future.

The apartment they so often shared was secure, access was by elevator to a floor unmarked on the panel; a special code made it stop; he had it changed, daily. Most folks flew by unaware a den existed on a floor and half, lap pool and all for exercising, relaxing and loving out of wedlock's bounds. His man looked after it and they had their own ways of dealing with one another.

Delroy MacArthur James – after the general his Pa told him - took care of the deliveries and the maid service; he was another guy from the Marine Corps and 'Nam. He'd done it all, or so it seemed, tapped his old sergeant for a job when age and booze took their toll. He'd lost a few fingers on one hand but he was equipped in other ways; being a construction worker and driver were only his day-time jobs. Some specialist skills he never forgot and after he had been cleaned up, detoxed and sharpened up he got his job, driving, tending and fending off any trouble. Manuel was the family driver, a grace and favour styled employment for him. By comparison, Delroy was a different resource, he was extra insurance; his boss could handle himself, he'd seen that often enough and he was lean; but there was no contest between them. Delroy had power and weight; as they often joked to each other, it was a kid's bike compared to a Harley.

Delroy knew the boss used the apartment to unwind in his own secure personal space. The pastel cream walls were meant to induce calm. The rooms offered comfortable but not lavish surroundings with sofas and bolster pillows, low tables and soft lighting, a few paintings or signed prints – a Warhol and Hopper amongst them. Put it all together and the space felt like a den; it was always cool in the heat of summer; discreet floral scents, the idea of a special *'space concierge'*, took away the stresses of the day. There was one large bedroom and bathroom; another room was fitted out as a small gym where his boss worked out alone or sometimes with him. He was well paid for his discretion and no mistakes; the line was narrow and very straight. His name was on the payroll, with a pension to secure a comfortable old age if he kept quiet. The boss was '*Mr* John' to him.

"Thanks Kelly, I think that's all for now." He put on his reading glasses that made him look older, the hair at the sides of his head pushed up by the frame.

"Can I get you a drink? Water…coffee…breakfast even?" She was used to getting in before him. Today was an exception.

"Later, when Ms Clarke and Elbee arrive…we'll work over breakfast." He looked down at the papers in front of him before scooping them up in a big hand. "There's a lot to get through. I'll call you if I need anything." He looked up briefly then tapped the pages together on the table.

He would protect the family wealth, the vast income from property assets in the city and beyond. That was family money, unaccountable to anyone but the authorities for a rightful due and no more; financial planners under his direct supervision took care of the detail. Trust funds had been set up for the girls – two of them were running them down too quickly and pre-nuptial agreements had been thought of too late. They'd been taken for suckers. Dayle had yet to draw on the first slug of money; she may be wild in spirit but she also thought of consequences and the need to stay grounded; excess was soon moderated. She took nothing for granted. '*What if scenarios*' seemed to feature in her youthful mind.

'*What if?*'…he thought of Joey. The intensity of the affair pushed aside any fear of the consequences but today was an important way-mark on the road he was stepping out on. Was it to be a new life or simply a new approach to how he should conduct himself? It would be a life exposed to intrusive observation, in the public domain, an environment that in many of its whackier features was quite alien to him. It required careful handling and management with finesse, skills he would have to buy into. Elbee had made little of his openly expressed concerns about FP or Flip Forsell. Dayle had said no more about him, but there was one thing he knew about his youngest, she always did her homework and made sure she was fully prepared to back up instincts. If a story existed she would tell him once she was "*good and ready.*" It had been a trademark phrase, carried over from the childhood jousts with her doting but often despairing parents.

Jacqueline Mary Clarke was no beauty, not in the coiffed, tanned and exercise–till-you-drop toned and firmed up sense. She purposely avoided the descent into that self-obsessed trap. Joey, as few were permitted to call her, possessed a vital spirit that had as its source a belief that each day offered a new opportunity for fulfilment and happiness. The half smile on her straight lips held a brightness that could also be seen in the keen gaze of her eyes. John had become enthralled, discovering that underneath all the hard business instincts that made her the super lawyer she was a deeply passionate and, at times, emotional person. Joey became a different woman after their first night of discovery. She had made love with a man in tune with her inner spirit. John pursued his own course for business success yet battled with a growing sense that he alienated many willing supporters by his altruistic streak; he touched consciences of those who felt better after a cheque had been sent. He approached the problem face on. It was not enough simply to make donations to favoured support groups for the disadvantaged; he could not remain aloof or remote from these deeds and discreetly pursued invitations to ensure a personal involvement. Personal involvement provided the near certainty that his funds were spent on those he intended to support, on folks that he came to see deserved help the most.

Sure, he had money, but he was not of the patrician class. It took some folks a while to see that truth in him.

Joey had been on the other side, protecting minority interests and lobbying for the assistance of big corporations. Financial constraints on the support groups she championed held back progress to achieving her cherished objectives. The step changes she and her committee agitated for in provision for the disadvantaged in the City were beset with what she had described to him as insurmountable difficulties.

That John had unexpectedly offered his help at first filled her with doubts; she viewed his motives with a deep scepticism that Elbee did not entirely dispel; her misgivings grew as no explanation for her business colleague's equivocal replies were offered. They were both to be confounded; neither understood why a man of John's wealth and status should seek to enter the circle of charity workers. Apart from a distinguished military service John possessed no obvious track record in selfless endeavour and they assumed an open pocket book and remote interest was more his line. That way he could maintain distance, perpetuate a divide that few sought to bridge if they possessed his pedigree. That was an Old World prejudice John had angrily barked out to her, only once, when she had dared to confront him and discuss his commitment and belief in her cause. She had asked him under her breath, the constriction in her throat a sign that she had no wish to deter him or jeopardise the prospect that he opened up to them for a significant change in their circumstances.

Surprise at an opening financial bequest was followed by wilder thoughts of the man himself. He forsook the seclusion of his home environment on two evenings a week to work in the charity's headquarters, housed in an undistinguished but welcoming building off 34th Street by Penn Station. His attendance in the hostels for disadvantaged or homeless families was muted and she came to realise in no time at all that his work with them suited him perfectly as the antidote to the high pressured life and world he inhabited. His soft-spoken observations on what he considered should be done to help were often accompanied by a disbelieving shake of his head at what passed for living in parts of the city that he looked out upon from his lofty vantage point. Usually, multi-millionaires did not put themselves too close to the tail end of the human chain of endeavour and possessions. Fewer still, none she could think of, took to offering manual help by way of a therapeutic diversion from their routine. Condescendingly she recalled, they had all given him time. No doubt John Kahn will come to his senses they told each other; he'll back off then fade away out of their circle. He offered no words of explanation and they had finally to concede to him, because his money made that vital difference but his commitment to their causes became a revelation. Grudgingly, at first, they had to admit that he made nothing of it, as they may have expected of him deep down. The man they had read about in the glossies was modestly in their midst, their prejudices were to be put on hold, confounded until some event would, they said, prove that they had been right all along. There had to be something to it, there *just had* to be.

She smiled at her own doubts and how the constituency he had been brought into provoked an awakening of deeper political senses and stirred their own for one another.

"What use is power…or money…if you can't bring good and real change to people's lives," John had said, "and not just to your own?"

He rarely uttered the sentiment but she knew by the analysis of the contracts he had to consider and then sign that he looked for the means to open up this vein of self-knowledge. It gave her the smallest clue as to the reasons she had become an advisor then with breathtaking speed a far more intimate and personal companion, someone who offered something more to him.

"I couldn't maintain the pretence and be myself with you only to leave and transform myself into another person," she had once told him when he had teased her on breaking a self-imposed rule to keep personal feelings under strict control. The intricacies of mentally adjusting to the habits and role of a mistress had to be convincingly learnt and emotion vied with her intelligence; she was torn between the love of the man and the circumstances of the liaison.

She felt like a dove released from a cage; nervy in the light, with no sense of direction then flying up and away sure of purpose until she faced the reality once more of their situation. Their nascent affair had ended in anguish; she had returned to 'her cage' to exist and survive within a barren marriage for a further year, outliving her husband Scott; it was but a short line on her life's resume'.

Her output intimidated, she put words into contract clauses that protected, defended, or reinforced her client's hard-won bargaining position, the corporate take on the world and what could be earned from the arrangement. Elbee's role was the one he had assumed from the first, in 'Nam. He was the enforcer; his seniority allowed no room for dubiety; transactions once made had to be followed through.

She could not endure separation from him and John succumbed once more to the soft look in her eyes, in the unblinking stare. 'Do *we hold this course or do we bear away and find a new way to our destination?*'

"You know me too well...far too well."

Joey had heard the words fall from his loving lips; every part of her knew that his taking hold of her once more offered release from an almost unbearable inner turmoil; his true marriage seemed to suppress all that burned inside him.

"I can't trust my instincts about this," she admitted to him in a moment when she had succumbed to the temptation to call him out of work hours, when no business matter offered any pretext for her contact.

"Cure me too, and help yourself," had been his reply and the thought of all that beckoned once more held her in thrall, weak with indecision, like a young girl and a first love. *'Pathetic'* she had said of her response to the renewed invitation of an adulterous affair, yet business and pleasure could so easily intertwine and opportunity to be in his company could continue without raising any comments.

A decision of hers alone offered a remedy, he had admitted as much to her. Friends were thankfully unaware of the man in her life. When she was not at home or in the company of women friends, she disappeared but not into the arms of a rich and spoilt philanderer who would tire of her. She had tried to escape once before; at times she felt as the insect caught forever in amber, on view but encased in circumstances she could have escaped, but the lure was too potent until the move to safety was denied.

"Come back to me," he had said. She knew before the 'phone fell back in its cradle that she had waited for John's unequivocal words to be spoken.

"Ms Josephine Clarke," the announcement was formal. John waited.

"Elbee's sorry, he's going to be late...fifteen minutes or so...he called." Joey smiled. Her voice could sound like small ice crystals when she was on business; he knew a different tone.

"We'll wait for breakfast, Kelly, thank you." He ushered Joey to a chair as the door closed silently behind them.

"You're early..." his fingers brushed against her throat.

"Yes...after last night it's hard to be close to you and obey some simple rules. I feel alone." She looked up and smiled wanly. "The experience is new...I was caught unprepared for the feeling. I can't go back now to how we used to be."

The makeup from the previous evening was gone from her eyelids. He drank in her fresh-faced loveliness. It was how he thought of her; Joey possessed an inner beauty and displayed an outer strength. When Joey dropped her guard he saw both, expressed in her stilled eyes and the confident set of her thin lips with the small creases to each side; he even loved the faint lines on the skin of her throat which she tried to smooth away. The bridge of her nose was pronounced, but it served only to make her open face so expressive of her character.

"Love at first sight," he stopped himself from saying it. The affair had been rekindled with an all-consuming intensity and in theatrical secrecy.

"Don't make it so obvious, what you're thinking, John."

"Mind reader too?"

"As what?"

"Exhausting...you were special last night," he murmured with a smile as he touched her sandy coloured hair. Finger dried it hung to below her ears, just. She had a relaxed sense of business dress, understated elegance. The cut of her suit was perfect, the material fine; she swore that the lining had to be right for the outfit to impress and justify the price.

"Can't see you often enough, John, to lessen how I feel." She stood up to put her case on the table and the catches snapped open like a whip-crack. The act was performed automatically, out of habit as she stared at him.

"We're going to burn up," he said evenly.

"No...we'll have to turn the heat down. One cliché enough for you?" She gave a little laugh that endeared her to him.

"Somehow..." They moved away at the sound of a knock at the door. "Think we can manage that?" he murmured.

She sighed. "We're gonna have to try, and keep something important from Elbee."

"Yeah...I loved the black dress. Will you wear it again soon?"

"Yes...lucky for me. It was an impulse buy at Barneys."

"It set my pulse jumping."

"And everything else," she smiled and gave him a slow wink.

"I found this piece amongst the press cuttings…foreign press cuttings," Elbee's baritone voice echoed in the room like a low distant rumble of thunder. He slid a comment on *'Charity'* across the table to John.

Joey scanned her copy. "You don't usually pick up on what they have to tell."

"No, but things are gonna have to change. It's been translated and syndicated. New York is at the centre…whatever London, Frankfurt…or Paris have to say."

"Or Beijing…and Moscow?" John smiled. "Want me to keep adding to the list?"

"John, "Joey looked at him, "I think Elbee's point is…"

"I know what it is, we're going to be in the spotlight and my meeting later today is only the beginning."

"Right." Elbee pushed the piece closer across the deeply polished surface. "Read it John."

"Global issues, pharmaceuticals…patents…Yep! I get the drift." He was impatient to get on. Elbee had made it easier, highlighting the key words.

"We still have to handle the issues John, for now. PulcriMed is in the firing line, make no mistake, just like all the other big players."

"We've got the patents and the intellectual property rights…we only concede what we can, or when we have to. We keep holding the line…on what's of greatest value to us…the patents on *our* ideas. That's my company's investment value…generic medicines is something else. I'll find a way through on that."

"Soon it may not be so simple John." Joey studied him and their eyes met. It was business necessity meeting inner conviction, she could recognise the look.

"You've got all of it on paper, but what of hearts and minds?" Elbee for once saw matters differently, aligned himself with sentiments rather than screwing the last buck out of a deal.

"Been there Elbee, remember you being there too."

"Forget that."

"No, we carry the scars. Instinctively we protect what the business has, emotion has no part to play." He shot Joey a glance.

"Tell the committee what your opinions are, what the line will be on social responsibility and the use of power." She looked at him and gave a half smile. "We've spoken about it."

"Can social responsibility…"

"I don't think so!" Joey turned on Elbee with a jerk of her body.

"We work to protect market share...stock value...that's what *we* are paid to do," Elbee forced a fixed smile then waved the paper at John. "Notice anything else in the piece, John?"

"Not especially...God even comes into it I see."

"It's a personal opinion, by 'The Owl'. See anything else?"

"Look, I haven't got the time to play a quiz game!"

"It may just be a coincidence...go on, check the name to it." Elbee said slowly looking only at John.

"What's your point?" Joey felt excluded.

"Nothing...other than we watch the press." Elbee said it casually and with a slight turn of his body towards her. "The foreign press too...John will get attention...in his case we manage output wherever we can. There's a lot to loose."

"Others may have something to say on that," John interrupted, "on what we put out and how it's done."

"Sure, but stockholders will begin to notice when the project you're setting out on affects them...negatively. Their investments dip...what we worked for suddenly begins to take a beating...they take unexpected hits and don't like it, nor do they expect little stumbles from a company like Kahn Inc. or PulcriMed. They're too big and grown up for that."

"We...PulcriMed never loose sight of the real world...and we're not too big to stumble. We work to minimise risk...all day, every day."

"I'm telling you of what's out there in the public's eye, John. I have people searching it out...information that may bite at you."

"Okay, we can speak about it again Elbee. In the meantime maybe we can check out how FP are going to handle things? Dayle's given me a few ideas."

"And the meeting later?"

"Kelly's working on something I wrote out before you arrived. Meet me there both of you?"

"I've got to pass on that...there's drafts of financial disclosures and earnings statements to deal with, John. Are you okay about Joey goin' with you, in my place? She can hold your hand so to speak if you need it?"

"I'll have to try that," John smiled in reply without giving Joey a glance but he noticed that she was looking at him.

22

"Lucky for me that Elbee had another appointment," John smiled. "Do you think he suspects anything of us?"

"No, even if he has been with you for so long…and might know the signs. No, I don't think so."

They sat in seclusion, behind a glass screen, in the cool rear compartment of the company limo' as Delroy drove them through the stop-start traffic, the honking horns and the bobbing and weaving throngs of pedestrians that braved the few crossings. Minimal lane discipline seemed to be observed thereby interrupting the flow.

"Elbee knows your taste in women, I'm sure," Joey went on safe in the knowledge that the intercom between them and the driver was off. "He's not going to put us two together." She said it with the down to earth realism that made him stare quietly at her profile.

"He thinks he knows that taste has changed an awful lot," he whispered, why he did not know, but, it leant more intimacy to the confession, or so he saw it.

"Oh, I don't think so. You just took your time to find it!" Joey faced him, twisting on the soft leather seats and smiled.

"Well!" John grinned back, somewhat ruefully.

"I don't mean Marie…she's different again I would have to guess; she means solidarity with you and the family background, just what the selection process is trying to discover…what are you really like?"

"Not what they see."

"And not so different in most cases than you may think, from them."

"I'm not going to be saying a whole lot on that, am I now?"

"No," she said tapping his hand that rested on the cushions between them. "Really! Here we are going to an important meeting and you're talking of the most *'unimportant'* things right now."

"It's always there you know…how we are, what you mean to me." John looked straight ahead as if to conceal that anything other than business conversation passed between them. "Scott…he never suspected, before he died?"

"No. I burned inside but I kept the intensity hidden. It was heart-breaking John, on so many levels. I can't go through all that again." The car swerved then negotiated a right into a side street. "Whoops!" she laughed softly as the car accelerated through easier traffic, then cut left again. "Just as well I'm strap hanging or I'd be all over you."

"Hey Delroy," John said through the small microphone fitted above his head, "what's the routine, man?" He flicked off the mike.

"Sorry Mr John, we gotta beat this if I'm gonna get you there on time."

"They're going to choose someone to sort it out, aren't they?" he laughed. Delroy gave him a thumbs-up and he could see his smile in the rear-view mirror. "You were saying?" John's hand brushed the side of Joey's leg.

"Behave, Mr Candidate hopeful. It's something you can tell the people we're going to meet – your ideas on traffic and transportation."

"All of it learnt in the back seat of a car, or a pick up truck...long ago, with a beautiful lady."

"Yeah, you said it," she teased. "Learnt with beautiful *ladies* more like," she added drily.

He let out his breath in a low whistle and laughed. "Hold up there! Not so many ladies," he said looking through the tinted windows that gave them anonymity. All the same, for a while overseas it had been squalid little houses, on a thin mattress with some girl whose name he soon forgot or never saw again; so many nights and different girls to chase, the business quickly transacted and a new trick learnt or refined.

"This meeting we're going to...," Joey began to say.

"I'll have to learn the rules of the game. I've got a few of my own and I'll have to help them to understand."

"Be yourself, easy for me to advise you but I know what kind of man you are."

"A guy who can't be with you as often as you'd like."

"Concentrate," she smiled. Her hand slid over the seat and their fingers touched. "We live it to the full when we can. Now, don't be distracted by all of that – I've learnt to live with it. For them, sell the family man stuff, the supportive wife whom you've been married to all these years. Bury everything else and bury it deep."

"They'll see me as money, buying into power and influence, squeezing out the smaller principled guy."

"And your answer is...to the question when it comes? When it hits you right at the beginning...not after an easy intro to the proceedings...your answer iiisss?" They had rehearsed a few and she prompted him. "It's not true...you're...you're...you're what?"

"Forgetful?" he smiled. She slapped his hand. "Yeah okay, that too! The answer is that the possession of money, and a knowledge of it can teach you the difference between the good and evil it can bring?" He went on when he saw her 'oh really?' stare, "what misery too little can bring? So I've learnt in business how to manage it."

"You may be up against a Comptroller of the City's Finances, he knows how to work with it."

"Sure...only he gets given it through taxes and so on; I've had to earn it...that's the difference. I'm going to manage it a whole lot differently."

"Okay, that's better…only just."

"You're a hard lady, but I'm glad you're with me."

"Stick to what we're talking about!"

They stared across the space between them. "You could leave me at any time, Joey."

"I don't think so, I tried it once remember? Near broke my heart…things were different then. I have my independence and I have you, neither of us can be completely free of the other." She fussed with her hair with a distracted flick of her hand. "Concentrate on real things for a few hours, please John," she whispered. "There's time later?"

"No," he sighed. "We had our special moments last night. I…I'm going home after the meetings," he said slowly.

"It's okay, there's no harm in using the word. Mine's empty, that's the only difference." The lot of the mistress, if she chose it although other thoughts had been coming to mind. She turned to meet his stare. "What have I done now to make you look at me like that?"

"You don't have to *do* anything…just be the lady you are, with the beautifully shaped head and intriguing face, your captivating green eyes and lustrous hair. You offer so much, what I need and love in you."

"Really, John." She looked at him abashed; he had never expressed his feelings so succinctly. "What a conversation to be having, now of all times," she smiled.

Marie had the natural beauty that she could only dream of but John turned to her for more than the physical distraction they shared. She had opened his eyes to another state of the union as she sometimes joked; she had brought to him the reality of life on his doorstep. He began to give generously to small City charities, supported foundations that were not mainstream and yielded no obvious payback for a man of his means – they had been organisations that supported disadvantaged kids on the edge of her neighbourhood. She and Scott her husband had done what they could to increase awareness. John had been in the background of these efforts.

"I never realised it quite so strongly as I do now. You have physical and intellectual beauty…you're so complete."

"I'm not so perfect," she looked away and squirmed in her seat out of embarrassment. "I….I….I can't listen to you say these things, John….I'll only play them back. I'll want you near me, to feel you close and to love me like you do, only you'll be far away…not so far, but distance is not the point. It's everything else…so, don't say it, please. I'll only remember the words and want you to touch me…only you won't be in reach."

"I needed to tell you…before *everything else* shuts me off from you for a while." He thought of Marie's admirable qualities, her physical attributes that entertained and brought delight to him still and the sense of long-standing companionship that kept him by her side; only she also had vacancy, no grasp of his deeper motivations in pursuing new objectives. She would be the ideal consort, photogenic and well-connected. Marie possessed all the attributes that the media would nevertheless dissect and comment upon after they were pictured together. Not the gushing coffee table society crap that passed for commentary but what their combined strengths were in the role they would have to play out. The paparazzos and columnists would try to dig beneath the surface. Was he, John Kahn a skirt chaser and attentive to Marie only for the public's consumption?

"And...I...I love you for it," Joey answered to break the silence that had fallen between them.

The mistress in his other life spoke softly from behind her hand; he had observed that Joey had kept it close to her lips since his unexpected confession.

"Do you want a child...my child?" He said it in a soft voice and looked unwaveringly at her.

"John!" she yelped her eyes widened in shock. No time elapsed for the question to hang in the air between them. "What?...Why?...My God," she whispered. "My God! Why now? Why ask me now?"

"You spoke of home, an empty home. I told you where I have to return to."

"Leave it...please John, leave it." He saw how hard a hand was pressed to her lips. "Darling...John," her hand drifted down to the space between them. "Yes...but as your lawyer...I wouldn't advise it." She gave him a half smile with trembling lips and held onto his unblinking gaze.

"Don't joke about it, I'm not."

"Please, John. Not now!" Her voice held a harder reaffirming edge. "This is madness talk, we're on our way to a big meeting, and you talk of this! I wonder sometimes what goes on in your head! Are you going sentimental?" She smiled and the grin on his face made it impossible for her to do otherwise.

"Ask Delroy what I was like *sometimes*...with the bullets and all a whizzing past our heads."

"Be serious John."

"I was then, and I am now," he said before pausing. "I think of what I need to be, and who I am, really am. The times we spent on the kids' charity work, a hands-on involvement with a project, making or doing simple helping tasks...that was the side I can't always show. I've done it in comparative privacy...maybe soon in full view, and still there will be doubters."

"Tell them in there, when we get to the meeting! Cut through all the partisan crap that the big parties always expect you to speak of, show them who you *really* are then, John."

"I've wondered who I belong to."

"A party that will do it right…"

"It's as well Elbee isn't here, he's hard line…no soft edges in so many ways. I guess I helped to make him like that, long ago."

"Leave it there then, out there, long ago. Be you…be yourself, now."

Joey remembered. Even Marie had joined in with John's new found philanthropic streak, only the novelty and the cachet of such an involvement soon paled in the face of more socially acceptable roles of gifting aid through donations at arts and fashion fund-raisers. John was different and it brought them closer, before the start of any affair between them; he persevered and put in real time by attending events and by being all too visible on the street.

"My John Lindsay moments you mean?" He had read the late mayor's biography, and all the criticisms of him.

Joey smiled. "Yeah, if that's who you really are…at least bring delivery to what he could only intend. Tell them that too…only don't mention the name, promise me that."

"Promise," he smiled. "Can't be long now…speak to you later? On the special number?"

"Yes." She began to study her appearance in a vanity mirror she had taken from her handbag. "Be my lover…stay as my lover, John please? Don't think of anything else."

"Remember what I said though? Will you promise me that?"

"How can I forget? What am I to do with the words you've spoken?"

"We won't take care of things. It's not a sure shot."

"With you anything is possible John. I've learnt that even on this short drive across town." She said it almost dreamily but reality and her force of intellect reasserted itself once more. The car had slowed then stopped at the last intersection before their meeting point. "We're almost there. Tell them what matters most now. Do that for me, do that for us?"

"Yeah, for us."

'For us all' he said to himself. Memories brought feelings of guilt, or pain, and imposed obligations that he did not go along with anymore. The means had to be found to express an altruistic streak and to combat the appearance of an entrepreneur trying to salve a part of his conscience; he could hear the voices now telling him of his good fortune. Soon, he had to go in there and explain himself; he had to go in there and account for his motives.

"Ready?" Joey asked. They were held up and she had regained control of her emotions.

"Yes, I'm going to need you." Both of you, he knew – Marie and Joey, and for different reasons that no prying news hound could truly understand or would be allowed to discover.

When he emerged from the meeting he would have to decide some more. Would he be a party man or would he go out there on his own? Should he use family money and be non-partisan, to wing it and to cut loose from all the historic garbage that had landed him and the country with its legacy, or could he find a constituency to believe in him? In his heart he thought so; he needed someone to sell him and the message. Joey would help him develop that; Elbee had to be talked to, but after he had spent some more time with his youngest girl.

The moved off slowly, held up by a rubbish truck.

"Stop the car! I've gotta make a call!"

Delroy obeyed.

"We'll be late for the selection committee, John. Not a good beginning if it turns out to be that way."

"I'm not going."

"Say again?"

"I'm not going." John pressed a number into the cell-phone's keypad, his pocket book perched precariously on his knee. Mobile communication, safety for some or reassurance to others, had been something another candidate in a previous election had thought to tax.

"Oh?" Joey looked at him coolly. "I thought we'd covered all the arguments and viewpoints before we set off on this adventure?"

"Yeah...but I've changed my mind." Annoyingly, he shrugged an apology to her. "Hello?" he pressed the set to his ear and held up his free hand in a soft gesture to silence her protests. "Frank? Hi, it's John Kahn...I've had a Damascene moment...no, I've changed my mind...I'm sorry but...I can't put my name forward as a candidate...for the party, after all." He listened. "Damascene...as in St Paul and his conversion."

John arched his eyebrows at Joey and smiled but she returned it with a fixed stare.

"Yeah," he turned back to his call.

"Yeah...I'm not withdrawing my candidacy from the election...it's more to do with the *who or the ideas* I want to represent and promote. It's about the platform that I feel I need to represent and that needs clearer definition." He shrugged, "I just need to be more certain of them all."

He listened to the reply, then resumed with a patient tone in his voice.

"Yeah...I'm sorry too but I may as well be honest about my concerns now...and cut out the cost of people's time. I'll make that up to you."

He paused again, an index finger tapping his lips. "Fine, make it personal to me and you'll get settlement...I don't think it'll break me."

He gave a low laugh then rang off, tapping the set to his chin as he thought over what had been said and the apparent impromptu decision he had come to. Only, he felt that his instincts to be different and prove himself to be so had induced him to make the call. It wasn't something he felt too bad about, the fact it had been a decision arrived at on his own.

"Well...John?" Joey looked sideways at him, her eyes very still.

"Hm?" he said in a distracted tone.

"What's the Damascene moment you've been through...so secretively?" She sat very contained now, tightened up, with the file held tightly to her knees. A perceptible space had opened up between them.

"It's not secretively."

"First I heard of it was just now." The voice was crisp and to the mark.

"First time it came to me...as we drove away from my office...ideas flying around in my head suddenly fell into place." John tapped the window. "Delroy? Back to the office please, the trip's over."

"Sure thing, Mr John."

"I wish it were...I really do," Joey muttered. "Nothing's a sure thing."

In spite of his efforts to make conversation Joey sat in silence. He had not seen the petulant and sulky mood from her before. She steadfastly refused to comment upon any explanation for his abrupt change of plan.

"Joey?" he almost crooned.

"Independents don't have so much as a toe hold in this City...much less in any District," she was finally provoked into observing. "Run as an 'Indie' and you'll be throwing away any advantage you have...it's madness...it's never been done before, never! None have ever come even close!"

"I didn't see that look on your face for long the last time you doubted my motives," he reminded her.

She waved her hand angrily in dismissal. "It was *involvement* even then... in high profile projects...you had, still have, *visibility*! Just who is going to pay you the slightest attention when the main parties have over ninety percent of the electorate? That's before the media even get to hear of you and this new adventure...or departure from convention."

"Ha! You said it...right there! Convention, and it's ninety per cent of the faithful that even bother to vote. What happens to those who feel disenfranchised by our processes...and those whom nobody bothers to poll or lobby?"

"I try...the charities you help, they try!"

"They suffer what democracy chooses to leave them...and for action groups like yours to deal with. I'll still be there, offering a hand in support if you need it."

Joey nodded her head curtly in acknowledgement. "We all have to make choices...that's democracy for you. You decide, individually in quieter moments if you want to vote...or you choose if you want to even bother with the system."

"I hear you...I'm going to try and break the mould and capture some folks' imagination. I'll take the field with a unifying ideal...try and find a consensus that is so different from the polarised views we exchange every few years and call democracy."

"You'll fail...that's what I'm afraid of," she spat out, angry now. "You'll waste your time and money...your talent...and for what? In the hope of being so different folks will open their eyes...miraculously and to realise that they've been fooled all along? Popularism doesn't work in these parts, got that?"

"That would be something...for sure!" He smiled in spite of the nervy anger that had erupted between them. A note of arrogant certainty had entered his tone; he had seen and heard enough of the early verbal jousting of potential entrants into the mayoral race to realise that he had to develop a distinctive voice of his own, forthright, credible and carefully considered. "But, they don't want to be confronted with their disappointment of past choices, I know that. You forgot to say I'd be failing the ambitions you have yourself for some change in the environment we have to work and live in. Maybe you don't want to be associated with that?"

She sat in silence with her head bent, serene in her contemplation of the remarks the situation had suddenly prompted from them. Delroy's smooth driving through the dense pulsating traffic was measured; it now bought them time to reflect.

"John, I...," Joey began but he had spoken too and she looked at him with unblinking eyes. She gave a sigh and said softly in concession, "Go on."

"I decided on it quickly...I didn't want to be a part of all the partisan primaries that pass for a selection process. Some say the city is a Democrat stronghold...while others say it has Republicans who masquerade as everything but that if it will gain some support for a cherished policy. I'd rather start from a clean beginning, say what it is I believe in and what I want to see changed. If I have to borrow a theology from each of the others, fine, let it be so. Opportunist, maybe...only, there's something unhealthy about the election being decided, some might say, before the day itself. I don't want to live in debt to highly motivated but unrepresentative cliques."

"Some will say you're a paid up member of them...you have been for years. Why should they believe you?" The frosty tone was softening, and she loosened in her posture, turning once more to him.

"I know you're angry...but don't be, please? I've got no secrets. I don't want to be in debt to some professional political elite, or special interest activists...or, dare I say it, to you...the beneficiaries of some poorly funded aid programme because the City has to listen to and help out in any way it can to so many."

"That's quite an admission of your core feelings...more than you've admitted to me so far. Is there anything else you want to tell me?" Her hand rested on the leather seat between them and he touched it briefly.

"Yeah, I don't want them to be owned by any one person or controlling group. Sure, it may be wildly optimistic...naïve, childish in its simplicity! But, they are private thoughts...many may share them but have no home to put them in or group through which they can speak out their ideas and agitate for a change in how we live and work...or look after those more disadvantaged amongst their neighbours. Someone has to pull all of those folks and their ideas together and make it happen for them...bring a real change to the city, for rich and poor alike."

"John, darling..." She couldn't keep herself from gripping his hand in surprise at the depth of feeling and how he had spoken of them.

"There's not much more to tell you."

"I was going to say you'll be torn apart, caught between the only two parties in town...they may still come back for you."

"Or after me!" he laughed but his voice held no concern at the prospect. "I want to appeal to people who believe as I do and who just might want to be part of a private institution or school of thought...lead people who are willing to take part in something new and very different."

"In a public...very public...and expensive election?"

"Yes...exactly." It grew quiet for only a moment. "But, I'm not going to throw a lot of my own money at the contest. I'll make a claim like all the other candidates and fight the battle on ideas and beliefs. So, can you see now why I had to stop the car and make the call?"

"Do one thing for me? Promise you'll leave the door open if you're asked to reconsider? Think it all through again...for me and those we both want to help and who have come to believe in you?"

"I promise...but it's 'make your mind up time'. That's what I feel right now. There's not a moment to let go of. I want to get on with building up my team, work out the details of the new project and get out there to tell folks, 'let's all try to make a real change more than a dream, or one man's wish...let's work to make it happen'."

23

New York – A Couple Of Months Have Passed

The electoral process was bizarre; to many it left a bad taste in the mouth, a sense that democracy was being denied its fullest opportunity to provide City Hall with the choice of candidates that represented a plurality of city dweller's expectations. Through his candidacy John sought to highlight all of its defects. The result might be his elimination from the preliminary round to select two candidates for the final run off. Why so few got on the ballot was seen as another convention, and one he felt motivated to assault. The attempt could be justified; he had rehearsed the arguments, analysing all of the reasons that had brought him to the decision to stand for office. He felt the need to effect real change, a democratic shift that others had for so many years sought to achieve through the Charter Revision Commission. The electoral process had to be '*freed up*'. Only, they ran into the immovable barrier that seemed to represent the vested interests of the two main political parties, and some public service labour unions that held the City in their grip.

"The Gotham Brotherhood," he murmured too loudly. "Breaking that is the trick...no mistake."

"What was that darlin'?" Marie came and nestled against him.

"Just politics, nothing for you to go getting in too deep with," he smiled, kissing her nose patronisingly and moved away, straightening his tie as he did so and checking for one last time that he looked as he intended. He was meeting constituents in another city borough, all with political allegiances. But his defences had matured very quickly; he had been coached long enough in Joey's communal action theories that charity work encouraged. Party allegiance often fell away when the broader interests were pointed out. Somehow, he had to appeal to a wider constituency through personality and the portrayal of a man-of-action; he would convert words into deeds and make a difference. That the major parties, Republican and Democrat, had their union affiliates and could wield power through them was something to consider carefully. How would he handle them and open up conspicuously closed minds? Some event, one single act had to be conceived to show things could be different.

"I'll help you in any way I can, you know that John, hm?"

"Yes...thanks," he replied rather too quickly and he saw Marie's reaction. I have another who is all too street wise to help me with the real fight, he thought, but he had to play several roles at once, and do it convincingly. Many would see the rich man and nothing more. The cynics would only see a man capable of '*buying*' his way onto the electoral ticket, a man who appeared '*willing*' to be a hostage to interest groups. They would expect their reward; discreetly, it might be through a policy shift, or an appointment, each granted in recognition of the value the political prop had been to his campaign.

"I've got one debt too many...before I even start," he said under his breath.

Anna Beth was evidence of a historical stumble by the family; sure they'd gained from that over the years, the past century and more, but that relic had to be kept hidden. He managed it with sugared efficiency, Elbee with brusque but lawyerly aplomb. He twisted his head jerkily as much out of discomfort at the thought as to settle his tie against the collar button. The legacy of how the family had secured its foothold in America gnawed at his conscience; he would make amends in his own way, God and legal providence permitting.

"I can make a difference to you John, even now...so, don't keep me in the shadows. The Hudson name still counts for something."

"Sure, but I'm not looking to rely on what we have or what we "*are*" in glossy magazine sense...it's what I have done and can do that is going to matter most...make it up to folks in some way...make it count and make it visible."

"You're in nobody's debt, John."

He laughed and took MC in his arms. "No, not really...just you, father, grandpa and even Dayle!"

"Dayle? We're all family."

"What would we have been without all of them...what would I and the family have become without you and the Hudsons? There's a debt alright, but it is not the one that I need to deal with most."

"What is it then?"

"It's dealing with the impression, that seems to run through some parts of City Hall, that you can be lazy, and get away with some things because it's always been that way. A select few hold the real reins of power...it's a form of cronyism, back scratching that loses you real, widespread support. To me, it's paying out on the belief in what needs to be done...no matter what your deep political allegiances may be."

"Wishful thinking maybe?" she smiled, "that you can change that?"

"Sure, but some time...some one...will come along and succeed, persuade voters that the electoral system can work like it does in other cities...it's not something that's untried or unworkable."

"It is here."

"Yep! It sure is and it's something to make a noise about…find and then elect someone unheard of so far in the political mainstream, but someone from right here in this City, someone with influence and who has seen things and knows of life. Elect someone who does know how it is out there on the street…I'm learning of it all the time, with the charity and voluntary work. Sure, it's small time, but it counts all the same."

"And that's where I may be able to help…if you'll let me. What do you say?"

Marie stood facing him but to one side and held onto John's hand. She squeezed it as if the effort to do so would persuade her man to bring her in close, join them in an endeavour that encompassed more than a physical union. His remoteness often left her with the belief that a *'skin-on-skin'* love affair was all that remained to them. She had picked up just enough from the few words he had spoken to understand that allegiance to a mainstream party was in doubt. It troubled her only for a moment. *'Her man'* was strong, independent in so many things that he did. The attitude often affected their relationship, she had to repeat the concern to him, *'don't shut me out'*, not now and at a time when being a minority-party, your own party hopeful or aspirant, needed all the help there was going.

The coffee table chatter was easily dismissed but a constituency, an influential one, with far-reaching influence could be deployed. There only remained an identifier, a label or pithy saying, a catch-phrase to bring him to the attention of others…the few, then more…then maybe, the many, the many that could make the difference. A difference that was large enough to win through, and get her man elected.

"I thought I asked you," he smiled, "not to bother with politics and things?"

"And I thought I said that I could be of help…some of the lunch groups, the coffee table meetings you dismiss…you do so at your cost."

"I didn't say that, or go so far!"

"You didn't have to, I could tell it from your tone…we're not a group of empty-headed women with no influence…just you remember that."

"Okay…I will! Now, I need to think of going." Marie gripped his hand again and made John look at her. "What?"

"Keep me by you…at your side in this?"

"Be my cheer leader with a select group?" Pillow talk, the favours and pleasures shared or dispensed to men-folk of her friend's acquaintance could be useful.

"If that's what it takes…initially anyway?" Marie tried to keep the note of irritation out of her voice. Her restraining grip had more effect.

"I've told you that I can use all the help I can get…so yes. I want you near me in this and your love and guidance."

"You have my love…you always have, it was never lost to you."

"I know…I know."

His voice lacked the depth of tone that conveyed a grateful acknowledgement of her commitment to him. An impartial observer might even note that it conveyed a hint of regret, that he had somehow to accommodate her true feelings with his own. Marie offered safety; condescendingly he thought, she was a haven in troubled times; with that condescension came the acknowledgement of security and the deepest knowledge of each other's frailties.

His devotion to Marie, it occurred to him suddenly, was borne out of habit whereas in his wife he recognised tenacious and resilient devotion; he still meant everything to her and he felt discomfited by his acknowledgement of the fact.

Joey offered the raw excitement of the new, and the consummation of an affair whose poignancy lay in striving to achieve a political goal and the shared experience of helping some disadvantaged fellow citizens. The Hudsons belonged with a political elite, a niveau that he had never sought to reach; in that he was *"below stairs"*, a product of a mercantile class that had made good or built on the fortune and good luck of another. The sentiment felt very un-American and recognition of this weakness in his origins often prompted him to look at the earliest family photographs and to devine where his true self could be found. Riches were bothersome, they bought everything and more; it could secure status, but he saw this as ill founded and instead he had always sought to earn his achievements through hard work and without trumpeting any of his successes.

He had to be seen doing things.

To the consternation of his parents and peers from High School, to the laughing derision of his friends he had accepted the draft, it had seemed like *'volunteering'*, and forsaken the route of officer school. By some perverse logic that he could only convince himself of he had seen the sharing of privation, fear and *'certain'* death in the jungle heat as his way of becoming more American than his birthright had bestowed. Until his posting overseas he felt "ordinary". Upon his return, the phrase *"my fellow Americans"* held a special resonance, much to the amusement of his buddies in the military.

For once, he felt included; the war had been a sort of Epiphany for him. He didn't go along with it all and took his own line whenever he could safely do so, but being as one with the men under his command had left its mark. He felt no stronger obligation to engage Delroy than that of helping a man who had fallen on hard times, self-inflicted maybe, but once he heard of it there was no difficulty in reaching his decision. He was in a position to offer help and did so, unequivocally and without any second thoughts.

The same was true with Anna Beth, but therein lay a twist. The family connection was vital; the origins of their arrangement and its continuance too embarrassing, lethal possibly, to his new dream. But pledging money to the kid's helped to assuage his conscience and there was every chance of a payback on events here in his own City. The generous act conferred nothing but good on his image, if he could find someone to create it for his campaign. The motives that lay behind the generous act weren't to be opened up to any kind of scrutiny. There was money enough to see to it that such revelations never happened.

His parting embrace was tender; how undeserving of Marie he was! His behaviour often told him that. She knew and had seen, to her pain, the difference between image and reality of the man, her only man. Tonight he was embarking once again to reinforce an image, manufactured in many vital respects.

"Am I so very different in that from any one else...anyone at all?" he said to the walls of the empty elevator as he went down to the street and Delroy who was waiting for him.

The car took him to another appointment, the outcome to be heard of in the coming days. His youngest girl was already helping him to get his message out onto the street; discreet information leaks on a new candidate, through un-attributed sources got the name John Kahn into corners where folks didn't think of a man from his part of town.

24

Dayle saw him first, exiting the building without a glance to left or right. He looked one cool dude if your taste verged on the smartly dressed roué' with a self-obsession. The tan was too deep, the gold bracelet for all its discreet thinness an affectation, and the Armani styled suit with the dark shirt too smooth for the hustling media types she knew. Turning on her heels she ducked away; even now she felt cold, in the midday sun; just how did a guy like Flip Forsell happen to be on Dad's team?

She didn't buy it, nor the story that Leandra recounted about her stalled career in fashion and lingerie and how Flip could be of 'help'. Her friend's drawing skills were rudimentary compared to 'A' list fashion designers but her enthusiasm shone through. Even the crueller jibes failed to quell the bubbly extrovert nature of the girl and modelling had become a whole new art form.

The allowance from parents out of town went nowhere near to funding the life-style she aspired to but she had 'friends' 'or dear ones' who helped her.

If that Flip guy was another considerate friend Leandra would be taking up with a man who'd allow her to burn brightly, but she'd be at his call.

She threw her bag onto one of the black leather sofas in Leandra's large living area. The apartment was an eyeball searing white-out that once you grew accustomed to the blaze of light felt comfortable; the sanitising whiteness, the calming atmosphere of the open space – she didn't like too many walls or enclosure – made you forget the heat outside. The street and the trash you sometimes stepped over could soon be forgotten. Pity, Dayle thought, that Leandra should want to bring it into the home. But then, the apartment was also an amphitheatre for parties and the occasional threesome and cosier wipe-outs.

They had become friends at college but since then their career paths had quickly diverged; they kept in touch, more than that, they often went to the same parties but could never agree on the best looking or most eligible guys to hook up with. She at least had kept hold of her scrupulous taste – that's how she described it – because looks alone counted for very little. Attitude was fine as long as you weren't treated as a piece of easy meat; nor did you give the guy any idea, if he passed the optical, that he had any chance of a trick with you. Just who was in control here? They could think what they liked, look at you as though you knew it would only be a matter of time, not so long, before you were on them and spiked for pleasure.

Leandra had lost that control long ago if it meant you got somewhere. Unkind, but true, Dayle thought of her wayward friend. The time spent would be worth the clean out afterwards; crude, but it said everything of Leandra's take on the world she moved in. She had the face of Audrey Hepburn and behaved like a tramp. And me, she now thought? Flip had seen her as easy but she felt like Audrey might have done, she liked her man to show some respect. Sometimes you had to look a long time, or compromise a hell of a lot. It would keep until she saw what she wanted for herself.

"Did I see right? Flip Forsell? He came out onto the sidewalk looking so sharp. He even had a car waiting." Any thoughts of meeting up for a cocktail had vanished from Dayle's plans.

"Yeah," Leandra paused for only an instant, "only the car wasn't waiting, not too long anyway. He brought me back…then stayed for a while." She gave a winsome smile.

"You didn't spend time with him? Make out…after the show last night?"

The smile broadened then became a deep laugh, fulsome in its sound of pleasure recalled. "Spent time…on, above and under him."

"Oh please!" Dayle answered in an exasperated scream on hearing the immediate and detailed reply. "What's got into you girl?" could have followed only Leandra seemed to be floating somewhere near the ceiling and couldn't help smiling.

Her hair was a black silky swirl above a sharp cheek-boned face with its narrow, perfectly straight, nose; it was coquettishly windblown, mussed it seemed for some effect. The small polka-dot dress in a soft pastel blue was stark against her pale skin, dusted with large freckles at her throat, like nuts on an ice cream sundae. The dress was a wrap, cut short at the knee, a garment fixed by a single button under her left breast and the belt fastened once. The large collar with its flyaway points was splayed wide to reveal an unsupported cleavage. Loosen it and she would be naked, an ample body to match a rather too 'come hither' look.

Instead, Dayle smiled to secure a further admission from her friend. "You look as if you've just got out of bed."

They'd known each other too long to believe the remark would be treated as anything other than a girly joke, a touch of awe instilled into the remark. Only now she felt none of the feckless union of wilder spirits.

"The guy can keep you '*up*' for hours, help or no help." Leandra fussed with her hair, the expensive gold watch slid along an elegantly thin and pale arm.

"You mean you weren't alone with him?" Her friend didn't even see the lead-in for information coming.

"Sure, mostly," she confessed. "There...there was equipment he likes to use."

Dayle couldn't help a soft laugh. "I didn't think he'd just look at you!"

Keep it coming girl, she thought looking at Leandra.

"But...he does!" she whooped. "First rhythm sticks...you know them electric toys?" She giggled in recall, "then the audio-visual with pause...and effect." There it was! Leandra's bubbly way-ward manner once again. Some men would find her irresistible in such a mood.

"Don't get you." Dayle exhaled slowly; where was this going now?

"You okay?" Leandra came over, smoothing the dress over her legs and abdomen. She had beautiful slender ankles, beautiful everything and wasn't afraid at the right party to let it all show. One pool-side frolic had even made a men's fashion magazine. Dayle had been told.

"Yeah, sure. I didn't quite copy what you meant by '*pause and effect*' that's all."

"He likes to put some of the scenes on film, turns him on. I got quite a freak at first but I checked it out." She laughed. "We did a few out-takes before we hit just the right spot…and he knows! The battery in his rhythm stick…his toy, doesn't run down so quick either!"

Dayle stared at her with folded arms across her chest. "And…I think I'm going to be sick."

"C'mon Dayle, a bit of fun and a break, I hope. I've got work out of it."

"What? Fucking on film?" she almost screamed out as she hustled into the kitchen, the heels of her shoes echoing on the tiled floor. You couldn't miss it even in this girl's love-trap. Only it wasn't love as she might learn to know it. The tap ran for a second or two and she saw her hands shaking. The creep had been in her home; his eyes had even scanned her. "Holy shit!" she cried out.

"It was personal, between him and me!" It was Leandra's turn to raise the noise count. "Don't get so psyched up!"

"You sure? Are you so damn sure? How many copies do you think he might make? A CD for a friend here, or there? A compilation disc maybe? Twenty greatest hits, and for all we know…you're only *one* of them!" She jabbed a finger at her.

"Hell, Dayle. What's up with you? You've never gone overboard like this."

She waved an arm impatiently. "You're a friend," she began. God knows why, if this was her idea of a career boost.

"And? So?"

"So…forget it, my hysteria I guess. I didn't like the guy. Just one look of him last night made me know it. I like him even less after what you've told me."

"Here, take one of these, calm you down." Leandra handed over a PulcriMed tube. "Goin' to work again?"

"I guess." Dayle turned the tube over between her fingers. "I don't do these tranx pills." Who have you got mixed up with Pops she thought and sighed. "I don't need them."

"I got them from Flip. He says they're a pep…when you need it most."

"I don't think so. I know the business, remember?" She raised her eyebrows to see if Leandra made any connection, but she failed. "Is this what you *really* took with him?"

"No, they were inside under cover…cover, that's all them pills in that tube were."

Dayle put her hands to Leandra's neck, held her friend gently but began to tighten her grip.

"Listen to me very carefully…the guy is *dane..ger..ous!* To your health and to your reputation." What she had left wouldn't be improved by this connection.

"I've got a modelling assignment booked because of him."

"Oh? You're on film. Was he the stud or did another guy come by and play the lead?" Leandra looked suddenly crest-fallen but her eyes resumed a sullen stare.

"Mostly him. Then the other guy came for a longer shoot, if you get my..."

"Who?"

"Miguel...Miguel Navarro."

"What! The show dancer from last night?"

"Yeah, the guy I samba'd with. Made me wet just to feel him against me. It was quite a surprise when he showed up, all of him." She stopped from spreading out her hands. Dayle's face was unmoving.

"You're unbelievable..." was all she could say.

That's how it went. Flip seduced them so that another could earn the real dough. Quite an operation to get the dancer involved; maybe his female partner in the demonstration fed male party-goers appetites. Any girl, Leandra this time, was there to provide the opportunity; a pill or two helped to blur the reality of what was going down, they loosened remaining inhibitions. Thank God she had avoided him all evening or she would have created a scene, for sure; keeping out of Flip's way was no big deal or so difficult; his mind was on one thing and with one person. Her association with Leandra was not made, they'd arrived separately and spoken a few times; she had left, alone. Before then, she had seen Flip talking to Leandra, a persuasive hand in the small of her back on the bare skin that her dress opened to his touch and teasing caress.

"Dayle, I..."

"I've got to go...I've remembered something I've got to deal with." She moved into the white-floored hallway with the zebra skinned rug as a focal point.

"Don't go frightening me, *you* hear?" Leandra held her arm but there was no strength in her grip.

"Don't go cheapening yourself, *you* hear?" Dayle shook with emotion. The guy had been so close, near to generations of *'class'* and her *'style'*. She felt dirty, cheapened even by association with her friend. "The guy is using you, will continue to do so if you go back, no matter how good the dicking was." Being crude was what Leandra seemed to understand best. "Can you remember much of it?"

She nodded. "The beginning, with him." Dayle saw the first up-welling of tears.

"Be careful, for yourself," she said softly. "You used something I hope...*all* of the time?"

Leandra nodded but went to her bag laid on an ebony trunk by the apartment's entrance door. She checked the contents, in case she'd got it wrong.

"They're gone...all used up!" She laughed. "And I took three with me!"

The story and Leandra's nonchalant attitude made the whole episode seem so gruesome. Dayle could only stand and stare at her friend; she prayed that it would be a social thing, only a few chosen viewers or a select audience if folks with seamy tastes could be described as *'select'*. She'd heard it said these things happened after dinners, set some freaks up for games later. The Latino star made her worry though, it could become more, a whole lot more; a discreet special delivery in plain envelopes, and at a high price, hand-picked players on film for high rollers to enjoy. Exclusivity brought its own rewards.

"Good girl." She hoped Leandra had used them, better still put them on the guy before she was spiked. "You got a copy of the film?"

"Soon..." The reply came with a defiant shake of her head; Leandra mussed the tangle of hair some more, studied her reflection in one of the mirrors that hung on the oh-so-white walls and gave a little nod of satisfaction. She'd brazen it out, even if Dayle acted as the inquisitor.

"Care to give me that tube of pills?"

Leandra shrugged her small shoulders; the dress wasn't quite fixed as she had planned it to be and the sudden movement revealed her breasts. She pulled the wrap tighter again before unscrewing the cap on the tube, shook free two pills into a long fingered hand.

"These are for me and the next time. The rest?" She held the tube out to Dayle, "Go on, take 'em, they're no good to me."

"Leandra," any conciliatory hand-hold was brushed aside. "Okay...use them if you have to...only with a real good guy and I don't just mean one that makes you holler for longer...and puts it on film."

"I did...he sure did!" she answered with a smile of devilish pleasure on her lips.

"You're proud of what you *did aren't you?*"

"Shut up! It's my life!"

"Sure is! A real career boost was it?"

Shit! Why am I getting so excited about *her*, Dayle thought. This is a situation that affects *me*, the family, even Elbee it seems, of all people! I was right three weeks ago and I sure am now. Pops had to be told.

"My business Dayle. I had some fun...some action. I took some product that you won't get near to."

"You got that *so right!*"

Dayle had never heard the word *'product'* used in quite the context that she understood Leandra to mean. She could only shake her head, unable to believe that someone in her circle of friends couldn't see what she was getting into.

"See you, Dayle."

"Yeah." I'll keep my eyes open. "Bye Girl, take care." She said it as an after-thought before opening the door onto the landing. *'Take care'* of what? Yourself and who you associate with, or carry on but take basic precautions? "There's not much that I can say it seems to make you think twice?"

"Guess not. It's a little harder for a girl like me to earn a living in this city."

You got that wrong too, girl. While you're body's available and with Flip around the good times could keep on rolling. She suppressed a smile as the thought entered her mind. At least I'm going to earn it standing on my feet! They stared at each other across the marble-floored lift lobby. She'd let the barb go and waved to Leandra before the elevator's doors shut her out of view.

"Hi mother! How're you?"

"Fine, darling...haven't seen you for a while. Coming over?"

"Soon, but not tonight. Say, is Pops in yet?"

"At this time? It's only seven...give it another hour or so. He's at some mayoral selection meeting...you can call it a beauty contest."

"Again!"

"Yeah...what of it? Want me to give him a message?"

"No, it'll keep." But not for long.

"I know what it is that's been bothering me about him. It was so obvious at the beach house a while back; I ignored it, what his look meant...but the feeling was there all the time."

"What, Dayle? What?" He had taken her call on his cell phone and stood by the office window staring down into the street, far below.

"Flip Forsell. He treats people, women especially as objects to be manipulated, he uses them, for pleasure...and, so I've now heard from someone real close, for profit."

The stone broke the surface of the pool, now the ripples.

"What!"

"You heard me Pops, and I told you before the Virginia trip. I knew it then. I have no doubts now. He's bad news. Fire him, and do it quickly."

"What have you heard?" he mused aloud then added, "It's too obvious..."

"Then side line him, make it slow. Give the work to another agency and make subtle changes to your strategy."

"I'm still working on that."

"Then you have time."

"Not as much as you think darling…gonna meet me soon?"

"Yes," she wasn't going to permit him to be distracted. "Pops? Do it, do it for yourself and do it for us, for me, please?"

"You were always special, oh so different," he said softly. "I knew it from the moment I first held you."

"Pops?"

"It's true, I love you specially. Come and work for me on this…better still I could tell Elbee to deal with your agency, but it would look like patronage and I'm not setting up any targets. I'll leave that to others…I don't want anything I do to look like favouritism."

"So, it's like the time we spoke of at the beach house, in the rainstorm. I'm better on the outside and looking in."

"Okay. Care to tell me how you found out?"

"Sometime maybe. All I can say is that a girlfriend likes to party, it went from there, it went a long way, way too far."

"I can guess."

"I doubt it."

"I'm old, remember?"

"No, I don't see it that way at all. Anyway, what the guy is…or may be mixed up in is too close to call, or to have associated with you."

"Dayle? I said I'd deal with it."

"Good…how was the meeting the other night? You get through?"

"Yes, a preliminary assessment to check the field for the special election… so they say…but…I have some more thinking to do, whether I want to be on ticket, do I really want to be one of *them.*"

"You've gotta belong to some one!" she laughed, "and not be entirely on your own."

"I'd get to feeling I was muscling in on other '*Indies*' who want to stand."

"They don't all have your pedigree, Pops."

"Or my money, they'd say…and so many of my other party opponents."

"Well then Pops…do it your way."

"Our way's what I want, darlin' and I know how I might do it, or show them how to do it."

"Tell me?"

"With nickels and dimes…with real hand work in the five Boroughs and in the districts…not multi million budgets and remoteness. That way the arguments come through."

"Then try it! You're the guy...the *man* that's gonna count! First off...fire that guy Flip! I can't bear speaking out the name!" She laughed and was gone, her spirited replies echoing in his ears.

25
Amsterdam

"Hello treasure." The silky voice held him in thrall. It was unexpected.

"Hey! Where are you?" His mind raced. I can't go there, I need to see her but can't concede to anything. One touch, what then? Edith was away.

"Close by. Does someone else call you that now?"

"No Monique, the label's your own." The word could mean avarice, keeping possession for one's own selfish pleasure or its denial to another, only it wasn't like that anymore. They had moved on, hadn't they? She had been tempted, considered the thrill of a new experience and finally conceded to another's seductive touch. He had seen it as nothing more than her defection.

"What are you called now? Lievert...or darling?" She gave a breathy sensuality to the words.

"Did you think I'd move on so quickly, after all we had?" He hadn't seen her for three weeks, not a call or a message had been taken or received; nothing, he'd heard nothing from her. Why expect that of her or feel disappointed? After all he had said, solace had been found with another.

"You're a loving man, a darling man to someone."

"Quite possibly."

"So, there is someone in your life?"

"Apart from you, you mean?"

"I'm not there now, am I? I made one fatal decision to that and finished it for us."

"You're still there in my mind and in my memories. Where are you now, who with? The guy you told me of?"

"No...it was a raid," she replied in a low voice. He found it a touching and, for her, a painful admission.

So, it was not the enduring seizure of what he had regarded as his preserve alone; Monique had shown endearing honesty in her confession to a drink and drugs induced deviation from their chosen path. As he waited for Monique to speak again he thought of Edith's whispered 'lievert' and the warmth of her breath on his skin when she had said it. He could feel comfortable with 'darling' now, 'precious' by any other name, in any other language. He might never grow tired of unity, togetherness and exclusive love.

"So? He just 'took' what he wanted, is that what you mean?"

"No…I played a part. I don't need you to remind me of that!" she cried out but with a faltering voice.

"That's true."

"Don't make me hurt any more than I do already, please Gerard?"

"No," he said softening, just a bit. "I haven't been able to work out, or understand, 'why'?"

"I was lost…"

"Lost for words…to describe what you had, then…with another guy?"

"No, and it seems I won't be able to explain it any better the longer we talk after we've been apart for so long."

"Maybe not," he replied. "I'll tell you this much…the pills? They were Ecstasy…or something close to it." He said it as if it were a commonplace observation.

"It's a peculiar kind of 'happiness' I feel now," she said in a barely audible whisper.

"You're clean…you're beautiful! Your body's your own…keep it unblemished, from now on." He poured out all the words and thoughts he had used to flay his memory of her with another man. You were born as 'pure' as he could imagine it to be possible, the work of some creative genius that he had little contact with, but who ordained a set of rules that he paid lip service to, call it a blind faith.

"I know, you told me so often…"

"Why are you calling me…after so long?" A bitter rage welled up inside him.

"It's a few weeks."

"Yeah, don't I just know it!" It had seemed an age to him, blank hours of not hearing her voice. "But why, Monique? Why call me?"

"To…to…to see you, and to hurt myself."

"Don't do that…don't do that." They were silent until he blurted out, "Don't, don't do that, and not over me."

"Anything, I'd do anything to return to where we were a few weeks ago."

"Why? Some would call it liberation from the routine of normal life for so many."

"Bull shit!"

He listened, then. "You were tempted away from what we had and I've picked up the pieces…I had to…and I've moved on."

"Have you, completely?"

155

That was a good one. The question brought him up short.

"It's unfair to compare," he said. The words rhymed, it could become addictive; 'enjoy and destroy' another phrase that succinctly summed up how he had felt on hearing her news. Another man's possession of her, humiliation and for all he knew subjugation – all of them seen as sources of fleeting pleasure. "You made your choice Monique."

"Oh! And how I regret it now."

He couldn't answer that one either.

"I'll meet you, somewhere close-by. I'm still in the office so you won't have to travel too far home."

"Okay," there was a trace of resignation in her lovely voice.

He pushed through the crowds in his haste to reach her. When she entered the restaurant the effect of seeing Monique was as it had been on that flight, to New York; there was the same shiver of attraction, a flush of adrenalin; no it was desire. Hypocrite! As she drew near and then held out her hands to him he saw for the first time tiredness in the slender face. She had changed; her features bore the signs of exhaustion. Gone was the vitality that he had loved but never spoken enough of. Their kisses became an embrace and as they were led through to their place he felt Monique's touch on his arm. They sat next to each other at the small round table.

"Missed you," he said as he took in all of her care-worn beauty. He held her hand. "You're safe…I won't make a fuss."

"I'd like you to…to make a fuss of me again," she smiled with a soft pout of her lips.

He held her gaze. "Excuse my outburst when you called…I knew then that I missed you…I was so bloody angry."

That was enough. He put a folder on the chair beside him; work to take home and to e-mail Edith over. He'd confess to everything, probably scare the hell out of her that he was *'distracted'* already.

"Missed you too." Monique's lips brushed his hand. "It was a raid… nothing more." Her eyes pleaded with him to understand. "It was over before it began, call it a temporary madness."

"I know that now…but it's changed everything, we can't put the clock back, we just can't."

"Why? You said we were…."

"Open? I got that wrong, so very wrong." He tried to attract a waiter's attention.

"Forgive, understand, but never forget?"

"Something like that, yes, it runs in the family. I've learnt about that too recently." They stared at each other then looked away. But, hands touched and fingers gripped.

"Ger..." She squeezed and pulled on his hand, to make him look at her.

"It wasn't easy, but...I'm not going to play the lovelorn injured party role."

"You don't feel loss?"

"Sure."

"So that's it? No second chances to make up?"

"Can't do it, someone else is involved." He let the words register. "It's early days, and I'm not going to admit I was distracted."

"Then don't...don't say anything. We see how it goes from here." She uttered the words in a rush of warm breath against his cheek before she kissed him. He sat quite still.

"That's how we got to be here...because of that attitude," he said loftily. "Shit! How pompous! How old and conventional!"

"A one girl guy...or is it only one at a time?" she managed to smile. "That's how you saw it?"

"Yes, I guess so. I should have told you. Do you reckon it would have made any difference? Would it have stopped you...going with that guy...pills or no quirky pills?"

"I was a distraction for him, a means to earn money I know that now, official and unofficial."

"I don't follow. The airline gave him a contract. What else was there for you to do?"

"Modelling."

"Oh God, that can have several meanings." He looked at her. "Tell me! Tell me that nothing is going to end up on the Internet. Tell me that...tell me! Please?" The waiter had left them a bottle of white wine and Monique held out her glass.

"To the brim." Her smile brightened as she waved the glass before him before looking at Gerard once more. "I saw the guy, after the photo shoot, why think of anything else?"

"Okay," he shrugged then poured out her measure. "I'm forgetting my manners." They clinked glasses. "Here's looking at you, beautiful lady. So tired, do you really need his sort in your life?"

"No, I told you. It was a ...."

"A raid; easy, quick and different?"

Monique looked away. "You have to keep reminding me don't you?"

"Oh yes!" He couldn't put any malice into his reply. "A drink, a few pills and...'*fait vos jeux*.'"

"I loved you…I still love you, enough to want to confess it all happened. No secrets, we never had any."

"I didn't want to hear this one."

"And I couldn't have lived with it for long, something would have shown you how I had changed…how it set us against each other."

"So spell it out, clear the air, clear the mind and then carry on?"

Monique's features hardened. "I never saw such conventional attitudes in you before," she hissed.

"No," he sighed, "and I didn't want you to die in our relationship, so I left you free. Only, I trusted in the unspoken bond between us…that was then." They lapsed into silence while he sorted through the papers in the envelope beside him. He then glanced up holding his glasses in his free hand.

"What?" Monique asked abruptly as she caught his glance at her.

"Know any of these guys?" he said casually. It was a very, very long shot, but he believed in the occasional coincidence, pre-destiny even. He marvelled at the unexpected, like hearing her voice after so long.

Her eyes widened and she glanced from him to the picture then back again.

"Where'd you get this?" Her glass tipped over as she took the picture from him. "Shit!" her chair scraped back. "Oh Shit!" He watched mesmerised as the wine trickled over the cloth then onto her neat tan leather shoes. Her finger pointed to one man. "Him, I went with him. That's the man you ask so much about," she said bitterly.

His fingers kneaded the skin of his forehead. "I know."

"Anything else, only I'd like to know why and how do you '*know*'?"

"I'm researching two of them, not your man." He refilled her glass. "I've got the pictures…there are several, I found them on the Internet."

"He isn't…*my man* as you put it!" She took several sips. "When relationships end, or hit the rocks it's a reason to be hard on one another is that it?"

"No," he paused. There was still a reason for them to be civil and show muted affection, in spite of everything. That at least was how he saw it but the feeling of anger at losing her for a meaningless squelch, or so it seemed, was never out of his mind. "Know the other two?"

"No, never set eyes on them." He held his hand to her face and she smiled. "That's nice…say something soft…just this once?"

"You're beautiful, a beautiful lady and…and…you're lost to me now."

"His name's Flip…Flip Forsell." She spoke abruptly as if goaded by his words, admitting to the condition of their relationship now.

He nodded. "Sh…I would have got our New York bureau to find out, eventually. With a name like that," he smiled, "I guess he does all sorts of tricks?"

"Oh, Ger!" Monique couldn't hide her tears. "Please, take me back?"

The simplicity of the plea touched him and he leant over to kiss her eyes. She conceded to his familiar touch, a habit they had discovered and often indulged in as if no one else seemed to be there.

"I can't beautiful lady, I just can't." He wouldn't explain it any further but kissed her again briefly, with a slip of a kiss to her mouth. "I can't lievert…not anymore."

For him a relationship now meant simply being of one body and mind.

Unwittingly, Monique had given him another lead. He would find the means to request that Nico looked into Flip Forsell's background before he wrote his next piece, or *'Comment'*. Ideas were forming but he would not commit to paper his initial thoughts; thorough research of the subject would be undertaken before Hans had an outline on his desk. The New York office would have to fill in a few blanks.

Monique's moist words, on the tram and as he courteously walked her home, wound up his clock but they only exchanged deep kisses and parted. *'Still love you, still want you'* she had told him. *'Still miss you, can't have you'* had been his reply. *'May I still call you, occasionally?'* she had asked him at the door of the apartment block as her hand gripped his jacket, tugging gently and coaxing him to stay…and stray. *'Yeah, occasionally – find the guy who can handle you and your beauty, not a spectacled beast like me.* He attempted to make light of the situation now yet all the while felt that he had belonged, not *to* Edith but *with* her.

It was a distinction he had failed to make with Monique.

"Could love you, Edi," he told her when he rang to tell of his evening. Look on the positives he had said to himself; he could put a name to the face in the picture; and, of even greater significance he could feel a motivating impulse to investigate still further a story line that now had a very personal association with a former love. The world seemed very small but Edith didn't see it as a definite lead, just a snippet of information; it was no big deal.

"Have loved all there is of you," was her distant reply. "Tell me again when I see you, in only three days."

"I'll have response from Nico Brant by then. Lots to say then and I hope lots to do."

"Just me and *just* you," Edith told him before she rang off.

26

The meeting had been arranged on what Marta Kahn described as *'neutral ground'*, the coffee lounge of a smart hotel near Wassenaar with its own sun-blanched terrace. The orange and white awning snapped and ruffled in the late summer breeze, the leaves of the silver birches that lined the roadside rustled conspiratorially. Edith's mother had been surprised by the call. Marta Kahn had said only that, based upon reports reaching her, Edith had grown closer to Gerard than ever before. The two of them were so often in each other's company, so her breathless call went, that she felt compelled to telephone and invite her over. A short train journey made the concession to inconvenience bearable; Marta had spoken of family history being under investigation and left her question of why hanging unanswered over the clear mobile telephone connection.

"I've heard some gossip. Edith and Gerard have become inseparable," Marta began as they sat down at the table. She smoothed the linen table-cloth with immaculately manicured fingers.

"They're busy people, so, not quite inseparable," Katerina answered. "Edith's still out of town a great deal, she works on EU projects as an accounts investigator, so she meets Gerard when it suits them both."

"That's not what I hear."

"From who?"

"Never mind that," Marta said abruptly but softened as she saw Katerina's reaction. "I'm sorry, it seems so sudden…and so unexpected."

"They have hardly seen each other since that reunion, how long ago was that?"

"I forget," Marta said.

"Never mind, it's of little consequence now." Katerina knew exactly how many years it had been. Edith had reminded her.

"They're having an affair, aren't they?" Marta said matter-of-factly when they were alone again. The waitress had left them to their coffee and patisseries that they had wondered at, before giving in. Will power had been useless in the face of such confection; they would indulge themselves just this once, meetings were all too rare between them they had conceded, smiling to one another; the uneasy silence that had fallen after the opening skirmish was finally broken.

"Oooh!" Katerina licked her lip as she put down her coffee cup.

"Okay?"

"Why yes," Katerina said. She kept her voice light and gave a chuckle at being caught off-guard. "I think I need more notice of a question like that." Marta was herself lost for words.

"Well?" was all she finally said.

"I don't know that they are," Katerina replied. "They are a happy enough couple, I could see that much."

"You've seen them together?"

"Yes, of course!" Katerina laughed at the shrill note of surprise. "Only once mind you, and it was some weeks ago now."

"And it was obvious to you even then?"

"Nothing was '*obvious*' as you put it. They were happy to be together and had made plans to go to an art gallery…come to think of it, there was a project they were going to work on."

"This so called family history, it's no more than raking up past difficulties," Marta almost hissed and without any attempt to conceal the tone of derision.

"Yes, that's a possibility but they're not likely to dwell on it are they?" Katerina gave a benign smile. The misdeed had not been forgotten. "This cake's delicious…go on, try yours?" She would maintain an equable tone, her earlier anxiety, at the prospect of meeting Marta, had vanished. "I see why you chose to come here Marta…it's so…sociable!" Her tone indicated a wish to lighten the mood.

Katerina fussed at pouring more coffee and glanced across the table then at the other guests seated nearby. It seemed pointless getting too enervated by the tale she knew only too well and Edith had devoted time to. Gerard's involvement had been a pleasant surprise; after all, the family split was regarded as a legacy that might yet be put right, at least in terms of renewed contact, however uncomfortable the early moments might be. She did not believe that Edith picked at this particular scab with any expectation of achieving some form of redress. At least the Dekkers and their large and immediate family were happily bonded, far enough removed from the Kahns to have little cause for worry at what might follow from Edith and Gerard being together or '*raking over the past*'.

The Kahns lived a separate life in very comfortable wooded suburbs to The Hague. The evidence of well-lined pockets was all about them but this had left no trace on Gerard whom she heard had overcome a disabling defect to his eyesight to achieve journalistic success thereby confounding all who met him. Edith had spoken much of him and spoke of a studious mind and her cousin's attentiveness. She had spoken with a song in her voice, making no secret that she found Gerard deeply attractive. If he succeeded in bringing emotional and physical fulfilment to Edith she would raise no objection to her daughter's chosen means of securing her happiness.

Katerina was jolted out of her reverie.

"Never mind all that, the cake will keep. I want to hear news of them."

"Ger must have told you something?"

"Nothing! Mind you his brother winds him up over all his girlfriends."

"Girlfriend…lover…I never said matters between them had gone any where near so far."

"And I know Gerard. If a pretty woman fills his life, and Monique the air-hostess certainly meets that need, then what can Edith possibly mean to him? A fling maybe?"

"I wouldn't gossip on the details, even if I knew them," Katerina bridled.

"You wouldn't see it as strange, cousins as lovers?"

Katerina closed her eyes and breathed slowly. "I told you before, I don't know any of the details…in any case, they're adults and times are very different, less judgmental…of everything and everyone, least of all it seems of moral behaviour." She would have to find out if Gerard was two timing Edith, but she doubted it; Edith knew enough from one wounding experience to see the signs. Damn! This is all going too far now.

"So, you wouldn't disapprove of them being together?" Marta sensed an opening.

"I've not seen Edith so happy for a very long time. If Gerard is responsible for that change in mood then, yes, I would not disapprove." You had to concede on some things, or else opinions were only to be seen as old-fashioned conceits or prejudices from the past.

Marta leant forward and rested her chin on clasped hands, looking at Katerina all the while. "All in the interest of mending fences?"

"That's not even been mentioned."

"Come on! Ger came round and asked straight out whether there was any truth in the tale," Marta said forcefully

"It's not a tale." Katerina replied in a voice barely above a whisper. In her case those distant events had almost been fed with mother's milk. They stared at each other.

"The only person to have told him is Edith, so what is she up to?"

"She's up to nothing as far as I can tell and, if she is, Edith…the two of them, seem very happy as a result!" Katerina put a napkin to her mouth to brush away the crumbs from the slab of apple tart, and to conceal a wicked smile. The story would make the Kahn's hop about a bit. Marta's stare provoked her to continue. "Believe it or not Edith has, with my help admittedly, put the whole story together…but that episode is just that, a moment of time in a long and eventful family history. I'm sure she just wants to piece the fragments together, knot the loose strands if you like."

"That's all?"

"Sure, I know and have told her of the pictures and the books, the songs…Edi's not intent on making mischief. We've been separated for far too long to go over all of that old tale again."

Marta began to fork some of the cake into her mouth. "We can agree on that!"

"Good," Katerina tried to make her voice sound convincing. The meeting had aroused her curiosity about the pair.

"Women always seem to be the ones to mend fences," Marta smiled.

"Yes." Katerina answered slowly as she sat back in her chair.

A woman had played a part in the deception long ago, inspired a trustworthy uncle to commit a heinous crime. The event contradicted what Marta had just said. Edith absorbed all that she heard; she had checked and rechecked every element but as far as Katerina knew there was no evidence, no proof and how could there now be, after so many years had elapsed? In spite of the collection of anecdotes and pictures, arranged in portfolios, they were all that she could have shown to Gerard. There must indeed be more to the relationship with Edith than events from long ago; he had shown utter disbelief at the tale he had been told; that much Edith had confided.

"Katerina?"

"Hm?" she looked up. "Oh! Nothing more will come of it than Ger telling Edith what he knows, isn't that it?"

"And what we have told him. It's not much, just a couple of letters." Marta laid her hand on Katerina's arm. "Ask Edith to stop?"

"Because she knows all there is to know?"

"Exactly! We're all okay now aren't we? Look around you? And…think of us. The family's moved on."

"Time has righted a wrong?"

"If you like. Is that how Edith may have been told of it?"

"Not exactly…the truth was that the deed was done, and," Katerina was not to be interrupted, "I've told Edith to leave it buried in the past. The personalities involved paid for it."

Marta laughed. "Judgement Day?"

Katerina nodded.

"I don't believe in that."

"That's your right. They may have suffered along the way, here on this earth, we'll never know, but our side of the family has had to deal with it differently. Their approach is influenced, entirely by what happened to my great grandmother and her children! Redemption follows the admission of a wrong and making up somehow, I'm sure of that. Edith wants the story to be a record."

"And Gerard is to help in all that?" Marta spoke as if the man had lost a sense of duty to his own family.

"No, I think he wishes to acknowledge it and then move on."

"I'll ask him."

"And I'll ask Edith about them, as *a couple*. That's fair...wouldn't you say?"

"Edi! Come back to bed!"

"I won't be long!" she called out happily, and under her breath, "you treasure." Edith smoothed the newspaper cutting over the coarse weave of the scrapbook's page. It's another piece by Gerard, *"The Owl"* to his readers.

"Edi!"

"Coming, you lovely man!"

"Like last night?" Their voices echo along the narrow hall way.

"Ger, really!"

There could be no one else, of that she was now certain; any obstacles to her passion for him, as her mother had alluded to in her call last night, belonged to another world. She was happy. *'I fell for your smiling directness and unruly curls long ago...you're still a student at heart, rebellious and no respecter of reputations if you see something to remark upon'*. She smiled as Gerard drew her down beside him under the thin covers. The intensity of their reunion surprised them.

"Last night, were you letting go at last?" she murmured, the bristle of his beard pricked and she pressed her lips to murmur against the skin of his throat.

"Ja!" he answered softly in a tone that admitted to his recognition of the fact, "was it so obvious?"

"Not until a special tender moment when you held me. I knew then that we were one. I could let go too."

"How will we be able to explain it? I had a call, about us."

"Ssshh!" Edith kissed him into silence. "We're not going to bother! It's our life."

"Tell them when we're ready?" Gerard could only mumble against her insistent lips.

"Yes, something like that...now, stay close. I love this! Just skin on skin."

"You've never shown me the scrapbook you left me for this morning," Gerard teased as they sat in the autumn sunshine on Edith's small balcony. "What do you keep in it?"

"Your latest piece."

"Oh, that!"

"Yes that! I've put it with my record of everything we discover." She watched him as he sipped on his coffee holding the cup in his large hand and dispensing with any need of the handle.

"Taste this for me?" Gerard held a piece of croissant out to her.

They had quickly fallen into a domestic routine and she was amused to think how comfortable he was in the role of looking after her. "You put into words what I often feel or think about when you're not with me. That's whom I love to be with."

"Is that allowed, after *all* the gossip?" They laughed and held out a hand to each other in affirmation that they would live for it.

"Some would say not…but it's happened."

He nodded. Gerard loosened his hold. "So, the article on the misuse of funds, fraud in high places, you've kept that? It's not one of my best, it's routine reporting."

"Perhaps, but it struck a chord with me after the week I've had. I'll be glad to see what's been discovered. Where have you hidden the papers?"

"Are they a welcome diversion?"

"From you?" she smiled. Gerard arched his eyebrows. "Let me see?"

"All in good time, have breakfast with me…and relax? I'll take care of you…in the meantime the story lives on."

The office of internal affairs and administration at the EU offices in Brussels had proved a fertile area to gain experience of the investigation and pursuit of those intent on malpractice. As a consultant she could provide an independent and often inquisitorial perspective. It was not an office that she ever wished to become a permanent part of, a well-paid and amply pensioned cypher. Political agendas were the most potent deterrent to that, also the many vanities and conceits that required careful management; she had neither the time nor the patience for it.

"Everything is as it should be in our new seat of government, is that what you're telling me?" he teased.

"No, but then whistleblowers aren't popular where I work. Those in power like to pretend or show us all that they're in control. Pointing out deficiencies is seen as de-motivating to their staff."

"Or plain disloyalty…OR! The disclosures upset career plans and medals for good service from grateful participating governments."

"Quite," Edith held a finger to her lips. "Sh! Cynic! Now, don't interrupt, or am I telling you something you already know?"

"It sounds so much better from you, lievert"

Edith pulled a face. "Anyway," she said forcefully, "those that tell tales or expose people in authority for mismanagement soon see their careers at an end, pensions all but gone...if they've been there long enough to qualify. I'm happy enough for now in what I'm doing."

"Here, take a look at these." Gerard handed a neat plastic folder across the table to her.

"Nico's handiwork?"

"Yes...with a little prompting from me. Published accounts of our dear cousin's companies. I've marked the pages of interest to me...see?" He put on his glasses before leaning across to flip open the folder to the donations page. "Start here...."

Edith pursed her lips softly together as she met his intense gaze, distorted by the lenses. Gerard hesitated. "Your handsome to me, with or without them," she smiled.

"Until recently they never bothered me...or what effect they had on another."

"They don't affect me...except to increase my admiration for what you've done."

"Go on, look through what I've brought for you," he said with a sigh.

"I read the statements first, at the beginning, and I also looked at the photographs, just to get a feeling for the ethos of the companies. I try to look behind them."

"Too one dimensional. The ethos is to make money, any way they can..."

"So?"

"So nothing, just an observation - an all too obvious one, I know." He watched as Edith bent over the glossy papers, her face hidden by the fall of her hair and brushed away by the occasional sweep of her hand. She turned slightly in her chair.

"Are you going to keep staring at me?"

"Yes," he smiled over the rim of his coffee cup. "Many must have done so long before me?"

"I wouldn't know or much less really cared, I told you." She turned to the printout that represented the bulk of Nico's e-mailed papers. "You spoiled me long ago," Edith said without looking up. "The amounts aren't big by their standards." She turned over the pages then back to where Gerard had marked them with coloured tabs.

"No...what do you mean spoiled you?""

Edith looked up. "Later, but can't you guess?" She looked down at the papers again. "The payments aren't so large or too frequent that they would draw attention."

"And that's precisely what they've avoided."

"Yes, until now, or until the pictures you showed me appeared," she said. Edith lifted her face to the sun. "Oh...I want to get all this over with."

"We will, I've had the photos checked out. Nico's followed up the names I gave him and the snippets of biographical detail."

"How did you come by that?"

"Trade secret...I can't tell you everything."

"Owlish behaviour?"

"Something like that!" he laughed giving her a sly wink but Gerard became serious. "Monique gave me a name, it was the lead that set me off on the chase."

"When was that...getting the name from her?"

"A few days ago, I told you."

"Not that part...the detail...not about her."

"Lievert, I'm with you, remember that. Everything has changed."

"Yes!" She flicked at her hair angrily. "Anything else I should know? I had a 'phone call too, about *us*."

"That you have nothing to fear...from her."

"And you?" Gerard stared at her for an instant. She had the loveliest of round eyes, bereft of all make up, and held Edith's gaze.

"I'm not fooling around...understand me?"

Without his glasses he was less intimidating and Edith relaxed in spite of the hard edge to his reply. She could infer from it his honesty; she had learnt that much of him in the short time, a few months, they had been together. She had sensed a unity of spirits

"It's happened so quickly for us," she answered.

"That doesn't mean the relationship's wrong...or the commitment's ill-founded."

"No, but time will tell."

"It already has, for me at least," he said allowing Edith not another moment to dwell on the words they often used to test each other's feelings. "Here...." A clenched hand was held out to her.

She took a small folded square of tissue paper from him. "What is it?"

"Open it carefully...then you'll see."

Edith's eyes widened and looked from him to her hands in quick furtive glances.

"Well?" he smiled. "I haven't done this before."

"Who's is it?"

"Yours, silly."

"I didn't mean that," she said in a voice just above a whisper.

"I bought it, guessed the size…I took a bit of a chance," he laughed. "Put it on…on your right ring finger."

"It's beautiful, so slender and discreet. What does it mean?"

"It's an eternity ring, two rubies and a diamond neatly set in a band of gold. It took some finding I can tell you!"

Edith stared at him then gave a soft smile at his evasive reply.

"Answer the question!" she laughed, holding her hand out to gaze at the ring against her skin. "What does it mean?"

Edith's sigh of unexpected contentment reached him.

"Okay, I'll tell you, but come to me…come here."

27

New York

"I'll change all of it, the perspective they have on me and my politics," John murmured in a low voice. The secret apartment offered him the peace and solitude to consider the primary tenets of his arguments for office, the reasons for his candidacy. It was a place for distractions too.

"What's that John?" Joey touched the skin on the back of his hand with a light brush of her fingers and they exchanged glances.

"Never mind, I was just thinking out loud." He slipped his hand from her grasp.

He would have to offer something that came as a surprise to them all, out of the blue skies that he would be expected to show could draw them on to him and his plans for office. He might be surprised himself, confounded by the unexpected that politicians had by some instinct to analyse and deal with, quickly. Afterwards, the publicity machine would make out they'd had it covered or in their sights all along. The moment for articulating the motives that made him stand for election would soon be upon him. Some would see the whole electoral process as parochial, a matter for a prescribed and small electorate; the turnout was never so high that the successful candidate could claim that universal suffrage had got him there, that an interested and diverse electorate had truly voiced its opinion. In modern times, cynics might say, those with the most to gain, or was it to lose, chose their man to walk up the steps of City Hall.

By going into politics he had something to lose for the first time since the heat and stench of the jungle and swamps. Home would not be the same in the corners of his mind where comfort lay; he would be outside that warming blanket. Once more, and quite unlike the business world he knew, the unpredictable would come at him and there would be little time to assess and respond to the situation he faced. It was combat but with words and ideas as the weapons to deploy. He had to engage a constituency with its own prejudices and a voice to catch him off guard; the tone and the content of his response was key, and a willingness to listen. The loudest voices, for him, did not always have the correct message.

"Know what you're going to focus on, darlin'?" she rarely used the word except in moments of cloying intimacy.

"The cynics will say "*he's done everything else, so why not this?*". I'll need to find an answer, quick and easy to understand for that one. On top of all that they won't like a rich patrician type hustling them for votes."

"Make them see you," she answered. "What I'm asking you is *just 'easy come-easy go'* chatter. Wait until some media type really grills you."

"I'll be ready."

"Hope so."

"I will be, you can bet on it."

His voice took on a harder edge that she had come to recognise only too clearly as John's adherence to a plan he had conceived.

Joey looked at him unwaveringly and could imagine that Marie would have done little to discourage his pursuit of a new goal. Business success and more money than you could ever spend would hold little attraction in later life. No, a new challenge offered the family the prospect of a presence in a wider world beyond their country's shores. But I haven't seen such an intellectual challenge in my rival for his affections she thought. It was instead a more parochial outlook she saw, as if the venture was the outcome of the combined Kahn and Hudson dynasties' natural progression to new heights. Reputations, especially of the Kahn's, were jealousy guarded, she knew that much of Elbee's work for them but little else.

John never spoke of it to her and all she would do was piece together a picture from the smallest fragments of news or comment he let fall from his lips. She divined what she could from the inflections or tone of his voice in reply to her seemingly innocent questioning. It was a small and subtle mosaic that she was laying down, with no motive other than to know more of the man she was falling in love with. She was complicit in acts of protecting him.

"Defy the critics," she answered him at last. "Tell them why you're doing it." She would provoke him into answers. "You're not doing it for the money."

"No, certainly not that," he laughed softly tapping her wrist in playful reproach.

"Status then, a few more lines on your life's resume'."

"No, not that either."

"Just for me, string a few words together, please Jack?"

"Love you...I love you a lot."

"Not that...."she sighed. Why did it always come to this? When she wanted Jack to consider the implications of what he was embarking on he took these diversions down emotion routes. They knew each other well enough now.

"I have my reasons," he smiled and held out a conciliatory hand, out of view. "If something bugs me or is important, thinking of something else helps me take it on....get me? Started it way back, in the heat and rain."

"Okay...talk of something else that motivates you *just now*."

"The main reason? The main one is payback time for a city, for a State that's allowed us to live life to the full and made us grow...separately and then with Hudson help." He turned to see if the mention of Marie's family affected her.

"You took what you could like everyone else...you were simply better at it."

She was right, but he was nevertheless surprised by the manner in which Joey uttered her matter of fact reply. The family had worked the system, unashamedly calling in favours or reminding others of a debt owed to them for past help.

"We were better connected too, don't you go forgetting that. And, we had help...some could say misbegotten help."

"Oh?"

"Forget I said that," the whisper came from behind his hand as he held it to his mouth. There would be work to do on a scale that would dwarf the boost the Kahns had received upon arrival. In this political adventure he was a rookie, a novice, a beginner who had it all to learn and do but he had put down a trail; community work, hands-on charitable work could be checked out by anyone and at any time. He'd see to it that others talked of his work.

"It came down to seeing an opportunity, is that what you mean?"

"Yes..." that's what I'll say, he thought. "It's now about making opportunities for all, a bit of social democracy with capitalism in the raw too, does that sound incompatible to you?"

"Not entirely, it'll take a special man to sell it and to make the message sound like it's no Democrat who's on the stump, we've had a few of them already...appeal to them on a different level."

"I'm not about taking from one group and redistributing the take."

"So? How'll you do it? Someone has to give and they will see it as losing out to someone less deserving." Joey spoke in a tone to needle him, to provoke a response, just as she knew the voters or potential constituents would work on a candidate.

"Everyone deserves basic rights…it's how you get there, or sell the idea. You've got to have a stake in the outcome."

"Ha! They all say that…sell it to me!" She laughed at him with ill concealed doubt in her tone now. "Make me believe in a win-win deal."

"Okay cynic…you disbeliever. Things have sunk so low have they?"

"C'mon, sell it to me! It's only what people will expect to hear from you."

"You're forgetting one thing. I'm thinking of running for Mayor, not the Goddamn Presidency!" he hissed.

"Good! You're beginning to fire now, sell it to me," she stared at him unflinchingly, "please?"

"You try to narrow the gap between the '*have's*', the so called rich…"

"They are," she interrupted but Jack held up his hand.

"Sh! You asked me, remember?" he said in a colder tone, "so, let me finish."

Joey sat back in her seat and visibly relaxed. She had achieved her purpose and Jack's eyes told her he was not too angry; in many instances he expected this agitation from her, realising the good intentions and the motives that lay behind them.

"Okay."

"You narrow the gap in relative values and perceptions. You have to strive to persuade the rich, in money and potential, that there are benefits in helping others move on or achieve their own goals…it's reconciling a lot of differences, it may help to make your neighbourhood a safer place."

"You'll come over as undecided, a motley collection of all party views under one skin. The constituents won't see anything to believe in much less vote for…unless you meet their expectations and you can deliver on the promises or pledges that you speak of during a campaign for office." Joey nodded at him as she spoke to reinforce her point of view.

"It's a puzzle and I'll have to work on it some more."

John sat staring at the traffic through the darkened window and shut her out. He thought of the diverse strands to his political beliefs and the influence of disparate ideas on what he regarded as social justice. His opinions seemed too diverse to enable anyone to describe them as John Kahn's political creed. He knew only too well without Joey's prompting that he had to raise a recognisable and distinct political banner.

"Independence," he murmured absent-mindedly. "Yeah…that's it."

"What?"

"I'll be judged and condemned, whatever course I follow, so, I may as well go Independent and give support to other like-minded citizens running for office and labelled as "indies"".

Independent thought had been his trademark and he had developed that character trait during his military service as far as its rules and regulations allowed. The legacy of his 'service to the nation' was to see both sides of the business case and quickly reach a decision. Often there was no debate; orders were given and the team deployed to get on with their allotted tasks, however frustrating that might be for those closest to him. But, he reasoned one side didn't have a monopoly on good ideas, it was just that one side might have the right team assembled at that crucial moment to allow it to secure a commercially viable outcome.

Some might describe him as a *maverick*, not a good label to pin upon a political aspirant, but it had been a credo he had lived and worked by. Elbee and Delroy had seen it in the field, rules of engagement were stretched but an objective was achieved, then secured. Values need not be discarded, they evolved with time to meet the circumstances of the day; gains were not achieved at the expense of core beliefs; rules were never quite broken.

"That's the inheritance of all politicians...to be seen, studied and condemned, for being too honest and direct...or too soft and unwilling to take the decisions that you said you would." Joey paused, waiting in case John chose to interrupt her, but he did not. "I guess you knew that before you embarked on this adventure," she observed coolly.

"Sure, but even the hardest guys expect the occasional nod of encouragement or gratitude that you were willing to try something different." He had lived through the post-war liberalism of John Lindsay and that had won the guy little or no respect, but that was not the way that he would choose to follow.

"That will come, if you're lucky and when you succeed, or deliver."

John laughed at her all-too-true remark. "Yes!"

"That's the bonus so don't go counting on any of it. That way you won't be disappointed or shatter the illusions of those that listened and voted for you."

He gripped her cool fingers but Joey did not respond or prevail on him to stop. "You're wise and beautiful."

"Not in the ways you've known them," she answered.

"That's where you're wrong, but I'll keep showing and telling you. Why do you make me talk of these things in the same breaths as business?"

"I don't."

"Well, you sure make me feel obliged to do so."

"Say what's on your mind, if it'll help...and, the truth is?"

He fell silent and tapped his feet in nervy spasms as if in synchrony with his thoughts. "The truth is…"

"Be still John…the truth is?"

He ignored her hand as it rested on his leg. "The truth is…the truth is that I'm going to do this on my own…quite independent and free of any other party structure except my own. I'll be able to live with that…outside the usual box they like to put you in. Only, it'll cost me some more in time spent, my own time. Others…correction, *one other,* has done it on his own but with a major party's ideas and a truck full of his private cash to follow him."

"You'll need some allies and you will still borrow ideas from them all, just the same…or you'll spin the web a little differently. It's human nature."

"We'll see…altruism and taking the best of each side to make it work for the many, that's an elusive prize and one to have frustrated so many and with greater experience than I can bring." Or, candidates less naïve had seen altruism for what it was and instead pursued their goal with a single-minded determination that others called selfishness and the really clever ones merely labelled pragmatism.

Joey read his thoughts uncannily. "Reality!" she laughed, "or as I'd call it the *real world!* It's life that's out there on the streets. It comes up and knocks you down. Everyone starts off with ideals, then…wham!"

"The cold douche of 'reality' as you keep reminding me?"

"Something close…if it matters to you that much and getting voted in matters more than anything else you're doing right now…then go for the prize…fight for your beliefs and make change happen."

"I'm through fighting…I had more than my share of that."

"You know what I mean, honey."

"Sh! Not that! Don't call me that, ever!"

"Lievert? I found a short piece in the New York Observer, their weekly paper. I'm e-mailing it to you."

"I like the personal delivery service better," Edith soothed in reply over the mobile 'phone connection.

"Or just service?"

"Behave!"

"Only when I'm away from you."

DEPEND ON INDEPENDENT JOHN
(*A personal view by Anita Maguire*)

I lost my pre-conceptions early on. Why had I fallen into thinking of stereotypes before my meeting? John Kahn looked fit; he wasn't paunchy, the muscle tone and reflexes overtaken by good wine and food consumed in wallet-busting eateries...or should I call them restaurants and glam night-spots taken in for purely business reasons? The man is rich, very rich, but the instant then a longer lasting impression was of a strong and yes, I'll admit to it, a charming handsome family man. His youngest daughter, Dayle, is on the campaign team. He's proud of that but the male line stops with him.

So, the fact that he's an aspirant in the mayoral race confounds most of my theories about such men, keep low and enjoy your life. Why put your head above the present day political parapet? Then I remembered the man's bio - he's a decorated Vet and unashamed of what he or his country tried to do in 'Nam. Apart from the admission that he took his place with comrades, (two are with him still) in an unpopular war, he tells you nothing more about it. He's proud and yet he displays a wide streak of modesty. You don't find that too often in a politician...but then you cynics or unbelievers out there will say, "what does he know?" or "he'll learn" (when it's too late to matter).

Okay...okay! That he is a politician and had this effect on me may shock you, but hey! Someone had to win me over to a reappraisal of the species and I'm not converted, yet. I liked the guy from the first then thought about his message, what he had to say in a few minutes. Finally, I tried very hard to find faults in his story; I looked hard to see any chinks in his defences or to discover some ambition-wrecking defect in his platform for election. Some of you will say I'm only a voter...I matter to him and other candidates. You may move on to tell me that those more experienced and accustomed to the breed will try to demolish him and his beliefs.

I hope we get to hear more of those before that day dawns because the guy used a word that you don't hear too often anymore...it's 'meritocrat'. A what, you may ask? When I heard him explain, the meaning became clear and it's in top place in his beliefs. To John Kahn it means a person who has earned his place in the sun, many of us...and he wants it to be an even greater number...in this City have studied hard, worked the hours and earned the rewards. So, they should feel no guilt. They have got there through your own efforts.

John Kahn's brave, unquestionably. The country thought so...he's got the medals. I found that out too, but not from him. He shyly admitted he had them, then talked of something else. He's come out...John Kahn's red-blooded, and very male, so don't get me or my words wrong...John Kahn's standing as an Independent. Yes! That's right! I also spelt the label correctly. Independent and a rookie! Scary huh? After all, who wants to be outside the comfort blanket that passes around the Democrat or Republican Party candidates? We've seen it all from them over the years, no decades. I remembered, but only after a diligent search of the web and I queried what they represented or stood for.

It was never any different. The apparent sameness of ideology held by these previous incumbents in City Hall bothered me, just a bit, when I read through the printouts and my brain cells rebooted the area of my personal recall.

John Kahn has one thing going for him right now…he offers the real prospect, tantalising to some, of CHANGE, a break with an all too familiar past and for all that many can see, or believe that they can, an all too recognisable future.

So, for those of you who like the idea of a smart and, yes, handsome candidate who has an unmannered…manner! (sure, he's rich but he doesn't wear it as a badge to intimidate you)…as your mayoral candidate then think hard about what he will come to say. He will no doubt talk of the City's ailments and how he plans to effect a change. In spite of status and wealth he spends many hours in disadvantaged neighbourhoods with his chosen charities and amongst those citizens he wants to help. He sees this as putting something back into the city that nurtured the hopes of an immigrant family…his family, way back in 1876. That's what his press office tells me, and I've checked it out. You can put a tick in that box. Immigrants made this City and this country; 'please don't forget that' he often murmurs when someone is seen doing the kind of work many folks now turn their backs on. John Kahn does so as a gentle reminder of our history.

So? John Kahn starts from way out of field, he's Independent and he's serious…and maybe as some folks are beginning to say a guy to look out for and take seriously. You can judge him for yourself at his next meeting…there's no grandstanding or wordy speeches; instead he's down amongst the crowds that have taken the trouble to check him out, discussing the issues face-to-face or hand-to-hand, as it seems he's known it from years back. Those that talked about him like what John Kahn has to say to them; take note of 'to them'; he doesn't lecture you or 'talk at you'. Some say that he takes risks mixing with ordinary folk on the floor of his meeting venues, but John Kahn looks the kind of guy that can still take care of himself; the medals and a way he has tells me that much.

Making enough people believe in him and what he has to say is going to be the trick of a lifetime.

28
Long Island and New York City

The days at the beach-house were idyllic; visitors were few and work was kept to a minimum. There they were, like on the days after the girls had left home, just the two of them with the house staff out of sight and of no concern. Marie had ordered it so, left her instructions in the nasally falsetto voice that she used to make her point and inviting no questions. Treece and her staff went about their business and left them with the orderliness that was closer to a first family in a state residence than a holiday retreat. But it was how Marie had learnt to interpret John's wishes, his desire for order, for process that contradicted the easy-going manner that she loved in him. But that was a front that she had learnt to live with; the smile of contentment soon faded with failure and was quickly and uncompromisingly addressed with words of excoriating criticism; arrangements had to be *"just so"*, or in his favourite phrase *"to the mark"*. It was a phrase she had heard him use after 'Nam but saw that it was his own. It set a standard that had seen him survive where others had not; he now lived by it and expected others to follow.

She had thrown the phrase back at him, when he had confessed to his infidelity. John had not been to *her* mark, deviating from the unifying commitment of their marriage vows that bound him to her. But, she knew that the neat scroll of the marriage certificate was just that, paper. She drew some comfort from the fact that he returned to her and that distractions elsewhere did not displace her in his mind. She remained a life's companion to him, still. Forgiving and making up with John for a subverted part of her life with him was never easy, but somehow she could draw strength from those reunions.

They were the renewal of a commitment to each other. John's taking of her upon his return from 'Nam had given her a clue. Difficult though it was, she recognised that his life could end at any time; the circumstances of war may have been very different but his service had changed him. John acknowledged openly that he never could see a life without her but almost in the same breath he could also admit to a 'legacy' from those times away on service. It was said as if to excuse his behaviour and to secure her understanding.

They sat on sun-chairs behind glazed screens that kept out the Atlantic wind, and talked of the coming week. Marie had been as good as her word. John had spoken to small groups of influential women the arrangements made with his office and Joey only too aware of the role his wife was beginning to play in his campaign.

So far they were low key meetings; the set piece events had yet to come and would be Joey's sole prerogative when it concerned interest groups that already had an association with John. They were people that Marie had no direct dealings with, unlike him. She made donations, some of them finding their way to the beneficiaries that John supported. The roles of the two women were distinct; they knew of each other but John had male advisors on his team so any more personal association between them was not made. She was a lawyer on Elbee's payroll, clever, and not a 'looker' that might have alerted

Marie to be on her guard for distractions or diversions that she knew John to be capable of.

The stakes were high; the press and radio showed greater interest and took his message with renewed seriousness; jokey comment on his platform for change was being replaced with closer scrutiny and analysis. He had a business brain and applied his knowledge to the affairs of the City; his electoral budget was deliberately set low; let the constituents see me, talk to me, *'press the flesh'* was his tactic, not the expending of flash money that raised doubts and lines of argument. Opponents had to answer questions on how they would meet the appeal of John's ideas. They had to deal with the man who had arrived from nowhere on the political scene.

But, Joey had secured one coup for him, followed up on one of his ideas, a comment thrown out to provoke discussion but which had struck a very personal note. She had persuaded him to stand in a "special election" for a post on a City Council committee. It had been a long shot, a *'hit from out of the sun'* but he had secured the post with a margin that left no room for argument.

"Folks will have to take notice of me now," he mused.

"What's that, darlin?" Marie held a hand out to him across the space between them. A scarf was tied neatly at her neck, leaving her softly tanned face clear. John smiled acknowledging that he could see the girl he had fallen in love with so many years ago.

"Oh, just thinking back…on that special election I was persuaded to run for…it gives me some credibility…they have to argue the finer points now…so the more coverage I can get the more they have to talk and debate."

Dayle would see to it; the girl was too bright, too up to the mark to let him slip back. Her ideas were giving his early campaign for City-wide recognition a much needed boost and people wanted to work for him; those that he took on were given the chance to prove themselves in his service.

"The times Dayle calls you," Marie drawled, "it's a wonder her head doesn't burst with all those ideas. Where does she find them?"

"Her Pa, that's where!" John laughed. He sat up and swung his legs down onto the stone flagged terrace. "She's going to run the whole thing for me, her and that company she works for!"

"You're doin' them a big favour with the work."

"Have to buy it…or into it, discreetly."

"And wait?" Marie smiled.

"You got it. That sort of media business can only grow…with the right ideas and finance."

"And you have both I guess?"

"Yeah…and the right management. People in business count for everything." Not like that Flip Forsell Inc that Elbee had brought to the beach house. They had served their purpose, limited maybe, and they were now dispensed with. Elbee was instructed to guard the fort; he didn't need any come-backs from careless mistakes being made.

Marie saw her husband's lips purse in thought. "What's on your mind?"

"What am I going to get out of the meeting this week…the one with your ladies?"

"And husbands…their partners…whatever you want to call them?"

"Yeah…they've heard it all from you already, I'm sure of that." He bent to kiss her and Marie's response re-affirmed the belief that she loved him and spoke up for the cause that she knew her man believed in now.

"But there's nothing like the personal touch, as I know only too well after a few days here alone with you."

"Just like old times," he said. The movement of his tongue and press of his lips intensified pleasurably. "Come back inside…relive some of them again…and again?"

"We've not been out here long," she whispered. It was always John's spontaneity that fuelled an erotic flame between them. Long ago she had given up wondering, let alone asking him, just where he learnt the things he often shared with her. "You give me fever…" she could just about murmur against the press of John's lips.

"So?"

"Enough is never '*enough.*'"

The word slipped from her mouth in a pleasured sigh as he found the means to caress her skin in spite of the wrap of clothing. She could never tire from the touch of his skin to her own, the enduring strength and tone in his physique, and her fingers still drew wondering circles over it, kneaded and caressed every hollow and fold whenever he pleasured her. She marvelled at the restoration of his spirit and soul after the torment of combat and the scarring to the mantle that had been her man's outer self.

"Right…what I have with you is still special."

'Ladies and gentlemen…friends…I can address many of you in that familiar greeting for we've known each other a long time. I…I was told to see a doctor today about something serious…I'm ill it seems." He paused and noted one or two listeners glance at each other then at him. *"Yes…I'm ill for wanting to run as an Independent candidate for New York Mayor, it makes me a suitable case for treatment."* His opening remarks raised a laugh.

The delivery was carefully controlled for timing, his voice modulated for effect. He felt relaxed; there was no specific or narrow brief to be followed;

there was no line to be trodden; he was his own man and tuning in to a wider constituency. Marie had cleverly cast her web of invitations very wide, over a disparate potential audience of ideas on local politics. Joey had told him it was risky, his delivery of the idea the key to success at winning some acknowledgement of the truth in the message.

"What I have to say may strike a chord…make you whistle the same tune with me…help you to learn a different refrain…that is my hope, my message. I express it very early…at the beginning of a brief address…a different refrain from what many have been accustomed to.

"As you can see and hear…I'm well. Independence is no sickness…it's a state of mind that the Settlers fought for; it's a state of mind in me that says I don't belong to one interest group or another; it says to me that I'm free! I'm free to borrow ideas that appeal, ideas that will make a difference and help people. Independence allows room to grow into a process that will help a disadvantaged group to settle and feel part of a wider community. It says to me…deep down…I can learn from others, the good and bad, learn from the workable ideas and those that failed, even miserably, and to do better…much, much better.

To me there's no shame in working for a meritocracy, in its widest sense. Everyone gets a chance, everyone. But," and he paused to let his audience wonder at the follow on, *"the word has different meanings to many people. For me it's earning what you have and allowing others the chance to do the same. Schooling, right here in this City, needs a fundamental shake up and shake down…those that can afford schooling for their kids of high quality…they continue to pay. They got their money through work…do with it what you want…but pay some taxes too so that the bright kids but from less moneyed families still get a chance…an even chance. You hear it from others, but there's a nuance; you take from the one's that have and give to those that don't. I take no comfort from those ideas and won't follow them.*

A better or improved education system helps to create a business environment that will help this City to compete…globalisation isn't a long word spelt out and understood by others. It's on our streets…in people's thoughts and affects their chances of work. Education gives citizens the chance…the rest and the outcomes are down to the individual character. No-one else can be blamed if you don't get there, or where you thought to be. Folks get the opportunity…we help those with talent but little resources…it doesn't mean nursing them, all it means is a safety net. Don't get me wrong…I'm not advocating a comfort blanket."

He drank slowly from a tumbler of water. The key points of his address were summarised on a single card; he had rehearsed the ideas and condensed them into memory joggers.

"Independence may also offer like-minded people the opportunity to form new alliances, to surprise themselves there are people around them that may feel and

179

think like them but have no natural home for those beliefs and feelings. They're abandoned by more powerful interest groups that follow their own agenda…they need you to vote them in…after that it's four more years…of what? A partisan snowstorm making those in power blind to another's needs or needs partially met.

Independence can mean new alliances…associations that spell community, a unity of purpose…for all, not the few this time and a few others the next, depending upon whom you follow…or voted for.

The Settlers I believe had another word for it…kinship. For some it has a religious meaning; for most…dare I say it? It's about community.

Get my meaning? It's working to the mark and it's a belief of mine that I learnt some years ago…I learnt it the hard way with a community of young men who wanted to be anywhere but where we were…I learnt it thanks to the War Department.

So for me…Independence and working to the mark means getting it right… not for some but for all…or for so many that no-one feels as though they are being deliberately excluded. It means working so that no one holds a grievance that makes them want to throw things at you, or shout things with a malicious intent that also incites folks to violence. Worse still it means not failing so that some one wants to take a shot at you…unless it is with words spoken or written that confront your argument.

The goal is simple…Utopia it is not…but we can aim for it, and for me it is getting names on a ballot paper that allows all ideas to be voted on…my Independent voice included. It is to get votes out of two deep pockets and out into the light…competing for everyone's attention, ideas brought to the notice of all citizens that have an entitlement to vote. Then we can call the result truly democratic.

I've taken a first step in the process…thanks to a Special Election I have a seat, a small part on a City Council Committee. It's up to me now, and hopefully some or many of you will think it over and join me, in voting for a change to how we do things around here.

Being Independent doesn't mean taking it all from one side and redistributing, nor does it mean ignoring the needy because one side has it all and leaves it to others…public spirited but separate…independent agencies …to deal with a problem. I know! I have direct experience…hands on, of what that work means and the absence of adequate or conditionally granted funding. The people who do it are heroes.

So! Independence means an environment where we can truly win hearts and minds and select…then elect the best man or woman to deliver on that. I believe that I have a role to play."

29

Dayle watched the assembled guests with relief and pride. Her mother had made the right calls and spread the word for Pops. His short address may not have roused them to noisy acclaim but neither had they sat on their hands. They had clapped and one or two had shouted encouragement. The message was out there and she had been paged, local newspapers had sent correspondents along and now asked for interviews. Her father's whereabouts concerned her just now and she scanned the crowd in the foyer.

"So, Miss Kahn…how was it for you?"

The smile was impudent and dark eyes stared, almost challenging, from a strong handsome face. She saw the furrowed well shaven chin and sensuous mouth. Her throat felt dry but she took her time; this hadn't been allowed for on the schedule for the evening, not one bit. The media types were to be kept to one part of the lobby where Pops could field their questions. That was after the cable TV interview. Who's in control here?

"Fine," she looked at the man haughtily. He had a youthful face, style and kept a polite distance so as not to intimidate. It was a refreshing and appealing change; against her better judgement she felt taken in.

'I can't go giving away any initial feelings at the sight of you', she thought. The all too formal but beautifully tailored suit, the crisp open necked shirt and waves of dark almost shoulder length hair did not look like "Press" to her. But, he had the badge of accreditation…it must be so. He held the leather zipped up notepad folder casually; his hands were beautiful with long fingers and neat smoothed nails. *'Oh God, I've seen all this in an instant and I can't help but look at him'*. Yep! it was useless. Surprise at being caught off-guard gave way to what she hoped was not a gaping stare.

"Who," she wanted to read the name on the badge, "who…are you?"

"Sorry, I should have introduced myself. I'm Nico Brant, of De Telegraaf… of Amsterdam…*Old* Amsterdam." He smiled again, beautifully she thought; the accent was light.

"I've not seen you before…" Why the hell should I have done she thought. We Kahns are all new members of the political circus but with a good looking guy like this to meet things could only get better, with less routine and lighter moods, maybe.

"No…we've watched from the outside 'til now. But, the political line of an Independent intrigues us after the two party routine that's gone before…we'd like to learn what it is that makes up John Kahn."

"Sure…who did you say you were?" She glanced down in irritation at the intrusive buzz of her pager; she wanted to keep Nico talking and to look at him.

"Nico Brant…Dutch press." His stare was unflinching. "You're not what I expected."

Gerard didn't know of the plan and Hans Blokman had told him to pick his moment to check the family out for himself, as back up or corroboration of Gerard's story lines. A second opinion would do no-one any harm.

"No…and you're in the wrong place if you want to ask John Kahn anything."

"I don't want any set-piece stuff. My paper, my Editor back home…he likes to get his information by less conventional routes…" Nico left the sentence hanging.

"Oh?"

"I could ask you, here and now. Have you got the time Miss Dayle?"

There! It was that impudent smile again. The guy's coming onto me!

"Just how did you get in here?" Dayle tried to keep the note of pleasure at his unconventional, even '*forward*,' approach from her voice. Mom had often used the quaint old-fashioned term and she smiled that it should come to mind now. But the sight of the guy, Nico, with the all too foreign accent, lifted her spirits. It had been a long day. She caught his mood of being at ease and went with it. "Don't worry, I won't report you. You've got the badge so I guess you're okay?"

"I am."

"Are you always so sure?"

"No, but then I haven't had to deal with a father and daughter story before."

"It's about the father…John Kahn. That's the story you should be after, nothing more." She shot him another glance then began to walk towards the lobby only Nico kept his distance and she turned out of curiosity. "Nico?… Come on? Join them, that's what I'd advise you."

"I've only got one question Dayle…may I call you that? I'd rather ask you about it out here."

"Oh? What about?"

"Yeah!" he said it in a heavier Dutch intonation. "Ja! Do you Kahns over here have much…anything to do with family that remains in Holland?"

The easy manner in which she felt tempted to deal with him fell away and she felt bolder now in looking at him. "No," she answered in a flat voice.

"Is that all the answer I'm going to get?"

"Ja," she replied in a poor imitation of his accent, "that's all!" The note of levity that had existed between them until then had gone.

"One question and you've changed," he sighed conspicuously with a theatrical shrug of his shoulders. "And here we were getting on so well."

"Says you."

Nico smiled and zipped up his notepad with an elaborate flourish. "What a fool I've been." He bowed his head then looked up at her again. "My apologies Miss Dayle Kahn for disturbing you." He walked past her without another glance.

"Hey...Nico?" she called after him, not too loud.

He wasn't listening and Dayle looked in puzzlement at his receding figure and the purposeful stride. Is that it, all he wanted to ask and to hear in reply? Nico had looked at her face; he made no overt assessment of the figure that was clothed in the fine outfit she had chosen for the evening; he was *different* from the guys who tried to come onto her. She liked his teasing way of speaking and the deprecating sense of humour.

"Just that one question...why?" she muttered as she caught sight of Elbee.

He'd figure it out but do I tell him and if so reveal the answer I gave? A telling reply had been expertly drawn from her, she now realised, and Nico's disarming smile had done it. On reflection she had been too direct, too honest; but, it was the truth, so why worry about that? Her interest in the man, the smile, his look...it all gave way to concern at how adept Nico had been in obtaining a simple piece of information. Her words of response had seemed important enough for Nico not to follow them up, or to just talk to her.

Why worry? We're Americans, over here and with an ocean between us and them over in Holland, whoever they were. She put any further thoughts of Nico Brant to one side. Pops needed her.

Nico picked the fax up off the floor. He didn't recognise at first the PR company's name but saw the signature on the scribbled footnote.

'Read the transcript of what John Kahn had to say a couple of nights ago. Your paper asked to know – if I remember right what you said in the few minutes we had - the political line of an Independent...after all that's gone before...we'd like to learn what it is that makes up John Kahn.' What you need is in the transcript. Anything else...make an appointment to see me. Dayle Kahn

"You did what?" Gerard burst out in anger and surprise; papers fell from his hands. The line to New York was very clear and he listened to Nico's explanation under the thoughtful gaze of Hans.

"I asked a single, simple question. I got a short simple answer for my trouble." Gerard looked over at Hans.

"Your idea?" The speaker 'phone echoed all that was said around the small office.

"Yeah, simple background stuff," Hans smiled. It was almost too provocative for its simplicity.

"A simple *signal* on what we're looking at?" Gerard retorted.

"Why the heat?" Nico's question boomed. "It's simple, we're filling in background, making good a few gaps in our knowledge…that's how she took it. It's filler for any other pieces you want to write."

"Jesus! I hope you're *right*!" Gerard couldn't sit still and began to wander about the office once more, scuffing the soles of his shoes on the carpet.

"Correct, Nico," Hans said pointedly before turning on him "What's bugging you Gerard? The fact I asked Nico to help us out, cheaply, or that you weren't in control of it?"

"You're the Editor," Gerard fumbled, then regained some composure in spite of what had occurred with Hans' full authority. "We're the business section and I'd be using Nico to help us out on the Kahn *business* interest…the personal angle I can deal with as a side show."

"Really?" Hans sounded sarcastic. "And what about the effect on your judgement?" Hans chomped on his unlit cigar and leant back in his seat. "We've been through this before Gerard." He came to a decision and sat upright with the chair making a noisy thud on its frame. "That's it Nico! Thanks."

"Wait one!" Nico called out before Hans could cut them off.

"No, that's it! I'll let you know if I…*we*…need anything more," Hans interrupted him.

"Okay Hans…Gerard? You've got the transcript, I hope, of the short speech?" He received no answer. "Gerard?"

Gerard stood by the window looking down into the busy street with its afternoon traffic. No foul ups from a simple question, that was all he wanted. He had run a biographical check on the lawyers in John Kahn's team, off the firm's web site, listing all the partners. Elbee was familiar from the pictures he had pored over with Edith. Jospehine Clarke was a stranger and one to keep under observation. She possessed intellectual beauty; he could see that from the look in her intense green eyes. Nico had done one thing right in sending a digital picture of John with her at some Charity event that he supported. Simple things, like her pose beside John, a glance, the whole composition of the picture intentional or not, it gave another person like him clues. Another avenue of enquiry had been opened up, and Nico had been the source. He'd have to give grudging credit to the guy and not be peevish about it. Their remoteness from the scene gave cover, a screen behind which they could continue to dig still deeper.

"Gerard, are you still there?" Nico's voice crackled once more.

"Yeah…I've got the transcript. Thanks for getting it to me. You charmed Dayle into releasing it to you?" He couldn't bring himself to go too far, yet.

"Everyone got a copy."

"Personally signed? I don't think so."

"What are you saying?"

"She's pretty…don't foul this up for me by getting too involved with her."

"I'll decide on that, Gerard!"

Hans booming laugh stopped them in mid spat. "Boys…boys!"

"I'm not doing this for fun Hans or as an interesting diversion," Gerard burst out. "The story means something to me…the whole story and what it may be associated with. I'm simply asking Nico to keep me…*me!*…in the loop. Okay, *both* of you?"

"Ja, Ja! Okay…okay. I hear you Gerard," Nico said with a sigh. "Just trust me a bit more."

"Okay, you're right. We're a team." Gerard smiled for the first time since the telephone conference began. "Is she as pretty as the pictures I've seen?"

"Who?"

Hans rolled his eyes. "Dayle's mother…who else!"

"Ja, of course!" Nico laughed. "Dayle is too…but, I can't go there."

"Are you sure?" Gerard asked in all seriousness.

Nico still wasn't convinced about what he was doing; he dialled and listened to the number as it rang, a distant trill on the land-line. Dayle had not written any other contact on the curt message she had sent a week ago; he thought of her and the portfolio of family shots that he saved on the database CD of John Kahn and the companies he and the family controlled. Amongst them were shots from a society magazine showing all too clearly the young woman with the blonde tresses he had met. There had been girls *like* her at College in Delft but Dayle Kahn, to his practised eye, was the real thing. The job with the newspaper and the real story, whatever it was, could become a complication, no mistake.

"Hi, Dayle?…It's me, Nico. You said to make an appointment…so I'm calling."

"I thought you found out all that you came looking for the last time we met, Nico."

It was not the start he hoped for. "I asked a simple question."

"True, and I gave you a simple answer. I then watched you walk away. What do you want now?"

"A new beginning…call it a fresh start? Give me the chance to say *'hello'*, *'how are you doing? It's great to see you again'*…you know? We say the sort of things everyday people do when they meet up. You may have heard of them." He was on the end of a phone line; all she had to do was hang up. He closed his eyes and waited.

"By the sound of it, even up in the clouds you think I live in you mean?"

"No…but come to think of it we're not talking like two people on the level with each other." Damn, I didn't mean that to sound the way it must do. "Dayle?"

"I can't begin to imagine why I should think that. How about you, any ideas?"

He seized the chance to make it up. "Sure, that night all I wanted was a hassle free few moments with you and to ask about a future political event that may concern your father. Then, I saw you and…well, you know the rest."

"Do I?"

"Yeah! I asked a question and you were kind enough to answer."

"Why the call, Nico? I'm busy."

"Too busy to meet me? I'll buy you lunch in some media place you people go to."

"We media people don't all do lunches in the same place. Anyways…I use media people…like you use subjects of interest…I don't see myself as one of them by the way."

"Thank God for that!"

"Oh, why?"

"We'll have lots to talk about."

"When?"

"Lunch…can you make it today…or tomorrow?"

"Hm…if I agree, should I come prepared with more one word answers?"

Nico gave a soft laugh. "No."

"First time I've heard you do that," she replied coyly. It was behaviour so unlike her. "Sure, we can meet but…make it tomorrow. You've got my address, it's on the fax…meet me here! We can take in a place nearby. It's clean…clean of media types, least it was the last time I went there."

"I'll be careful not to be predictable, or make it obvious what I do."

"What do you want to know, or to ask me? I want some prior notice this time."

"Hm," he delayed. "Walk first then run."

"Sure…look Nico, I said I was busy, so tell me please, and…make it quick."

186

"Okay, I'll tell you. I research companies for my paper. I could ask your father's company press officer for all the numbers and facts I can't find in open records, but it's…"

"It's the personal thing again? The same type of question as last time?" She became defensive.

"No."

"Good, because you've got your answer on that so I won't be wasting my breath anymore…or my time, going over old news. Get it straight, now…we're a New World family. Understand?"

"I hear you Dayle…can we deal with the rest over a drink, face to face?"

"Like I said just now, maybe I should come prepared? Care to tell me what we'll have to talk about?"

The reason, or excuse for his call had come to him. Hans had agreed on the line of enquiry; Gerard would have no reasons to blow a fuse like the last time, he had received the pictures so it should be a measured follow up, filling in background. But Dayle's unprompted reference to a 'New World family' was an interesting remark in itself, and one to store away.

"Charity," he said bluntly.

"You in need of a helping hand, Nico?" Dayle teased.

"In a way," he drawled. "Listen, it's your father and why a CEO of a major business does the charity work…the reasons why he gets his hands dirty so to speak."

"Nico…I'm glad I asked 'cos I'll know what to say. Just see it as the difference between *doing* and *being*. John Kahn explained it in the transcript. Read it again Nico?" Dayle paused. "Nico…?"

"I'm here…"

"Take care now…see you tomorrow, 12:30, here." She hung up.

The conversation had given her an idea for promoting Pops' work; she could talk to Nico of that; the financial details of the business were up to him to find out. She tapped her fingertips together lightly and thought. Nico's call had pleased her; in spite of the apparent stand off between them it held a tension that she wanted to break. Her initial mistake in answering so directly the first question would be her last, she'd work on it. The answer to the *'Charity'* question would be easy to give; after that was dealt with *business* could be put to one side, if she read him and her own feelings right.

30
Amsterdam

"Thanks, but I read the signs in the pictures a few weeks ago and made a first draft then. I saw the possibilities for another story, or article. I'm ahead of you for once."

Gerard smiled fixedly at Hans. Nico had sent another e-mail with information gleaned from his association with Dayle Kahn. Unsurprisingly, no detail was mentioned of that.

Hans picked up on the tone but they had a way of dealing with each other now that sparked good work. There was no malice. "I said some time ago, Ger, that you'd get too close to the story and your work would suffer. What have you got there for me?" He held out his hand and Gerard noticed it shaking, more pronounced than usual.

"Are you okay Hans?" Their eyes met and any belligerence between them was dispelled.

"This?" Hans held out his hand again. "It comes...then it goes. It comes from working here...with you," he winked and gave a laugh. "Only kidding." They held each other's stare for a moment.

"Yeah...I know. Take it easy man...we won't know how to go on without you. Ease up on those little smokes we can't hide...do that for us?"

Hans shrugged. "I'll try. Now, what have you got?" He looked at the pages neatly clipped together with an orange paper clip and threw it off. "Very patriotic!" He tapped the pages on their edges against the desk top scanning the text quickly. "Still here?" he asked without looking up.

"Yeah."

"I'll call you. Let me *enjoy* this on my own." The laugh at his good-humoured sarcasm lightened the atmosphere.

"As you wish...but no smokes? Deal?"

"Go on, get outta here!"

POLITICS AND BUSINESS - DOING AND BEING
Gerard Kahn©, – A personal view.

'Business is interesting, often on account of the people you can see involved in the pursuit of its goals. To witness a fellow human being setting out to become a politician is also intriguing and writing for the business section of a newspaper allows me to study and comment on both. My Editor is very understanding – I have to say that you'll think, but we debate the issues often, before I write my

piece or the blue pencil suggests improvements. At times it feels as though I'm still the pupil.

So, what is the difference between doing politics (and business for that matter) and being in politics? The distinction may be arcane and your eyes are beginning to glaze over at the thought of making the distinction, but read on, please? You can be doing politics and mean it. On the other hand you can be something and those who look on you may begin to wonder. They can't help it. You see, in politics or business the 'doers' have a visible, a tangible, or a measurable result to show for all their efforts. Being in politics or business isn't quite the same. See what I'm getting at?

Someone can play at being a politician but that's only the start. Putting into effect what you're being takes courage, commitment or staying power; it requires a thick skin or a defensive shield; it takes vision, ideas, and a route map between your jumping off and landing points. Being a politician requires persuasive powers and yes, it requires integrity.

Above all, it costs money, or does it? The elections in New York next year are of interest to me. The city's cosmopolitan, it's big, it's brash and many races rich and poor live close by to each other. It has a huge budget (and deficit) like a nation and boy some thinking is going to be needed on how to run that "nation". It is the setting against each other of those that believe in 'doing politics' and others who think of 'being in politics'. The city has over the years swung between the Republican and Democratic parties. Like all politicians who rip apart their opponent's policies the scales rise and fall between 'doing' and 'being'.

And who suffers? Right! Those that thought they were voting for a doer but got a being instead; or was it the other way around? Some say, and I read this somewhere, Democracy suffers the most; you get what you vote for; cynics may say what you think you're voting for. But what am I getting at in this piece?

Well, along comes a business-man, rich of course; he's from New York and he's standing as an Independent. He's more of a doer in politics – so I am led to believe – and business. He's said to be all-action at work and commentators on Wall Street seem to like what he does. He is also into charity work and putting a little bit back into what others have messed up. I have to assume much of this because you don't get told everything do you? A judgement has to be made, for instance at a critical time when you have to place a tick against a candidate's name on the ballot paper – you and your beliefs, at the pencil tip. Are you casting a vote for a doer of politics or a being in politics? The difference between reality and illusion is often too close to call.

I've come to the conclusion that the quest for public office, and a business's share price too come to think of it, is often simply telling the story with some spin or a carefully managed nuance. It's winning hearts and minds…for a while anyway, for a few crucial moments. There's plenty of time afterwards to rejoice or rue the

189

decision you came to. But, I'm also told and have learnt the hard way...'That's life for you'!

I will watch the progress of this aspirant with interest and hope that he achieves (does) with his company's wealth and products what I believe being in one of his businesses is all about. DOING health, good health at an affordable price – home AND abroad. When pharmaceutical cartels (and their bosses) succeed in persuading governments that being in politics and doing business is about 'inclusivity' of all people, then I'll sit up and really take notice. If they continue doing good and solving mankind's manifold problems and not simply swelling the bottom line, then I'll believe in them - wherever they originated from or obtained their start in business or politics.

To conclude, to me the doer in politics takes everyone along with them; the being in politics is, to my cynical mind, in it for themselves however strong the protestations to the contrary may be.

[The views expressed here are my own, not of the newspaper]
Gerard Kahn ©– Amsterdam 2002

"I've taken a call from a New York TV station...God knows why, but they want an interview with a guy called Gerard! Know him?" Hans breathed heavily down the 'phone; the guy was killing himself with those little cigars. "I told them to piss off...until they could talk properly!" He guffawed with a hacking bellow.

"Sure you did," Gerard answered, "and in the nicest way possible." Hans was quite capable of such a blunt reply to a request if not so crude in the chosen language; that would keep until he at least knew you.

"When another outfit wants to interview one of your reporters about their work you know you've made an impression."

"They're second to getting the idea?"

"Right," he wheezed, "you're learning my boy." His mock condescension was a loveable trait.

"It's about time...eh Hans?"

"Don't get clever with me. Don't worry...I said they could come over, that's their local guys, or gals...hopefully...and sit at the font of perceptive writing."

"Yours then?"

"Easy, I said don't get clever. No, they want to speak to the writer of yesterday's article...the doing and being one...I'd rather have called it '*Seeing is Believing*'...but I gave way as you do, one cynic to another." He sighed as if in despair.

"The message amounts to much the same thing," Gerard said, agreeing with his mentor. Economy in the language used, it was Hans at his perceptive best again.

"Well, at least your work has stirred up a few brain cells, that's what pleases me, Gerard…even if they are possessed by people across an ocean."

"Oh?"

"Ja! Intellectual rigour…we'll get a name for it."

"I thought we already had that…over here anyway." Hans had always kept him to the mark in the nicest way their working relationship and deadlines made possible.

"Ja! But then you're the first to be interviewed by that crowd."

"I'd better smarten up…when are they due?"

"No idea, just play it cool," Hans said turning almost fatherly, "and don't go getting all clever and tidy. On second thoughts," he mused breathily.

"I'm not always both, and at the same time."

"Right…we want them to think *'ragged exterior.'*"

"But *'ordered mind'*. Am I right?" Gerard couldn't help laughing at the all too downbeat approach of his mentor and friend.

"Ja! I'm glad to hear I'm teaching you something useful."

31
New York

Dayle was utterly devoted to her father; an affinity existed that to the observer bordered on obsession. Over the course of a carefully managed campaign John's youngest daughter, a girl of strikingly beautiful features attracted much media interest, not all of it savoury. But, no one could discover the faintest trace of scandal about her and instead attention turned to the unconventional nature of the father-and-daughter relationship in the context of a mayoral contest. Deliberate or not, the publicity John gained was as much the product of Dayle's ingenuity at provoking debate on the issues she knew her father sought to canvass support upon as the acumen for promotion in her young mind. Press releases spelt the message out quite clearly; directly attributed quotations were few; the agency she worked for and who won the commission managed everything; her father had no organisation behind him, yet, other than what she had helped to establish. He could make and keep to his *'mark'*.

"You taught me to speak my mind," she said to him as they drove to another meeting.

"Be honest…"

"Right, so keep doing it…"

"I have to find the right language now, darling. I need to learn a new skill or nuance it more than I would normally." He held her hand for a moment's unobserved intimacy.

"Keep the message, strong and clear."

"You're some girl, a fighter from the first scary seconds I held and prayed for you." He wanted a son, for the line, but there could be no regrets.

"You made me," was all she could smile in reply. "Don't get side-tracked," she continued, "or worry about the 'papers."

"Some of the papers," he corrected.

"They're fishing, and Elbee will handle it."

"As always."

"Yes," there was a note of hesitation, "only he could finesse things better."

"He cuts the deal…to the bone, he always did."

"Just mind he doesn't attract unwanted attention."

"He won't…he's an expert, remember?"

"Sure Dad." The tone held modulated criticism but he allowed her some leeway. Dayle had earned her place on the team following his one lapse of the campaign so far, the choice of an earlier media consultant with a sideline in personal videos that featured people too close to call – one had been a girl friend of Dayle's. "The more important problem right now is handling the Virginian relationship."

"Taken care of…I made a donation to Anna Beth's school foundation. She'll be satisfied with that for a couple of years…the school will grow further and I'll be able to claim some credit for it."

"It's too far away from what matters to you here…and, you're laying yourself open to prying eyes and inquisitive minds."

"Buried deep."

He knew only too well, from his own Dad's last letter of advice attached for him personally to read. It was money paid to buy silence.

"Don't bet on it. I want you to be…" She was momentarily silenced but Dayle moved her head away from the press of his fingers to her lips. "Clean…that's what I want them to think, you've nothing dirty that will come back to haunt you."

"Sh, honey. When I'm elected…it'll be taken care of."

In the meantime they would follow the press agency bulletins.

"That went better than I dared hope for," John smiled with pleasure.

"Come on! The real man came over and you did the right thing going onto the floor and mixing with people and just talking with them. You were a natural…gifted even."

"They don't expect it," he said wondering how his daughter could have picked up the tricks of the media business so quickly. "You're a natural too, honey," he smiled in admiration.

"I don't know about that. What I do know is that I could see it with some of them…what you did is what they will remember of you, and the words you used."

"A suit talking to them you mean? A Teddy Roosevelt moment."

"I wouldn't know Pops. I wasn't around then…neither were you!" They laughed.

"No, I sure as heck wasn't."

"Well, you did it…and I bet they'll remember and talk about it."

"Just dialogue with potential voters, my constituency…people in the Borough." He thrust a clenched fist into his other hand. "They also need to remember what I have to say."

"The flyers and leaflets we left them, they will help. We don't want others trying to copy you…they can try but I'm beginning to see the news footage."

"Me too…"

"Yeah…the others don't seem to fill the venues…or pick the right ones to get attention. You're selling the idea…independence of thought and action."

He had noticed the changes too; subtle at first, just a few more faces in the crowds, but the numbers seemed to be growing.

"That's something else, another surprise."

Dayle looked at him; in any other setting her father had no difficulty selling himself. But in the febrile world of politics, local politics, the street-to-street quest for votes he still gave the impression of a man on new ground, a rookie or a novice. The candidate braced himself for the introductions, the ice-breaking moments before sheer personality and the inner man came through. She knew her father had other sides to his character, she had heard that much from Marie; it was not so very long ago that she had heard the raised voices of argument when her parents must have thought their daughter to be deep in sleep. They did not take her into full account when the verbal jousting began, the slamming of doors and the heavy tread of feet escaping…or was it to meet once more, the all too vocal onslaught on each other, the defender's role played by Pops.

She knew there had been others in his life; friends had spoken of him with admiration on their lips, expressed all too vividly an interest in a man who combined physical attraction with a capacity to appeal to their intellect.

"Open eyes," she murmured.

"What's that darlin'?" he asked. Dayle looked back at him, startled. "Thinking out loud?" His arm went about her shoulders; his youngest occupied a place in his heart like no other.

"Yes…I must've been." She lowered her eyes than looked up frankly at him. "I hear things. I know your appeal runs deep with many that you would not see as your natural followers."

"Is this some sort of *'class'* thing?"

"Not entirely…not completely, let's say."

"What of it then?"

"It's the Independent thought that spooks them…so looking good helps, with the women folk!" She winked.

"Don't go telling Mom," he said as his eyes became stilled and held her smiling gaze.

"She knows Dad…it's no secret and never has been, has it?"

"Dayle…"

"Don't go fooling around, that's all." She gave a short gasp at the casual manner in which her deepest fears for him had been expressed.

"There's only so much we can talk about, Dayle." He answered without any anger, simply with a heavier tone of decisiveness. "I never *fool* around, as you tell it, with anyone…or anything, come to think of it. Everything has a purpose."

"You and Mom matter to me…to all of us."

"And nothing…no-one…will ever be able to change, completely…what is between all of us."

"Okay," she answered slowly picking up on the words he had used, or one in particular. *"Completely"* was a word that had fallen from his lips, perhaps unintentionally. Only, she had been woken by the rows between her parents before, when they believed her to be soundly asleep upstairs. With child-like fear of the raised voices between those she loved and a mind receptive to the smallest signs of a deeper discord she had held her breath and listened. Pops had strayed.

"Does that exclude someone coming into your life who'd make you think on that?"

"I've told you before Dayle…some things are out of field, even between us…I meant it." His embrace fell from her shoulders and his face set in sudden fury.

"I never could live with your anger," she said softly.

"Leave it," he said over his shoulder as he turned away.

"Dad? I'm sorry…"

"I know why you said it. I never made out I was perfect, but you're right about one thing…I'll have myself to blame if I fail at this because of weakness in my character." His breath momentarily misted up the window he spoke against and he absentmindedly drew his fingers over the surface. Delroy would have to clean off the greasy smear.

"You're not weak."

"I'm only your father and you seem to know enough of me to feel obliged to tell me what's on your mind…otherwise, why are we having this conversation?"

"Because I want you to succeed…give this election business your best shot." She grimaced at the use of the overworked cliché.

"So, just in case, you reckon now is a good time to tell me how to behave?" He smiled at her now in unexpected and wry good humour. "Like I said, I'm not fooling around…"

"Okay…I heard you."

"Come on? We're nearly at the next venue. I've got work to do…press the flesh and smooze the words."

"Yeah, but make them believe what you believe in."

"I'll keep doin' my best."

"And the rest?" Dayle whispered in a plaintive tone that took him back so many years.

"Is my business." I'm not going there, he thought, no way.

In his youth he had taken his pleasure wherever he could secure it, with any woman from whom he could seduce a concession. It seemed to epitomise the times they lived in. The slender, smooth legged girls of Asia had taken his money and filled his time; one had held him in thrall for too long and as the frequency of his letters back home fell away so the emotional enquiries from MC began, for page-after-page.

32

"The meeting's arranged…I'm on my way, lovely lady."

Nico imagined how Dayle would be dressed. The formal business pose with neatly combed hair, as a complement would, he hoped, be discarded; instead the wilder child of his target man might make her appearance. The flash of temper and exchanges of their first meeting indicated an inner heat; their revelation had tugged at every fibre of his memory since that night. There was a job to do, but he had made the rendezvous with longer term intentions, as a part of his personal plan.

The team in Amsterdam had their own game in sight; his quarry was all too feminine and, he guessed, free-spirited; he would do what was expected of him but any out-of-hours endeavour would be devoted to an altogether different pursuit. The trick was not to come onto her too strong; the conclusion had not been reached by guesswork alone; no, discreet study and a few 'phone calls had filled in the background detail. It revealed Dayle to be unattached and for all he knew right then she wanted it that way...this was New York, another day and so many ways to meet her man. Another explanation might account for her singledom...not every man would take to the political firebrand, ingenue or not, and with a cash-rich pedigree to complete the set of hurdles to be overcome.

It was a challenge, so bring it on!

Nico shook his head, clearing any lingering doubts. There she was! The reasons for meeting Dayle Kahn stood before him. Absent was the floaty dress he had briefly imagined she would wear to show off her softly tanned skin with its dusting of freckles. Instead, she wore an eye-popping outfit of casual chic, figure hugging black trousers and matching sleeveless top; the ensemble was carefully contrasted by a flowing patterned over-garment, sleeveless too, and embroidered at the neckline by midnight blue sequins. The mane of blonde tresses was drawn back from her face as if in a casual after-thought to enhance her fresh-faced beauty and to show off the large pendant circles of twisted gold band earrings.

"Hi, you made it," he beamed and held out a hand, but out of an impulsive greeting that lacked all formality.

"Yeah...what was a girl to do?" she smiled.

Could being with Dayle Kahn get any better than this?

"Here's looking at you." Nico raised his glass in a toast to her.

"Who said that?"

"Captain Hook to Peter Pan?" he ventured and Dayle laughed.

"Too gay!...How about Bonaparte to?...to?...to his many female conquests?"

"You've got me...I can't name them."

"Mussolini?...to his many lady friends...truck loads of the darlings?"

"Got it!" Nico laughed. "Lord Nelson to Lady Hamilton...with his one good eye!"

Dayle met his gaze with an unflinching stare, only her voice held the soft note of embarrassment.

"Don't look at me like that..."

"There must be someone who does…someone who finds you entrancing?"

"Yeah," she shrugged rolling her eyes as if to make light of the compliment Nico offered. "I've only just met him - 'walk first then run' was what he told me. I think those were the words he used." She held her glass out to him. "May I have some more of that wine?"

"Good advice," Nico smiled as he poured out the measure. "I'll have to remember the words."

"Be sure that you do."

Dayle's choice of eaterie, *'Retro'* the sign said, had been smart; the simple décor and dazzling natural light filtered through blinds above them rendered the candles a superfluous extra. Informal simplicity was no disguise for quality; the room was full and Nico noticed that Dayle was a well-known guest, acknowledging those that greeted her with a winning smile.

"Wondering at how we managed to find a place in here?" she asked, observing his attention to her.

"I don't think we'd have got in on the short notice I gave you…and my press accreditation card wouldn't open these doors, so tell me."

"Pops owns the building, one of the few on the Lower West Side he acquired. I guess you won't find that on any information sites you've trawled to check him, or even me, out on?"

"No, but then I wouldn't choose to find out about you in that impersonal way. I prefer sitting here with you."

She gave a soft pout, but not one that Nico could mistake as any acknowledgement of his remark. "Want to guess what some of the folks in here do…or don't do to get the money to live so well?" Even as she spoke to him a sixth sense made her turn and suddenly smile. Dayle lifted a hand in a discreet, almost genteel, greeting of an acquaintance across the room. "Lady I haven't seen in months, but with Pops and the campaign there'll be more *"shakin' and greetin'"* I guess."

"Develop and maintain the network?" Nico caught her eye. "It doesn't matter whether they live from honest or dishonest money, the name of the place suggests that folks like a "retrograde" way of life…could that be it?"

"Hm, possibly. How about 'retrospective', a looking back at what's been missed…or used to be so good…but, maybe that's too obvious."

The emphasis on 'retro' held up many visions for him. "Accurate though, a look back to the past…or maybe, going back on the past?"

"Reetro…visual? Is there such a word?"

"Not that I've heard. You've made up a new one!"

"Yeah, thank you." Dayle smiled. Nico's attentiveness felt as if he was courting her and the waiter was left with nothing to do for them until they ordered lunch. It was a new experience, a compliment expressed in few words and by the smallest sign of intent. She averted her eyes and again took to discreetly pointing out people in the room that were known to her but, after noting the diversity of the clientele and Dayle's irreverent bio of the subject under review, she again became the centre of his attention. "I asked you not to look at me like that."

"Okay. Here's another word…retro-viral." The tone had changed to one of matter-of-fact enquiry. Nico sat back in his chair and twisted a signet ring on his left hand. He waited.

"What!" A disbelieving laugh escaped from her softly tinted pink glossed lips. "What!" Dayle clapped one hand to her mouth and stared wide-eyed at him. "What's the link? Tell me that?" she said at last.

"KPM Inc? They're big in the manufacture of retro-viral drugs, aren't they?"

"Yeah, so what?" She stroked away strands of wispy blonde hair from her freckled face. To him it was unnecessary, yet he watched the graceful movement of her hand in fascination.

"A mayoral candidate has an interest in the business I hear," he said casually.

"So?" Dayle shifted in her chair and put down her glass with deliberate care as if thinking over how to set the tone of any further reply. "You sure know how to bring a girl back down to earth!"

"I can also…" he began but instead of finishing the line he gave her an impudent grin.

"Oh, that *is* difficult! Let me guess…take her to…heaven? Is that it?" She paused then laughed with him. "You're running now!" She shook open her napkin with a noisy flourish. "Can we order and eat? Too much wine and no food will ruin the afternoon…and there's work to do."

"That's the busy, go-go world of a politician's acolyte…I guess."

"Yeah, you said it…what does 'acolyte' mean?" she smiled teasingly. "I also have to keep my mind focussed on off-the-wall questions from a journalist."

"Not enough to go answering him. Want to try now? Remember what I asked you? It was about KPM Inc and retro-viral drugs."

"Yeah, how could I forget? The company makes them," she said defensively in an attempt to think how she could get him to speak his mind, where the drift of his line of questioning was to lead their conversation. She would rather speak of them, what could become of the time they spent together. In spite of Nico's almost gentlemanly attentiveness, it was unusual for her to experience such behaviour with the air of ambivalence Nico also projected; she could discern no believable flirtatious intent in him. The words seemed a competent means to an end, to seek information.

"Yes, I know...it has done for years. The disease...Aids, has developed and spread ever wider...tens of millions in Africa are afflicted. Yet, all some companies do is offer first generation medicines...old formulas for new strains."

"It's a start...and PulcriMed isn't one of them following such practices."

"You sure?"

"Look? Are you some narco guy on a mission but dressed as a journalist? Or maybe you're a crusader out to change the world?

"No..."

"Question my father's business style or his hopes in some way...by questioning his ethics? Is that it?"

"No...I'm just after a few facts, ma'am." He tried to make light of her annoyance but failed.

"Look Nico, if we're here just to talk of KPM Inc and the god-damn drugs they make, I'm leaving."

"Hold up!" he replied in a voice that made her think again. "Without them...the real drugs...the folks they could be used on are all but condemned, that's for sure."

""That's it! I'm going Nico," Dayle said flatly placing her glass perfectly in the centre of the coaster by her right hand. "What we're talking about is a little...how shall I put it...limited."

"Or boring..."

"Right...lighten up, or I really will go."

"Never accept lunch invites from a journalist."

"I thought it was lunch with *you*...but I'm learning it's different and that I am wrong about *you*."

"Maybe you are," he answered before pausing. "I just wondered...in a round-about-sort-of-way...is there an altruistic streak in him? In John Kahn?"

"Look," she began but changed her mind, "there sure is another side to him."

"Do you know what my 'drift' is?"

She nodded. "Yeah, but go on...tell it to me anyway."

"Look after your own, those near to home...the world beyond is for someone else to deal with. That's what I mean."

"The company has world wide concessions...that's what John Kahn and the company KPM Inc means to do."

"But patents stay here...in safety, closely guarded in the U.S. of A."

"It is capital and knowledge invested; it's time, success and occasional failure…then, success again after you've sweated to get the formula or product right. All of that effort has a price and a cost; KPM Inc paid them both until commercial success came along."

He couldn't help but be impressed; perhaps condescendingly, at first, he had thought of her as a vacuous and rich fresh faced beauty; some might yet describe her as eye-candy with spirit. Instead, he came to realise that John Kahn had invested time and love in the education of his youngest, she was well spoken in the realities of business.

"Your Dad must be proud to have you on his team," he flattered. A jigsaw of information that she might offer could yet build up into a clearer picture that Gerard could use.

"I believe in him and the platform he represents, in the ideas and ideals he wants to present."

"The ones to make up for other disappointments, is that why he's doing this mayoral campaign…is that who you are to him?"

"Meaning?"

"Meaning he's got a large, loving family…of which he's proud; he's wealthy from a large business concern…but, one thing's missing…there's no son to carry the torch after him."

"No," Dayle bridled. "So what? Where's this going, Nico?" She looked at her watch impatiently. Their meeting was too intrusive and far too personal, and for all the wrong reasons. She also wanted some lunch, anything but this invasive line of questioning. With a growing sense of disappointment she realised that their time together was leading nowhere; she studied anew the well-dressed good-looking guy across the table from her.

"A large, healthy family…unlike some folks elsewhere…here or in Africa, say?"

"Fuck you, Nico!" she hissed then looked down, a shaking hand covering her forehead for an instant.

'Yes please', he thought but regarded her with stilled eyes.

"Pardon?" he asked as she met his gaze.

"I'm not granting you any *'pardon'* for tricking me into coming for lunch with you and listening to all this bullshit…all these round-the-park questions. Come out and just tell me what you really want to know."

"Can your Pops do politics or is he simply being in politics?"

She shrugged, irritated.

"You've seen and heard him speak! He *does* politics…follow carefully, if you can, what he's involved in out there on the street and in the neighbourhoods. He takes time out from the business to be with others. Compared to what it means to be Mayor it may look like small time stuff…but he's learning,

learning fast from all that he gets involved with…out there on the streets. It's low level experience…call it a learning and training period in his life, but with the potential for a high level pay-off."

"Okay, I understand the message you're telling me."

"It's not 'okay' and for once I don't believe you." She leant over her folded hands and spoke directly to him. "He associates with all sorts of people and learns from them. He understands…John Kahn is not the kind of man to look down on the street, jingling money in his pockets and thinking 'here I am, lucky me; I don't have to sweat and grab what I can to survive out there on the streets. Divine right to be who he is or wants to become doesn't figure in his ways of doin' things… that's not what I see in him at all.'"

"A view with privilege."

She looked at him coolly for a moment. "Sneer and provoke me, if you dare. I'll tell you this one last time, then I'll go."

"I'm just putting another view of things…go, or go on."

"You're not really a journalist are you?"

"No…a researcher, but I'm learning what the rest is all about. Never mind all that just now," he finished with a dismissive flick of his hand. Dayle saw that there was no anger in the gesture yet she persisted in a harder tone.

"Fine…so it's not what I thought when I said 'yes' to seeing you. Our meeting's purely business."

"Dayle, I didn't say that…and I didn't intend our meeting to be so formal." She remained silent. "I'm sorry I've annoyed you…maybe we should keep it that way, just business?" He waited then gave a soft smile. "When it's done you can decide what to do."

"John Kahn doesn't rest on privilege…he doesn't wear it like a badge either. He's down-to-earth and, I believe at least, he has a common touch. The people he meets see a different man behind the clothes and media stuff put out on him…by others, not us in his team. Like it or not, we can't control everything that's said."

"The power of free speech…and a free society?"

"Sure, put it that way if you want."

"It's one opinion against another…that's all. You can spin the web how you want to suit the quarry you're after. You can embroider the detail to make the story being pushed."

"Did you hear what I said, Nico?"

"Uh-huh."

"Good…his credo, as an Independent, is quite simple. Level out the obstacles and give everyone the same chance and rely on individualism. If you've really earned your share, then he would say *good for you*. Keep what you've won the hard way…only pay your dues, and never forget where you came from. Do your bit to help others…that's his line, he practises what he says…only don't expect somethin' for nothin'."

"It sounds like good old-fashioned right and left wing politics to me. It's nothing new, he's just going to come over as all undecided."

"I don't think so!" she said derisively. "It's not the word of someone who takes from one side and gives to the other, then…all change! My group is going to keep it all now and you can all swing…that's not the line at all"

"Utopia, that's what it still sounds like. Who does he think will buy into all of that?"

"Plenty…those that feel their vote doesn't count, or they don't even bother; people who are on the edge because of some colour or employment disadvantage, or some hang-up by Government or City Hall on community investment."

"It's all of the defects you have with two party politics, the Republican and Democrat way of doing things…in Europe some call it *'first past the post'* politics. It breeds all kinds of resentment at the system…a low percentage share of the vote and you still hold the power. Crazy stuff!" He shrugged expressively.

"So? What you're telling me now is that *just maybe* it's worth arguing and standing for change. Am I hearing you right, Nico?" She looked about her, frowning. "Are we *ever* going to eat?"

"Yeah." He had a charming way of taking the heat out of her argumentative ways of talking. "I'll call over the waiter…made your mind up?"

"About eating or staying?"

"Both. I'll be honest with you…"

"That'll make a change…from before."

He smiled thinly. "I may deserve that…only you could have left me long ago, before the discussion of your father's politics began."

"True, but a girl doesn't always walk away from someone different and interesting. Beginnings count for a lot…"

"This experience, with you…it's something else."

"So? We get the politics out of the way and see what gives?"

"Yes."

"John Kahn's candidacy is not about wild swings like you might find with first the Democrats and then the Republicans, though the Democrats don't always do so well around here in spite of the problems."

"The apathy of the *'no-hopers'* or the *'unbelievers'* may be the answer to that."

"Right. So the message of being steady, on the level, will register with those that feel that way…at least it'll make them think twice about not voting at all or the same as last time…a vote again for disappointment. He gets it from his business life where unexpected or un-planned change affects the shareholder, so…he sees the constituents of the City affected in just the same way. It's not just about 'doing' politics, but 'being' on the level in word and deed…that's what his candidacy is all about. He's sign-posted changes he wants to make already." She gave a deep sigh. "Enough of all that…least ways we got off the retro-viral thing!"

"Dayle…" he smiled.

"Let's eat, and fill this up while you're about it?" She held her glass out to him once more. In spite of the exchanges, debating the foundation of John Kahn's beliefs with him, her hand did not tremble; he's my father and I believe in what he's doing, she thought. "Find out from someone else what John Kahn's about. Verify what I've told you. He's not ashamed of what he's done in the past or what he plans to do. KPM Inc works for many, both here and in Africa…your favourite subject. The value of the stock tells it all, people aren't disappointed in what the guy's doin'."

"You've been very eloquent…don't say anymore. I won't ask and we'll see where it all goes to."

"Promise?"

"Yeah, mind over matter."

"I don't follow."

"Brains, or passionate belief, over beauty," he laughed disarmingly and held out his glass in a gesture of reconciliation.

"Oh well…I get it from John Kahn."

"Let's hope others see it too and get him to where you want his journey to end."

"City Hall and Gracie Mansion? They will…I believe it. Better still, if you have any influence print it in the 'paper you represent. Tell them outside of here that someone else is in the race, that's all. Plenty of folks'll have to make their minds up to get him elected…and he has plans."

"Later…right now it's me with you…person-to-person."

"We'll have to see about that," she said almost coyly. The smile on her lips told a different story; it was merely a teasing gambit.

"You must have heard it before…from someone else, but…but, I don't want to be anywhere you aren't." He uttered the words clumsily but she was enthralled by their surprising directness.

"Nico…" she looked away sighing softly. "No, I've never heard it said before…like I said when we arrived, what was I to do?"

33

"She's arrived, I've seen Jacqueline drive by…I hope she can find a parking place for *that* vehicle!" Joey laughed.

"And it's still there when she leaves," John replied.

"Not too many wisecracks, hon…" Joey responded primly, but there was a smile on her lips.

"Okay, in poor taste…sorry."

He seemed to be in an up-beat mood and at such times could say things that often confounded those in his company. Was he serious or not? Those that understood him knew the score; Elbee had it too, a tongue to talk away the stress of the moment. They had learnt it or grown into the habit long ago and the manner of speaking never quite left them.

The campaign office was nearly full and peopled by the right person for each important role – tell the message wide and clear, manage the funds, deal with the issues confronting their man. The team was small, composed mainly of freelancers who had heard the initial call of the message being put out and pressing résumé's into the hands of staffers at the earliest meetings, or mailing them directly to him. He payrolled most of them until he could convince administrators of the local campaign finance laws that he was not pouring his undoubted wealth into an electoral war-chest all of his own.

Instead, he agreed to abide by spending limits – four to one public funding to his own would be a good match. The message counted more than the bank roll; to make sure of every cent, experts in budget control were on the team; there had been no pressure, but they were on release from KPM Inc.

What he missed was a political thoroughbred, a staffer who knew the routes and dead stops, a street-wise political alley-cat who could work out the opposition's strategy and '*play*' with it. By his side he could do with someone capable of trading verbal blows if it came down to it, and who could keep him to the mark.

Joey knew of one, a lady with daunting political and administrative credentials. 'Almost intimidating' was how she had described Jacqueline Purcell – only those who worked with her and referred to Jacqueline as 'she' of the Housing Department, knew the bark to be more than what was chewed on. Jacqueline projected the image that John sought for the campaign, of others seeing you do what you said you would do. In one word, she had told him when the meeting was being set up that his candidacy was about 'delivery'.

"Show her in straight off, please. I can introduce her to the others when we've talked."

"And got her with us, on the team."

"Right…" he heard voices outside the room followed by a discreet knock.

"Here goes…with you John," Joey said quietly.

"I know…and I'm glad of it…show you later?"

Joey nodded then winked as she drew open the door to the visitor.

"Often."

"Are you looking to join a coalition of those that are disenchanted with the way things are done around here?" Jacqueline moved quickly to the substance of their meeting; she had picked up early on its only real purpose.

"Or not done," John smiled by way of reply.

"Adds up to the same thing in the voter's mind, only 'til now there's been two parties to select from and to really take seriously."

"Are you so sure?"

"Yes, you can't name any others in previous contests that threatened to upset the status quo. So…yes, I'm as sure as history has told of it so far."

"So far," he picked up on the words. "I'm nowhere near to being defeatist! I'm not even close to feeling that the system will get the better of me. You look at the percentage of the vote cast and wonder how the winners can claim a mandate. It's my job to go out there and secure a real consensus…and to try everything, legal." He arched his eyebrows as if to seek acknowledgement of a truth. "The idea may catch on…if not now then next time." He laughed as an idea came to him. "The pioneering spirit, you might say."

Jacqueline regarded him thoughtfully. She had come prepared to provoke, to test his resolve with the simplest of questions and to learn if the man had the vaulting ambition that she regarded as the essential ingredient to the successful conduct of a bruising political campaign.

"I wanted to hear you say that," she smiled. "The election during the final run-in will just be between two candidates."

"Or, three…if I upset the status quo! Whichever way you look at it…I sure as heck intend to be one of them," he continued allowing her no chance to interrupt, for only a moment, "one of the candidates. I'd value your advice on the ways to making sure that the day comes."

"And, I wanted to be sure your ambitions were for real…that they could be trusted. I may as well tell you of my concerns, bluntly." She looked at him with stilled eyes and met an equally unmoving stare.

"You may."

Jacqueline acknowledged his reply with a curt nod. "I'm…I'm taking on something new myself, breaking with the past and a traditional way of doin' things."

"I know."

"Oh? How's that?"

"My advisors, and it's a small close knit following, have researched what some people for my "dream team" have said recently...I've read a target's commentary on the ideological detours from the route their party chose to follow, and they don't approve of. We've talked about them...but of them all we've spoken about you the most." He looked enquiringly at her. "We wondered if you could find a home with us...we recognised the risks of an approach and what you would have to face. But," he said, lowering his voice to make it sound more reassuring, "I'm not doing this for fun, and it sure as heck is no diversion from what many may see as my real '*day*' job."

"I'm glad to hear it. If your constituents saw that in you, that all of this was an interesting change, they'd drop you. You'd be no more than dead meat to them."

"I hear you...it's what I figured out long ago." He then added, "I'm not setting out simply to rebel or out of any wish simply to create anarchy. I'm not looking to help the other two change their ways."

"No, but the folks you want to come over to you will be rebels..."

"I hope not! I'd like people with convictions...wanting to share ideas and aiming to change how we do things around here. I also need some more allies...like asking the Independence Party if they want to play."

She allowed the interruption gracefully. He'd made a good point and after a further moment of reflection conceded...the guy she'd come to meet had thought it all through...far as she could tell most of it. The edges would be smoothed over. She guessed that was the reason she'd been picked to meet him and for her part that she had agreed to consider the idea.

"Okay but you've got to go out and sell the message still more forcefully. Spread the word and tell 'em why you're doing it...to break with convention and work for a plurality of the vote...a real majority if you possibly can win it. Explain still more strongly why they should look to you and what you stand for...what you want to do for them. They've got to see the world with new eyes or open their minds to a different way of doing things."

"Enquiring minds...make them open up to the possibilities you mean?"

"Precisely that, John."

It was far too soon, but he sensed already that he was close to winning her over to his side. "I'm ambitious...if saying it don't sound so arrogant!"

"Not to me, but you've got to join sincerity to your ambition...and, you've got to mean it, consistently. There are enough disenfranchised voters...or people disengaged from the process out there to count in this, so, mean it for them." She knew only too well that low turnouts spelt out the message all too clearly, '*none of you address my concerns*'. A new voice was long overdue and it was time for more to hear it and feel included by what the voice had to say to them, and take on their concerns. The ethnic mix of the City was changing all the time; social pressures were being compounded by immigration.

"I spoke recently about '*doing politics*' and '*being in politics*'. I told of how I saw the differences."

"Yes, I know John, I listened to the programme…but did the audience really understand your message?"

"Not at first," he replied with a sheepish grin. He had worked hard to get the true significance over to the listeners. "But I got through, in the end…the questions that were fired at me told me that."

"May I see a transcript?"

"Sure…I'll ask Dayle, my daughter…she tracks everything I say and do. She minds me." He felt proud to admit to the contribution his girl was already making to his campaign.

"I know, Dayle's made herself known. I heard about the strength of feelings and interest in your platform from others and thanks to her and the company you've taken on for the promo work," Jacqueline spoke tellingly of the contributions being made to the cause already. "I saw it was more than a passing fancy you were engaged in."

"Thank you," he said pleased at the uninvited commendation of another's efforts on his behalf. "As I was saying…I can send a transcript over the wires too you."

"Okay…where would be without technology?"

"Knocking on doors and meeting even more folks…but I'm gonna be out there doin' that anyway."

"Technology saves you time for that."

"Sure, but to *convince* them," he began, slapping his fist into one hand, "I need to be on the street! I need to be talking to the families who want a place of their own…or who feel it's theirs and who want to feel they belong. I've got to convince others that they won't lose a firehouse, because of budget cuts. And, there'll be others who have to know that there'll be funds for schools, so that their kids can get the best start in life we can afford." He sighed on recalling recent work in a community centre. "It's achieving little things for them that get the juices flowing, the achievement of small ambitions that they have held on to for so long."

"I'm with you on that, John."

"Good…I've got some of my own projects as well. I don't settle easily for bureaucracy so I find ways to get things movin'…some don't like me for it, only those I help have the only answers I want to hear on that."

"You'll have to make them believe that no matter what they will get to where personal ambitions and hopes take them...or you've got some explainin' to do."

"Yeah..." he smiled ruefully in acknowledgement of her remark.

Their conversation was getting deeper into his credo or touched on his core beliefs. Joey had helped to open his eyes to what passed as life for so many, way down there on the street below his apartment or office window. He had been on the edge of that world; he had realised that all too clearly when Joey came into his life. And Delroy, he told him of many things but only in reply to questions thrown at him to make easy conversation. The comfort zone that he took as normal life had been acutely challenged once they had each in their different ways pointed out the reality.

But, talking to Jacqueline was one thing. Laying bare his intentions if elected was fine, if she was with him. It was a risk speaking so openly but the content, the words, were hardly real news; he had articulated his ideas often enough; he had them on a web-site that took so many hits that he saw the need to improve the messages held on it. The responses varied, from the obscene and ribald commentary on his candidacy to the more thoughtful observations on the comments he regularly made on City governance.

The daunting task now was that others needed to be persuaded to follow, local councillors and support groups who rallied in too small a number around the Independent Party banner. Jacqueline's membership of the team would be a great coup and a potent signal of intent that John Kahn was in the race aiming to deliver on his ideas.

"The street's taking notice of you, I found that out," she said as if to help him understand that she was being converted.

"Good...the tracking polls are encouraging, but I don't want to be seen as the fun part to the election; I don't want to be seen as the guy that stirs the mix only to have folks put a tick in the same old box they've always done."

"Chance."

"Yes. But...are you with me to try and change conventional thinking? I'd see it as making chance into certainty...or gettin' darn close to it!"

"Yes. See it as a mix...something old, something new?"

"Something borrowed...?" he laughed now.

"Sure, but not just red and blue...the usual party colours. Check out the whole spectrum!" she said in a voice stronger for it's unexpected enthusiasm.

"My line exactly. We have to win a large enough consensus to turn history up-side-down."

"Not all at once, John! Just make a start, enough to cause a real shift in allegiances and open eyes to other ways of doin' things around here." She seemed to have worked it all out now and had even borrowed one of his phrases.

"So...you're with me on this adventure?"

"Yeah, I told you. I've been waiting for someone with the strength of character...a 'newee', someone with a fresh vision to come along, only..." she gave a flutter of her eyelashes as if a qualifying remark would deter him.

"Go on...I can take it."

"Only, I didn't think it would be someone from way up Park Avenue who'd come along and tell me of it. That's all."

John laughed. "I don't eat off a silver dinner service and...I walk the same streets as many folks here. I know what's out there...or enough to know there's work to do."

"I know, I kept reading about you in the press briefings. It helped to persuade me. Philanthropy can be done..."

"Like I said, it's *doing* not *being in politics...or business.*" Jacqueline nodded.

She had read most of it on the web. The sentiments struck a chord and she wanted to find out if reality would match the words and that a cherished hope for a change would register with enough folks in the city to count in his favour. On the way to meet John she had debated how the irony of his candidacy would be handled and if it weighed against him. The tone of his opponents and some media commentators was not hard to imagine. His advocacy of core values or beliefs would be seen as new blood challenging blue blood. But, in the public's eye which side would he be seen to champion? She had heard from him of a campaign strategy; it was a challenge to the status quo and the dominance of a two party system; she saw it characterised as the blue bloods against his new blood. Political pedigree was being confronted on the streets by a spruced up mongrel. Okay...okay, can the clichés she thought to herself only that's the world we're going to be living in for a while...dog eat dog, insults being traded in coded language, ideas torn apart by a counter-argument.

"Substance over spin," she murmured as her mind cleared.

"That's right, that's my ambition...what I'd be measured by," John answered.

He had allowed Jacqueline her moment's reflection on what they had so far discussed.

"A small team on the inside, but not many out there in the city?"

"Yes and...no, or not yet," he answered. Before Jacqueline could question the ambiguity in the reply, he added, "we'll have a close knit team at the campaign office...the rest is dripping out the message to the electorate. They're the real team, we get to them and they will do our work for us. It's selling the idea that's going to be the trick! The people out there will talk one-to-one, then some more. Somehow we've got to make the wave and then help it grow...pulling in a few like-minded councillors will help too."

"Network time...spread the word whichever way you can. Leave that to me...okay?"

"Right. Help me with it...show us on the team how best to do it."

"You've done right so far."

He took it as a further compliment on Dayle's enthusiasm and the efforts of her agency. He'd buck her up with the news that someone with Jacqueline's experience had noticed the media campaign so far. A web of valued contacts was established and could be called upon; others were political mavericks but he'd get to them, or Marie would 'speak' to their wives. The charity work had been his way of putting something back into the community, he had done so for years without any further thought of seeking any pay back on it. And now? The work with neighbourhood action teams in all the Boroughs could be called in, but only to lend credibility to his nomination as a candidate. Joey would be by his side too, spreading a particular message and the revolution, if it came, would arise on the street and would not be dispensed by some party grandees, from the top down.

As he studied Jacqueline's pensive face he rehearsed once more the thoughts that lay behind his decision to run for Mayor. He had confronted doubters once before, when he had been a draftee and turned his back on officer school, preferment and position. It was a life or death decision then, or so it seemed to his immediate family, but who was to tell him or those that believed in change that he could not pull through?

"When do we start?" Jacqueline said as she made to go.

"We already have...just talking as we have done. We've just got to make the ideas fly some more."

He took Jacqueline's outstretched hand and he shook it.

"Right."

"We talk again in a day or so...I'll call you. Think over what we've said and if there's a weakness in the argument or manifesto..."

"For change...for doing things right?"

"Yeah...if there's a weakness, just call and tell me. The 'phone's always on."

She did. Jacqueline had consulted Joey on his ideas for increasing the candidate's pool in the Borough Elections and whom it was that John might count on for support.

"There's one thing in the political process here, in this city, that I can exploit, and that may be of help in my candidacy. We bring a new party's organisation and some financial muscle, discreet support, to other Independent candidates...we make a team, unify the separate parts to give us a bigger voice."

"I thought we were doing this from way out of field," Joey interrupted.

"We are," he smiled and held up his hand to keep her from continuing. "Hear me out first...please?"

"Go on..."

"Say for a moment I have a name in the city, I'm known and as a businessman I can claim to have some social prestige...and legitimacy. In business you make a profit either by having rock solid copyrights on a product and you're a sole, even monopolistic, supplier...or leader in the field, or you keep your costs down...you're ruthless in that. PulcriMed have been no different from many other companies...we've just been doin' it for longer. Now, you compare that with local government...your costs rise, you can't always control them...but your income's fixed."

"So services suffer...you can't put your prices or taxes up so easily," Jacqueline offered as her opinion.

"Right...higher welfare case loads mean high costs...for some their quality of life gets squeezed...you start to argue with your neighbours, you play hardball with the authorities...you may make some trouble, and so on."

"And your solution is?"

"I've been doin' it already...small time, but my soft investments in your charity, Joey or supporting BIDS...it all helps to show I've been doing something to make it better; it's not all talk. What I say is tied up to some action, out there on the streets."

"Go on?" Joey prompted. The two women listened, he had finally begun to articulate some heartfelt belief in what he was now a candidate for, his platform for change or making an improvement in the City's governance and the creation of opportunities for others.

"Here's the reason for rallying the Independent candidates and 'believers' under a flag...if they want me, I'll lead them."

"Who else is there with your name or reputation?" Joey smiled at him.

"No one credible," Jacqueline nodded to her in affirmation.

"Okay, so here it is. The two main parties have vacant space, in their organisations...their recruitment doesn't show me to have much control. You get folks to turn out for you when the need arises, or the call goes out...then it falls away. What we've been doin' in the Boroughs is to develop the nucleus to build around..."

"Who do you mean, John?"

"Joey, it's all of the folks we help in charity work...or in their business ideas, that's who."

"They're a few..."

"A start, and they're more than a few. The word spreads...when you put our leaflet in their hands that sets out our message there's another chance to hook them...or bring them on to us some more. So...we go out and sell the message even harder." He moved around the small office talking out his ideas with rising enthusiasm. "Then, there's the party grass roots organisation, or the lack of it; there's no real structure, not to my eyes anyway...not to my way of seeing it. We keep expanding the core organisation, the hub, so that we know everything's that out on the streets bugging people. We analyse it, think on it and...we get an answer out for it. We take small stakes in all the areas and build on them...we work with existing people, the 'incumbents' in a district, a street or a Borough. People there know them...if they get to hear that there's a city wide organisation out there, then folks'll start to take notice...they hook into each others systems by talking it over, they share ideas...we build on a small stake."

"Stakes? What do you mean John? Money...give them help out of our pockets?"

"No, least no more than what we're doing already only we're so quiet about it."

"It would be bad news to have the charities we work with associated with a political party."

"Sure, but the help I give...the people who come to join and help us because we 'sell' the ideas of Bids and self help with a supporting charitable hand, that's what I reckon it's gonna be all about. Don't see it as folks in city hall and borough offices working to some agenda of their own! We show folks that they can take charge and work to make their own futures. The local government departments are there to help and serve the community...to guide the ideas into a unified policy, with direction from the Mayor."

"What they don't do is rule so that others in the street have to follow. I'd like to think we'd get a consensus at some point in my life" Jacqueline observed.

"Right, a dictatorship of ideas it isn't, democracy isn't made of that...not in my book and that's what I'd tell other Indies who wanted to be part of our grouping...we're *persuaders* for people out on the streets and in businesses nothing more...not their bosses." He paused for a moment. "Know where I got to see some of this persuasion? In 'Nam...once an idea takes hold no amount of muscle is going to stop it. Ideas...new ones, persuade folks to think afresh."

He sat down heavily in a chair and raised his eyes towards the ceiling before closing them. He ran his long fingers through his hair.

"John?" Joey voiced soft concern. "Okay?"

"Yeah...I was just thinking back. Lots of kids, guys as old as me, then pushed against ideas and persuasion of others. We're still doin' it now...I'd rather get it straight here first before we tell others how to do it. We've got to make the City work for everyone, not by bossing people about but by persuasion that certain ideas will work. Persuasion...persuasion...still more of it, persuasion...not telling folks this is what you'll do or how it's going to be."

"We've had all that...seen it done...and seen where it's gone to," Jacqueline mused. She looked at him and laughed, clapping her hands in glee. "It's great! A Great idea...a great idea to go and shout about on the streets...persuasion, by soft sell."

"You've got it! It's through right, the right ideas...not might. And, we have to keep on working at the idea that folks can have their own hands in the changes they make by working through the Right Aid centres."

"That won't change John, but you keep a distance so that no-one comes looking for a weak spot in your defences."

John nodded to her. We're so close in this Joey, he thought. He marvelled at her stamina, working at the law firm, looking in afterwards at the centres and helping to manage them and their work. Best of all, she found the time and devotion in attending to his need of her. He cleared his mind of the intrusive thought.

"Posters...billboards, small hand outs...flyers and tickets...car stickers... most of all, me telling it that way. Follow me?"

The women looked at each other, and Joey frowned.

"You still have to lead, John...consensus is fine but people will look to the Mayor for guidance and leadership, otherwise they'll go about wondering, 'just who's in control here'? The city's too big and complex to let the people alone decide."

"They can taste that for a while," Jacqueline said in reply. Her intent was to pursue the earlier themes of their conversation. "Write it all out...that's what I'm going to do, John. Keep it all in the eye and mind...from a small seed the big tree grows."

"Exactly, but I want to draw the Independence Party to us, and I've got an idea where to start." John smiled at Jacqueline and stood up. He had a meeting of his Board to attend now. Enough time had been spent on his political life, his other life as it might become. "It's how it's always been, starting small...or modestly," he said finishing off his train of thought.

213

It's what Grandpa Frederick would have said, more, he would have done. From a small beginning he, John Kahn, was the inheritor and guardian of a large business empire. His eyes and attention would move to a new horizon but not at the expense or loss of the past, his and the family's heritage.

34

"This will be something else for the voters in the City to think on." John held a newspaper cutting out to her. Dayle had done exactly as he had instructed, calling just two correspondents to tell of the meeting. The word had spread to others but by then the interviews had been given; the 'scoop' was for them to make of what they could. Follow up interviews or carefully controlled press releases would serve to keep the story in the news.

"You're learning all the time," Dayle replied with a proud grin on her face.

"Yes, thanks to the good people I've got on my team now," he acknowledged before reading the piece and thinking back on the past few days.

Independence Party finds new Leader's Voice

They're the third largest 'party' in the City of New York but in the past they traded their own independent voice and lent support to another party or its candidate. It won them few friends among those who wanted their independent voice to really count. One of the incumbent main stream parties – there have only ever been two you'll say – criticised them for siding with the other. Some called it fusing with a likely winner, otherwise you're left out in the cold.

Well, that's history! That's what John Kahn plans to do, change the way politics is seen in these parts. Together with lead helper Jacqueline Purcell, a recent recruit or convert to his cause, he called a meeting, to pull everyone together and to draw up an Independence Party campaign plan. Okay, okay…there are some that will say everyone who's not a Democrat or a Republican is an Independent. If so, the Independence party will say, register your name, enrol with them and do it quickly! It may mean greater choice of candidates on the ballot papers when the election days come.

John Kahn's come onto the scene from nowhere and the other main parties will no doubt hope that he'll go back to political anonymity real soon, or after the Primaries. That'll be hard, losing a guy of his stature. He's 'only' the CEO of PulcriMed and that's no place to run and hide because the company's known the world over. He's high profile and that's where he wants to put the Independence Party (or a party for independent thinkers if that's what you prefer) and to break the political stalemate that passes for democracy in these parts. Fusion politics, tagging your votes onto another candidates so you can bask in another's glory (if they win, of course), is to be put to one side.

John Kahn's aim is nothing else than to shake the political foundations of New York City.

While others find ways to throw mud and stones at them the Independence Party has a new figurehead. They agreed to it; some might say they had to; he put up some money, his own money, just to make it happen. What happen? Why, he put up some of his own money to get a new central campaign office set up to co-ordinate all the smaller ones, the satellites, in the cause for spreading a new message.

Others, before him, have put their own money up front for the good of their cause, but not like this man. He's putting it all into funding back-office costs, not marketing or pushing out his name. That, I'm told will be for later, when the Campaign Finance Board checks out his claim for funding just like everyone else. Every one will be playing off the same handicap, so to speak, so the candidates and their prospectus will be all that matters to the voters.

He's quite open about it; the campaign's to be about ideas and personalities fit for the job, not about the money they have to make their case. He has his own ways, and John Kahn intends to follow them.

The invitation was simply presented and printed on a neat card with a red, white and blue band to one side; it was of a convenient size, slipping easily into a jacket pocket or a handbag. It had been mailed following a 'phone call to all Independent candidates for local office in the City's five Boroughs or to picked names off a contacts list. Jacqueline knew where to look for them, and John asked no questions. This kind of *'callin and haulin'* to a meeting was not his way of doing things in his pursuit for legitimacy as a candidate but she had political pedigree, and experience. He deferred; she was on his team for a very good reason, she had knowledge that there was no time to gather.

"I'm doin' it simply as a means of persuading them to meet and listen to ideas," she explained.

"And I'm through with any ideas some may have that I'm just 'being' in politics. Let's go out there and make it happen…a real change."

"No trade-offs?"

"Heck no! I'm tired of them too, or reading of them…least ways, in how a candidate gets chosen. They say New York's a Democrat Party City, that the Republicans hold off and so…everyone watches and hears of back-room deals bein' done…or it's the other way about. Let's be different, let's go out and connect with others who don't follow that line and make for a fresher political reality."

She met John's gaze as if he challenged her to comment on what some might see as a naïve remark, the observations of a political ingenue, a rookie. She made light of it, sensing deeper held beliefs in what he'd spoken out.

"Power to the People?"

"Yeah! You got it in one!" he laughed.

"I'll tell them we're building an alliance and will fund some of the effort ourselves."

"I will, you mean?" he smiled in good humour. John knew what she meant but reality was somewhat different. "We'll keep on the right side of the Campaign Finance Board…we're doing this with ideas and policy. I'll spend my share on back room staff, building up from near to nothin' an organisation that everyone can work within and we do it for one reason, to best the others in how we take on the opposition. We get through to folks on ideas and policy; we give them answers on what we see is needed to help solve the problems in the City. We don't do it by simply shouting the loudest and spending a whole lot more; we fight them on equal terms, and that way…if we win, we know how we did it." He paused to see if another opinion would be expressed. "Right?"

"Right…we think City wide but act locally."

John held out his hand. "Go on shake it…I'm real glad to have you on my team, we're going to make this work!"

A mutual strength of feeling could be expressed to one another by this simple gesture.

Yes, he remembered clearly the efforts that Jacqueline expended in making the calls, to overcome doubts and to handle the dismay expressed at a novice in political circles calling them to a meeting. More, he was suggesting a union…a union of kindred spirits. One had laughed at her suggestion of it.

'We've already got a union, it's called the Independence Party, you know that Jacqueline,' she'd been told. And he had heard of it from her but curiosity would get the better of them.

"No, I think it will be your persuasive message and the offer of some campaign support…money. It may help to draw them in."

"I didn't go too far on that, John. I said we had a message that had at the core the making of a change, a big change. They knew your name, they realised a bank note might help…above all, they knew that a 'heavyweight' name might draw more people to the flag…so to speak."

Well, however the message had been put over Jacqueline had succeeded. The room was full; a buzz of expectant conversation filled the air; ideas were being exchanged, speculation on the events to come and wonder at the nerve of a stranger calling them to order.

216

They heard a commanding but respectful voice. "Ladies and gentlemen, shall we begin?"

John studied them all, his smart and curiously attentive guests, but turned to Margaret Lightart, their party leader. He had noticed, from the corner of his eye, how she had studied him thereby allowing others to talk and make themselves known.

"I owe you an explanation...but first of all," he smiled at her before looking at the seated onlookers, "I want to say thank you for responding to an invitation to meet up with me."

"We're always glad to welcome new members to the Independence Party," Margaret smiled in her own acknowledgement of the circumstances that had brought them together. "What made you change your mind and do it?"

"Do what?"

"Leave you natural political home...the Republicans. We checked you out...we looked in the archives. You had an association with them."

"Long ago. Life and events change you."

"And making money helps too," someone chipped in.

"Nothing wrong with that...we all get a chance."

"Some more than others, John."

"Yes...but that is one of the reasons for my candidacy, my wish to stand in the mayoral race...it's what I'm all about, improving the prospects for change and the opportunities for many more."

"With our help." He couldn't make out whom it was that offered these observations to test him.

"Care to identify your self? I'd like to know who's heckling me." He made light of it.

"Frank...Frank Swartz." The man stood up briefly.

"Okay Frank, if we agree to help each other...that's how I'd be seeing it, a union of effort."

"Why would we want to do that John? We have our share of influence."

"Where's that?" he asked directly of her and Margaret met his look.

"We've helped others get through their primaries and then an election."

"And your prospectus, what about that, hm? I read and know of your want to widen the appeal...to broaden the constituency you'd be calling on and who can be persuaded to vote. We've all got to find a way to make more people take a heck of a lot more interest. We need many more to enrol...with us."

"And you're the guy to do it?" Frank chipped in once more.

"That's why we're meeting...to think it through, yes."

Margaret looked at him calmly. "We only know you from the business press...maybe a few pictures on the social pages of a magazine...of you and your wife. What we don't know much of is the political part of life…the being in politics part of it all."

"I believe I've gone further…I'm doing the politics thing…and I don't go for simply being involved."

"Oh?"

"Heard of KIDHS?

"Sure…there's inclusionary housing schemes around the city."

"Not like mine…they're inclusionary housing and development schemes, and I started them a little earlier than most."

"So, you're claiming to be a pioneer?"

John shrugged. He had a soft smile on his lips. "I won't go so far, I just read a few signs and took the opportunity; you know, folks have got to live somewhere, and work…the closer you are to your work the better it is for some lower paid people…everyone in fact."

"Yes." He saw how Margaret sought the reactions of her followers.

"You've heard of Real Chance, a charity?"

"Sure, what of it? It's small time…and local." He recognised the subversive tone of voice.

"It's not small time to the folks being helped, Frank…it means a lot to them."

"He's made a difference," Margaret told his inquisitor, "I've heard about it…even went to see for myself what's being talked about. I did it out of curiosity…before your call came, or Jacqueline's."

"Good."

If he was being interrogated, in a hard and soft shuffle of speakers the plan was only just working. He had been prepared for a mixed reception.

"Thank you…I was intending to say that it was by 'doing' politics that we make a difference to folks. The two organisations help in showing the message isn't empty words. Sure, what I do to help with those groups is small time, but…the word's out on the streets." John allowed time for his message to be considered. "I'll keep doing things out there. In the meantime, I hope we may be able to join all of our ideas together into a respected and credible platform. Then, we'll go on out there and create a storm!"

"Of our own?" Margaret had been drawn in by his enthusiasm.

"Yes. Why help to make it happen for someone else? Why fuse your membership's vote to another's when we should sell our own ideas and grow our own following on the City's streets and in the Boroughs?"

"It's our way of facing the reality of political life," another voice piped up.

Margaret held up a hand to silence interruptions for an instant. "John, we've got our own ideas. Tell us of yours…spell them out for us…maybe then we'll see how we can mesh them with our own."

The meeting had evolved into an inquisition of his ideas and political credentials.

"Try this? I'll work within strict financial limits."

"Why?"

"We'd be campaigning to win on ideas and policy."

"Everyone does that," Frank muttered loudly, "it's called politics."

John noted the impassive expression that Jacqueline gave him when he caught her eye. He was on his own in this; he had to win this debate alone.

"Sure," he replied easily, "only some…many maybe, they would expect someone like me to throw a few barrow loads of money at the election… promote the man and the image…ignore the reality or the message at the core…the very reasons for my candidacy."

"Are you saying you're gonna ignore that little benefit, your own financial situation?" More voices were directing questions at him.

John looked about the room; he felt calm. Shareholder meetings were tougher than this and he got through by being well briefed, to his mark.

"Yes," he replied flatly.

"Why? Work the system as best you can!" The question was coolly delivered and John asked himself if it was a trick, a co-ordinated test of his integrity at its basest level.

"No, I won't be doing that. I don't intend to win, or support anyone, through buying my way to success. It's about ideas…not the weight of dollars." He could have added, 'I'll do it by force of character'.

"Very principled," Margaret said flatly.

"Yeah…maybe." He waited for an instant before continuing. "I'd call it simple democracy…the winning of hearts and minds, just what your web-site proclaims to be your party's big wish."

"Our party, John" she corrected.

"Yes, our party." He had to admit to the slip but there was also the hint at a unity of purpose.

"So?"

"So, my way's to organise, to fund the back office and get teams set up that can tell the message out there on the streets. We show what we've done, till now, but we really talk and sell what we can still do…what we have to do, for everyone!. But…and get this, we do it on our own. It is high time we broke the monopoly, or the stranglehold the other two seem to think they have."

"They've got the right to think it."

"No Frank, not the right…we and others have let them get so far."

"We've not been blind to the obvious…to the reality." A woman who had sat very still and silent suddenly felt emboldened to speak out raising her hand to draw attention to herself. "We're outnumbered hereabouts."

"I don't see that less than two million people taking part in a vote, in a city of eight million or so as being outnumbered…I'd call it closing off all the options. So, we stand up and make a lot of people believe in turning out to vote."

"We're still outnumbered, until that day comes," the lady persisted. Others nodded in agreement with her.

"But not out thought! Never think that!" John blazed out his response. "You don't know who's on the edge. They vote one way because they don't see a real choice. All I'm saying is…let's all work together to give those waivering people, or the unsure, a choice. Let's all work to give voters on an election night a choice. We need it in the Primaries…first of all we need to give them a name in the nominating primaries, a name that will make folks pay some more attention…and to make them register before the day."

"A big name," Jacqueline spoke out at last. She had waited to put his case before them.

"And you're telling us, all of us here in the room…"

"Suggesting to you, Margaret…suggesting."

"Okay, you're suggesting that we pull together and work with…him?"

"Uh huh," Jacqueline smiled, disarmingly. "Got any better ideas, or a better person with the profile and big business experience?"

"Business?"

"Sure, business. The city's like a business, a corporation…it has income and expenditure…they're out of balance, seriously out of balance."

"Stop!" Margaret exclaimed, "stop! We sure as heck know all of that!"

"Sure…sure. Okay…okay. No more reminders or stating the obvious is necessary," Jacqueline conceded with a softening in her tone.

"You got that right."

"So, what's it to be?" John asked.

"You mean…who's it to be. Right?"

"No, Margaret…to my mind it's *'what'*. What we do is the first call. After that we decide on *'who'* is to lead the united party, or pulls the campaign together as its focal point…its leader."

"I thought we'd all come together to talk about it, or…for you to tell us, John?"

"No, I invited you all here so that we could meet and talk…think things through and…see what came up."

"And who stepped up to the plate…or offered themselves."

"Sure Margaret, there was that too. But, it's our first meeting…so, we don't rush it, too much." John saw Jacqueline nod slowly as he turned to her. They were on the same page; what they spoke of had to sound true, from both of them.

"We'll think on it," Margaret said and prepared to gather her few things together.

"Fine, have a drink before you go? I've arranged a buffet and some drinks…we'll lighten the mood." He stood up as Margaret did so. "I'd like to be part of a change, Margaret…I want to make the changes we've touched upon, happen. My team does too and we want to work with other like minded groups…make some new friends."

"Make *many* new friends," Margaret said and took a moment to consider his confession.

"We weren't expecting any of this, John," she said at last. "We only heard that you'd developed an interest. We all agreed…all of us after Jacqueline called that it would be worth meeting up…to check you out and see if there was anything to your proposal."

"It's becoming an obsession," he laughed engagingly but his stare on Margaret was unwavering. "It's all about doing politics…"

"And we'll have to learn how we can work together on it."

"Sure…only, and I'm sorry to put it like this…make it soon, please? Names have to be in next month…in the ballot for nominees."

"Is tonight soon enough?"

"Tonight?" He couldn't conceal his surprise at Margaret's answer.

"Yeah. We came here ready to listen, to talk and to bargain. We'll take you up on your offer of a drink…but we'll go somewhere and talk it all through."

"Fine. Call me when it's done?"

"Yes, of course." Margaret looked at her neat gold watch, slipping it round a slender wrist. "It's nine o'clock…so, say, we come back at ten thirty? Can we meet up again then?"

John caught a moments glance from Jacqueline. An arcing movement of her hand suggested tomorrow would be better, a few hours respite would allow all of them to think and talk it over.

"Tomorrow, make it tomorrow morning? I've set out a summary of my ideas, to help you. Look them over and we could speak again tomorrow." John took a folder from beneath his chair. "Please, take these."

"We will, John…but the time remains the same. We settle things tonight. We know exactly what we'll be up against if we decide to follow your lead…or ally our efforts to yours…and we produce a joint manifesto. Who knows?

Other groups may join up…we all fuse ideas into a concerted strategy to challenge the incumbent political elites as they like to think of themselves."

And their decision was reached by due process and in the time Margaret had told him. A momentous outcome for all concerned had been reached in just ninety minutes, an hour-and-a-half. None on his team, not even Jacqueline, had expected judgement quite so soon, but Margaret had a ready explanation and put it to him succinctly.

"You picked your moment to call us very well, John."

35

The review of promotional strategy, the meetings with Independence Party candidates and canvassing their views upon his leadership under a unifying banner counted for him. The media had someone to concentrate their attention upon. John Kahn, a mayoral candidate? Why take on that kind of heat? They all asked the same questions and received the carefully worded and controlled answers; the party machine was quickly at work. Margaret Lightart and her closest associates saw only too quickly that they had found a guy to bring a very different, a stronger and credible message to the city's electorate.

John Kahn was as good as his word; he listened to ideas and learnt from them. He didn't dictate terms; he persuaded all of his workers and others that they were in the electoral race together. The prize was too big to waste energy on internecine squabbles; they'd save their energy for putting the case for change wherever and whenever they could.

"Pay off time!" John whooped.

He saw the impact of the news that he was standing as a candidate very quickly; the invitation to appear as a guest on a Cable TV interview was announced a day after the story broke in the New York Times. With Jacqueline he worked on the main questions that he might face and brainstormed the rest; they took anything that came to mind and wrote it down, checked the list for any "stumblers"; she called them "ball breakers". Margaret, discreetly called them 'hostages to fortune'.

Jacqueline suggested the venue, his low-key campaign office and certainly not the headquarters of KPM and the executive suite. His background was on the public resume' of him, the man and the candidate. What he stood for and offered to the voters had to be projected from altogether different surroundings. His hitherto low-key and un-publicised involvement in City-wide projects would count for him; any publicity that showed the candidate in the neighbourhoods to be helped wouldn't be filled with 'plants' to speak of a man they knew nothing of until the promo team showed up. He had 'form', a word he used to great effect...and there seemed to be plenty of folks readier to speak up for him than before.

She could hardly believe it; as the days passed since joining the team she came to realise his appeal. Where had all these folks been hiding? The old party, as she referred to her previous political home, hadn't found them a voice...but, John Kahn, a political novice somehow achieved what had eluded them.

You only had to hear the best stories once to remember them.

"So, what's the philosophy, the political credo of John Kahn?" the interviewer began. "What comes out of the lamp, if you polish it? A genie or a real picture of reality?"

"The election should be opened up, make voters feel what is available to all of the people. I'd like to see that everyone has a stake in the outcome. It's one of my main motivators for standing...for the Independence Party."

"At most you will split the vote. Do you really think your candidacy has any validity? Can voting for you make a difference...even win it?"

"If the vote is seen as available only to a privileged few, or a coterie of what many see as a privileged few then it's bad news. If the election excludes those who seem to believe that the main contenders, in their eyes, are talking over them to another constituency then I think it will do nothing but harm to the whole city and its boroughs. I stand as good a chance as any other candidate in the early stages of the process...win through and the voters will have a stark choice to make."

"So, your candidacy is more in hope than conviction?"

"Oh no, not at all. Where'd you get that idea?"

"From you."

"I don't think so." He shifted in his chair looking at his inquisitor all the while. "I'm not out there selling something or being nice, but pitching for every vote against all-comers. I've taken the hits and come back for more. I can take the disappointments along the way, the comments of those that won't give me or my ideas a second thought."

"That's too honest!"

"Cynic," John smiled. "But is it? You're not out there simply to manage a core vote."

"Do you have one?"

"Sure do. I'm not just managing that but working to take it from my political opponents, in other words working to win the argument and the battle of hearts and minds...it's a contest of ideas as well as substance."

"It's a fight for votes…nothing more or less."

"Exactly so, but before that moment…it's about winning on ideas."

There was only a second's pause before the interviewer altered his line of questioning. "Some accuse you of being a control freak…people in your business life say that of you."

"Do they?" John tried to keep the tone of mock surprise from his voice. "I like to compare the way I manage those I work with to a ship tied to the quayside with a length of rope. When the engines are running the rope's taught…it's stretched and wanting to be loosened and to progress; if it's slack there's no drive to be anywhere. In my book there's a big difference…if the rope's taught you're working to effect a change. If I control anything it's the direction I wanted my businesses to take…when elected it would be no different…my attitude that is. I'd want people to see the difference and not talk of *'when is it goin' to happen?'*"

"Okay, I understand the analogy…so, if you're not a control freak then as a manager you avoid confrontation. Is that what you're telling the audience? You've got to have ownership to achieve your target results."

"Business clichés."

"Yeah, you can't get away from them can you?" The interviewer looked down at his pad, for his prompts. "To get back to the question…you're either one or the other…control freak or a nosey manager."

"Democrat or Republican, you mean?" He waited for any riposte but none came. "I don't agree, and that's why I'm standing as an Independent candidate."

The interviewer looked baffled. "I don't get you…"

John smiled. "So I see."

"So explain?"

"Sure…you become a control freak, as you put it, if the team you work with either haven't bought into what your plans are or worse…they are being instructed to implement a policy the beneficiaries haven't been consulted on. If you don't go out and meet the people, sell the idea and explain how it may affect them what hope is there? Things get outta hand…policies rebound on you. Then you're seen as an interfering, nosey manager. I saw and learnt much of that the hard way…thanks to Uncle Sam," he finished ruefully.

"Politicians intuit it."

"They what?" John laughed. "Whatever the word means, I don't!" He leant forward and asked in a friendly tone, "What does that word mean, *exactly*?" His host had a colourful turn of phrase; it sounded like he had invented a new word.

"You rely on *intuition* and what you learn from your political organisation. You know? Your few workers out there on the street. They're intelligence gathering…discovering for you what the issues are out there."

"Oh is that what you meant, what we learn from the so-called *'few'* workers, that we have?" John smiled as he heard the unflattering comment on his campaign team. "The group I and the Independence Party have got is big enough for the task ahead. If you load yourself with extras you lose the message…you're diverted from the core beliefs. You spend more effort micro-managing them than the policy and putting over the ideas you have. I won't be going down that route."

"Isn't this a lonely road you're stepping out on?"

"Not at all…the party's membership is bigger than you think."

"If small is seen to be beautiful…you would cut the City's payroll maybe? Reduce the numbers?"

The questioning was disjointed and not the seamless scripting that Jacqueline had advised him to expect or prepare for, but, old habits never quite deserted him and he had mentally prepared for what he now faced. He was learning; in business he would liken the preparations as *'thinking outside the box'*, one of the few mantras that resonated. He knew. It was a practice that paid off for PulcriMed many times and left Wall Street wondering just how they had done it…more like how he, John Kahn as CEO, had dreamt up the path to glory. Only the successes had been all too real and the rewards handsome.

"No, not that either. I *chose* and now I've *got* a great *small* team with lots of ideas and all of them displayed on this wall and out there on the street being pressed into hands and through doors of affected people and neighbourhoods. If the message is clear and you have something to *really* say then the message will just fly! You can't hold it back…voom!"

John's enthusiasm was evident as one hand made a swoop then rose gracefully in a short arc to emphasis his point before he held it out to the host as if to say, *'it's that easy, see?'*

"But out there you're faced with conventions…you're trying to break all that down…and persuading people to change personal voting habits while you're doing so."

"I've changed too! Don't forget that!"

"Did you? I thought Independents were just borrowing another's ideas. Underneath they go with one or other of the main stream political theories or parties. What's the word…fusion?"

"Yeah, I heard that too…once. Something borrowed and modified in the face of reality or experience; it's also about something new…look on it that way. You may get through to the message then. In case you forgot, progress means change…conventional thinking giving way to the new, or adapting. That's all."

"If that were so why have we all been waiting so long for these ideas to reach some kind of prominence?"

"Like being voiced on your show, you mean?" John tapped the fingers of both hands together. "Look? Democracy is for all the people…it's not about making deals behind closed doors. The ideas, or philosophy has been out there for quite a while…I thought I'd take a tilt at them windmills of entrenched political interest…and, I don't give up so easy."

"You're the man of the hour…is that it?"

"That's for others to decide upon, in the voting booths. They've gotta grab hold of the idea first."

"Change is going to take time and a great deal of money, isn't that the case? Your time and your money…it'll take more than one campaign to carry it off, to secure the prize you're after."

"Quite possible…it's quite possible. I don't take or expect any special favours. It's convincing people of an idea with just the same budget as any other candidates have at their disposal." His host attempted to interrupt him with a disbelieving question but John silenced him with an almost imperious wave of his hand. "The difference, if I may be allowed to finish, okay? The difference is that I'm out on the streets, wearing out shoe leather and so is my team. I'm out there talking of the big ideas, be they on schools, budgets or minority interests. Those with philosophies set in stone, Democrat or Republican, won't change…but you never know. Those who are still outside all of that can hear me and think on my ideas. If it strikes a chord…"

"Let it play?"

"Yeah…more clichés, and here's another!" John laughed quite naturally. "I'm enjoying having a tilt at these windmills but the intention is all too serious."

"You're in a political game, there are rules to follow…you mean?"

"No, I'm not in a game! I'm in a contest, I mean it and intend to win it. The only part of the analogy that fits with a game is that there is a winner at the end. You can check my business record…any record for that matter, even my charity work record…you'll see how often I've been on the only side that counts."

"What you're telling me may sound over-confident…arrogant even."

"I hope not…what I mean to tell you is that I am not playing at my candidacy. It spells out in my book a belief that politics is about working for people…all the people in the city and boroughs…and it's going to be very different, but not scary. It's just going to be different and measurable."

"How so?"

"I read somewhere, in a foreign paper's article to be precise…a Dutch one as it happens reporting on what I said early on in the campaign…that politics is about '*doing not being*'. It's doing politics and getting results, it's not about being in politics simply for the appearance of it."

"Have you got anyone in mind when you describe your philosophy like that, in a neat summary of your own *different* political credo?"

"No, I just feel that convention needs to be broken and we head off into new territory but we still keep our eyes on what matters *day-to-day* in the constituency…the widest constituency possible, in *all* of the five boroughs. We all have a duty to persuade a majority of registered voters to turn up at the polling stations and vote, not just a quarter of them."

"It's still democracy."

"Yeah, but disinterest on that scale breeds trouble and resentment. Why have that when you can work with many others to effect a real change…for the better?"

John Kahn won his nomination to run as a candidate. Enrolment for a rejuvenated Independent Party voice exceeded all expectations. *'Seein is Believin'* the Independent Party car stickers said. He hadn't sanctioned their use but he knew who was behind them. Dayle had told him of a slogan…she even sang it out. *"You aint seen nothin' yet"* as she showed him the artist's mock up ideas.

The radio and TV stations sought him out. They couldn't resist the novelty of a charismatic businessman being questioned by political pundits or commentators on the elections that grew nearer every day.

"Let's err on the cautious side," he told his opponents. They were seen as the front-runners, the candidates representing each of the main stream parties, the political establishment to many. "The disconnected voters or those that don't turn out at the elections is what…50% or so? Some times less than 40% turn out and vote for the candidates on the paper. I got through the nomination primaries…the race is on for the primaries. I've got where I want to be…at this stage of the process."

"It'll get tough now…two go through in September."

"Usually, it's two. But, yeah…two months or so from now…so, in the meantime we all put out our message…there's plenty to debate and discuss… the team's in shape and the base continues to grow. It's what I wanted from the beginning, a real election…not with two to argue it out but three or more."

"That must be a good thing, some real competition," the interviewer asked the others.

"Sure…it'll still come down to two parties." Steve Cruz was the public employee's candidate, the union man with a Democrat label.

"The question will be which two." Beejay Newhouse had the Republican support

"And then there's one that might really represent the majority view of how things are to be here in New York…the voice of those who haven't taken an interest until now and represented by a *third* candidate." John made his contribution sound light, he hadn't got the measure of these two or the rules for these face-to-face exchanges. Like in the military, he guessed the best form of defence might be to go for your opponents, but he'd wait it out, and see how the game was to be played by his opponents.

"Cutting taxes won't get things done…boosting investment will." Steve Cruz eyed him provocatively.

"What's your record in managing public money? What's your plan for that?" he was asked by the show's host.

"Collective investment schemes…"

"What? What are they?"

"They're schemes, call them projects, that I've been involved with for some little time. It's caring for the lower income groups, it's a small beginning for many but it's important; it's an idea you might have approved of Steve, only your party blocked any radical proposals my business and the charity I supported had for them. So, I went and did it in my own way. We called the place Independence House. You'll know it, up on the Upper West Side. It brings work, homes and some hope…better still it encourages self-belief. The folks being helped owe everything to themselves, to their work ethic."

"And your controls…and what your companies make out of it. Altruism it isn't." Steve waved a hand in dismissal of the proposition.

"Wrong! We earn from a part of it, sure…it's investing in places and people, in dual risk asset classes. The city could do it just as easily…it needs a real political will and the support of a wider electorate."

"Vacant lots are being brought into use…we're planning to re-zone areas too. What you're suggesting is nothing new." Beejay offered.

"Sure…the thing is I get things done quicker. You both, in your own ways want to exercise control, to stifle initiative…a bureaucratic mess."

"Nonsense…we aim to help all to get it right."

"You sure of that, Steve? By my reckoning you want to control things just as you try to control the electoral process…you and the other party…that way you narrow the field…eliminate real choice."

"Once again…nonsense! In any case your newly discovered party, when it comes to you in particular, had no concerns about joining up with another… just to get by."

"And exercise a fingertip touch on putting over new…newer ideas. That was then…keep up, Steve. Things are changing and are goin' to change a heck of a lot more. We're pitching…"

"But you guys drop the ball often enough…and you'll be no different."

"We've got new policies, fresh ideas…we're where we are because of them. The enrolments are rising daily…we'll get the numbers needed."

"But John, we have the experience of government…of being in office. What have you done in that?"

"I've made work and money, for a business and people that work for the company," he smiled in answer. "If you've got a handle on things, why the mess? We're free-thinking on the important issues…independent in thought and action where we can exert some influence…above all, we're open."

"The whole system is open."

"Are you so sure? It's not what we hear out on the streets, or see in the papers…or on the web logs for some stations."

"The system brings stability…" Beejay began but John interrupted him.

"It's brought inertia and an inability for change…real change, least ways until now. We'll be taking you on to make real change happen…count on it. The status quo is all shook up…and we've only just started!"

"Stability…we've got that and will continue with it."

"Beejay? Folks haven't really seen or believed change was a possibility; they had no one who shouted out the message to them…BELIEVE IN IT! VOTE FOR CHANGE!" John looked directly into the cameras as he spoke. "Well, they have now."

"They'll compare what they've had for so long, the stability and the certainty of having people in office and in the Mayor's chair who know what needs to be done, how to do it and who is to do it. What we're not in for is daydreaming and airy wish fulfilling promises."

"Don't you go counting on it, Steve…none of it!" John spoke out firmly. "Folks will soon have a choice, they'll be able to contrast and compare, think and then decide what's right."

"The nominating primaries have come and gone, ladies and gentlemen, and I'm still standing for Mayor of New York! My eyes are still wide open and my opponents know a new kid's out on the block!"

"Kickin ass!" someone shouted.

"Only," he said wistfully, "we know we may have to do that some more to open eyes to what's really goin' down."

"We need someone to lead us on that!" a woman screeched out.

Some in the hall clapped and he gave a beaming smile.

"Thank you…and thanks to you and many others there is to be a three candidates race! That's right, at least three names. Many said we didn't have a prayer, or the Independence Party would have to do an awful lot of that, praying and for a long time before we got a look in and broke entrenched habits.

Well? We've taken the first steps…big ones, to giving a voice to those that may have felt disenfranchised…with no vote that really counted in these parts. For those of you here in this room who felt that way…maybe your silent prayers have been answered…just a bit. Other voices are being heard on the streets and they're calling for a change.

It's great! Join me and let's all work to make a dream come true!

Historical precedents, how things were done in the past…well they're just that, heading for the past and the history books. The Independence Party has found its voice and it speaks for its manifesto and for smaller groups who have ideas and who have endorsed my candidacy. Thank you for doin' that…I aim to make this Mayoral Election one to remember. We made others think and widened the choice…of candidates and ideas.

I'm standing for office and I'm working for change!

Change…don't go bein' frightened of that!" he laughed.

"Let's all work together to make change happen, for those not here tonight and for all of you who have turned up to listen. No one can say that their voice isn't listened to or their concerns have gone unnoticed. The elections are for everyone to give voice to their hopes and their fears. If a candidate or the party's policy isn't goin' to light your fire then don't enrol with them!

Join me and give voice to different *ideas*!

Join me, and others, around this City who have turned their thoughts to different ways of *doing things* and don't look to others to make it happen! Together, we can do it!"

His voice sounded confident and enthusiastic as he thumped the lectern; it was a prop and he had no real need for it. There were no notes to refer to or spread out upon it. He was at ease and spoke to his audience in confident eloquence.

"The Independence Party! It's an association of ideas, of freedom to think and act differently!"

"Just like you and your fat cat buddies do at PulcriMed?" a dissenting voice called out to him now waving a publicity flyer to draw attention to himself and looking about to see if others would join in the heckling.

None did, to John's surprise.

"We all work hard and we work within the law…corporate governance is key. It'll be no different if I was elected Mayor. There's no room in my business for breaking the law…"

230

"Yeah sure!" the dissenting voice continued, "The law? You just bends it."

"No...we have Stock Market rules to comply with. I see to it that we follow them to the letter. We do that and make money...I'm not ashamed of that...I can run a business and make my staff feel that they're valued. What they put into the business...they get back. It'll be no different in City Hall. The only distinction may be that employees of the City don't run the Boroughs to their own rules...the Charter, you the voters and citizens do."

"Let's all see that Mister!"

"You won't have long to wait."

"And you've got to be elected first!"

John laughed. "That's what I figured too! So...play your part, if what I'm standing for chimes with you...in some way, vote for change!"

What he was speaking of had been said many times but he never fell into a routine that seemed as if he spoke something off by heart. Practice was developing into a new skill, judging his audience and speaking of concerns aides had told him affected the audience of the district he was visiting.

"If you're listening out for new ideas, please listen to ours, the Independence Party's, listen to me and speak to my team, my great team! They're here, in the room...tell them what bothers you about the way things are goin' down here, in your District. It all gets back to me. I think on it, and give you an answer."

"We'll see, Mister!" someone yelled out. "You'll cut it for all of us, will you?"

"Yes, count on it!" John cried out, looking in the direction of where he thought the call to him had risen. "We don't do 'skin politics'...colour, background, and so on. Ethnicity doesn't figure with us except that some policies aren't working for you in a city where the population is changing. The Independence Party is no longer about maintaining a two party system in the City of New York. We're working to effect a change so...help me and my colleagues, party candidates in the borough elections too, to make each and every vote count.

What that means is...casting your vote! It means getting down to the polling booths and pressing the buttons, pulling levers, or marking a ballot paper. Vote for change, vote for what the Independence Party stands for...if you're persuaded that a different outcome is possible and isn't just your long held hopes said out loud in a prayer once again!"

He paused to draw breath.

"What about that God you're calling to help you?" someone shouted out to him amidst the whoops. There was laughter and John took it to mean that the tension had eased and some had been willing to really listen; it was a good omen.

"He may hear you, listen to us all…but right now, your votes count. So, join me if you're out to make a difference and to make yourself heard…get out there!

Be different!

Vote for a CHANGE!"

Many laughed at the turns of phrase used to end his short address. Some waved papers at him, others used the flyers or a handout that told of the man who stood before them now. This was no remote guy, detached from the reality that was life for some. Joey had made sure that the beneficiaries of the charitable work he supported were in the audience.

"Hi, how're you doin'?" John was standing amongst them now, just talking and passing the time of day.

He could say 'hello' and some could see that he meant it; this was no moneyed guy talking from a stage at them; he was talking with them, on their level and eye-to-eye; they sensed that what he had to tell them, John Kahn meant. He was not afraid to look you in the eyes for a while…a while longer, as if to say 'a few moments with you matters to me.'

36

His workload was prodigious; he survived on the number of hours sleep he had last endured in the jungle and swamps thanks to Uncle Sam. It felt like he was working at two coal faces, mining the returns for shareholders and the Wall Street markets on the one side and, on the other, the demands of a questioning but more receptive electorate.

The days drew into night seamlessly. He left the house and Marie's warming embrace early, worked at the office for as long as his diary required attendance. Then, Delroy drove him to the campaign office and the noisy preparations for the night of speech making, working on text and delivery; then, it was moving on to the meeting and ideological combat.

At last, a return to small talk in the arms of Marie, or divertingly the passionate clasp of Joey's hands and legs. The risk of discovery was intensified by the poster campaign that he had begun to notice and over which he had no control. Elbee asked him if he wished any spoilers of his own to be pasted but he shook his head. Free speech and all…it allowed him to put forward his ideas; incumbents got financial support so, he reasoned, they could resort to the tactics his team railed against.

The pithy captions were critical and unflattering; his candidacy was being dismissed so the line went; it was an affront to any thinking electorate's intelligence. 'Independent'? They collected a few derisory percentage points in any vote – what the people needed was independence from the quirky ideas espoused by John Kahn, the pot-pourri of political tenets that passed for a policy to govern millions of City dwellers. New York was a world-renowned City, a magnet for the tourist and employment seeker, a mine to work for riches, each-to-his-own; or, it was a vault for storing away your gains.

What did John Kahn know? Someone had to govern the place and look after the interests of its multi-racial, multi-cultural and multi-denominational inhabitants. One guy you couldn't trust was a certain John Kahn, a parvenu if ever there was one in city government. The language may not spring from the page so fluently as his inveterate critics might wish it, but the main opponents saw him as an interloper, a danger and verbose threat to their carefully managed and assiduously guarded territory. A choice from two was enough, wasn't that the truth?

He learnt of this from the few posters that were pointed out to him, and some of the flyers that landed on his office mat; he could only laugh at the comments made and reassured both Dayle and Jacqueline that he was unmoved, unbothered by the assaults on him. Dayle's sensibilities, hardened as they were, took a beating none-the-less. Her language on seeing a newer version of the deriding prose grew more colourful and was perhaps best suited to the mouth of a disgruntled road worker.

"I must be getting to them, darlin'…there's no other way to explain it," he now said reassuringly and to convince Dayle of his untroubled take on the negative campaign that seemed to be springing up. A few anti-globalisation tracts and 'freeing up' patents in pharmaceuticals had suddenly appeared at his office; the use of threatening language was a development to be watched, nothing more unless Elbee's intelligence network produced evidence of clear intent at mischief.

"Yeah…that's my take on it too," Dayle said grasping his hand and responding to the squeeze he gave her. "Be careful with your self?"

"Yes, you know I will." He bent to kiss her. "So? Tonight's interview or the panel game if you want to call it that…it's an opportunity to *'swing the lead'* at my opponents, so to speak…but in the nicest possible way."

"Shaft them Pops."

"Not my girl's usual choice of language," he smiled, "but I get the general drift." He took hold of her hand once more as it rested on the seat between them. "Are you keeping the right company when you're not with your old Pops?"

"Yes, the best…and as I keep having to tell you, you're not old. You're in tune with what a younger generation is beginning to believe in and wants to hear."

"Is it anyone I know?"

"Who?"

"Your *'best'* company, next to me."

"It's far too early to say, or talk about," she answered and took her time to think on what more to tell him of Nico Brant. "I can discuss things with him…cuss at him and what he believes in; or, he provokes me into telling him all there's to say about the road to follow."

"Just talking and cussing…no loving?" he said, and gave a sly wink.

"Dad!" Her grip tightened. "No, I'd like to but he's someone I need to meet often and get to know real well…better than any other and more than just skin-to-skin, for both our sakes." She signalled between her and the father she adored but was not in thrall to.

"Oh?"

"Yeah, if it works out I'll be choosing for keeps…I feel he could be that important to me."

"So you won't go throwing away what's best in you…your feelings?"

Dayle slid across the seat to sit still closer to him. "No…you're the only one I can really talk to; you're my true soul mate when it comes to learning of life."

"I've only been here a little longer than you darlin' that's all; I've seen and done some good and bad things. I keep working to earn new credits for being here. So, the political thing…Mayor…that would see me through, in this life anyway."

"With us all around you."

"Yes, I'd be nothing without you and a few others."

He gazed on her with deepest affection. Both Jacqueline and Joey had deferred to Dayle and she now accompanied him to the studios and the three-way parley between him and the Republican and Democratic candidates. Joey had spoken for both of them, saying that Dayle was just the youthful company that he needed to be seen with and photographed arriving for this evening's show. She attracted the right attention, her sense of dress for the occasion perfect and seemingly untutored. The lemon yellow billowing blouse accompanied well-cut and close fitting jeans and pointed lemon yellow sling back shoes. Dayle could bring him to the attention of a segment of the constituency he needed to draw in.

"Secure a victory and there'll be more people than you can thank."

"I can only achieve that by doing what I said I'd do for them."

"Well, where we're heading is the place to win some more to your side of the line."

"Make some more cross their own Rubicon?"

"Yeah, I'm sure you're right there." She raised her eyebrows as if despairing of him. "Where'd that come from?"

"Rome and its history. If I were you I'd read a book or two from time-to-time, darlin'." He squeezed her hand in affirmation.

"Yeah, good advice. Once you get elected I may be allowed the time again."

"Don't go counting on it. You'll be in demand…at work and with the man who's next best."

"After you?" she sighed almost in resignation. "We'll see."

'Right Treatment' was the name of the charity, a fund managed by benevolent people and with his money at its foundation, and very few knew of that. Five facilities had been built so far, one in each city borough had been the plan; more would follow. Those that devoted precious time to the endeavour knew of his connection – only, they knew he was there helping not bank-rolling the effort.

The men sitting opposite him in the uncomfortable studio chairs were unaware of this direct and personal commitment. It was his money, doin' good. Independent Commissioners for Charity had run the rule over the organisation, for more than three years; they were clean, every cent accounted for and testimonials to the charity's work hung on the walls of their offices. Jacqueline had heard of its contribution to rehabilitating some disaffected youths and men; she knew only of his day-to-day involvement in operations, in person or by 'phone asking questions and offering some direction.

He had not been the one to shout the charity's achievements from the rooftops, nor had he, so far, spoken too much of his place amongst those offering help. However, seated in the studio's waiting area with his two most likely opponents in the contest he decided that the moment to 'come out', so to speak, had arrived. Jacqueline had advised as much when she learnt of the heights his true benevolence reached.

The negative poster campaign had provoked the idea. Seeing them had touched a nerve and the moment to eyeball and payback his detractors would not be passed by, not this time; shame it was cable TV, but the word would spread soon enough if he got it right. Against all advice he'd given them their heads; he chose walkabouts at every meeting possible to rebut any allegations of his candidacy's failings – his inexperience of political realities – that were asked. Meeting constituents rather than talking at them would bring hope. Nothing had happened to change his mind on that.

So, he held his tongue, uttered no harsh words reviling his opponent's slogans or rebutting the innuendo as to his character to govern. Instead, he ordered photographs of work being undertaken by beneficiaries of the charities and work groups he supported. There! He was amongst them, the black, white, Asian youths and young men…any guys needing a helping hand onto a different road from that they'd trodden 'til now. Without any evangelical overtones the candidates were being encouraged to mend their ways and community fences. The only words to accompany the pictures were simple and held a consistent message:

> 'New beginnings – Help <u>and</u> Independence
> Doing things John Kahn's Way'

The smiles on the faces about him told it all; they were confident but not cock-sure, aggressive or challenging. A closer look, better still word-of-mouth, showed the real message. Disaffected youths had faces showing grudging respect; there was no distance between John Kahn, 'candidate', and the young men the charity prepared for work.

Commitment to a new life, the "right treatment", was being developed; the first rule was to consider them as adults and to devolve responsibility to them; it was treating them as adults and hoping they didn't screw up too often on the way. They took on responsibility working with dangerous materials in the course of learning a trade; respect for themselves and others was dripped into them by quiet but unmistakably firm voices; mess with equipment and fool around and you could end up dead, your new buddies along with you.

In essence, "Right Treatment" was about painstakingly teaching respect for others; being sociable meant more than jokey capers and wrecking things; right treatment meant a community of spirit, learning to rehabilitate and grow communities. That way they might just hold back the process of gentrification and persuade people like them not to keep moving on – from one squalid street to another as developers cleaned up…and cashed in.

Jacqueline had checked him out; KRE, Kahn Real Estate was clean; no accusing voices could be raised to say the company destabilised communities by keeping lots vacant until the market rose and a marginal scheme became a "cert". Delroy had pointed to sub-standard housing and semi-derelict shopping areas as the main contributor to the mayhem he had sometimes endured around his home. KRE had spread the risks and the word…you didn't all need to live in condos and pay galactic food prices to play your part in the City's life.

"You gentlemen ready?" Another political joust was to go out on the air.

"Wishful thinking, that's all I can say that's polite, about John Kahn's approach."

"Dreamland," said another.

"Yes to both of you," John replied without rancour. "There's no harm in wishing for a better city and for being the person to work at making it happen. As for dreams, well…one constituent I spoke to told me I shouldn't use any words like *"I have a dream"*…'cos a better man in his eyes spoke them long ago."

"So?" the show's host intervened, "how do you answer your critics, or opponents, who accuse you of wishing or dreaming of a better world or way of doin' things?"

"Yeah, they do don't they?" he said then added suddenly, "but it's nothing new to want that. Ask anyone in the City and they're sure to give you much the same answer; some give me both, that they're wishing and dreaming. Many more cling to the belief that the to-and-fro of the two party system could do with a change…maybe stop it altogether for a while and introduce some competition. They tell of having had enough of the mean spirited trade-offs that happen along the ways…someone always looses, often those least able to take care of things."

"Many folks call it politics John, in case you forgot!"

"Or never learnt it!"

John fixed his two opponents in turn with a narrow eyed stare. "Snipe all you want…in my book your way of doing things is from *way* back. Compromise gets things done…not just talking about them but really achieving your goals. That's my dream and we'll see who wins the arguments at the Primary. Getting nominated was the key! We made it, on our own…the Independence Party! That party stands for fulfilment of personal goals for as many folks as possible…that's what I want people to see as the cornerstone of my candidacy."

"Talking as you do…it's departure from reality, how it is for real people out there on the street and in the neighbourhoods," the interviewer felt prompted to intervene. So far he had taken no active part in leading the debate; the mayoral candidates had done the work for him; they were pretty good at swatting the arguments to-and-fro between them.

"John Kahn has no experience of real politics, or dealing with closely guarded territories, the neighbourhood priorities that exist in the five boroughs. He hasn't experienced, as a worker within the City system, the effects a budget cut has when Albany decides plans have to change and the Mayor has to handle it." Steve Cruz looked to another for agreement on the new line of attack. Steve once again regarded John Kahn as an interloper upon the political process.

"Our parties have a history of working in that real world…maybe mine more than most," Beejay volunteered.

"You mean pedigree counts for more than substance? Well, I guess voters will be interested to hear it spelt out in that way by you both. I'm not sure it ever really counted, and Divine Right went out of fashion some time ago…in England I believe. Being a managing mayor would be more my style instead of a ceremonial mayor…I'd put that idea in the trash can of history."

"Fine words, but the voters will decide between today's kid and the man who has got history and experience behind him."

John's answering smile was captured on camera. "You forget one thing, I happen to be part of a business that addresses people's daily concerns…even their lives, and," he paused for some effect, "it makes some money. I've got a track record…call it history and experience. I'm just gonna channel it in a new direction."

He made it all sound very reasoned and believable.

"With a party behind you…if you can call your collection of followers a '*party*'?" Beejay almost sneered, but he had a smile on his lips.

"How'd you answer that?" the show's presenter laughed and acknowledged the barb as a means to expose the true scale of John Kahn's support. He had failed so far to introduce the numbers aligned behind the candidates into the discussion.

"Like I do when I have many adversaries facing me, like I seem to have now in this studio," he smiled raising his eyebrows in enquiry as he did so and looking at the interviewer. "It's all very homespun, but it goes something like this…pull back the drapes or the misty net curtains…open up the windows and let in the bright light…and *fresh* air! Come on and breathe it in!" he said with a shouting laugh. "Many may recognise the message, history or pedigree is just fine…as long as you read about it. I'm working hard with my team to make it, history, really *happen*! Many support us…and the pledges of signatures just keeps on growing."

One of his opponents gave an audible snort of derision.

"Let's hear what your opponents have to say of that. Who's going to try?"

"I will! The history made will be another term for the Republican Party," Beejay smiled.

"Oh no! It won't be the status quo," Steve Cruz called out. "The Democrats bear all the influence, we make things happen by rock solid local representation. In the end the Mayor's something of a figurehead…he may promote the policy but our party workers implement it and get it through by their votes on Council."

"Is that elected representation you're talking of or union influence?" John asked reasonably.

"Both." Steve Cruz replied.

"Excuse me?" John intervened before the show's anchorman, or Beejay, could react. "The citizens of New York should be voting for representatives to act on their manifesto…on the policies they were voted in to office to implement…on that alone. "

"That's very…very, uh…" Steve Cruz.

"Democratic?" John prompted with an impudent smile.

It made Beejay laugh quickly but he realised, too late, that his candidacy had the support of unions. By association there was little to distinguish his stance with Steve Cruz.

John made the most of his opponents' discomfort.

"Let's work to have a *real* party contest between candidates that started off as two or three of many…and from different points, and who finally earned their spot in the line." John said it equably but his eyes were very still. "Let's make it a real political contest rather than government by a circle of connected insiders all working in the heady atmosphere of political egoism."

"Better that than corporate egoism, which seems to be your platform," Steve Cruz was goaded to reply.

"Well now…it was about time we got onto *political* platforms. You say where and when and I'll be there, we can debate them rather than throwing clichés around at each other." John made his voice sound reasonable. There was no sense in coming over all touchy with these guys.

The host of the show again intervened; it was easy going; he had little to do, but the antagonism of the two regular parties against the newcomer was evident and the sparks seemed to fly without too much prompting on his part. He turned to the other two and the camera held them both in shot.

"The tracking polls show that John Kahn's message is getting through… the figures register that."

"Right on," John was prompted to say and watched his opponents with a smile on his lips. A political career could yet be nurtured from last week's success in the nominating primaries. The media spotlight would be on him even more the like of which his opponents must have hoped he would fail to secure.

"It's early days," Steve Cruz smiled, "by how many points does it register?"

"Enough," the show's host began but John finished for him.

"By enough to make us start a debate or try and debate the issues. You name the day both of you…singly or together. Maybe *together*…that way it would be cost effective…we got to think of the money, haven't we?"

"That won't be a problem for you."

"Prudence ain't just a girl's name," he smiled thinly. "I'll work within the allowances we all get for this. Money ain't the issue…it's winning on ideas, get it? I'm here in a studio so my views and those of my supporters are beaming out…the constituency will grow. Being here is enough, for now." John finished in a voice that was almost a growl; his intent was unmistakable and the viewers would see it. He had caught a glimpse of his image on the nearby monitor screen.

"Your platform lacks breadth and there's no depth to your policy, like those of the main parties…ours in particular on social and neighbourhood issues. We connect with residents and with the voter's needs, with their hopes and fears. Voters hate remoteness from them. A man with a corporate…moneyed background fits their image of an opportunist, a bored mid-lifer with no real experience of what they have to face but wanting to meddle. You'd be seen as *'outside it'*…someone unable to deal with the political realities."

John gave no sign that Steve Cruz's direct and personal assault had wounded him. He was not conflict averse as some commentators would have it said of him; he worked to a slow burning fuse and the moment to reply would come. A reaction before the show's end would have to be found, and quickly, for the viewer or listener to ponder upon. He needed to find a way to have the last word.

"Well?" the show's host prompted him. It was both a question and an expression of surprise at the verbal barbs directed at John who scribbled in his pocket book as he was spoken to.

"Well," he smiled as he raised his eyes from his notes, "all I can say is that to me arrogance breeds contempt and closes minds. Far from being *'outside it'* I'm on the street talking to the very people I aim to be of service to. I'll also continue working with local action groups in neighbourhoods that need more time and resources devoted to them. As for political realities…I don't come with any political baggage. I've seen you people at work from the outside…I've run a major international company from the inside. All I needed was a public affairs expert to confirm to me what I already knew and to remind me what past mistakes have cost the City and some of the people in it. As you know I've got Jacqueline Purcell on my team…and it's not so small now. So, you'd better keep your eyes open…I'm not on the outside looking in anymore, but right here amongst you two and your parties with a message. I'm not going away because of others thinking they have a claim or a divine right to the status quo."

"And the rich folk, John Kahn's kindred spirits? What about them? Are they with him on the Odyssey to get elected?"

"You don't get it do you? *Inclusivity*, or everyone together, that's what my platform is about, not division or the setting of one group of people against another in some kind of social struggle. That's passe' and will get the city nowhere. If that's what you're peddling I aim to make you fail. The mood's changed hereabouts by my reckoning…maybe you should try to switch on and tune into it!"

It did not take long for reaction to the evening's current affairs show to come through. The office called saying breathlessly and against the din of ring tones in the background that the *'phones were a jumpin'*.

"Let them ring…make 'em hungry!" John laughed and looked for agreement from his team as they hurried to another meeting. But it was coffee and donuts first. It was scheduled as a low-key meeting but he was prepared; he never let go of hard-learned lessons, either out in the field where it could get you killed if you screwed up or in the business world.

"If I may say so, you're gripping things awful fast John," Jacqueline said admiringly when they had a quiet moment together. His cell-phone trilled in his jacket pocket.

"Thanks to you, Jacqueline…anyway, the longer they wait the more time I'll get on air. Spontaneous questions will give way to a more planned interview." He looked at the screen of the 'phone. There were calls waiting, from two of the women in his life. "Speak to you later, hm? I've got these calls to take?"

"Okay…and, you're right. Make the callers think you're in demand."

Yeah, he thought; one or both want a piece of me and there are only so many hours in a day or the night.

37

He had made a short set-piece speech and now turned to a questioner who asked him of his experience, what he had that made him a credible candidate for the Primaries. 'They're the ones that count' he added mischievously.

"I have the credentials…the business experience to run for the office of City Mayor. You can look back at some previous holders of the post…they came with political pedigrees that withstood all scrutiny but they still failed to deliver on what they promised."

"So!" someone in the crowd called out, "trying and failing is a recommendation is it, pal?"

There was laughter at the inquisitor's disrespect but interest was heightened in how this new Mayoral candidate would react.

"I don't have a hand-book of well worn clichés and orthodox…well-worn and outdated phrases and ideas to call on. Ignorance of the failures of the past I don't have either. I live and work here in this city, remember? I help out in good and not so good…not bad, but tough and hard-to-get by neighbourhoods. I mix with and talk to folks that see others getting on with their lives and wanting the same! They don't ask or talk to me about any special favours. They want a floor, some solid ground to stand on that gives them a steady step to set out on a path…then a wider space and finally, a road on the way to what gives them the same chance as anyone else."

"Man! You mean a comfort blanket!"

"Heck no! That's too comfortable and childlike…I'd call it a foundation on which those less fortunate can rely…to me a comfort blanket means treating folks as incapable or defenceless."

"Some are buddy…read the papers…speak to those you walk…or drive by."

"Listen up!" he couldn't help falling into old and he thought forgotten habits, the way he used to talk to men under his command. "Hear me out, please? I mean defenceless in the way some folks believe others have no inner will to succeed or deal with what they have to face; but they have! Only the politicians I've spoken of…"

"You're elite man, officer class…what you really do in 'Nam?"

The interruptions broke his rhythm; he would have to get through these and make his point when the antagonism had been quelled by his answers, if those that he gave were accepted.

"Sergeant…that's what, with a bunch of grunts! I took the heat…I've stayed on the street and heard what it can be like for many folks in this city. I learnt it in the front line then and I'm doin' so again now. I learnt in the MC and since…if you get the basic tools to win through…a helping hand…nothing soft mind, then the rest is up to you, each and every one of us to take the chance that comes our way. You can see it as a comfort blanket if you want. To me it's a rain-sheet or a shield, anything to keep out what may harm you while you set out on making your dream, however big or small, come true. Or it's something to help you get so close to your wish that you can almost touch it, to work at making it happen. It's no substitute for your own will…what you've got deep inside you…that inner spirit We've all got it."

"Right man…"

"Yeah, that inner spirit or engine that drives you on. We all have gifts so don't go looking on any help as a substitute for what you've got. It's for many a jumping off point, security for them to get up and fly a little ways…to rest up…then fly some more."

"Right again man…you tell 'em." There was one supporter who helped him along; John nodded in acknowledgement of the support he took from him.

"The city can't live on just relying on one group with "money" as some see it, to keep the rest or help them out…all folks need to play their part…some more than others."

"So who pays man? Who gives and who takes, some cut the deals while others suffer?"

"Sure, but we'd all work on that…you and me, all of us in our own ways…in bigger or lesser shares, not just in cash but in muscle and effort…by using our heads…dispense knowledge of how it works to make it better for many."

"Yeah sure…"

"Don't laugh, man," he smiled at one tormentor. "I'm sick of hearing and reading about one group settling scores with another for what they did…or didn't do…years, weeks or months ago. It's negative and divisive…see my point?"

"That why you're Independent?" another voice below him struck up. He was glad others were engaged.

"Sure, I don't have to follow all of the rules someone else made up so that we all run on the same track, on a different engine maybe but with the same smoke coming out of the stack. I'd prefer to check out the good and bad in an idea, pick up on what works…or works a little better and bring fresh enthusiasm…and watch it roll on, better and straighter…"

"Higher even…"

"Right…or faster and further. There's only so many ideas and beliefs you can have…you cut them or slice them any which way you want but the basic material stays the same, people have their wants and it comes down to how you can deliver on them."

"What you know about that? You've only been in business!"

John smiled. "At least we're having an exchange of ideas. Yeah, I'm in business, and I know what it's like to earn the dollars to pay the wages of hundreds of folks. I keep on learning how hard it is to…to think ahead, to think smarter and avoid the traps that can foul you up or slow you down in achieving your goal." It was all too conversational but he could see from his vantage point on the stage that his audience were willing to listen; it sounded too homespun but also there was a visceral flush of honest intent, in a core of beliefs that he was expressing. "It's living as honestly as you can and avoiding the traps."

"Like history coming up and biting you! In the butt!" someone called out.

"Yeah," he let the words out real slow "that's right!". Anna Beth suddenly came to mind in a split second moment of recall. It threw him off guard to think of her in these surroundings. "Right…" he said again absent-mindedly then shook his mind free. "I'll work to avoid repeating the mistakes of the past. The juices don't flow in me from the hard graft of just politics, that's for those who want to talk not act. I'd rather ride a raft over the rapids of problems, find a course that settles differences by the strength of argument or commitment, it's not for me the stronger man that wins but the one with the better and deliverable ideas."

"Or some new ones!" yelled a woman from a group at the back of the small meeting room.

"I'm glad we agree on something, ladies and gentlemen!" He laughed then paused to take a deep breath; the water in the tumbler that stood shielded from view on the neat podium tasted well on his dry lips "Consensus ain't such a dirty word when lives or the environment folks live in is at stake."

He caught sight of Jacqueline waving her papers and drawing her fingers across her slender throat. Okay, cut it short now was the message but the audience seemed to be of a mix that he had to appeal to, a varied constituency who relied on the support of the city and Federal handouts. He sensed he was amongst a constituency that remained to be persuaded and the interruptions had lessened; yet he could not dispel the impression that he was a rich boy coming to tell them how to live their lives; no, maybe even to lecture them. I'll have to try and make it even more conversational, the approach was beginning to work. A willingness to meet the interruptions that came his way head on had won him a few friends. He could see it on the faces of those seated closest to him; the lines had softened, they sat relaxed in their seats and earlier belligerence was now muted. They *'cut him some slack'* and he even dared to hope that he had won those over to his side; he had given voice to his ideas and they had begun to listen.

"Anything else you gotta say, Mr John?" a woman in the front row waved enthusiastically at him.

"Yes ma'am," he smiled, answering her in overdone politeness, but it scored a mark. "I'm almost through talking…remember this of me…I want to persuade you that there can be another way to govern this City. We don't have to polarise views…folks in opposite corners of a ring waiting for the bell to chime. For me there's another way…independence of thought and action that gets to the objective your aiming for. It spells out freedom from the signs of four years of doin' things one way…followed by four or more years of doin' it another…like some crazy metronome swinging this way then that. I'm not finishing our meeting by asking you to ignore what's gone before…just weigh up how it's been and wonder at how it could be…a new beginning. Take time to compare that with how it's been before and how it's going now. Is it better or does it feel like all your yesterday's repeating on you, and not for the better? If you're persuaded it could be different…that it *will be* different, then join me? We'll work on it together."

"Right!" said the woman who seemed to be on his side.

He waved to her and then to the crowd.

"Thank you for your time! If you've got a concern or want me to think about something that affects your neighbourhood in its own distinct way then let me know…the address or 'phone line number to contact me, and my staff, is on the paper some of you are waving at me. I hope it's to say *'good luck, we're with you'*?"

With a lightness of step he jumped down the short flight of steps from the stage.

"Phew!" Jacqueline smiled at him, "that was spontaneous stuff…grade A."

"Thank you."

"Dayle…hello, stranger."

"Nico…this is a surprise."

"It's been a while, I know."

"But you got through…"

"I still followed your star."

She gave him a winning smile. "And it brought you here?"

"Clever…"

"There's always the 'phone Nico, only you didn't call."

"No."

"So, what brings you to a meeting hall, in the Bronx of all places? I thought this kind of event was strictly for your syndicated boys…your correspondents?"

"Not always. Besides, I get the chance to see your man at work, on the political hustings."

"And?"

"He's quite something…not like the guys I'm used to seeing or reading about. The political game takes on a new dimension over here. And…I see that he's very controlled, nothing gets to him."

"Or it doesn't help to show it…even if something did, or someone managed to."

"Is that a secret?"

"No, it's a statement of fact. You don't go showing any weakness…that way you're not exploited."

"I'll bear it in mind, Dayle."

"And, what I'm saying might apply to quite different circumstances." She looked around but nothing seemed to hold her attention for long; she met his gaze once more. "What are you really doing here?"

"Noting everything down…the upbeat mood, who is here to see and listen to your man, the mix of people taking an interest." He spoke in a matter of fact tone of voice but looked at her all the time. "And, I've been taking a few shots on this camera…I can mail them on."

"Who to?"

"Interested people…those back in the office, in Amsterdam. It's archive stuff…there's not much they don't already have, on all the candidates."

He wasn't sure if he should go into all the detail. The deal had been to follow this guy who was running for Mayor; he had been told, *'keep checking him out'*. There was an upside to the instructions; they gave him every chance that he'd meet up with Dayle Kahn. He'd struck lucky that evening.

"I can imagine…"

"Tonight it's the scene here, at other venues…maybe something else catches the eye and it's different." Nico shrugged. "I never know until I'm at a venue what's going down. Tonight's fresh…get me?"

"No." She was made to smile on seeing his impudent grin. I sure have missed seeing that, she thought.

"Well…right now it's listening to him and picturing how John Kahn looks. He's a changed man…"

"Is he?" She turned to follow Nico's gaze.

"Yeah, he seems to have his policy all worked out…or he's well briefed."

"Both…the team's bigger and even more in tune with what's goin' down out there."

"And you're at home with it too?"

"Sure."

"I see and read about it. I know your hands are on some of the publicity stuff he puts out. I guessed it was your idea…the car stickers?"

"Jokey fun…"

"But the message is clear…"

"Nice of you to say it…but a lot of what you see or read is put out by the Indy Party…it's not an individual thing."

"But someone has to get the sparks flying…get the ideas out there." He moved closer. They were jostled by the crowd as it slowly began to disperse and he had reason to think why that should be. People talked in little groups and held onto leaflets and gestured, as if to make a point about something that had been said to arouse their interest.

Dayle kept looking from him to the stage. Her Pop stood in front of a camera crew and was in conversation with a reporter. She was holding a wool-covered microphone out to him to speak into. He looks so at ease she marvelled, it's as though he's become a new man. Others wanted to talk to him too; the night would draw out unless he did something.

"He's full of ideas...he's kept this side of him from everyone." She beamed with pride and waved to John as he looked down in her general direction. He felt prompted to wave back and she saw him make a further comment about who it was in the crowd waving at him.

"I guess you've got to go?"

"Yes, I may have to. There are other things to see and do before this day's through. You?"

"Got a few moments to meet up with me?"

"No...no, I can't." She was taken aback.

"Okay...just an idle thought."

Her mind cleared.

"That's how I see it too, Nico." They stared at each other in silence and Dayle watched him put away the camera and belt up the bag with his notebooks. "You really do say the first thing that comes into your head don't you?"

"Meaning what, Dayle?"

"You tell me? You ask me if I could meet up with you as if there are other things just as important just then for you to do."

"No finesse," he said in a light self-critical voice.

"You said it...I didn't have to."

"No."

"Just ask me, and do it nicely," was all she said and stood closer to him once more.

"Okay," he smiled. "Meet me for a drink later? Will you do that, please?" he finished with a soft plea.

"Yes, I will but, there will be no talk of this, any of it." She waved her hand to encompass the venue. "It's just us two, talking and being together... listening to what we can say to each other that does not include work...any of it, yours or mine."

"It would have been so some time back, but you're a busy lady..."

"I'm too young for the word, *'lady'.*"

"Pretty woman then?"

"Better...that sounds better, Nico."

"I'll call you." He prepared to leave.

"Hey, when?"

"In an hour or so, say ten o'clock?"

"Don't you go bothering with that." Dayle waved at her father who beckoned to her. Jacqueline was close by arranging interviews. "I'll go and tell him I'm leaving now...the rest of the evening is prepping for tomorrow. I'm not needed for that...but I'll check what the plans are."

"And we've got a date?"

"Looks that way. Wait here, please?"

"I've lost the will to move," he laughed and made out he was rooted to the spot, helpless. She met his intense gaze and touched his arm.

"I won't be long."

I've got to live separate lives she thought as she made her way through the crowd. The life I've been thinking of as he spoke to me, one that may include a guy like Nico. That life hasn't even begun yet but I know where I can make a start.

Dayle hesitated as she approached John.

The crowd gathered about him was bathed in the glow of bright TV camera lighting. A microphone was thrust from behind the first rank of onlookers before the reporter could be fully seen.

"Your platform is based on change...trust me to deliver, is that the message?" she began.

"Shelley diMarco...watch out," Jacqueline whispered. He gave a curt nod to acknowledge her warning.

"Mr Kahn...John...do we need to take your word about your service record, all of it? Some politicos throw that out in their resume' to create wider credibility...the safe pair of hands syndrome. Is it true of you too?"

"Directly put and yes, it's true. You could look it up but to reassure you I've got a better idea." John turned to a close aide. "Hold this?"

He gave the man his jacket then pulled at his tie.

"What...?" the interviewer began but her eyes looked intriguingly at him, at the slender fingers unbuttoning the shirt. She avoided the insistent, penetrating stare of John Kahn's eyes. "There's no need for that..."

She realised too late where her words were taking him.

"There sure is...you started this and I'm sure as hell going to finish it. Some just *talk* a good fight. I got *involved* and took the heat, I accepted the draft!" He sneered. "But then your researchers must have told you all about that?" The interviewer looked back dumbly then shook her head. "I thought so, sloppy work ma'am," he said concealing his anger. "Anyway, it was to many people at the time a damn fool thing to do...taking the draft, but you'll understand when I tell you that if you believe in something you'll do all you can to achieve it. Get my drift?"

"Sure. Achieve your ends by fair means or foul, is that what you're telling me?"

"No it isn't, not at all! What I'm saying is you devise a policy and you work to see it through…if it's hurtin' folks you're big enough to make corrections, so you don't make your way at the expense of innocents."

"The history of that time didn't come over to me like that…not at all."

"No…and the history lessons you read clearly didn't tell you how I and many others dealt with orders. I listened and found the route through to the objective; whenever I could I followed the line of least cost to the people with me."

"Eliminate the opposition…talk later?"

"No…not always. In my field of experience lives lost was an argument lost…that way could have cost me…cost me more than I was willing to pay at the time. I had to find another way…most times I did, but one time other hearts and minds thought differently from me and I nearly paid for it."

"Meaning?" The interviewer stared at him, off camera. Her dishevelled crew looked on, keeping him in shot and tightly focussed. "What now?" she asked him with the hint of a curious smile.

"This!" He bared his left shoulder and revealed a neat smooth skinned depression. "Any lower, just an inch or so…either way…and a telegram from the WD…the War Department…"

"I know, what 'WD' means."

"Good. I'm glad to hear it. Any lower and a telegram to my grieving wife and family was on its way."

"I don't think we need go into all that," she said coldly looking away but the camera stayed on him; Shelley's team had seen the moments as an opportunity not to be wasted on idle interview speak. They read the signs like him; the pictures saved a lot of breathy words.

"Why? Too close up and real for you?" He deftly fastened his tie. "I didn't raise the war issue, you did. It's history! Talk to me of what gives here in the City, or what my plans may be. Ask me any question you like about what I've had to say tonight in this room! Above all, leave out events that don't concern younger folk anymore like they did for me and my buddies of the day."

"You broke with what your contemporaries took for convention," she began but whatever line of questioning the script told her should be pursued John did not allow her to finish.

He interrupted with a flourish. "Right on, Shelley! You've made an important point for me! Thank you, people will come to see that a break with convention is not something to be afraid of, but for me that meant doin' something different in very distinct and dangerous circumstances. What happened then was not the time to stand aside and let others take the heat."

"It's a raw thing with you...even now," she taunted.

Her station represented another view and the tape could be syndicated. John heard only the one word of whispered warning from his aide and acknowledged again that it had registered.

He kept his cool but answered her unsmiling. Sure, he was riled deep down, but she or the audience if they ever aired the full interview would see the calm exterior.

"I'll put the record straight Shelley...let me repeat it once and for all. I went. What others chose to do in my family or beyond that circle is for them and their own conscience. Mine's quite clear and it has been all these years since I took the draft. I came through and I learned from it...I stood by some comrades and they're with me, even now."

"Mr Kahn...John."

"I hope you've got what you wanted from this unscheduled moment," he smiled, interrupting her. "I sure have, Shelley. You've done me a big favour...my team will agree on that too, I'm sure. We can talk, babble words as long as you have time but a picture tells it all so much better. You have a nice evening, now?"

He turned on his heels.

"Mr Kahn...thank you."

"Gladly done," he said over his shoulder then turned. "And any time," his lips barely moved. "Only, next time ask me what my plans are for the City...that's what folks really want to hear." He gave a curt nod, then smiled. "Never mind me...some things run deep but it doesn't give you or me any reason to talk about it." The interview was at an end.

"Where to now...what's the next venue?" he asked his aides as he strode away in the direction of the exit doors. "Where's Dayle?"

38

"Would it bother you if we hitched a ride, with John Kahn?" She tilted her head enquiringly. "We can go so far as Kahn Tower, we'll be at the centre of life there."

Nico had watched Dayle almost from the moment she had left his side only to be delayed by the little media scrimmage on the platform. The girl, or 'pretty woman', had been engaged by what had unfolded before her eyes and he had turned his attention to John Kahn's over-reaction at the line of questioning; it had clearly provoked him into turning the event into a publicity stunt.

"It doesn't bother me, much," he began.

"Good…"

"The thing is I remember us saying that we'd leave all this behind and have nothing to talk of except what we could think up…the spontaneous to-and-fro…boy-meets-girl stuff, on a date."

"Charmingly put…so, not such a good idea to you?"

Nico shrugged. These are Kahn's you're dealing with, man.

"It puts both of us on guard."

"I don't follow you…against what?"

"I get asked questions about what I do, and I'll be tempted…against my promise to you and beyond enduring, to ask John Kahn some of my own."

"So? It's what you paper guys fret over…you'd do anything for a few moments alone with a '*name*'…and with no interruptions. Here's your chance, almost gift wrapped."

"And I get to be with you," he went on. "You forget…I'm different."

He could imagine his interest in this pretty woman, in Dayle, being compromised or affecting his work…even his loyalty. He had no doubt that Gerard or Hans would seize the moment, but he would feel torn between doing right by them, the people who paid his salary, and the woman now standing before him. Yep! She was a feast to the eyes, chic, sparky and so feisty, and all of her beautifully wrapped. At first, he had pursued her to gather news and to persuade Dayle to reveal some anecdote that would help his inquiring bosses. Now, as she looked at him and waited on his decision to travel with the mayoral candidate, securely enclosed in some utility vehicle, he knew that he sought her out, the woman, for her company, hers alone.

"Well, what do you say?"

He listened to her and it occurred to him that he could liken the situation to the princess and the pauper, only, he'd have none of that. There was no sense of inferiority at work in him at all; they lived and breathed in the same air. John Kahn's message was to reach out across social divides and personal circumstances featured in policy pronouncements. He could see what needed to be done and was in the Bronx for that very reason. No area of the city, no street or sidewalk was seen as no-mans land to him or the Indy Party, as they were being called. The shortening of the name held its own message; people used it as a sign of affection or recognition, not disapproval or distaste.

"Sorry…" he said at last. The flurry of thoughts seemed to have silenced him for a long time.

"What's it to be Nico?"

251

"We take the subway, or a cab. We see the city under the lights and travel through the places to be governed by John Kahn, if he makes it to being the Mayor."

"I don't see why you're passing up the chance…"

"There's a reason…" No time remained for him to offer an explanation.

John Kahn now stood behind her with Jacqueline, the aide who had delivered a rousing speech on the party's organisation and the help citizens could find at the *call in* centres. She had made it very clear, they were places to meet and talk with real people, not a disembodied voice to speak to on the end of a phone line. What Jacqueline hadn't told the gathering was that these call in places were also where persuasive arguments were deployed to increase party enrolment. From what he heard they were succeeding.

"Hello, pleased to meet you, sir."

The formal mode of address echoed his upbringing and the Dutch way of greeting a stranger. Okay, so John Kahn didn't quite fit that description but there was no sense in forgetting his manners. He was learning all about the guy through his own research and enquiries, but he wanted all the time available to be with his girl, Dayle.

John's handshake was vice like and the inquisitive look unwavering. "John Kahn, glad to meet you. Foreign press, right?"

"By association…I'm research and investigation. I look at the background… see what's in the public domain."

"Or what's not." John winked at him

"Yes sir." Nico spoke out involuntarily.

"You're offered a lift…a ride, with us if that's what you want. It saves Dayle some time…she works too hard."

"I know…but, she knows it's for a good cause."

"She tell you that?"

"In her own way…"

"Okay…sorry, but I've got things to do. You're welcome to come along. There'll be no questions asked and no favours given. It's just a ride. Delroy, my driver…he's over there, he knows his way around these parts like no other."

John gave Delroy a 'thumbs up' sign to acknowledge that he was ready to leave.

"And I'm learning about them too…so that my paper understands and can write about how your policies aim to put things right or help people."

"Both…we aim to do both." John spoke confidently. He still had an audience. "How far we go and how we set about doin' it is why I'm here…folks can tell us, or me, how it's got to be for them. It's also what we find out for ourselves. At the root of it all is partnership."

"Which paper did you say you're from? Jacqueline asked.

"I didn't."

She let it pass. "The story's out on the streets and in the Boroughs."

"That's right." John looked at Dayle. "Decide on the plan and do it quickly…please?"

"I'll be with you…give me a minute?" She waited until she was alone with Nico once more. "Why are you making such a big thing of the ride? Take it, take up the offer? Besides, I thought we had a date."

"Sorry…but no, no thanks. Family and transport arrangements got in the way."

"You give up too easily."

"Oh no!" He shook his head and gave her a rueful smile. "I bide my time, that's all. Tonight wasn't right. Take care of yourself?"

"Yeah…will you follow my star?"

"Yes, I will!" he laughed and Nico saw that her disappointment, even anger, at not going on with him had lessened. Then, he did something impetuous. He kissed her.

"Don't get lost," she whispered.

"I think I already am."

Dayle nodded. "Then we meet…some other time, real soon maybe?"

"Yeah count on it. About the lift offer? It was too close and personal."

"Explain it all to me, some time, *real* soon?" She touched his arm and left without a backward glance.

39

Amsterdam – Gerard's Flat

A frown of irritation briefly crossed her face and left it just as quickly. "Sorry."

"Okay…is it too sunny out here?"

Edith shook her head. "No…it's wonderful to be able to just sit here with you and take pleasure from these quieter moments."

"Oh…are your thoughts on another time then?" Gerard had come to recognise the look, but for a pleasant change they had not yet discussed her 'cause celebre' over breakfast.

"Yes, but not that long ago…just a time when there was peace and not the piercing drone of scooters, a time when I didn't feel so irritated by the noisy intrusion of machinery all of the time."

"Easier to park mind you…and it's mobility for the not so rich amongst us."

He thought back to the previous evening, before they had tumbled into bed and pleasured each other. Edith had arrived at his flat and gazed in wonder, first at the surroundings she had been brought into then at him. It sparked a passionate reaction that seemed to confirm in her the decision she had reached about their relationship only a few months previously. She waltzed past him, taken in by the 'riot of colour, the use fabrics and the items of pottery' – the words came in a bubbling flurry. Edith said she felt so at home, nothing appeared to be synthetic.

"It's all natural…I don't have anything that's man-made, well," he remembered adding quickly, "man's had a hand in it obviously…little is made by machines, let me put it that way."

She had marvelled at the earthenware, the large jars he had found in Italy, the leather chair on it wooden staved frame he had picked up, in Paris was it? He couldn't quite remember the market where he had been persuaded to take it from, for a pittance it seemed to him. Some poor Mexican family had made it and probably earned little for their trouble and considerable manual skills of creation.

He heard Edith's calling to him. "Sorry…sorry…" he smiled.

"I was saying, lievert…what mobility? Nose to tail and it wrecks the Old City…"

"Yes…yes," he acknowledged her observations but his mind was still on someone, somewhere, taking advantage of another and the extension of entrepreneurial zeal to everything, almost to the act of just living.

"…it spoils the quiet even out here." She gave a derisive laugh. "Listen to me! I'm sounding old and crusty…"

"Look as beautiful as you do now and I'll be with you forever…crusty or not."

She smiled then turned her head away, lifting her face to the warmth of the sun as she did so, eyes closed.

"I want to go there…the USA…on holiday, with you," she said without moving from her pose.

"Why?" he replied before pausing. "And…is that the sole reason, a holiday with me?"

Edith pouted; it was her way of acknowledging his directness. "To take in at first hand what they possess and the world they live in. Collections of pictures and files of papers is one thing…seeing will make it all seem real."

"Lievert…" he was unable to give voice to the nagging doubts that remained. Edith turned abruptly to look at him.

"I'll feel closer to the people and the path they've trodden since Frederick took Margaretha and they went their own way...that's one answer to your '*why*'." Edith gave no sign that she would soften the tone she had begun to answer him with.

"Fine."

"Is it?" she asked before they fell silent.

They sat and a few rare moments of peace could be enjoyed, no sounds of cars in the street below or motor scooters rose up to disturb them; they could just make out the twittering of sparrows in the plane trees beneath the balcony, even the cooing of doves.

"Do something for me?" he asked gently and, leaning across the narrow table, he brushed her face with his fingertips. She pressed against the caress.

"Anything, you know it..."

"Write down and seal in an envelope what you want from the trip."

"We're going?" she smiled, happier now at this concession from him.

Gerard shrugged to indicate an enigmatic answer. "Write down...your expectations and your fears. Note also how you believe deep down in that loving heart of yours...your true feelings about outcomes, and...whether you think your feelings will change from what you discover."

"Why should I do that, Ger? I prepared myself for months not to gain anything...then you came to me, we found things out together. So tell me why I should write anything down...like some testament."

She had used the very word he had thought of.

"I want...I pray...that deep down you will remain the person I often see...that I want to remain with. Once the pursuit of closure to past events is done with I want that little testament to be opened and that you will have no regrets, none at all."

"I tell myself every day...I lecture the image in the mirror each morning that I am after fairness, the admission that a wrong was done and that somehow we can hold out hands to each other and bring two sides of the family together again."

"Write it down, lievert – 'my hopes, my fears', put it all down; above all, Edi, 'this is me...this is how I feel.'"

"And you? What about you, what will you do?"

"The same."

"The same as what you're telling me to record?"

"Asking you...suggesting that you do it."

"Why?"

"To make it clear in your mind before we go 'on holiday' what you are going for and why. Call it self analysis."

"I'm not so introverted..."

255

"Aren't you? Isn't there just a trace of wish fulfilment about all this?"

"No!"

"What we have is anecdotal, just a few snapshots of historical events; there's a thread binding them but," he added directly, "it's so loose...the intervals between any significant events are too long to make a solid or even believable case."

"We found a receipt!" Edith replied as she shook out her napkin. "It's a start and makes a point."

"What else?" Ger paused, provocatively, but she remained silent. "That's right, we have little else, or not enough to make a solid case." He nodded sagely as if to reinforce the correctness of his analysis. "A receipt is all we have and a few stories about what happened...or what we understand some folks were told had happened...none of that is *really* going to hurt him now."

"Except perpetuating a lie...being complicit in that will count for something! He's part of a routine that still covers up a misdeed! There's been no effort over the years to try and make good the hurt."

"And why should he do that, hm? Why should the family over there think about doing that? There's been a de facto divorce...a schism between the two sides of the family for what...how long?" He shrugged for some effect but Edith merely stared sullenly at him. "It's over a century ago when it happened...and we don't know for sure that the money was never paid back."

Edith's eyes widened in surprise. "You've kept your change of mind very quiet! I didn't realise you were having second thoughts!"

"I'm being practical," he replied evenly. "I'm really trying to find the way to obtain some redress for past events. How to make them...John Kahn himself, if he's so involved with it's concealment or paying for silence...it's how to have them make up to your side of the family. Edith? To me, succeeding at that is the trick...the goal or objective to aim at. The fall-out from any revelations is the follow up story." The journalist in him would be rewarded.

"And it risks opening up an old wound with your side of the family." Edith brought him back to the reality of the possible outcome their disclosures would provoke.

"Ja! There's that too, but we were going to make up for that weren't we?"

"You're talking in the past tense...as if it's all over."

"Was I? I'm sorry..." he held his hand out to her in reassurance. "It's not over, lievert...only I can't break a carefully learnt habit or forget a lesson."

"Oh?"

"Ja," he sighed. "I'm taking stock and checking what we have…where we really are with this or where we can go…what we have on him in that little knowledge pool of ours that can pay some kind of dividend."

"We can go out and expose him and the family he represents for what they are!"

"But he…John Kahn…he didn't *commit* the crime," Ger answered too reasonably.

"Oh? Are you now telling me that being part of the cover up doesn't amount to complicity? Everything he now enjoys began from the head start that family got at the expense of our family…at a cost to my side of the family…mine, over here!"

"And? And so…?"

"And so?" she spoke in a disbelieving tone and in a softer voice, "you're teasing me. I never thought you'd do that, not over something that you know means so much to me."

Edith left him sitting in the sunshine and shuffled about in his cavernous living room. He really had bought a wonderful apartment and she marvelled at the collection of artefacts on the shelves and the pictures hung on the high walls that showed the extent of his travels and Gerard's tastes. She laid face down a small, framed, picture of Monique glancing at it only briefly and thinking *'you're history too'*. Her absence did not persuade Ger to come inside and make up.

"I'm not teasing you," he said in greeting upon Edith's return to his side. "I'm just being analytical; it's the reason why I disfigure my good looks with these." Ger smiled weakly and pointed to his glasses.

"It's the man inside…the real you I want to know not the outer shell."

"And you've got me…a man who has to weigh up the evidence and see what we have and then considers…with you…how we can achieve an objective that on the face of the evidence is getting more difficult. So much seems to be going John Kahn's way…"

"Is it? He's riding a small wave…"

"But he's not way out," Ger answered and thought of how he could expand on the metaphor she had brought to mind. "The ocean's floor is shelving, the beach is getting nearer and the wave is growing higher. Here, look at these?" He tossed over a small bundle of papers clipped together that comprised newspaper cuttings that Nico had scanned and e-mailed to him overnight.

"More work for me, instead of…? " Edith smiled suggestively.

"Later. Look at them! Our John…our cousin John…he may be a rookie at this political game but experience and reading these articles tells me that we need to take the man and his message seriously…very seriously. Others seem to be doing just that. I know some of the writers of the pieces you hold… they're not easily fooled. The audiences he speaks to and the reports of those meetings tell of a man in whom others are taking more of an interest."

He loved Edith's almost child-like obsession, the search for the truth and the *"righting of a wrong"*. Why was he so cynical, so gnarled by experience that he distrusted still his own instinct for the story? The simpler the language used to describe the wrong the harder it would be to refute or deny. The years had passed and no-one had sought redress. But times and people changed, the mistakes of the past had to be revisited, the story had to be retold and an ending put to it. The world had grown small and communication shrank distance until it felt as if everyone was your neighbour…just reach out and touch, you could almost be that close.

"Put it down on paper, lievert. I'll do the same and when it's all over, with an ending or not, for better for worse," he smiled, "we'll open the testaments over a glass of champagne, here…in my apartment…or in a restaurant on Crooked Tree Water…if there is one. We'll remind ourselves of what we noted down and felt about it then."

"Accord! It's a deal!" Edith smiled brightly.

"That's better! Do that again! Now you're the girl I'm falling for," he smiled back at her.

Gerard viewed the short video clip the New York office had sent him. Nico was out-of-the-loop this time as Ellen Maguire's covering e-mail had told him that Nico had been pictured with Dayle Kahn at a 'party'; it was nothing heavy, the Home & Lifestyle researcher had said, but for him an association was being made of a couple out together. He would not involve himself in any enquiry of its seriousness or question his colleagues integrity; the girl was gorgeous and Nico a good-looking guy; but, he had voiced his misgivings about getting too close to the subjects under investigation and personal entanglements led to conflicts of interest.

"Time now to take charge myself," he muttered as the mail was put away in the ever expanding file that contained a diffuse collection of social snaps of the "target" and his business dealings. Anecdotal the information might be, yet it all counted. He would have to pursue Edith's money and John Kahn, the family Kahn, in his own way.

The interview clip was brief and yet there was another clue that he could focus on out of the few exchanges that had been recorded. He had to listen to it again to make sure. Ellen had been asked to record any interviews or news items she came across without any guidance being given on the content he was really looking for. The outwardly worthy still had *'prior'*, as he had once heard an entry on a life's register described, happenings or deeds that had yet to be discovered. The unlikeliest event or the answers to a line of banal questions could still yield vital information. He had listened to the clip twice; this time he made some notes as it played.

John Kahn said he was 'in trouble'; the revelation of the cause followed quickly. He had taken the draft to *prove his citizenship* of the family's adopted country. From that time on, until he declaration of intent to stand for Mayor, he had worked on business and the acquisition of private resources. As these grew he became more 'troubled'. He read the 'papers and heard the news. Making it 'big' was fine but he recognised a continuing need to give something back, on a personal level.

"Meaning what...?" Gerard said out loud as he continued scribbling down the words spoken in his scratchy short-hand.

'Doing citizenship meant so much more than simply *being* a citizen' he heard John answer his questioner. It was the reason for his involvement with charity work. John Kahn had not dissembled or moved his eyes on giving the short reply. He had done the 'journalism thing' long enough to see in the absence of the shifting body language that John Kahn was on the level.

"You're saying it often enough," Gerard mused. "People are beginning to believe you." He was following John's progress, the ratings followed an upward trend; his enquiring e-mails to contacts on Wall Street from earlier days in the City confirmed that much.

"So, you won't be too surprised when I come knocking at your door, will you, cousin John? When the moment comes, you can *do* the family thing!"

40
Getting To Know The Family

The heavy framed glasses detracted from his rugged good looks and the lenses distorted the gaze of Gerard's eyes. Edith had noted their intensity so many times but she loved the admiring stares he bestowed upon her. She had learnt that they were but an outwardly serious manifestation of a high-spirited loving man.

"Okay?" she smiled and wrought a smile from him as they sat close together on the flight to New York. They had been airborne for an hour, leaving Schiphol Airport on a late afternoon flight. "Do you need to look at all of those now?"

"Sorry, I just want to be sure I have everything." He kissed her forehead.

"It's too late to do anything about it," she told him simply.

"Ja!"

He took the notes and carefully rearranged them in the folio; it was a jumble of papers, collected photos and contact lists he had assembled in the months leading up to the nomination primaries. The whole project could now be over in days; there would no longer be any need to write any articles about John Kahn and his business interests and how they touched upon his Mayoral ambitions. That would all be consigned to history. Nico could chase after Dayle and his investigations into the man and his story would be consigned to background detail.

John Kahn would be the leader of a world known pharmaceuticals conglomerate who could act almost imperiously to protect intellectual copyright against all those who chose to take him on or who took issue with his company's policy.

"As for me...what then?" he spoke out softly.

"Hm?"

He would have no tag line for his stories about John Kahn. The conflicting morals of the man, as he perceived them, would no longer provoke the fierce mental conflict in Edith. Her quest for redress, or the admission to a family wrong, remained an endearing obsession and contrasted with his own calmer and considered assessment of their chances.

John Kahn had to become Mayor, a figurehead in a wider social context, if he was to be of any real use to Edith, or to him.

"He's quite a man, isn't he?" Edith whispered as she took a slip of paper with a picture of him from the folder.

John Kahn was an exception to the rule, considered by many a persuasive performer if all that he had seen and read about the man was to be believed. Independence Party candidates, well intentioned but often seen as no-hopers and with scant support had taken on a new prominence; they might yet win through in the elections for a borough post. They seemed to ride the wave that John Kahn's candidacy had generated. Some had called him a cool dude, to borrow a very old cliché, and these weren't comments on his dress sense. No, it was about his attitude; nothing seemed to rile him so he left little for people to use against him except his political argument and policy.

From that perspective he was an ingenue...a new kid on the political block.

And...the questions remained; why was he putting himself up for this and the aggravation of public office? It had been a phrase that he had seen in the newspaper cuttings e-mailed to him, commentaries printed by the local press and appearing with noticeable regularity; it seemed that others were acknowledging that the status quo of political life didn't need this kind of well-meaning but misguided intervention. Third parties formed alliances, they didn't go taking on the Establishment…or, not unless a heap of money was being thrown at the process because the candidate was on an ego trip.

Only, that wasn't the case here at all.

One correspondent had picked up on the theme, expressing disbelief at the reasons for John Kahn's candidacy. He had said *'it was to be different'*. It sounded trite, a cliché that fell from the lips of any aspirant for office. Didn't they all say that, and didn't everyone hearing it reply, 'yeah sure, you guys all say that as we learn to our cost later'.

"Well, we're going to find out soon enough about the man and his situation." Gerard took Edith's hand and kissed it. "We'll find out about the man together."

"Hm?"

"I said we'll find out all there is to know about the man on his own turf. Then after the next round…when the Primaries are out of the way we can decide again what's to be done."

"If he gets through."

"Edi…the man has gained momentum for his campaign…read the cuttings!"

"Easy to say."

"No doubts! He's a believable candidate…the papers are beginning to say it too. People will soon have a choice…they'll have to face up to the prospect of a complete outsider making it to the final election."

"And then?"

He couldn't understand her doubts about the man she had devoted so much time to. Tracing the bloodline, of being convinced that she had found a relative, and a man now absorbed by the pursuit of high office had been all consuming. They had even found each other again because of it.

"Edi, lievert…it's a choice between change and more of the same, a choice between a two party system or something new and very scary…government of New York City by a consensus of ideas and ideals."

"Isn't that what all elections are about?" She gave him an enquiring look but only saw Gerard's smile in reply. "What have I said that's so amusing?"

"Nothing lievert."

"Don't tease me." Gerard held a hand out to her. Edith moved but then changed her mind, lifting the armrest between them before clasping his hand to nestle closer against him. "That's better."

"There will be a shock to the city's political system. The consensus will be broken…or the belief shattered that only Democrat or Republican policies will work...and no one else's. It will all be shaken up if an interloper, a guy peddling a change of beliefs gets in...by splitting the vote. Better still, if he wins it by pure argument and belief in a policy shift. The consensus will, instead, be a mix and he will have forced people in the city to look at the political situation through new eyes. They'll have to make a real choice."

"Do you believe it'll happen?"

"There's no saying where it will go...but, it's getting interesting no mistake. It'll have to be a ministry of all the talents to get the people of the city on his side...he'll have to find people to work for and with him if John Kahn gets through to the very end."

"And that's it...IF he gets there, to the very end."

"Yes, possibly." Gerard gripped her hand tight. "Come on, let's hope for him...for your project, and that by getting this far others, many others are beginning to believe in our cousin John, the man. They may even think he can do it."

He spoke of it with wonder. Success on that scale would really be worth writing about.

"And we'll have to believe in it too, otherwise we won't get to where we want to be."

"You want to be," he said.

"No Ger, where *we* want to be." It was Edith's turn to squeeze a hand tightly, to reinforce the objective and aim of their trip. "I want John to succeed so that I can pursue my own ambitions for him...and, you so that a good story comes out of it."

"Okay lievert, okay. We're on a voyage of discovery, look on it that way. Even I can get excited about that."

41

"You've come a long way missy," Anna Beth observed with a slow smile on her lips. There was also the suspicious glint in her eyes, so still as they looked on the unexpected visitor. In her shaking hand she held the grainy family photograph that revealed the confidence on the faces of the sitters.

It had been Edith's best idea, a calling card that showed the early bloodline and used with great effect to hook her host. Time and distance had been no barrier to their meeting; the gambit had paid off.

"Yes aunt."

"I'm not that!" was Anna Beth's gruff reply. "Don't you go startin' me off on that journey!"

"But you are. The picture on the piano tells the story without any words from me…or you, from anyone here in America."

"Which one?" she asked. Suspicion of the beautiful young woman before her remained.

"Why, the one of Frederick Albert Kahn…there, the one in the gilt frame. It could almost be the one he packed when he left Amsterdam, all those years ago. My mother has one just the same…handed down through her side, my side of the family."

"I guess they made a few, more than one, anyways," Anna Beth said warily but in the strong voice she resorted to when she wished to intimidate. Only, this time the visitor's returning stare held no fear.

"Yes," Edith said gently.

The shock of her arrival was evident on Anna Beth's lined face but consideration for the woman gave way to excitement that even with the smallest piece of evidence close-by on the piano she felt wholly justified in making the long journey and calling by, unannounced. Surprise had been key, and it had worked.

"Why Frederick Albert alone, why not a picture of him with Margaretha? They were a couple, joined in wedlock."

"She's in our hearts and minds, even now. Our work here is a memorial to her and what she started…from nothing! Pictures of her are in the hall, you must have seen the portrait in the lobby? 'Twas painted by a man who recognised distinction, he had a feel for human permanence. Margaretha's work carries on, through me."

Edith thought on it; running off with your deceased sister-in-law's bequest to her children was not the act of anyone she would describe as distinguished or kind-hearted.

"Yes, and you have help."

Anna Beth snorted. "Course I do! The place is too big now to handle on my own or with a few helpers. The kids we help cost…they cost us all in time and money."

"Lucky for you that the family here helps out with the money side of the work you do…it must be a relief to know others care so much."

"We get by on gifts, that's true."

"Generosity of spirit is always welcome…"

"Yeah…"

"Even from those you might think were too far away to really gain anything from it except a good feeling…or, to make amends for something."

"You ain't been here long enough to go pushing your luck…get me, missy?"

"Edith…"

"Yeah, Edith...what you say the last name was?"

"Dekker..."

"Can't say I've ever heard it mentioned."

"Well, I'm glad you have now...and that we've met."

"What you got in that bag you hold so tight?"

"Pictures, of family...my home. They may give you some contact with the other side of the family...where your ancestors...and mine, come from."

"Only two started as my ancestors."

"One, Frederick Albert..."

"No! Two...both of them. Two ancestors by my reckoning...got it?"

"Yes, aunt." The word did not provoke another outburst, just the same wary glance of Anna Beth's eyes.

"They both left to start a new life...over here."

"Yes...from the little I know you have all done very well."

"Matter of opinion...but yes that's so, in spite of everything and anyone. Those of us here got on with it and made a life."

"And to think it was all done with little or no help...just a small stake to gamble on that new life...way across an ocean."

"Uh huh! You're the first, far as I know it, to even bother coming over here to find us."

"That's what I hear...still, special times need a special person. What do you think aunt?"

"I told you...once already, we don't know each other so's you can go calling me that."

"Well, you may get used to it?" Edith smiled, encouragingly. She was still in the room and would gradually get to say what was on her mind. "It's a shame no-one followed up the break after it all happened."

"Too far...any ways, folks here wrote back until the ties were loosened."

"People drifted apart..."

"Something like that."

"Or...others came between the early settlers and broke up the family who fled Amsterdam...with another's dream in their pockets."

"The family, as you call them, was not large...and they had their own dreams. We're few and we're spread out now...each with their own lives and interests to follow."

"And look after..."

"You can see what I do! This is what I look after...and the kids."

"What of the others in the family? Do you know much of them?"

"No."

"See much of them?" Edith asked directly. She looked at Anna Beth with unflinching eyes and took in every line on the majestic face before her.

264

"No."

"Okay..."

"Time and happenings saw to that...I reckon you know more than what you're tellin' me. Am I right or wrong, missy?

"Edith...and wrong. I don't know everything....wish I did, mind you."

"And you won't find out...from folks that we hardly know ourselves."

"I'm sorry," Edith smiled touching Anna Beth's arm briefly in an effort to calm the tension between them. "The excitement of coming here and seeing you for the first time...any relative over here...it's made me talk too much."

"An' ask fool questions..."

"Curiosity, that's all...to find out something about you all."

"There's a limit...get me, missy?"

"Edith, try calling me that?"

"Depends..."

Edith reached into the bag that she had clutched so tightly and prompting Anna Beth's earlier observations of it. Gerard had laughed at her in a gentle tease as they set off for the school and Anna Beth. *"Just like the first time we met, lievert,"* he said and finished with a gentle kiss before dropping her by the path leading to the school's imposing front door.

"Here, aunt...a greeting from my family...from way out there across an ocean."

"More than a hundred years," was Anna Beth's mumbled reply as she took the envelope with a card inside. It also held a photograph of Edith with her parents and a view of the Amsterdam street they lived on.

"Pardon me?" Edith had already picked up on the expression during her short stay in The States.

"I said it's a long time since anything like this was done."

"Times were different then, folks too as you put it." Edith's accent gave a homelier intonation to the word.

"Volk," Anna Beth repeated smiling.

"Ja!" Edith laughed. "Volk...people! We're just people over there and you...you're over here."

"Memories fade, people lose touch or they are lost...but, not quite all of them."

"Not to me...they won't be lost if I can do anything about it or to make up for what happened."

"Yeah, I can see that now, missy."

"Edith?"

"Yes, Edith." Anna Beth pushed a bell button set in the wall near to her favourite chair. "I'm forgetting my manners. Care for a drink? Tea is it you folks have at this time of the day?"

"Ja, graag…uhm, yes please."

"Got you the first time Miss Edith."

They laughed.

'It would work out', Edith thought.

'What's she after coming here out-of-the-blue like that, family or not? Anna Beth wondered as she studied the attractive and smartly dressed young woman before her.

"No one came looking, not even out of curiosity," Gerard mused, glad to have Edith by his side again, "until now."

"Yes…here I am, dragging you along behind me."

"Hardly!"

"Yes! It was an effort to persuade you, remember?" she smiled.

"Well you've put in its place another piece in the jigsaw, it'll help…it will demonstrate that we've done the necessary background checks to the story, and done them properly."

"And now? After all that I've told you, what do you think now?"

"We've a few more days, we can be tourists and still make some calls and read the papers…watch the TV bulletins and see what's being said. We'll get more when we finish the trip in New York…on his home patch."

Gerard leant against the door frame and called out to her above the drumming noise of the shower.

"It's not all going his way! The labour unions seem to have doubts about our cousin John!"

"What?"

Gerard peered round the corner of the screen; Edith's silhouette was enticing but he preferred the real thing.

"I said the unions are voicing doubts about millionaire John." He put down the 'paper and caressed soap-suds onto her back.

"Come in here with me?"

"Oh no! That's much too distracting," he laughed and slapped her buttocks gently. "If I did then where would we be?"

"Late, that's all," she said in a matter-of-fact voice.

"I'll read you an extract…"

He lifted up the 'paper and scanned the text. The article had been spotted in the local journal, syndicated news from a City broad-sheet, that carried the piece because a well-known local business owner was featured. He read the piece through shaking his head; the use of English was very particular, quirkily American and at odds with how he would have written the article. The very 'out-on-the street" use of slang would not be tolerated by a Dutch readership although he knew only too well the lapses that his paper fell into; colloquialisms gave authenticity and modernity that might hold the custom of an otherwise fickle readership.

"Ger?"

"Ja…Ja! Listen, if you can!"

"Connecting with all the city's people is my aim and to encourage the belief that we've all got to play a part in solving the budget problems. It's not to be a case of I've got my share and I'll defend it…I'm not concerned with others."

"Easier to say if you've got a few millions tucked away," Edith said loudly before her voice dropped as if in tune with the reduced noise as the shower was turned off. Gerard looked up from the page; Edith held a hand out imperiously. "Towel, please?"

"Would madam like a hand…some attention?"

"Yes…but it was declined," she replied with an overdone sigh. "What else does the article say?"

"To balance the books or get anywhere near to realising such an ambition requires a few "give backs"…quaint Americanism, Gerard said and pulled a disapproving face. "The writer then goes on to say *"someone has to suffer, though how a person with John Kahn's money, if he ever gets to be elected Mayor can convince voters that he'd follow through is an open, and as yet, unanswered question. Labour committees want to know what the Independent's views are on this."* Gerard laughed.

""We're not a group of stiffs who'll take anything that's handed down, mandate or not,"…that's a union leader's quote. There's more! *"Folks have a right to be consulted in the widest sense. This mayoral hopeful's own wealth perhaps inclines others to look on his candidacy with a great deal of scepticism, if not down-right hostility.""*

He held the newspaper loosely to his side and watched Edith massage cream into her skin before wrapping a dry towel about her body, tucking the fold neatly between her breasts.

"We've not seen much in that negative tone, have we?"

"No…but it's out there. I'm going to check the web when I get connected."

He looked at Edith reassuringly; her hopes and plans all but depended on an election victory but he had other ideas. A successful, conclusion to the campaign was a bonus, but a 'Plan B' had also to be in place. The guy was a political novice, and this was the USA; the two party system worked everyone out of its course long before the real votes counted and told for one or the other. The habit of making a follow up plan had got him out of a few scrapes before. There was no danger in the whole escapade, merely the exposure of a man and his family for not being quite what they seemed. Everyone had a secret; how they were exposed to scrutiny or the story put into the public domain was something else.

"Any more…?"

"Yep! Listen up. *'As in business so in running the City, you don't always get to say what the answer may be…you have to decide on action…you have to make a choice. It's in every businessman's or politicians risk profile. If your decision has a successful outcome, in spite of short term pain, then everyone give you some [grudging] credit."* The article has John going on to say *"If you screw up, then they're goin' to be after you."*

Gerard laughed. "I'd be fired if I wrote this! *'Poor John, it's a crock, alright…'"*

"What does that mean, *'crock'?"*

"Lievert!" Gerard exclaimed but he saw it rang no bells for her. "Shit…it's a crock of shit, uhm…a poisoned chalice is a better way to put it."

"Oh!"

"You look beautiful!" he said softly as the paper fell out of his hands onto the floor. "Has anyone ever told you?" Gerard placed a soft kiss to her lips.

"Only by the one that matters to me," Edith answered sweetly.

"You've written about this!" Edith exclaimed as she watched the candidates on what seemed to her an outlandishly large TV screen set into one wall of the hotel bedroom. Her comments interrupted his reading of the 'New York Times' and their assessment of the campaign and the most likely candidates to feature in it. The note of surprise that John Kahn figured at all had caught them unprepared; they were big enough to admit it.

"John's campaign has developed a momentum all of its own…here, read it? The report's balanced and gives him credit for what he's achieved so far."

"I thought you wanted to see this programme?"

"It's drawing to a close." Gerard threw the folded 'paper onto the sofa beside him. "Are you going to stay sitting so far away from me?" He held his hand out to her as he spoke.

"No," she said flouncing down on the seat and curling up against him. "Now listen…."

The TV show's host had played the all too-familiar controversy card, propounding a theory on good governance that he knew would provoke a heated exchange. Added zest was to be found in the form of John Kahn, a parvenu in the political game, but a player who was making his presence felt. The ploy had worked before with John Kahn taking the hits, a target for malevolent diatribes against his personality, his credibility and his integrity. Ger watched fascinated. Only American TV had the balls to invite candidates into a studio and then putting them through the grinder.

'*What's left to ask him? The state of John Kahn's virility?*' One newspaper critic of the previous night's viewing had commented drily.

'*That'll come*', was one correspondent's observation on the letters page the next day.

Gerard didn't doubt that for a second. Someone would be out there sleuthing around for the smallest piece of news that might bring him down in one hit, or to fatally damage his poll ratings that made continuance of his candidacy fruitless. '*Keep your eyes open, folks*' was his take on proceedings.

John Kahn's integrity was the target of new invectives against him, or more particularly the company he still commanded as its CEO; it would be a role he would retain if he were not to be elected Mayor in the Fall.

Edith's exclamation reflected the nature of the debate they were watching unfold; corporate responsibility pitched against social responsibility, it was an all too open attack on the fundamental principles that underpinned the ethical foundation to John Kahn's candidacy. Aberrant feelings and deep-seated prejudices could be voiced, if not by the studio hosts then by callers to the follow up radio show. It made for a political dogfight, in the raw, for John Kahn could not escape his background, the family history or the name he had already made for himself.

"I can take it," he laughed in a manner that was becoming a trademark of the man and his character. "I've dealt with worse *incoming* than what you can throw at me," was all he said to shut them up and move the debate onto a subject that would hold the attention, on him.

"Good answer, cousin" Gerard said with an admiring nod of the head.

"Are you buying into it?" Edith unbuttoned his shirt and ran her hand over his skin but Gerard pressed it to stillness.

"I only said we should believe the evidence of our own eyes, or ears…that we should also believe it once we had seen good being done…really done, not just talked about."

"They're not on about that though, are they? It's more to do with being able to fulfil your obligations and save the City some money, lots of money."

"Yes, I'd gathered that much!" he pushed her playfully. "I've been here before, lievert, remember?"

"Sure, but he hasn't. John's got through this far but he's up against the pro's now…the big-hitters, and it's showing."

"Really?" he said surprised. "Don't you go betting on it…just wait a while. He's shrewd and draws them in, I've learnt that much of him just watching. It must be his military training or an acute and finely tuned business sense. Let your opponents feel it's going their way, make 'em drop their guard, even only a little…then BAM! BAM! Over and out! Just a few shots to make your point and one there's no return from."

"You're impressed," Edith smiled.

Ger shrugged as if in grudging acknowledgement. "I've grown to admire what he has managed to achieve so far from a dead political stop."

"How do you rate his chances?"

"Forty to sixty against…he's an outsider. He says the right things but for most voters he's saying what they prefer to hear from their own kind, the guys they usually vote for with a recognisable label pinned to them. I don't know that they can cope with a schizophrenic…a potpourri of political ideals all in one person. They like it simple…all dress to the left, or to the right…none of this *'take it from both sides and go down the middle'*. It confuses them, poor things."

"Then why doesn't he get on the ticket that he's at home with? Show them in that way what he's made of…and can do?"

"He's discovered benevolence, charitable deeds…it reads well on the political resume'. Besides, Mayors don't usually come from his background… the main parties don't like patrician types showing up at local elections and, as they see it, buying their way in."

"You told me he wasn't doing that, 'buying his way in'."

"No, he isn't…or it's not so obvious."

"What then? The voters like the more parochial, down on the street, touch? Is that what you mean?"

"Yes…and that's where he's getting to them. They don't understand him," Gerard explained further as he saw Edith's frown. "They don't know what to make of a guy with a few hundreds of millions behind him in personal wealth dishing out food at help counters and talking with them, one-to-one and actually saying something they can tune in to…he resonates with what gets to them." He laughed, "not my words, it's in the paper, but I can well believe it…"

"There's more," Edith said and sat up closer to him. She tapped her lips with an elegant index finger. "Please, Mister?"

"Oh yes, there's more…always more," he whispered before kissing her and then drawing away. "There's always more…"

"Of where that came from?"

"An inexhaustible supply," he said before they kissed open-mouthed and with flicks of tongue.

When they were finished Gerard held her face gently and looked into Edith's eyes. They gave so much to each other yet the nagging doubts returned; first, there was the small item of where they would get to in the quest for restoration. Then, there followed Edith's haunting of him, how intimately joined they often were and the joyful flaming spontaneity that they could discover. Man to woman, a beautiful woman, fine. But, cousin to cousin, was that fine and okay? It nagged at him and yet he knew that they would deal with it individually and as a couple. Convincing others of the legitimacy in their relationship, now that would be the ultimate test.

"Have they finished yet?" Edith asked in a bored tone. "Has he finished yet?"

"Kissing...you mean? Are you asking *'him'* that?"

Edith gave him a squeeze. "Never that, no."

"Our cousin's a fit looking man, he'd win on that criterion alone... compared to the other two...they're okay, I guess, but John Kahn stands tall above them."

"He speaks as though he knows how to manage a big concern..."

Gerard looked at her and smiled. There was in Edith's tone a hint of admiration too. "You're not weakening are you?"

"No."

"Well that's okay...his companies are capitalised in billions of dollars, so competence is not the issue here, for us."

"No, I'd call it provenance, where the seed corn was first harvested."

"Lievert," Gerard whispered, his lips pressed against Edith's hair.

"I know, I know," Edith said and broke free from his embrace. "It always seems to come back to the same question...or the beginning of their journey, the Kahn journey all those years ago...with someone else's money."

"Well, the run-off's in less than a months time. Can you wait that long?"

"I'll have to, with your help."

42

"Hello, how're you doin'?"

"Fine thank you. You're on the air in sixty seconds, on the Max Benoyt early morning show."

"Got it. Okay...thanks for the wake-up call," John chuckled.

"You're welcome!" said the warm voice in reply.

"I said if there's a problem then we're going to fix it. We won't be working at the edges too frightened to get to the middle of things. Oh no! It's to the heart of the problem. That is where I intend to fix it."

Max had come straight at him with quick fire questions and he was glad now that Joey's liveliness so soon in the day had sharpened his senses. He sat on the edge of the bed and clasped the cell-phone with one hand while he tried to towel himself off with the other.

"Brave talk…but you've not been a politician…or an aspiring politician for long…you're a rookie."

"Direct talk," John answered evenly before his voice dropped in tone to almost a growl. "Impolite too."

"You get it out on the street…when you're on the stump."

"Yeah…" John let a silence fall between them; he had enough experience of these types of interviews now. By comparison the incumbent politicians, those with time on committees or city departments, had it easier. Max clearly believed a crack at a patrician aspirant for office would liven up the show, make the listeners eat their breakfasts a little slower. But John knew that Max would have a schedule to keep and to make him talk. 'I'll let him wait…'

"Well?" asked the voice over the 'phone

"I'm still here."

John raised his eyebrows in response to Joey's quizzical look

Max came in again with a hardened insistent tone to his voice. "Anything else to add to the little you've said so far?"

"Sure…I'll help you out Max, shall I do that? There'll be no concessions to constituencies who's interests have to be finessed first…we've seen and heard from them often enough over the past years. That way you simply postpone what you know has to be done…you increase the pain, but…it's usually after you've gone…it's your bequest to the future."

"When you've left office, you mean?"

"Yes… you also show yourself to be 'chicken' and I'm not settlin' to learn any of those tricks."

"Stay yourself…believe that you're right?"

"No…," John paused and drew the interviewer into him before adding quickly, "*do* what I believe to be right. I'll stay *'me'* and get on with what has to be *done*." He'd have to cut out the emphasis he often placed on words to make his opinion sound more convincing.

"A politician…in the UK once said, "*if it isn't hurting it's not working.*"

"Not my choice of words…"

"But the intention behind them? Does it chime with your way of doing things?"

"No."

"Explain?"

"The sentiment behind the words were only too different…there was another intent…call it political point scoring at someone else's expense…a fellow human being's expense…families, and so on."

"So, the listeners should think you'll go steady? What you've said doesn't sound like you'd be tough to deal with."

"Check the record...just try me! My companies don't hit their targets without some one driving them or motivating them to stretch the boundaries... ask those that work for me."

"We may just do that," Max replied.

"Fine...see that you do. And, when you're through...call me again. Have a good day now."

John hung up before the interviewer could close the call.

"That was abrupt..." Joey's hand slid across the skin of his thigh as he stood up.

"Yeah, I said all that there was to say to the guy."

"It's not so long before election-day, you ought to be leaving the listeners with a more positive memory of you."

"Rather than my reactions to what that guy...how the interviewer approached the call? And at this time of the morning?"

"You were wide awake..."

"Thanks to you." He bent to kiss her.

"Don't let the radio people, anyone...get to you...or tell them what they think you're made of. Go out and show them, John." She sat upright now and drew the sheet to cover her nakedness. He had a way of looking intensely at her that provoked a flush of unease; she knew all there was to distinguish her relationship with the one he held on to with Marie Christine.

"The time will come...but not in the meeting halls, or not in them alone."

"Important as they are?"

"Sure...but not only in those places. It's got to continue to be out there, on the street where my true character has to be shown...that's where I can show what I'm made of."

And, his girl Dayle kept him busy. There was no easing back on the interviews or the times spent in studios for radio or TV. They looked for folk to fill the time slots and who could be better than an aspiring politician, a businessman trying to sell the city something it hadn't bought in years, so the lead ins went, independent action and a new message from a clean cut new guy.

They just had to have him on the show, staked out on some political idea while experts picked over theories that folks had to buy into. It was a new face with a different message. Was that it, really? Or was it a well-known guy using new words, for him, to sell old goods?

"Forget it…such ideas never rang any bells with me. Neither of them… money or people, should be wasted; I never once thought there was enough, or as little, of either that we in this City could afford the luxury of wasting them."

"But you did, in the military…"

"I said we wouldn't go there…but, I never held with the phrase of 'wasting' another human being…either in the taking or the abuse of a precious thing. Of the circumstances you keep trying to get me to speak of…an individual and collective choice was replaced by bombs, the bullet and the knife. Only, you couldn't hold down ideas, and that is where elections play an exceptional… and I'll say it again, a humbling role."

"You've made a lot out of encouraging local enterprise…" It wasn't the most subtle change in the line of questioning.

"Correction," John interrupted now, "I had somethin' to say about encouraging businesses and people in their neighbourhoods to work on getting their BIDS recognised. It's also what the Mayor's there to do…to help out with."

"You were too quick jumpin' in…"

"Let's start this talk off right…"

"I was going to say, or tryin' to that you've promoted the idea of local enterprise as a means of helping to solve problems in neighbourhoods… through business improvement districts?"

"BIDS, yeah that's right…the effort's in promoting, not making a lot out of them…there's a difference."

"Yes…I think we've sorted that difference of opinion out."

"Not opinion, fact. I'm working and seeing to it that people get the message…take hold of your neighbourhood in any which way you can and make it work for you. If you've got an idea BIDS are the way to go…you just do it under the eye or guidance of the City and the Mayor. The idea's to keep the area alive and prospering."

"They've got to get a start first,"

"If the place is making some money then it's goin' to be looked after…you take some pride, I hope, in where you're livin' and you take the heat off the City budget. You take control some more and the City keeps a hold of the finances…they've got to…they're at a stretch so we'd not be looking up the road to Albany for help. We'll do it our way and in the best way we can."

"You'll still need them and no one's come close to really making the City pay its own way. You even called it a 'dependency culture'…"

"Did I now?" John laughed as if it were a secret he'd let go of.

"Yes, in an interview you recently gave on ABC."

"You listened?"

"No, I heard…research."

"And more have heard of it now," John smiled at the interviewer, "on your station."

43

For John Kahn the day job continued, but not as before. Shoe horned into the day's itinerary was the personal quest for a political life. The interviews, the canvassing for votes and walking the neighbourhoods, meeting people out on the street, they were activities pursued to deliver a personal message…and, it all had to be fitted into a wakeful sixteen hour day, or longer.

The meeting with Elbee, in his office suite was simply a routine to be followed. They had got the signing of commercial contracts down to an art. Usually, no 'phone calls interrupted them; even the mobile 'phones were switched off. There was little time set aside for diversions…least, not in the working hours of the day.

"John Kahn's office, may I help you? Kelly speaking."

"I'd like to speak to John Kahn."

"May I ask who's calling him?"

"Is he in? Is John there?"

"Yes, he is ma'am…but, I need to know who's calling, please?"

"His aunt. Tell him it's his aunt, Anna Beth."

Kelly heard a matronly laugh.

"Right," she answered slowly unable to disguise the doubt in her voice.

"Believe me. John Kahn knows who's calling…just mention my name."

"Very well, I'll let him know you're waiting." Kelly put the call 'on hold' and picked up another 'phone. "Mr John? I have your aunt…Anna Beth, asking to speak to you."

John laughed. "She doesn't call me, it's usually the other way about."

"I can tell her you'll call back…when you're through with the meeting?"

"No, it's okay. Put her through. I'll deal with it now…it'll be one less thing to remember for later."

"Okay, Mr John…line two."

"Hello! Aunt…what can I do for you?"

"I don't believe in coincidences John, but…a girl called by here, uninvited and unannounced…said her name was Edith…Edith Dekker. She said she knew you."

"She doesn't, and I don't know her." The lady was direct, no mistake, so he fell into step.

"That's what I figured. Strange though…she said she'd flown all the way from Europe…she was making a visit to these parts. Said she was checking up on family connections."

"I see." John motioned to Elbee to come by the desk.

"Do you?"

"Sure." John prepared to turn on the speaker 'phone, to low volume. "Listen in?" he told Elbee. "And…how'd you make out?" He tried to make his voice sound interested in the tale she had to tell

"Edith's well-informed."

"On her own was she?"

"Far as I could tell. A car called to pick her up…couldn't see who it was that she may have arrived…and left with."

"Right…"

"I just thought I'd tell you…to let you know, seein' as you're in this political game. Neither of us wants the past coming up and biting our hides, or nixing either of our plans."

"What plans?" John answered obtusely. "We don't do plans, we do charitable giving…call them gifts. Remember that aunt…and, remember it well."

"Okay…"

"Anything else?"

"No, John…I could ask how you're doin' but I guess I'd be interrupting a hot shot meetin' or the like. You're big time, or soon will be…mayoral candidate an' all."

"I'm fine…and I hear you're fine too. Yeah, I'm a candidate…but it's early days and too close to call." He moderated in his manner of speaking to her. "Knowing how it's goin' is some way off."

"Not what I read…even down here."

"That's good…people are taking an interest."

"I am, boy!" She gave a noisy laugh and he responded.

"You're fine…I'm glad to hear it. So, how are those kids of yours…how are they getting on?"

"They're getting by. That's why we're here, giving a helping hand."

"Just like me then aunt, with my charity work."

"I'm almost one of them," she said quite clearly.

"Yes, in a manner of saying. We won't forget that now, will we?"

"No."

"So, when anyone calls on you…you know exactly what to say, isn't that right?"

"Sure, John…same as I always do. We may be family but the tie is not so strong…or how it used to be."

"No, that's not what I meant or wish you to say, aunt. The relationship's primarily charitable."

"It's hard to think of it in just that way, John."

"I know aunt. It's legacy, but maybe it's for the best."

"Yes…" was the whispered reply.

"You take care of yourself, now?"

"I will…and you too. Watch out for yourself and your folks. These political things don't get done like they are with family."

"No, you may be right…but it matters to me. Now, I have to go. I'm sorry, but how it is may be for the best. Bye…and take care of yourself."

"Good, that's the line to take," Elbee observed when John put down the 'phone and sat still, thinking over what had been said.

"It's what I always try to follow, but personality and feelings get in the way too…I can't overlook that." John stood up. The call made him consider options but he dispelled them just as quickly. What's there to say, what is there to show or prove of what happened? It was such a long time ago. Most folks move on and forget…only, only we don't seem to.

"It would have been useful to know who this woman…Edith, who she's working with." Elbee intruded on his reverie.

"She's on a visit…I don't call that work," John said absentmindedly.

"And I'd call it more than a visit, more than a simple coincidence she's here. Something like a pattern's emerging."

"Easy…how so?"

"Head up, John! Think! Think John! Articles appear in the business pages…all of a sudden, in an Amsterdam paper. The correspondent's even got your name. Then, Hey! We get a visit…"

"Where's the connection between those articles and the girl? They've got nothing…we've got nothing, by way of any evidence to get in a sweat over. The business press takes an interest…one of their subjects of interest moves into new territory! So what? It happens…and we manage what there's to come out of it all."

"John? Please…don't go kidding yourself, don't do it, not now. In politics anything and everything's tried just to screw you up…or to see what you're made of."

"Easy, I said."

"Listen John? I've still got my senses of what feels right and what's beginning to pull at the wires…the trip wires, the outer warning signs…get my drift?"

"Me too...only I'm thinking that we've got it covered. Anna Beth gets her shots of cash to meet the school's build programme and we get some publicity, the company and me. We can all make some use of it."

"And we need to keep hold of it...real tight. Meantime...we work on what's here, on our doorstep...out on the street way down there below the window. We don't go about drawing attention to anything else...take my advice on it, John, please?

"Sure. I will...I'll do that." John took his seat once more. "Now, shall we move on?"

"With no sons to pass on my business interests to, or to succeed me I'm looking for a new job and a new direction, but I have the qualifications to serve. The company I might leave for only a while, the valued employees we have and the products and investments we've made in future knowledge...all of it is in capable and dedicated hands. I'm sure of that. From here on, I'll be following a different path and if I succeed I'll be working for and accountable to a different constituency. I may be on call to constituents with more to lose, some may tell you than those I've worked to look after until now. If I were to be elected it would be a new day, a more uncertain dawn for me...but I've known many moments like that before, in my youth."

"Oh? In what sense, do you mean, in the Army?"

"Marine Corps," he corrected, "but yeah, only I'm not going to speak of that. It's something else...for me there is something very humbling in the experience of being elected to an office...it will be quite different from being a CEO or President of a large company. In that situation you may have earned the promotion by what you have done first; your peers have chosen you to lead them."

"Whereas in politics you're chosen? Is it really so very different?"

"'Tis to me...there's a distinction. Your constituents, or those that are persuaded to vote for you rely on your word," he began to answer but was quickly interrupted.

"Folks aren't that gullible! They know politicians too well!"

"Excuse me my belief then...they may think that of the status quo, of those that have gone before or some of those they have to deal with now. Whoever gets elected, the constituents buy into the trust they're selling... they're persuaded by your conviction and ideas...that's what I hope for."

"They're also looking to a belief in your competence to do the work that's needed.

"Agreed. So, it's like I said...the humbling part of it all is the knowledge that to fail, or go to go back on the word you gave means it's *"three strikes"* against you. Lose that trust or your credit rating and you're yesterday's man."

"With those who voted you in...if it happens, and with those that didn't?"

"Yes; for those that didn't cast a vote for me they would have confirmation of their initial assessment, so..."

"That is where the *'doing'* and *'being'* in politics comes into your beliefs?" The interviewer was being unusually helpful or his subject's candidacy was founded on a shallow and easily understood philosophy. "Are you telling me you understand what failure will mean?"

"Sure...when you've been elected and you mess up a great many people could get hurt. If you don't make it...well, the message didn't get through or you failed to convince enough people. That's the way it goes...only you get hurt, pride and all."

"And to those that didn't vote for you, enough to make you lose...they could say they had a lucky escape."

"Luck doesn't figure in this."

"Okay! In that case...if you don't get elected, would you put it down to their good judgement of the policies you were trying to sell them? Is that a fairer assessment of a likely result?"

"I don't intend to even contemplate that outcome."

"Every politician, successful or otherwise looks beyond the day the last vote's counted. They look at their future...the listeners aren't going to believe you're any different."

"No, that's true...but I don't go into something with the idea I'm going to fail. What you have to say is contradicted by what people see in your eyes...in your body language. If you enter the contest with that baggage you're wasting everyone's time. I hate, just hate waste...of people and of money."

"To some the city has enough of both depending on where you are, in which Borough you are. To others there's never enough, you've seen the deficits. The Community Reinvestment Act and policies that flow from it... they divide...and they create the waste and tension between folks."

"There's still a lot to be done, that so true," he concluded.

People expected it of him.

Being conventional and acting the part of an aspiring politician from the moneyed classes of Manhattan was easy; it was far too predictable and in his case way *'off the mark'*. Many would think that conformity was a prerequisite for a man like him if he was to stand any chance of progressing beyond the first ballot. They were wrong there, too, and that was before folks took in that he was not aligned to one of the two main parties. But, his own canvassing returns and intelligence off the streets told him and his followers otherwise; in spite of what many might regard as a patrician pedigree he had no intention of using *'too much'* of his private wealth to gain any electoral or promotional advantage.

"Are you lost, man?"

"What's a guy like you doin' on a street like this?"

"Checkin' out where the next buck's gonna come from?"

They were some of the more polite and friendly comments that started off a conversation out on the streets of precincts where he walked. He walked in boroughs that many, no…most of his social equals would only drive through. Spending time with ordinary folks seemed to be working; sure, it took time to break down barriers in neighbourhoods where the inhabitants might feel disenfranchised because no one really came to listen to them or ask the really important question; 'what matters most to you?' Talking with them, not at those he met, won a grudging condescension. At least 'the man had bothered', was something else he heard or got told about.

But for some the uncertainties remained.

"What's a guy like you doin' on a street like this?"

He had lost count of the times the disbelieving question had been fired at him but the famous face was not all that constituents and key voters came to see or recognised. The guy was on foot, there on the sidewalk just walking into stores and talking to them…to just about anyone who happened to be there. Nothing pushy, just a quiet 'hello', 'I'm John Kahn', or 'I'm running for Mayor…there are lots of interest groups talking about their story…is anyone talking or speaking out for yours?'

If no one engaged him in conversation or debated the issues that affected, or screwed up their daily lives he'd leave, handing out a leaflet and the invitation to call his office and make their point if that was how they preferred it. But, for many that he met the opportunity to talk it out face-to-face, or mano-a-mano, overcame any reticence or inhibitions. He needed no reminders, New Yorkers were like that, they told it to you, straight.

On walkabouts his clothes were low-key and did not create an obvious divide between him and constituents; gone were the jacket and tie, and an entourage that declared some authority was amongst them. He only had four followers in attendance, and the car nearby; they wrote down the questions called out to him, recording too the measured or reassuring responses that he gave. A break with the past way of doing things was something he thought worth talking about and voting for. Partisan politics was a way of doing things that held no appeal for him any more and he read often enough that the population mix of the City was changing all the time…and fast. Special interest groups still tried to rule their corner of the street, or the City, but a coalition of new ideas was for him the route to a different future.

'Inclusivity' wasn't a word that you heard too often, and certainly not from a guy like him and with his background. But, they couldn't spook him; he knew his brief and folks fell silent at the straight answers that he gave them. Sure, he was a Manhattanite, but they came to see and hear that he was a New Yorker too.

What did the label hold for him now? It meant rejection of the machine politics and overbearing party organisation, kickbacks and paying out on a favour owed that had characterised past elections. Just like forging a new career path, or getting a good job, it meant a struggle to regain the necessary control that enabled everyone to make choices. In his case, it meant stepping out on the route to a political life and canvassing a wider constituency who at first might see a rich boy trying to make up for the guilt at having had it so good for so long. But that would have been to misread him, the man, the Vet who'd taken no favours and granted few…or none at all. He had earned all that he now privately possessed through sweat, and no insignificant loss of his own blood; he'd won the right to be the man he was today.

Success in life, as in business, had come through ideas and self-belief, from the role to be played leading and helping others. He'd kept his side of the deal for long enough to be known on the street; he continued to do it now. He had learnt through hard experience and pain how ideas overcame power, how human muscle and fortitude in adversity overcame raw might. Yeah! He had learnt one hell of a lot in the jungle, with ordinary guys; so, machine politics was not a commune of ideas that he could subscribe to.

The team was small, way too small for folks to take seriously…or so he was told. But, he'd seen arrogance, even that myopic self-confidence in the military that appeared to hold the line until events on the ground, amongst the tall grasses and swamps persuaded them otherwise. Hearts and minds were like an unstoppable blast wall following an explosion and moving towards them. It was a case simply of taking shelter, bending with the wind, or being blown away.

The appointment of Jacqueline had brought other defectors to the flag. Ideas bubbled on how to take on minority interests; the socio-political records told anyone who cared to read them that the pattern of long-term interests being high-jacked for short-term needs would continue for a while yet. Why wait for history or get labelled, like so many others, that minority interest votes had secured your election? No, he had other ideas.

'Real communities work by sharing out the hardship.'

That had been Jacqueline's mantra when they had first met. Only, his political opponents would say that with money you had a better chance to get through the hard times.

'After all that the good times feel rooted in community…we went through the pain but now we can all share in the good times, together!"

'Together'. Yes, that was how he had seen it too, first in running a lean company making the dollars they earned go that much further and the staff working that much harder and keeping the payroll numbers tight. He had followed that road long before they had met and it wasn't an idea that he readily talked of save with Joey, or later with Jacqueline.

By then he had become involved with local action groups facing up to neighbourhood problems, pledging funds in support or lobbying district politicians to take notice some more of what was happening outside their doors. He was building his web, making the contact network, finding support for ideas even in those that regarded him with suspicion…at first. It took time making the links and strengthening them. A physical presence, putting something back in the time allowed to him counted for more than simply showing up at a fund-raiser. He had seen that presence *and* money were the key contributors to success in the poorer neighbourhoods. So, he'd made political friends and though local decisions were reached by folks of differing political allegiances to his own he learnt quickly enough that alliances did not always follow a simple pattern or come out of a recognisable mould.

As in 'Nam, he had kept his eyes open and senses finely tuned to keep hold of life as it was lived or endured by so many he encountered. Another lesson had been learnt; it was that everyone could be or is willing, at least, to consider being an ally. Years of quiet, unremarkable and publicly unrecorded work had built a reserve of knowledge that could now be turned to his advantage.

To his opponents he was a 'rookie', new to political gambits and melees. But in terms of knowing the battleground and the tactics needed to confront, hold and then beat a stronger enemy, these had all been learnt long ago. They had even gained for him and KPM a new place in the business world. Time could be an ally and he had seen and heard from VC political commissars that the erosion of a comfortable status quo would take place through the knowledge gained of neighbourhood issues. In his own city, concerns that appeared unique in one Borough had its likeness in a neighbour and beyond.

The white population dominated the voting returns but Latinos, Africans, West Indians and many others were changing, or had already effected change in the political balance of Borough representation. The importance to him of recognising the facts came in a heated exchange with Joey and Jacqueline on how he was to be seen…was John Kahn responsive unequivocally, to minority interests, all of them? Could he be all of those things and still remain a credible 'white' candidate?

"You've shown them…shown them!" Joey had yelled at him, finally exasperated that he could doubt his own achievements in being seen to work for the very people he now sought votes from.

"There's nothing to be ashamed about now…you're stepping up a level, that's all!" Jacqueline added. "The support groups Joey's involved with, others have put time to…they all know a stronger and visible voice is needed now… you're the guy to try and win it for them!"

"Right," Joey had agreed with a laughing acknowledgement of Jacqueline's words. "That's right…let some more, a heck of a lot more know what can be done, what you've helped to do!"

"We've all done it, Joey," he corrected.

"Okay…" She'd done it for others; she'd done it for herself too; she'd done it to be with him, so much more.

"I'm glad you're on the team, Jacqueline…best move I ever made in the last few months."

"You persuaded me…now let's all get on and do it!"

"Or scare the hell outta a few people on the way!" He laughed before looking at each of them in turn. "Only…I'm not foolin' in all this…we're goin' to win it…and we're goin' to do it from nowhere."

"Yeah…and it's goin' to happen soon, a movement for neighbourhood change but on a city wide scale." Jacqueline's defection had brought a few powerful allies, strategically placed, some might say. "Yeah…we're goin' to show them all!"

"I've shown them," he had said to Joey when they were briefly alone after one such debate on strategy and canvassing votes.

"Yes…yes you have, my darling man. Don't doubt yourself."

"But…but my work at KPM puts a whole sharper perspective on caring… for minority interests. We make medicines and hold onto the patents…in some cases medicines that could help minority interests one hell of a lot…only other interests hold sway…get me?"

"Shareholders…and their investment?"

"Right…"

"What you're doing now is different…so distinct, John."

"Is it? Is it really so different to anyone looking from the outside…in at us?" The contradictions had bothered him before. Now, they were raging more brightly. "I'm not seen as an *TWAP* any more."

"A what?"

"I saw a car sticker…Dayle showed it to me. It said, *'John Kahn - An Indie Without a Prayer'*. I also saw it on one of my posters. Just the letters, painted on. The team knew what they meant a second or two after me!" He had laughed on recalling the moment of revelation.

"Many are said for you, believe me."

"Okay, only, to me there's contradictions that we need to guard against. It feels like I can try to look after minority interests on the streets while back on the company floor an industry I've been part of can hold onto to something that some minority interests would give almost anything, if they had it, to get their hands on. Then it's minority interests versus investor's interests."

"Oh…John."

She had looked at him with stilled eyes. Conscience and political ambition didn't come to mind too often when she thought back to other elections. He had spoken before of machine politics and a party line being walked. The very idea of them seemed to cause offence and Jacqueline had heard of it from his lips too. Only, she seemed to have an answer for his disquiet.

"It's nothing more than a Board of Directors to a business…the machine controls the outcome. See it in that context."

"I don't see it quite like that…there are things called scruples that sometimes come back to bite you." He felt uncomfortable at being reminded of Mary Beth's little payments and the family history.

"I don't remember ever working with someone who had these scruples when it came to being elected."

"You forget…defence follows attack. Any way, for me it's a serious principle. I'm not just *talking* about improving the circumstances of minority interests or to lead the City to a more inclusive form of politics…I'm looking to make it happen. Independence means just that, for me…making it happen, not just talking about it in cosy clubs and diners. I'm looking to tap into a wider constituency…we've got eight million people or so in the City, and only a quarter seem to want to vote or believe in doin' it."

"I know…I know." Joey took hold of his hand and simply held it to her cheek.

"You okay?"

"Yeah, sometimes I can't quite believe you're doin' this."

"Yes…but get this, I'm fully engaged by it. I want many folks to take part in the vote…not left to wondering, 'Why man? Nothin' ever changes.'"

"Well," Jacqueline answered, "I know things aren't going to be the same in a few weeks time…you're goin' to shake them up and make them think! When that happens…"

"Anything's possible?" he laughed back teasingly. It occurred to him, as he said it that he'd have to be prepared for every eventuality.

"That's right…start believing in it," she smiled in reply. "I have."

"Well, after next week and that programme we'll see how we're set up."

"I have a call for you ma'am. It's Mr John Kahn."

"Thank you."

"Hello…Anna Beth?"

"Yes, it is. Mornin' to you…what's brought you to doin' this, John?"

"Curiosity…and passing the time of day with you."

"And when did you ever do that?"

"You've got me," John laughed. "Okay, this is how it goes…have you had any visitors in the days after we last spoke?"

"No."

"Heard anything from the lady?"

"From Edith Dekker you mean, the Dutch girl?"

"Is that her name?"

"Yeah…I had a call, just to say she was leaving…I had that two days ago. She told me she'd seen you on some TV show."

John laughed. "Yeah, there've been a few recently…so, that's okay."

"Is it, John?"

"Sure it's okay. Now, about Edith," he went on, "I'm a little surprised… about the easy come then the easy go kind of visit."

"Well…that's how it is for her it seems and I'm not gonna fret about it. We just look to what may happen to us from now on. That how I see it, John. I'll still sleep easy."

"Yes, Anna Beth…nothing can happen." He paused. "Now, how are you keeping?"

"Fine…the same as always and considering all this new interest and 'phone calls from you." She always found John polite; it was a quality that she admired, in spite of the things she could say to provoke the man.

"It's the first for quite a while, that's so."

"Yes, and that's what makes it interesting to me sitting here. We're not goin' to get all wound up about one unexpected visit now, are we?"

"No…no, we're not. We've got things ordered just as before…we've been that way for a long, long time and long before my involvement with family affairs. By my reckoning of it we're just goin' to keep on living as we always have."

"Apart," Anna Beth said in a flat tone, "and with silences, long periods of quiet in between."

"Yes, that's so."

"Right, that's how it's been. Take care of yourself, John," she said then asked him lightly, "how is the mayoral thing going?"

"To my plan…as I see it. Coming second is not part of my thinking."

"No, I guess that's so, but time will tell, John. Will you think on it?"

"I sure will, and I do. Now, I've got to go. You take care of yourself and those youngsters in your care?"

"I know no different," she agreed with a chuckle. "You'll have a few to look after if you get through all them election things."

"Yeah…"

"Well, bye now…and thanks for the call. You really are a surprise to me sometimes," she laughed. "Take care of yourself…and your family. They count above anything else…do you follow me?"

It was the first time she had spoken out anything quite so familiar to him and without any *'edge'* to her words. It almost felt as though she had found a Kahn with a real conscience about things.

"I certainly do *'follow you'* Anna Beth. There are plenty of reminders for me to deal with."

44

"I'll say this…money, technology and lots of feet on the ground don't mean success, they guarantee nothing."

"You have an advantage," the interviewer began but John already knew where the line of questioning would lead.

"No…it's not about money at the candidate's disposal or the number of helpers! That kind of argument…it's not sustainable. The Japanese used bicycle troops to invade parts of a country and outflanked the Brits…an easy and cost effective way to out-manoeuvre your opponents! They gained a flexible tactical advantage. And then there's the VeeCee, I got to know a great deal about them…they, the Viet Cong, they came on foot. And there we were, the guys who seemed to have it all…only, there were times when we were chewed up, by *simple* warfare." He got no reply from the interviewer. "Enough said?"

"On history…yes."

"Oh no! You think again, please? Elections are about winning hearts and minds."

"Another old phrase…."

John shrugged. "Sure, it's another old phrase but it's still relevant here in the city. In the ways of this election it's not about how much money you spend but on the ideas and programmes you have to deal with some of the city's problems."

"The theory still has an old and dated ring to it."

"It's relevant, even now and right here in New York. You look at the numbers, at who the voting majority is…they're not whites. They may think they have the last call, in the end…but in the Primaries the whites are outvoted."

"If that's so, your policies are going to be dissected by those that know the streets and districts so much better than you. They've been working on them and with the problems a whole lot longer than you."

"Maybe." John gave a phlegmatic shrug of the shoulders and a look that indicated he didn't go nearly so far in believing what he'd been told.

"Why say that, *'maybe'*? It's a fact…the voters will follow the guy who's in touch with every day realities for the people. Isn't that the truth of it?"

"Not quite, in my opinion."

"Explain," he was asked bluntly.

John flicked the interviewer the smallest glance to show his manners had not deserted him.

"Sure…how come only a quarter of those who could vote actually believe that it's worth bothering to do so? Something isn't right, even if you're trying to suggest otherwise. To me there's everything to work for in this election, and a whole lot of people to do it for."

A pattern seemed to be emerging; he showed up at a meeting where he had been invited to speak and after a short address he dispensed with formality and simply talked to anyone that asked a question. It was living on your wits and sharpened political reflexes; he listened and answered on any subject put to him; you couldn't know it all but you could express an opinion, or you promised to get back to the questioner when a more considered response could be given. People seemed to like the arrangement, some became known to him or his small retinue of staff and attended other meetings. They wanted to make sure they had got the measure of John Kahn; they said that was why they had come to see and listen to him some more.

Initial impressions don't always give you the true picture they said, and these constituents held a special value; they confirmed that a question posed had been answered within the time slot agreed.

"I call it keeping my word. You may not like what I have had to tell you in reply, but a reply is what you've received."

"And we can always talk some more?" one had asked him.

"Sure. My candidacy is all about keepin' an open mind about policy issues that affect you…constituents and citizens. It's a cliché and I'm sorry to use it but - one cap does not fit all folks. So, the Independence Party, and my candidacy is about listening to people and managing change. The world out there is changing, it affects all of us out on the city's streets in some way…if the other parties don't meet your ideas of how it should be then listen to us, vote for us, vote with us. We can manage change rather than being forced to adapt because of the circumstances creeping up on us...only that's not how it is. It's happening but some took their eyes off what was there for them to see...only, they were too scared to really look...or, entrenched attitudes got in the way."

"But that's all we've ever had in these parts...in this city!" Someone had yelled out to an accompaniment of murmured assent.

"Yeah, it is...or rather, it was like that!" he had yelled back with a laugh.

"So?"

"Let's change it! Independence means you're free...free to pick and chose what you want people who represent you to do...free to pick economic or social programmes that suit the most, not put one group against another, then swing round and settle scores!"

"See to it that everyone with their names on the roll gets out and votes, man!"

"I agree...but we don't force them to, we do it by persuasion and ideas that meet the present needs of the city and represent all the people...hear me? Represent a majority of the people."

Exchanges like these made him believe that being seen, in the flesh, outlived the expensive TV commercial campaign others were so reliant upon. He had the money to follow them onto that trail but word of mouth and eyeballing folks counted for so much more.

Dayle found a word for it after the nomination primaries were over. She called it *Proximity*.

"Your arrival on the political scene is like a stone dropping onto the smooth surface of a pond." Joey spoke, warmed by John's embrace. "No one saw the consequences...the ripples got bigger and spread so far that you've reached a constituency that people had all but given up on."

"Or they on the main parties did little to help...or really reached out to."

"Well, it took your candidacy and way of selling a new idea to really make it happen, John."

"Before it was too late."

"You said it."

"And I've said quite enough...in the circumstances we have here," he whispered against her skin.

Joey laughed with pleasure. "It's been a while."

"We've had things on our mind..."

"But never quite to the exclusion of this…one-on-one."

"No…but the opportunity for us to be together is becoming a problem."

"I'm with you whenever I can be," Joey said turning to meet the renewal of his passionate kisses and she felt compelled to speak of her devotion to him. "Help me make another great moment, John? I want that of you, only from you."

'Okay, there's only a week, just a few hours left before New Yorkers go to the polling booths and vote in the first round of the Mayoral Election, in the Primaries. There's a new twist to the story this time…a fairy tale for one person, and for others, the Establishment, it seems like a mis-print on the papers. We have the prospect of three contenders for the General Election! That'll be some change! There's more! There's even a chance that one of the candidates is none other than John Albert Kahn, or JOHN as many are beginning to call the candidate for the Independence Party.

John Who? You may be saying…or might still be saying. His main opponents Steve Cruz (Democrats) and William J. Newhouse, or 'Beejay' (Republicans), hope he will soon be somewhere else…in a place called Political Oblivion!

We'll just have to wait and see!

Right! If you've got a question call us!

If you've got a problem about some policy issue…or the candidate's style and attitude, you can still call us!

Can your fears and modesty! Let us hear it!

The lines are open and we're goin' to take the calls!

Be patient! If it's a sure fire thing…a great twister of a question, well…the questioner goes to the front of the line!

They're the rules folks!

In the meantime, we'll be asking each contender for their last minute pitch… we'll be asking them to tempt us with their ideas of how life in the City may change once they get their hands on the levers of power. And, if they don't…we'll be asking what they see as the consequences that a bad night for them may have on others and the City's progress.'

The intro was breathless, confident and measured. Jay Kovacs was the anchorman on a show that pitched contenders together for one purpose only, to make the sparks fly and the debate between the studio guests either like a street brawl or a thought provoking exchange in University Chambers. It didn't bother Jay that much, the show made the contenders look like crass vaudeville acts spouting rehearsed words or they came across as polished performers. One of the studio's guests might yet turn out to be a master of a political craft that had as its glaring associate, its consummate and polished affiliate, a quick brain and command of language. Such a combination might yet persuade doubters that a vote for him would after all not be a 'wasted vote'.

Jay's notes said it all. John Kahn was well briefed, prepared and looked the consummate businessman and leader. As he looked at him he noted the contrast with pictures he'd seen on video news clips and in the street press. Gone were the casual clothes that marked him out as a man of the people, out on the street with them talking and helping out...working with them and lending a hand. It was not such a smooth hand some remarked who had taken it. The guy was not just 'talk'...or style, nor smooze over substance.

Oh no! He worked at what he also spoke about. It struck a chord with folks...only many still didn't quite understand it. Why get involved? Was it for real? Could you really believe the guy?

It seemed that you could; it wasn't simply anecdotal evidence that the guy was out on the street. The studio had sent the reporters out there to find out for themselves. Sure, people knew of him, his reputation and presence was noticed, city wide, but unlike the other contenders his presence was still low-key. But, there was no way of ignoring a simple truth; John Kahn *did* what he said he did. Yep! What was turning out to be good PR for the guy was bad for his political opponents, those sat opposite him in the studio. The seats were arranged just as the electorate might perceive the contest to be; two versus one; the pretender versus the establishment. It didn't seem to bother the guy one little bit. Why? It seemed that they had little ammunition to fire at him that didn't sound trite, or condescending, the kind of arrogant *'I know how it's done better than you'* kind of put downs that had seen their day.

No one took account of boredom until maybe it was too late. Some had already figured it out...they were on John Kahn's team and between them all they were shaking the tree. So, anything could happen and the uncertainty made for wider interest in the outcome, not just of the kind that saw one group doing better at the expense of another. John Kahn had somehow opened eyes to all that and it wasn't his wallet that had drawn folk's attention to the message.

John Kahn had gone out there and done most things; he had seen it for himself and not relied on some tyro to brief him on what they had read or talked about. John Kahn had been out there and shared in the work. It had been an education and the opening of his eyes; the experiences had been without question more informative than the newspapers and their slant on the story or their perceptions of the truth as the readers might want to note it from the words.

'God! Where'd he gone and found the time?'

Many asked but few could doubt the guy's commitment. All that, and he was a guy with a vault full of money and a view over Central Park. It couldn't be right, or could it? Someone was there on the streets wanting to give something back to his home town.

Move on folks you're being had! Was that it?

Looking at the guy, it didn't seem to be that way.

Many that met him and understood what the man had done thought otherwise. It was kind of disconcerting; the studio audience's response to him let them all know, and John Kahn in particular, that he was no Lone Ranger.

Jay laughed out loud as he read the closing words of the briefing note, '*Lone Ranger*'! He could understand now the strengthened feeling of anticipation, the quiet confidence in what had been worked at and planned for, and the expectation that had to be burning bright inside this guy called John Kahn.

His opponents had something to really worry about it seemed. History was about to be 'all shook up' if the polls were to be believed; they were all looking out on new political territory. The conventional way of doing things seemed to be under threat or in need of a shaking up.

The unknown beckoned.

The station hoped the lines were going to be full of doubters, faint-hearted believers, or those willing to buy in to a *real* election, a voice for new ideas as well as 'new' people. There was the hint of *real* change, a realisation…to work the word '*real*' to its thinnest…that maybe, just maybe, the election for a New York Mayor was going to be so very different this time.

45

"This is a call for John Kahn…"

"Go for it…you're on the air."

"The question's this, John, 'why go on'? Your candidacy's going to fail… all you'll be doing is splitting the vote further and disenfranchising those that don't have much of a voice…so, why do that?"

"I'm not…and the people I meet and speak to don't see it like that either. I'm giving many of the people you say '*don't have much of a voice*' that very chance to be heard…through me. The registrations…those that support me and the Independence Party are all the proof you need."

"Convince me…I'm not, so far."

"I see it in my voting base, in my voter registrations and their numbers… they stretch across all the Boroughs and all groups. There are Latinos, Asian Americans and Hispanics amongst them. I have colleagues on the team who have put in a lot of hard work with a number of smaller groups to fuse their votes to the Independence Party line. They're coming in behind me. Why? Because they see that the other parties just don't have all the answers they're looking for. They've waited only nothing's really changed."

The caller didn't buy into it.

"Do your work some other way, John…why don't you support the party that holds to your principles? Tell me…and everyone else what they are, by the way. We don't hear much of them."

His opponents in the studio laughed and nodded at the observation. Their gestures were picked up by the studio cameras and fingers pointed at him in defiance. He said not a word.

"Well?" Jay prompted.

"I'm fine, thank you," John replied with a smile and paused. "The abiding principle I have is 'one man one vote'…the casting of a poll by the majority of the people in this city with a right to vote." He held up a hand and quelled an interruption. "I know what you're goin' to say. 'everyone wants or has that'…only the figures from past elections don't show a whole lot of folks turning out, or bothering to turn out to vote. I'd like to see a change in that and be a part of it when that moment happens."

Finally, he had to give way.

"Air, just air…listeners and viewers want to hear some facts on how you're goin' to make a difference," Steve Cruz said interrupting. "Speak out some real facts!"

"I hope the cameras picked that up?" John answered looking at Jay Kovacs. "The voice of the arrogant few, those that trade influence to hold onto power, for a minority it seems…"

"Plenty voted last time!" Beejay observed.

"Less than a quarter who could vote did so!"

"Policy? Are you going to say *anything* on that?" Steve Cruz interrupted once again.

"Bilingual education support, more of it, that's one," John counted it by tapping his index finger. "Two, health care…make some changes in that. Three…housing, make improvements in certain districts where there's a chronic need…stop gentrification, or too much money going in and forcing up prices so the local people get moved on or moved out."

"Nothing's new in that," Beejay told him. "We've supported policy on that for years."

"But you haven't actually done it. I have…on my own through companies I work with."

"So there's a private money-making instinct?"

"Yes Steve, same as in any business if you and your kind ceased putting up local taxes and making it still harder for well intentioned companies to make something where all sides can benefit. At the heart of what I'm standing for is breaking up the monopoly of so called big ideas you both claim to have. I'd go further, I'd say let a wider…much wider constituency decide upon a broader democratic reform in the City." He paused for a second only, for dramatic effect. "In my book, my small political dictionary compared to yours, gentlemen, it's spelt out clearly, it's DEMOCRACY!"

"It's worked long enough here and long before your appearance on the scene. The city's a Republican or Democrat party city."

"There's been some re-districting, as you may both know," John observed lightly and keeping hold of the impulse to be sarcastic. "Areas of the City are being brought into more economic and social harmony."

"Man, where've you been?" Beejay called out.

"Let me remind you John, both of you, the last Mayor was a Democrat…he started the process, my party, the Democratic Party started that re-districting process."

"But you still talk down to folks, you don't talk with them. That's all I've done…I've listened, and what I've heard hasn't surprised me or my workers. It's those concerns, of people standing outside the real democratic process as they see it that I'm addressing."

John smiled, shook his head and waited, to see if Beejay or Steve Cruz would offer any other reason for the status quo remaining unchallenged. He pointed a finger at both of his studio opponents in turn.

"Lost your way haven't you gentlemen if you're denying folks their wider constitutional rights to have a vote? I'm for giving as many candidates who are willing to put their name forward on the ballot, and who get through, the chance, a real chance to…to make a difference."

He sat back and put one cupped hand to his ear pretending to wait for an answer.

"Community based organisations are working fine, they serve their neighbourhoods well. What John Kahn's proposing is a break up of these organisations…" Beejay's comment made Steve Cruz nod.

"They're the organisations that control lives, that suck in government money or are voted to you if you're very fortunate, are they whom you mean? I'd call that the beginning or sustaining of a dependency culture…"

"There! We've heard it from him at last! Cut off the money to the more needy of the Boroughs that make up the City of New York! We heard him… you all heard it from him, from John Kahn, at last!" Steve Cruz almost shouted it out.

"No…no you didn't, not at all!"

"Let others be the judge of that, John! Some of the folks you seem to dismiss can't do without the agencies you want to abandon or abolish so easily...so carelessly."

"I want to do neither of those. Sure," he said wishing to debate the point, "I'd be working to lessen their hold and give neighbourhoods all the freedom they needed to encourage investment in their broad based community. I wouldn't be working to extend the *dependency* on others that takes away all hope of an individual's right to make their own future."

"Easy for you to say...from a haven up there on Park Avenue."

"You're from a comfort zone...what do you know about inner city living?"

"I've been associated with a charity, Right Treatment. You may have heard of it...they deal with the kind of issues you talk so much about. In contrast, those people work with the problems...talk is for others, your party it seems."

"Nonsense..."

"Complete fabrication...a story for people to hear and be frightened by...that you and your policies will deny them basic life needs."

John smiled as these jibes were directed at him in raised angry voices.

"On the second point, inner city living? The charity work keeps me in touch with that. As for the first, where I live, well...it's been worked and paid for, just like so many settlers did before...just like so many who come to the States and to this City long for...the chance to do it and do it in their own way. Are you sayin' there's harm in that, in being proud to have worked and got your dues?"

"Still easy for you to say...dependency, or the way you tell it is a slap in the face for those unable to get by. My party recognises the fact...ours more than most. At least the voters tonight got to see what you're really all about." Steve Cruz sat back, his smile the acknowledgement of a point scored.

"You didn't answer my question," John persisted, "but I'll tell it this way...lookin' at dependency and support for those really in trouble are two very distinct and clear policy objectives. Dependency means different things to us round this room."

"It's based on need...to look after those in real need," Beejay offered in his attempt not to be sidelined by the others in their heated exchange of political views.

Steve Cruz turned on him. "It sure does, it means helping those less fortunate than yourself!"

"I agree...we can agree on that...in part anyway." John paused once more to see if his opponents would respond further, or jump in at him again. "Only...there's a part to the statement that you guys conveniently forget...it shouldn't be about paying out so that the incentive to really work and control your own life is not in your hands anymore. I'm looking to other ways, the independence route that both helps those really in need amongst us *and* creating the environment, city wide, for folks to get on by themselves. I'm not peddlin' ideas in supportive neighbourhoods alone just to get on…I tell people I meet what my policy objectives are, incentives to get on by your own will and help if you need it, truly need it."

"Means testing? Is that what your proposing?"

"No, Steve. Help where it's due and really needed, not to secure a political position."

"Fantasy…a tale all made up in your mind, John! It's not like that, not one bit!"

"I ask myself, then, why is it so many unions support one party when their jobs are paid for by *all* the citizens of the City? The City Government and workers are the servants of the people, not the other way around. It's something you both forget, and you Steve in particular."

"Jeez! You're just repeatin' old prejudices!" Steve Cruz's look of sudden anger left John unperturbed.

"We'll see, won't we? In just a few days, we'll see…if the voters will buy the same goods but in new wrappings, or if it's to be a chance for a real change."

"The City's run just fine…two distinct party allegiances working for the good of the majority." Steve Cruz had calmed down.

"Funny how you keep talking of a majority…"

"You said it to us both before…DEMOCRACY!"

"Yeah, I did Beejay," John smiled. "It doesn't mean we can't try to improve on it. How sure are you…really sure? Hm? If you are, tell everyone out there that's tuned into the show how it's working. I don't hear it out on the street, not in the parts I've been workin' in and helpin' out on. They see it oh so differently! To them…to me…Democracy means of the people and of all the people…*all* of them, or as many as you can get really motivated to believe that a vote cast will make a big difference to their lives and neighbourhoods…how they feel about themselves and their neighbours."

"Those that want to, or are willing to go down and vote in the booths," Jay interrupted.

He had allowed the debate to flow with minimal interference. The calls put through had been few. He had heard over his head-phones that callers observed that the debate was going along lines they had wanted to provoke by their own questions and so they rang off. He'd heard something else; John Kahn seemed to be in touch with the mood out on the street. What was more, they surprised everyone who took the calls by saying that…he seemed to be speaking *for* people not *at* them. You had to *stay* silent and listen.

John Kahn even got in the last word.

"Sure, but folks need the motivation to do it…to go out and vote. They need to be motivated by the feeling that their vote, put in the box for the guy and party they can believe in, will make a difference or maybe provoke a change in their lives and neighbourhoods…he will do something they can feel part of. They don't want to go out and vote to reinforce a cosy status quo. I'll correct another misconception…food stamps? My work and support of a charity, Right Treatment…they make sure that people eligible for them take up what's their due, and I ask that they tell me if things aren't working out. They aren't…your two parties suggest they are available, but tell folks to get them for yourselves. My party, the Independence Party makes sure that they get them…and we support the charity and other groups in their self-help, in getting the stamps to those that need them most."

"Quite a speech," Steve said acidly. "Can we come in on that?"

"No…sorry, time's out." Jay shrugged apologetically. "Next time, maybe?"

"Count on it, John! We'll debate that issue next time."

The microphones picked up Steve Cruz's angry admission of the last word being with John Kahn; he, Steve Cruz had been bested. John Kahn, to many listeners and viewers was learning to be a seasoned *'pol'*.

"Quite a performance," Gerard observed as he switched off the TV, "and here's a guy who's never done serious politics before."

"He's in business, at the top…he's no 'ingenue' as some of our friends might snootily say, across the border…south of here." Edith gave him a soft smile. "Hurry back from your trip? Next time, we go together…for the real thing. I can trust you to watch the Primaries can't I?"

"Yes…and you can see how it all goes from this cosy little apartment. I'll be thinking of you…"

"Alone…"

"It's not for long…Hans wasn't in favour of it but I was lucky. There's a conference I can cover and play the detective or be the advance party at the same time. I can even see if Nico has any more leads with that girl of his."

"Dayle Kahn? It's nothing to get concerned over is it? It's not so close and personal."

"Like us you mean, lievert?" Gerard smiled.

"You know *exactly* what I mean."

"Ja! And I think I know what he means with that girl…but I'll check it out, somehow, so don't you go worrying about them, at least not now.

296

We have someone to bother with…John Kahn and those Primary Elections coming up."

46
New York

"Lievert?" Gerard called out with a laugh. The mid-afternoon flight from Amsterdam to the Big Apple had been uneventful and he was now settled into a hotel close to Times Square. "I'm glad to hear your voice! I thought you'd be asleep."

"Alone here?" She gave a little gasp. "What a row! Where are you?"

"On the balcony of the hotel, I have to see the view, just to confirm I'm here again!"

He liked to simply stand on the balcony to the restaurant and bar and to take in the sights and vibrant sounds. The traffic below him in the streets never, quite, grew silent, no matter what time of the night it was.

"It's quiet here, in my place. Come back soon?"

"I will…promise. It's only a few days."

"Long enough."

"Well, depending on how it all goes we may both be back here again soon."

"Let's believe it will happen? You believe in it!"

"A miracle?" Gerard laughed but he did not wish to tease her. "Okay, I will…tomorrow I'll see Nico and we can talk it all through, whatever it is he's found out, and that we don't already have."

His voice was raised in order to make himself heard above the rumble of noise below his 'perch' and he noticed one or two other guests look over to him. That's why people come here, to experience the hustle and bustle of the place, he thought.

He noted the contrast with the city of his birth; everything, just everything, had an 'other world' feel to it. It was a city where he had work to do; other than that he could not say that it held an enduring fascination for him. The visit with Edith, only a few weeks ago, had not changed his opinion of the place but together they had seen the city through the eyes of tourists and there had been no deadlines to meet. For once he could relax in New York; their joint quest to find out all that they could of a distant relative, a certain John Kahn, had not spoilt their short break.

"Call me later?" Edith seemed to shout before she was gone.

'Miss you...wish you were close beside me.' He sent a short text message for her to read when she woke up.

But Edith's reply was quick. "That's what I'm thinking...I can't sleep wondering what you'll be doing over the next few days."

"It's quite a performance that man puts on." Gerard gave Nico an enquiring look as he swilled his beer round-and-round in his tall glass. For him a light lunch was finished and they were talking of the short video clip that Nico had recorded.

"It is no performance or an act to con the voters," he replied easily. "I've seen it for myself, with my own eyes...I've seen the looks of doubt that the audience may start with when he appears on stage or amongst them. It seems to vanish..."

"They're converted to the cause," Gerard smiled, "is that what you mean?"

"No...not quite. They give the guy a chance to tell them what he's all about. You've seen the political reviews on the man..."

"Mixed...nothing to really get on fire about."

"Maybe not, but he's a fighter, he takes everyone on who has an argument to pick with him. He takes the hits but always comes back."

"It's in the genes. You'll do anything or put up with almost anything if it means in the end that you get your way."

Nico nodded in agreement. "Well, I'm glad that the information I sent to you has given an insight of the man."

Gerard shrugged. "I've followed his progress," he replied without any sign of appreciation for what Nico had pieced together of the man's background. "I've also seen the contributions...or read about them, those that key members of his team make. Jacqueline Purcell is a star...no mistake."

"She's got John Kahn to where he is...she's coached him along, I'd say."

"Well, she's been an asset to the campaign, Nico, I can see....or have read about that. But, John Kahn has all the attractions of a new guy to the game...he speaks directly and tells you what's on his mind. People have to get used to that...people in business expect it, more often than not. Politics is different...as he'll keep learning."

"Very wise," Nico told him with a smile. Gerard had made it sound as if he had a wealth of experience to draw on.

"No...just an opinion." Gerard paused. "Dayle Kahn's a help too... wouldn't you say? You know her, don't you?"

"I've met her," Nico answered easily, but he now decided to wait on where the questions were taking him. "I can't claim that I know her. That family only shows you what it wants you to see, no more...and no less."

"And you and I have to put the constituent pieces together, of the businessman, the family man…and now, the aspiring politician."

"Sure. Which one do you buy into?" Nico asked.

"The business man…unquestionably. Then…the politician, I'm learning about John Kahn the politician all the time."

"And the third?" Gerard had left the opportunity open for him to be quizzed.

"The family man? Oh," he sighed casually, "there's always something hidden…the past's checked out. But, as for the present…?" Once more he left the question unanswered but Nico stared back at him and picked at the bowl of salad that he had sent out for.

"There's nothing to the present." He crunched on a portion of carrot noisily, indifferent to Gerard's observation of it.

"Are you sure, Nico?"

"Yes, Gerard, I'm sure." Nico pushed the meal to one side and opened up the folder of cuttings and pictures that had become his research folio on one man and his family. "You've already seen many of these," he went on, "but, here…check these out."

He resumed eating in his leisurely way as Gerard looked at the pictures of a family at the Beach House, then at another; it was of John Kahn at an office. The banner, hung on the wall behind him, said "Right Treatment".

"What about her?" he asked and Nico saw the stab of Gerard's finger onto the picture. As if to reinforce the asking of the question his other hand pressed his glasses tight against the skin of his face. "Josephine Clarke," he announced, "what of her?"

"She's a lawyer…his company lawyer."

"I thought Elbee was the man to do all of that…not this strikingly attractive woman."

Nico studied the picture once more. Gerard had a point. "She's still his lawyer…a partner in Elbee's law firm. That's all I know…or have been able to learn."

"I know," Gerard said slowly, " it's just that she appears in quite a few pictures I've got of him…from my own sources."

"Which are?"

"My sources…uncomplicated by any entanglements."

"Just as mine are Gerard." Nico gathered up the collection of assorted papers and pictures, gossip column froth and the more measured analytical pieces about the candidate. "Your quest, if I can call it that…for some inside news on that man John Kahn…it's still in tact. I don't speak of the detail with anyone."

"Not even Dayle Kahn?"

"Christ, no!" Nico laughed.

"Oh?"

"Don't look so surprised!" Nico laughed again. "That 'association' if you want to call it that…is more like an occasional hello…it's me seeing her at a political meeting of some kind that Dayle sometimes gets taken along to. It's the family thing…John's wife isn't into all that political stuff…she's high society and shows some involvement…when there's a party to enjoy…she's not so involved."

"Not out on the street, so to speak?" Gerard smiled at the image his words might conjure up.

Nico laughed. "Something like that…"

"And Dayle? What about her?"

"I've told you," Nico replied with a harder tone of voice, "there's no association that goes anywhere near compromising what I have to do as a journalistic researcher." Nico shrugged. "I'd like it to be a little different, but then Dayle Kahn's protective of her man…"

"So, she's wary of the press?"

"You could say that…but we have our uses." Nico looked at him as Gerard lounged against the wall, his chair tipped back. "Why the grilling?"

"Oh…I was wondering, that's all." Gerard's chair settled onto its four legs once again. "Seen this?"

He slid a picture from under his pile of papers and across the space of the desk between them.

"Where'd you…?" Nico spoke out slowly as he looked at the photo then at Gerard. "My own time is just that! And it's private!

"Sure! As long as work doesn't get compromised by entanglements, do you *follow* me?" Gerard thumped the table, but not very hard. She was a very pretty young woman, and Dayle Kahn seemed to have an interest in Nico. The look on her face and the clasp of her hand in his as they danced at some club said it all.

"It sure as hell won't…and it doesn't!" Nico hissed. "We're not all obsessed by the journalistic game to the exclusion of anything…or anyone else! Do you *follow* me, Gerard?"

He took off his glasses and looked at Nico. "Good. We can get down to work now that's cleared up. I'm going to watch that clip again."

"And I need some fresh air. I may catch you later?"

"Sure," Gerard replied casually. The dust would settle.

According to observers of this year's mayoral contest John Kahn's been very clever.

He has drawn on all of his experience as an astute businessman and considered the electoral process in the City and seen the opportunities presented by a political process that is dysfunctional, pre-determined (almost) and in truth undemocratic. New York is regarded as a Democrat party city, yet we've seen candidates who changed sides before the election and after they had drawn in voters from other constituencies not so closely associated with them before. It was an exchange of political chips.

It all became a complete turn-off for everyone but 'prime' voters until someone new arrived on the political scene.

What's John Kahn done? He's only gone and tapped into a huge reservoir of centrist voters who like policies to be aimed at them, or for them, and not at a political elite. They're also folks who think that they have concerns that should be heard…better still, to see that something's done for them. You'll know that the percentage of registered votes actually being cast falls with nearly every election we have in this City.

John Kahn has also gone out and created his own political brand image, sold the idea and it seems to have worked – at least, so far.

Sure, he is an Independence Party candidate, he's truly independent and has single-mindedly set about selling the message that the City and community come before party. Things had to change he and his supporters told anyone who asked them; if they didn't like that message then they need not have turned out to vote in the numbers many have so far for him.

And they did! They turned out in thousands and no one can say that he and the party he represents bought their votes. Oh no! They were persuaded of a change being necessary; better still many seem to have agreed that supporting a rank outsider might focus a few entrenched minds that have kept the city mired in old political ways…maybe not of so many years ago.

John Kahn can say he tried, if the results don't go his way. He can also say 'what is the use of being in office when only a fraction of those who could exercise their vote bother to do so'?

But, he doesn't go for such a negative approach to the contest of becoming Mayor. He and the Independence Party keep working on the idea that partisan elections are okay just as long as all the parties take an active and committed part in the whole process. The people of the city should expect one hundred per cent effort from all aspiring candidates.

That's how John Kahn sees it and no one seems to be arguing too strongly with him on that…anymore.

Many of those disinterested voters had never bothered, or so the stats told us, until now. The registers of voters have seen a dramatic rise – is it merely a coincidence? I don't think so, and the other two parties know that if their candidate makes it to Gracie Mansion he'll have done it the hard way.

301

How has John Kahn approached the case? It's simple, now that we've all seen it in operation. It went something like this…he persuaded people to register by having a check in desk by, or very close to his company's stores. You have to buy an aspirin to get through some days here, don't you? Or you have to clean your teeth before a date…or get medicines for a close one. He was smart. John Kahn didn't use his money in such a way that the Campaign Finance Board would feel obliged to take their glasses to what he did.

Oh no! He was smart; like any businessman or retailer, he made the customer stop and look at the merchandise, only in his case he was selling an idea. People passed an Independence Party stand. There was no pressure; absent too was the hauling in for a talking to by a high-pressure sales pitch. None of that for him! The party simply had an eye-catching stand, a quiet presence, and a slogan to make you think over as you walked on, by, or up to the stand. The crisp banner in a subdued green seemed to say it all and it seems to have been extremely effective:

MAKE A DIFFERENCE - FOR YOURSELVES
BE DIFFERENT – JOIN US!

People had to stop and look; the leaflets said where in your neighbourhoods you could sign up if you were thinking of buying into the ideas being peddled. I stopped and checked out one of these stands, just to be sure of what I felt inclined to say on seeing it for the first time. There was no hard sell or the sign-up-or-else-move-on kind of stares. I was left alone to think over what the leaflet had to say. I only asked them 'how's it going?'

The answers were direct but not in any gloating or boastful way, it felt very un-American for its quiet modesty. I found that a little disconcerting. 'Surprising, phenomenal, unreal, too good to have believed in when John Kahn said to us go out there and show the people we're in their neighbourhoods.'

That's all I heard from the helpers, all volunteers from mixed backgrounds and races. The Independence Party, John Kahn no less, has taken in a lot of folks who might not be entirely at one, or comfortable, with his core beliefs but we're all looking and wondering where's it going to end? He's on a roll, even if the platform for his candidacy is a little hazy on the detail.

He's got many folks, registered voters, thinking that he can really make a difference, and the elections are certainly going to be like no other. The Independence Party is on the ballot paper as a challenger, not hanging on by prayer alone; they're proclaiming themselves as a force for change.

They're doing it the hard way but folks are really taking notice; making a difference has already happened. The nomination phase saw a surge in membership; they were scrupulous in their systems for registering support. Now, after the Primaries there are likely to be three names up for the General Election; one of them is going to be an Independence Party candidate. You can't ignore twenty five percent plus of the electorate so easily, that's what the end of poll figures in the Primaries came up with for him and there's everything to play for now. Those who are undecided have a new name to think on.

Many will say that it is a change from the usual election routine, so it's a great deal of fun and a diversion from reality. It's a mighty tall rock face that the Independence Party will have to climb but they're not bothered by the challenge. Electoral Reform, it seems, will have to be achieved by the 'people' voting for a choice of candidates, and in sufficient numbers, to make a real contest. In doing so the voters, not political party mandarins or vested interests, will decide the outcome.

John Kahn merely put forward a different way of making political dreams come true.

"Where's the fun in it all if success comes easily to you?" he said to me with an engaging smile. Many have seen the look on his face to know that the guy isn't going to go away so easily and commentators like me have something new to talk about.'

He was in the City when the news finally broke. On the TV stations, the radio, and even the buzz in the bars was all too real. Gerard witnessed it all and shared a drink with colleagues in the office. A certain John Kahn had confounded the critics and won the right to be a part of the General Election. It was something to talk about and to speculate how the story might end

"History's been made…and I suppose you'll want to go back for the real thing?" Hans laughed over the phone.

"You bet! My namesake's a part of it now! I can't miss it!" Awe and disbelief at what had so far been achieved could be heard in his voice.

"At least I'll know where you are, Gerard." He heard the booming laugh and imagined his Editor's face, every hint of his sarcasm to be seen upon it and in the look of his eyes. "By the way, I haven't read any copy about the conference you were covering for me, Gerard."

"You've got *some* copy…what more do you want?"

"I was hoping for more insight and investigative rigour."

"You'll get that too. In the meantime, I've written something else…it was an impulsive, spur of the moment thing."

He acknowledged that Hans had indulged him by allowing the trip to proceed. But then, Hans knew a bigger story required adequate preparation and of Gerard Kahn he had no need to be concerned.

"When did you ever do that?" Hans laughed, teasing him once more.

"I know, Hans…only this time someone close…closer, say, is making some news."

New York, September
Political Travel or One Man's Journey *by* Gerard Kahn©

'It doesn't seem so long ago that I first wrote about a namesake, John Kahn, an aspirant for the job of the Mayor of New York setting out on a journey. I also wrote about my expectations of him. What was he to so many people, then? Was he a political hopeful, a parvenu, or simply an opportunist? The answer's 'no', now, to the first point and probably 'yes' to the many who didn't vote for him, a 'chancer', in the Primary Ballots yesterday. They're the means for each party to choose a candidate to go through to the General Election in November.

Whichever way you may look at the contest, convention has this time been turned on its head. The General Election for a new Mayor has an outsider as one of the candidates, a rank outsider. John Kahn has a reputation but until the Primaries this was not regarded in any political sense as truly newsworthy or to be bothering yourself with. Wrong! Oh so wrong!

This is New York, so everyone takes an interest…even more so now.

Many, very many people, have been proved to be way out of touch. Many more, more than enough have taken to the guy and his message. No-one can really pin him down on the details of his policy or gain any insight of his political credo. He simply believes in doing things differently and doing them right. His critics in the Primary Election run-up tried to point out his failings; he did the same of his opponents but there was a difference; he argued the case rather than shouting the opposition down. To change poignantly an old phrase from the 1930's 'might was not right', or, put another way, 'I'll shout you down until no one else can hear the real and true arguments for change'.

John Kahn found a voice, and a potent one at that, to express the hopes and ambitions of a far wider electorate than many thought would turn up to cast a vote. He can boast of one significant achievement already – more people bothered to register with a political party, the Independence Party to be exact and to make his candidacy a cause for celebration. Democracy means 'of the people', and he has certainly spurred many more into taking an active part. Many will say that is for the good of New York; others will say, sure, but John Kahn's not the man to really deliver on their hopes.

He told us himself during one of the staged but extremely effective TV face-offs (yes, sorry, I fall for the occasional American cliché) with his opponents that things could, and now had to be, done differently. Too many people were out of the loop (OK, I'll stop it) or on the outside looking in (I must stop, now) for the political process to feel truly democratic.

Political pundits or theorists may dispute this last claim. But, one thing is certain, the City of New York faces a period of change, changes of mind and perception, changes of people for all we can tell right now. Most of all, there's a change of attitude. If he achieves nothing else, John Kahn has provoked people to look at themselves and the political processes, institutions and personnel that have governed them for so long. What John Kahn may have started is a change in circumstances, and for all anyone knows the changes may yet affect John Kahn most of all.

He must be a happy guy this morning, as on most mornings over the last few days since he got through the nomination stage and now the Primaries. He may well say to himself as he shaves, 'you ain't seen nothing yet!'

We'll see.

There's not so long to keep us waiting now, is there, John Kahn?'

"Edi, I'm coming home! Our man has made the cut! He's in the play-offs!"

Gerard didn't quite know why he taken to using golf parlance to set the scene but it seemed entirely appropriate. The newspaper, opened at the place where an article had caught his eye, was cast aside for a moment. He sent the text message before the mobile had to be switched off. The aircraft doors were closed and the flickering cabin lights indicated that the engines were being started.

"We can book our next trip…to come back here, together! For better or worse!"

JOHN KAHN – A MAN ON A MISSION
By Anita Maguire

I last wrote about John Kahn and expressed the opinion that here was a man to be listened to. It would seem that many New Yorkers have done just that. They've listened to him, questioned him, thought about his message and what opportunities may open up for them and their city; and then, they went out and voted for him! The guy has gone and achieved the unthinkable. He's broken what many regarded as the stranglehold of the two main parties on this City. Remember? I said that John Kahn was a man who would be difficult to ignore; it seems that I was not the only one to think it.

I was told that he wished to make a difference, to deliver a shattering message from voters and constituents in the city that things had to change. It was time for new ideas to see the light. New faces were needed of those that governed the city; new people were needed to deliver on the expectations of so many for learning in schools, for a chance to get a good job and a better or improved living environment.

305

Remember? He said those in power should listen to the people they served, all of them, those people who said do it "our way". Well, the result's been a wake up call. He is seen as effective; he must be, as John Kahn is the CEO of a very large business that produces results, consistently. He's convinced enough people that he's believable because he does not thread political clichés into his every-day speak; he doesn't dissemble in his conversations with voters, or in his interviews. He may be rich but he has made no show of it during the campaign so far.

Instead, he wears out shoe leather, shakes hands and talks to people out on the street at their level, face to face. He's not remote as you might have expected of a man with his wealth and connections. He plays all of that down and simply tries to debate the issues and see the problems many of the city's dwellers confront every day. What is more he works long hours; after all, he still is the boss of a very large company. Read into that what you like, but John Kahn's not afraid of hard work. Those close to him say he thrives on it, and they are the ones trying to keep up with him!

Most of all, it seems from the result, the guy's different. He's not a product of the two-party system many would have expected him to rise up from. Deliberately, he put all of that to one side, he played down any connection voters may have made between money, a high flying job, and an apartment up on Central Park…so the list goes on. He simply chose to pursue his electoral ambitions in his own way. He aims to succeed (or fail, as he may yet do) by force of argument and personality.

There's no hard sell of his political philosophy; some critics say you hear little of that in any discussions with him, either on the street or on the TV shows when he's invited to appear upon them. But, some are tired of the tub-thumping rhetoric of former elections. He seems to be there to talk a different message…to contrast and to compare.

The message, to many, sounds banal and over simplistic, trite even. But, it's worked, twice. And it is? "My candidacy is about the common good." Simple? It sure is! Obvious? That too! Credible? Ask those that have voted for him so far. They repeat the message he has articulated so well during his minimalist campaign, compare his budget to the other parties and where has it got them? Right! Do you see, now? The mayoral contest has developed into a three horse race of ideas not just personalities! 'Two party infighting and posturing is not the surest way to bring the services and organisation many believe this great city needs,' he told me.

I learnt something else from the people I talked to, people who until now had remained loyal to the system that governed this city or bedevilled it (depending on how your life's been affected). A few laughed, cynics that they are as I had been until I took the time to think it all through and restrained myself from flushing John Kahn's opinions down the memory pan with everything else I had ever heard from politicians. One word kept me, and many others, from doing so. I think; it was the use of the word "altruism". Ok, sure! The cynics said, of course the guy's altruistic; he's a politician, an unknown one, and he's on the make. He'd say just about anything…well, almost anything just to get your vote.

Do you know who to put your money on in the next and decisive round of voting? I'm not sure I am now; it's too close to call by my reckoning. And altruism, what about that? After I had thought all his ideas through, and listened to others in the hall where he had spoken on the eve of the first round of voting, they weren't indefinable ideas expressed on hot air. There was intent and a commitment to hang a substantive policy on the framework he spoke of. You know why others felt that way? Because they had thought of the man again; he's out there on the street, talking to people, telling people what motivates him to run for office, he talks they all say, with us not just to us! Yes, he talks to us, voters and citizens.

For him it seems that 'altruism', or dual purpose, needed to be explained. You're working on something for yourself, and yet…and yet, you're thinking of others, those less fortunate than you or with a start to life that was harder than you had. Those cynics in the crowd that didn't interrupt him laughed all the same. Easy, when you've got a wallet full of dough! Altruism is a few coins in the basket…then, get on with your own life.

It doesn't come down to money alone. Sure, it helps one heck of a lot but for John Kahn it is also about opportunity. That's what John Kahn's candidacy is all about…the message has been sharpened up but it has been there from the beginning of the campaign. The guy's learnt a lot and enough people saw it in the man to vote for him; John Kahn's someone whom you can't ignore or relegate to an also-ran. Altruism has a whole new meaning and John Kahn spelt it out during his campaign; he spoke of it out on the street but most of all it seems that people saw what he had done, out on the streets.

Do you understand me now?

It's not just talking up altruism, it's about doing it as well! He doesn't shout it out loud, he simply 'gets in there' and works on the problem, with folks, and for nothing; it's working with local charities and being committed to a cause rather than simply throwing money at the problem. It's what this city over the years has been very good at…when it has the cash, only folks don't want too many strings on the hand-outs. Instead, he calls them NAGs, one of the groups that he works with so effectively it seems. He calls them Neighbourhood Action Groups…they get some cash but they get local folks believing that the heavy hand of local government, and their 'apparatchiks' as he often describes them, don't figure nearly so prominently as before. It's local folks that get the work done and so build a community spirit that fights against areas sinking into no go areas or ghettos, as in the old days. You have a stake in your neighbourhood, you own a bit of it and you get some pride back. Another organisation he works with is 'Right Treatment'…that's where he learns of the problems unique to a Borough and some of the districts within them.

The other candidates have a record in city government; they have an advantage over him in that. So, John Kahn studies, listens, and according to many he learns. He spends time on the project, he doesn't buy knowledge as his critics or doubters might believe of him.

"With other people's money ideas come easy! You spend it and hope for more of where that came from! What I'm talking about is that everyone in a Borough has a stake in the outcome of their own efforts to improve where they live." That paraphrases the underlying message of the guy. I'm not talking him up, I'm merely explaining what the guy has secured for himself in the Primary Elections for Mayor and what others, many others, seem to have 'bought into'.

So, it's like this. Enough folks have listened and thought through his ideas to get him on the final ballot paper in November. What about next time? It's too close to call…but nothing would surprise me now about the man. Some call him John, or Jack, but, he waves such calls aside. There are no similarities, and he's his own man. He copies no one; that's why he's an Independence Party candidate for New York Mayor.

47
Amsterdam

"I'm listening to a programme…it's a political dialogue in the studio and out on the sidewalk. It's about the election and the main question seems to be *'why is a guy like John Kahn even doing this?'* It's another view of *'what's out there on the street'.* He faked an accent and broke into English as they spoke.

"You're beginning to sound like a native," Edith laughed softly. "Miss me?"

"Just a bit."

"Oh!"

"Silly question…sillier answer."

"Oh, okay," Edith went on airily. "I guess it is when you make it so obvious…that you do."

"Sarcasm gets its own reward, lievert."

"Promise?" she laughed brightly now. "I'll soon be home."

"For those tuning in…the question tonight is *'Who's going to run New York?'* Many of you will have a point of view so let's all share and talk it through. Call the number and join the line. In the meantime, folks are telling it as they find it for them…we're not being polite or following any structure. There's no rules, just say what's on your mind in answer to the question. And, for those of you just joining us…we've heard the first joke, so no more word fests, no more *'Who's going to ruin New York?'*"

"John Kahn's not the man!"

"If he pitches right the city will function with Steve Cruz as the new mayor!"

"Let's have someone…and something new! Please, please, please! We've had Steve Cruz's type before and the self interest groups he represents…and those un-elected jokers he speaks for…all of them meddlin' in our lives!"

"At least we've got a contest and not a two horse race with one of them a lame runner!"

"You're right there lady! Beejay will see them both off!"

"Garbage! That's what the last caller's just spoke!"

"Really? Least ways Beejay has experience managing budgets, looking after housing needs and the work needed for disadvantaged kids and families."

"Let's all vote in someone who reminds us of what Democracy is all about and leaves folks to decide how the city should really be governed."

"I can answer that last remark…let's pick anyone BUT a guy making medicines that the poorest in the world, or the sickest can't buy."

"Right! The previous caller…that lady, she hit the bull's eye! We don't need another corporate big shot. We need a guy from the streets and known on the streets and in the Boroughs…in them places that fat wallet John Kahn never set foot in…or been to 'cept in a limo."

"Jeez! What a jerk, that previous contributor…open your eyes, man! Read what's said about John Kahn! Sure, he's made it but he's not too proud to lend a hand…or give a buck."

"Did I hear you right?"

There was a laugh. "You did! The guy cares…so he *'gives'*!" There was a louder knowing laugh. "Get me man?"

"The guy's not real…give me, give the city, Steve Cruz."

"Status Quo, lady…the guy's a comfort zone baby. He won't do the real work for those that really need it…those without a loud voice."

"You think a guy like John Kahn will do the real work? He's all show…he wants to lead and see that others follow…put down the orders while he takes the credits. He's got no important friends."

"Save the people who follow him…and believe in him."

"One of the previous callers? He got this much right, John Kahn leads…"

"That man Kahn? The difference with him is that we know he's got everything figured out and knows what to do and who to call on. Above all, a guy like him was willing to step up to the plate...c'mon, throw it at me! I'm ready for ya! That's what he's sayin'."

"He holds out a plate, sir...corporate profit over social and human welfare."

"Bull crap! Sorry...sorry! That's just plain wrong! The guy's working his butt off running a business that takes big risks. When did you ever see Steve Cruz do that? Like a previous guy said...he's a comfort zone baby...while John Kahn ain't that, no way!"

"Steve Cruz don't exploit other folks lack of money...profiteering from sickness! What kind of example is the guy to our kids...tell me that?"

"Loads of folks do charity work and give money...it don't mean they're gonna be good Mayors an' all. We need a guy who's worked on it...long and hard and learnt...then learnt some more. Steve Cruz's the guy, folks. VOTE FOR STEVE CRUZ! Don't waste a precious vote on a Park Avenue smart ass!"

"Beejay's got so much experience goin' for him. He knows the City far too well to need any training for the job...not like a guy of John Kahn's background!"

"John Kahn's smart all right! Way too smart to bother with all this name calling and throwing dirt! I haven't heard it from him, not once. He speaks out what's on his mind, sure...but he's on the level...he meets and greets, I've seen it, he's on the same level as those he wants to help and to change what gives here in the City. He wants a new start on how we do things 'round here."

"Right...I'm with her, the smart lady...the previous speaker. It should be about US, all of US."

"Us! What baloney...since when was democracy about all of US...it's about a majority, stupids...a simple majority."

"Great! We're all stupid are we, for wantin' things to be different and gettin' a lot more folks involved in the politics of the city? Maybe...just maybe...we'll all get a new sense of community by voting...for whatever guy we believe in."

"Agree! I agree! It's about US for a change...that's ALL of US!"

"Right! All of us in New York! If it takes a guy like John Kahn to open eyes and change things then I'll be voting for him. What have we got to loose?...Ha! Only the costly old ways of doing things around here...the UN DEMOCRATIC ways of doin' things 'cos some of those guys and gals telling us how to live and breathe here didn't get my vote or anyone else's...they appeared!"

"Right on the button, man! We're ruled by apparatchiks, you know? They're the appointees of some self-interest group or union…they don't really care about most of us folks. Independence of thought…a change in voting style and choice…that's good and John Kahn made it happen, he's given us the chance…just by working and being there. Like him…we've gotta be brave and help to get it right."

"We gotta believe it'll be different…"

"It will be…vote for Steve Cruz! He's the right man!"

"Get real lady! We're goin' to upset the status quo and move on to doin' things different…the people will vote for it…they'll vote for John Kahn!"

"The drugs peddlar?"

"Be careful, man! His companies make things we have all used to get through the day…some cost a little more."

"Like a few thousand lives you mean…in Africa?"

"Why go so far? Look closer to your own doors, folks…since when did rich guys care for anyone else out there on the street…way below them and their Park Avenue apartment?"

"Since four years ago, ma'am, when John Kahn and the charities he helps made a heap of difference…in the Boroughs where you say men like him don't go. You got that wrong…I knows 'cos I've seen him do it with the charity helpers…I've seen 'im with my own eyes!"

"Sure lady, the one's likely to fix things for him…he's not been in all of them harder boroughs and neighbourhoods, showing his face and talkin'… like Steve Cruz has gone an' done."

"So wrong…ahhuh…ahhuh!"

"Enough ain't ever enough…sorry…but the guy don't just talk about doin' good…he's out on the street workin' on doin' it! He's helpin' out in any ways he can. He just don't talk about it much."

"Until election time!"

The show's presenter interrupted the volleys of opinion that flew over the airwaves between unknown constituents of the three mayoral candidates. He had allowed the fire to be exchanged between the camps and followers of them all, and yet could not resist the utterance of a closing observation on the night's proceedings.

"Listening to all the previous callers I guess Steve Cruz and Beejay have a real fight on their hands."

"Guess so," he was told by an unmonitored intervention. "An' it's time… real time, for change."

"Thank you…whoever you were."

"I'm still here," came the laughing rejoinder. "Pull another plug! A big change, that's what's goin' to happen...it's something else that's good to tell everyone, about John Kahn!"

It wasn't over, not all the lines had been cleared; a willingness to show support, to score points or throw an insult at the candidates was too good an opportunity to miss; so, the show's presenter "butted out" for a while longer.

"The only good thing about John Kahn's candidacy is that he'll get beat, by political argument...it's not somethin' we've heard too much of from the guy."

"With Beejay...with William J. Newhouse you get to hear all the arguments!"

"But none of the answers, lady!"

"Where have you all been the last hour or so? Callers have been saying they want *change*...no more cosy fix its or patch ups by an elite of *'socios'* in the Boroughs."

"Oh! I get it! Keep it tight, keep it restricted to one *socio* group, the ones that live off Park Avenue...is that it? I thought we'd been talkin' about Democracy earlier in the show!"

"Sure we did, the right of the majority to vote for change...open change... a vote for the opportunity to take a chance that the future will be different...in time may be better...and one hell of a surprise, for all of us!"

"And I'm one who likes the Kahn do mentality!"

"Give us a break lady! It's funny enough having a guy like John Kahn coming onto the scene trying to sell us something we don't want!"

"Like real democracy, a people's choice? Is that it Mister?"

"Thanks to all contributors...we'll soon know who's got the keys to Gracie Mansion. Good night...keep talking...put down your vote. That seems to be the message comin' out of all your calls tonight."

There had been no carefully worded arguments or thoughts deployed by the callers, just a visceral intent to express an opinion. The show's presenters wondered, at first, why so many contributors insisted on leaving a voice message for the three candidates to hear. Then the last caller's words delivered in a polite and calm voice came to mind; they felt compelled to play them back and did so before the closing music began.

"There are many of us in the city who like to hear another voice putting out an argument for change and showing us a different way to look at our so called 'democracy'. The fact that it's someone unheard of in political circles...but very well known in business, does not mean that he should be ignored. He's holding

up a mirror and maybe some of the callers before me don't like what they've seen staring back at them."

48
New York

Elbee entered the office after a perfunctory knock on her door.

"Hi?" Joey looked up from her papers. "We'll finish this in a moment or two," she smiled at her assistant. Nothing else was said until they were alone; Elbee even resorted to seeing that the door was properly closed.

"I thought you might like to read this. I have people check the web...the press...anything that has John Kahn or his business in the public's eye. I call it keeping one step ahead, only this guy's taking more than a passing interest in John."

He held a newspaper cutting in one hand while he pointed to the article.

"Okay, don't get jumpy about it...or the newspapers. They'll do anything for a story."

"Easy to say. There's a pattern...it's beginning to show. The guy writing that stuff is with a Dutch paper...but I've already checked them out. They have a New York office and...they have researchers there."

"So?"

"So, here's the good bit," Elbee faked a smile, "one of their researchers just happens to appear in a photo with Dayle."

"So? John's name is out there and everyone wants to know about him...his family, gossip about him and the girls and so on. It's society gossip stuff...it also helps to show the guy has more to his life then just business."

"Well...I'll keep checking on things and recording what I can. You never know when it'll become handy...as a lever for those out to get him."

John had often spoken of the roles that Elbee assumed in guarding him and his business; he likened it to the work of a gatekeeper. John had made his remarks not to diminish the loyalty shown to him but out of respect that Elbee maintained an extensive contact list that enabled him to obtain information that could one day be used to defend his friend and client.

"Where'd you get it," she asked him, "the picture?".

For once the answer was not what she had expected to hear. "The Internet."

"It was that simple?"

"Yeah...a society page, web chat rooms...they tell it all, what's going down...who's doin' what and to whom. Get my drift?" he said needlessly. "Dayle featured as the lippy kid that had John Kahn as a father."

"So, I guess it was nothing complimentary."

"No, Joey. That's what I keep on telling our man. You just don't know what's out there...being written or recorded that may come up and '*bite*' you."

"I'll let John know, and Jacqueline..."

"Just John!" he interrupted sharply. "Never mind telling her! She's not part of everything we speak to John of! She has her uses...but only as a part of the Election for Mayor thing. What you're holding onto for him...as I am, is business, his family concerns, nothing more. The guy who wrote it is in the business section of that Dutch paper. While John's workin' on how to become Mayor we're working on the patents and his pharmaceutical company's interests. Politics and that side of his life aren't goin' to be the best of companions...so I want to be prepared, for anything."

Now she knew why he had been so abrupt when he called on her. His moods could be unpredictable and she sensed that Elbee was not at all comfortable with John's political ambitions.

"So we keep watching him, this guy...Gerard Kahn...and what he writes," Joey made up for an earlier remark. "We can all help you in that".

"I watch him, what he puts out. I'm on to it. You mind that John's business interests are sealed up...real tight!"

She gave Elbee a moment's stare. "He matters, to us both...and to a lot of folks that have met him and seen what he could achieve. The tracking polls tell their own story...John's competing with the main party candidates...no question about it."

"Right...so maybe we've got to find a way to let Dayle know whom she should hang out with," he said.

"What I know of her that's the last thing we're about to go and do, Elbee."

"I'll go and find a way to tell John...he's working like a man possessed. The ground game has got them all wondering how he does it, and finds the time to take care of the stockholders' interests."

"People see a guy who's not all image...playing a part in the election. They see him walking the streets and meeting folks. He's shown the others that his ground game is as good as spending all the money they have on advertising or selling their ideas."

"Well, whatever the secret...I don't want any personal entanglements getting in his way or fouling up the work he's down to. I'll take him up on that...on Dayle and the newspaper guy."

"Mind how you do so," Joey said without blinking as she stared at him.

She too could be regarded as a 'personal entanglement' but John sought her out; a close working relationship was seen as the perfect disguise for a deeper association. Over the course of their relationship she had become adept at controlling what was at work between them.

"Hi darling…it's your Pops!"

"Hi."

"Bad time to call you?" It had gone past eleven and John sat in his 'den' a glass of beer in hand. "It's kinda late…"

"No…I've just arrived home. What's up?"

"Nothing girl…nothing serious. Got to ask you somethin'…"

"Just don't know how to start?" Dayle gave a teasing laugh on hearing the hesitancy in his voice. The mobile 'phone was cradled between her cheek and shoulder as she shrugged off her jacket and kicked off her shoes. "I'll help you. I've been out and I'm still behaving myself…I'm a good girl."

"Out with anyone I should know of?"

"You know him…least ways you've met him, just once."

"Who? The newspaper guy? From that Dutch 'paper?"

"Why think it's him?"

"I wasn't," he replied unconvincingly. "I just had to ask."

"At this time of night?"

"Okay," John sighed, "it could've kept until I saw you tomorrow…only, I keep getting these newspaper articles, pieces about the Election. They're to the mark…I just wanted to warn you."

"Not to get used by anyone…is that your take on this guy?"

"I've been round the block a few times, honey."

"And I've been around you long enough to learn something…even at my tender age."

"Okay, suitably told off."

"Dad…" It was said slowly and not in agreement with his remark.

She strode into the small living area of her apartment and flounced onto the sofa. Great place, up-to-the-minute furniture, pictures on the walls some would give a heap of money for and that Dad didn't want; all that and yet her bed was cold. Nico was either playing very hard to get, not a trait she'd seen in him the first time they'd met and on their dates, but maybe it was all show, or there was something after all to Dad's question. Go one step further, was he '*really*' warning her?

Maybe Nico cared enough for her not to go compromising the family or his own feelings by using their hitherto platonic relationship to serve his paper's interests. There, that might be the reason why they had so much fun together and got real close, but not so close they shook off their clothes and took a tumble. She'd break him, such were the feelings he aroused in her by his look or an occasional touch on her; his teasing, perhaps, was part of the routine, extended foreplay until consummation in a few days when the spotlight was finally off them. She'd seen the society snaps, of them at a party, and the speculation that ran with the pictures about their relationship. Nico didn't look like a newspaper guy, that's what they all said, and he was open enough to admit that the work didn't course through his veins like in some he could mention, working for his 'paper.

"Dayle?"

"Yeah?" she said absentmindedly.

"Okay, I won't bother you any longer. Have a good night…see you tomorrow?"

"Yeah."

"The last week before election day starts then'."

"Yeah…Dad?"

"Yes, girl?"

"I just meet the guy and we go out. There's nothing more to it…no secrets are given away across the pillows, understand me?"

"Yes, darling," he replied making it sound as though he was apologising for his intrusion. "I'm real sorry to have bothered you…over a fool thing. There's some ways of asking that still don't work for me."

She gave a soft laugh on hearing his admission; it was so utterly touching and so like her father.

"Don't go all political on me, Dad…be with me as you always were, straight out and to the point. We don't…we never did finesse things with each other, did we?"

"No girl," he agreed. "You're a wonder…and I love you."

"I love you too Pops. I never grow tired of hearing you tell me."

"Many years of that to come…and not just from me. That's what I hope for you."

"You never know," she said in reply before he rang off.

The New York Mayoral Election – An Outsider's View of the Citizen's Choices
From an article by Gerard Kahn©, De Telegraaf of Amsterdam

Funny, if you've never been in politics or run for office you're nothing but a rookie, a guy who's ignorant of the real political world, how it clicks and turns, and how it's lived out there on the streets and in the neighbourhoods. Whereas, if you've grown up in politics, cut your teeth on the dogfights and trades, you're

*supposed to come from a political class (say it softly, a proclaimed political elite...
or, ayleet as they say it over there) and so you know it all. You play by familiar
rules and so you bite your tongue or finesse the words when you have to. You know
someone else is right only you have your own agenda to follow and you'll see it
through, somehow.*

*It's a learning process. Many may ask, 'when are the lessons going to sink
in'? Isn't that 'funny', or does real change only come about when the comfortable
status quo is overthrown?*

*It may go something like this – 'So, mister or misses constituent, you floating
voters or undecided residents...vote for us and we'll see what we can do to really
make it work. Trust us...believe us...vote for us...it'll be as we say. If it isn't,
well...we tried. We didn't go givin' any guarantees! We just told you things might
be tough before they got better. In the end it'll be thanks to us that we made the
changes. Anything's better than what's gone on before, isn't that right?'*

Well?

Okay, I hear the doubts in your voices, but you've got to believe in someone.

*It's simply a choice, the taking of a calculated risk. You're only casting your
vote. It isn't as though you're playing a game of Russian roulette!*

*You've seen the faces, met the candidates at rallies or meetings. You've seen
or heard them, on the TV or the radio; you may even have met them out on your
street. They're no giants, just ordinary folks, some with more money than you or I
will ever see in a lifetime and beyond, but heaven can wait. As a New York citizen
you may say, 'We need to get by here first and we'd like to do it in a peaceful, clean
and prospering City, fit for all whichever Borough we live in.'*

*And so people will tell them, 'Where's the danger? Are you worried about
making your choice?' Is it wish-fulfilment over substance, the new guy on the
voter's register against the wise guys who will claim 'we've been there and done
that'? Heck no! You're faced with a choice so what's the difference between three
and two? One! You're right. You only need one right choice to make it work out,
after that where's the risk?*

*I don't see it. Whether you've got a new guy or older experienced ones in
the game, it comes down to the performance in the job. So what if there's a new
candidate to choose from? It's a new set of ideas, in a new body, with different eyes
to see what's going on, under everyone's noses...and, for all I know before those
with myopic vision. What is it they say? Oh yeah. Familiarity breeds contempt.
You could put it in another way; you get complacent.*

*Democracy's for everyone, top down to the grass roots or from pavement level
up to the sky, the tip of the Empire State Building and beyond. Pick whichever
cliché you like or fits the situation, only pick the person too that will deliver what
you believe in and what you think really needs doing.*

The winner's a servant, nothing more. He may be in it for the ego, the next career step, or for a genuine belief in what is good for his fellow man. Maybe, there's a bit of each motivational instinct in all of them. The right person for you is the one whom you believe has these three character traits in balance or weighed up carefully, one against the others.

Whoever wins it the burden of delivering on their promises is heavy. Sure, you get help, but you have the expectations of your supporters on your shoulders. Then, there are the hopes of those folks you persuaded to vote for you, maybe against traditional voting habits or their better judgement in the heat of the election; you hold all of that in your hands too.

Take the chance!

You never know. A few citizens may make all the difference, to how it is for them in that world-renowned City and for others. After the big day they will all have to learn to live a little closer with a new Mayor in City Hall.

It had become common practice; candidates for Mayor took part in a debate of the issues, on TV and before a peak audience. The announcer on WCBS calmly observed that this year the event had a special significance; three candidates were in the studio whereas in the past only the front-runners from the two main parties attended. The station specialised in hard news and pursued its own investigative trails but the progress of John Kahn onto the General Election ballot paper had them perplexed.

There was nothing new to say about the man. Viewers of their nightly headline show would have regarded him as a long shot, a rookie, and a candidate whose only purpose was to make the main contenders think through their own policies. He'd be long gone when the real day dawned, many said.

Yet here he was in a TV studio; John Kahn stood before them, his place conspicuously poignant. Whether it had been a premeditated act to place John Kahn between the two main party candidates would soon be revealed when the show began. Maybe the producer had seen the Independence Party candidate for what he was, newsworthy but caught in between two hard hitters from the political establishment. He would be questioned and taken on, from both flanks; it made for greater visual interest. If John Kahn stood to one side he would face both opponents at once; it did not make for the best disposition of the political contenders.

No, the staging was ideal. He was, still, the interloper.

Michelene Danvers, the pushy presenter of that evening's show even made the point as they prepared and undertook minor last minute adjustments.

"Glad you could be here," she smiled, speaking in a remote voice to John as if the moment was a matter of routine for her.

"And I'm pleased to have earned the votes of my supporters." He gave an easy reply, adding, "it's thanks to all of them that I'm here."

She turned to the other candidates and greeted them as one who had known the 'players' for some time.

Sound checks were completed, the lighting for the opening credits set and the large screen behind the candidates paled until the station's logo appeared out of a mist, WCBS.

"Clear the floor," someone called out. "Candidates stand still...face the cameras and watch the monitors. Remember! Look up and to your front! The viewers want to see your faces!"

"Joyful and triumphant," Beejay muttered, prompting laughter from his opponents.

"Still!" came the order once more.

"Too soon to speak of it, Beejay," Steve Cruz whispered, loud enough for them to hear it. "First, it's 'oh come all ye faithful'."

"Only they're changing sides, Steve," John observed lightly before looking him in the eyes.

"We'll soon see, John."

"Count on it."

"Face the cameras...keep still, gentlemen! Please?"

The TV channel was one that John often tuned to and he had prepared for the evening. He knew that his image on the screen had to be clean cut, visible and crisp. So, he had dressed accordingly, in a dark finely tailored suit, a bright striped tie and a shirt that showed off a robust, still youthful and healthy complexion to its full advantage. Jacqueline had given her own advice, don't merge into a light background that the TV channel so often used; *'stand out and make yourself heard'* had been her recommendation and he had taken it all in.

His planning for the show had gone further; he considered all the likely policy issues that might be raised and he produced 'flash cards' on each topic. They had served as an aide memoire and had been studiously read through. They dealt with the issues in a question and answer style. If they came at him on any topic he had a response, or a reasoned argument that prepared him sufficiently so as not to be caught off guard.

The lectern before him was bare. He had decided upon projecting the image of competence by being fully informed on all that *'was out there'* or *'in play'* for him and the other candidates to deal with. Only, he had his own take on the situation out on the streets, gathered from the host of walkabouts and meetings, some impromptu gatherings, that he had gone through.

He was prepared; he would listen and express his views.

'Speak to your unseen audience, out there, as you would do if you were in the meeting halls with them, Jacqueline had advised him. *'Use your direct way of speaking so that they know you mean what you've got to tell them'.*

Man, was he pleased to have got that woman onto his team; Jacqueline was invaluable and he had prepared thoroughly for the debate. Yes, he would speak out and in the direct language that he knew the circumstances now required.

"Good Evening. Welcome everyone! Welcome to 'Have your Say' the programme that tonight brings together three exceptional candidates for the General Election. The prize is to be Mayor of New York." Michelene's enthusiasm set the mood. *"The citizens of New York have voted in the Primaries and the candidates with me tonight are the voters choices! William Newhouse…the Republican Party candidate, Steve Cruz…Democrat Party…both of them are familiar faces, and then we have the Independence Party candidate…a certain John Kahn."*

She was held in high regard by the station and viewers, so, Michelene could phrase her introductions as she pleased.

"The format of tonight's programme…a debate of the issues facing the City of New York, in all of its five Boroughs…is, first of all, for the candidates to make a short personal statement…that's followed by a debate. My role is to watch the time, ask the candidates to play by the rules, but I won't be too strict!" she laughed, *"for once. All I'm here to do is to see that the candidates spell out what they stand for and that we get through an interesting range of subjects. You will have noticed that we have made a bit of history! We have three candidates…and I'm holding three envelopes."*

Michelene walked by each lectern and held out the envelopes for each candidate to choose from.

"Thank you, maam," John said only to be met by a moment's startled reaction on her face. He tore open the envelope, out of curiosity, then placed it on the ledge before him. A small card was clutched in one hand.

She gave them all a glance on returning to her seat; Michelene faced them but to one side so as not to interrupt the camera's view. A trivial moment of theatre followed.

"Open your envelopes…those of you who could wait…and hold up the card inside, gentlemen. It will show who opens tonight's debate." She paused for only an instant. "You're making news all the time! John Kahn, lead on!"

"I'm a certain John Kahn," he smiled, looking down at Michelene as he spoke, "and I am the candidate for the Independence Party. As you can see, I stand here tonight between the two political parties who have considered themselves as the incumbents of the city's political stage. I'm taking this moment to thank all of you who voted for me in the Primaries and who I hope are persuaded to do so again in a week's time, in the General Election.

"On that day, the choice will be between managed change and a departure from the usual way of doing things, or, continuing as we are with the to-and-fro of old political arguments. A vote for the Independence Party is a vote for giving a voice, democratically heard, to many more of the city's citizens. Many of you have already gone out and done it!"

He held out his arms and moved them in a way that seemed to draw people closer to him but he quickly resumed a more authoritative posture. What he had just engaged in seemed too staged, sentimental and ridiculous.

"You've taken your chance and voted! More of you have done so…and I hope that the idea of change will enthuse many, many more because democracy is what we really need around here, not a vote of thirty or so percent of all those who are eligible to do so. Many of you have done it," he told them in a voice that rose to reflect his acknowledgement of a task achieved. "You see? Casting your votes doesn't cost much and you have a stake in the outcome."

John gave an engaging laugh and looked ahead, directly at the camera before him.

"And, what are you deciding on if you cast a vote for the Independence Party? I'd say it was a vote to see that you all got the right return on your investment, call it something real…of value to you in return for the taxes that are paid. You can call it a payback in services for those that need them most right here in the City. I'm for making every cent go that little bit further and to waste nothing.

"So, it means that your kids get schooling, a proper and credible education; you get clean and safe streets. It also means that you get a neighbourhood where you can keep hold of the stake you have in it, be it a family connection, work or the environment you live in. You look after your neighbourhood you choose to stay in because it's become a part of your life and you'd like to see it get well, and then a whole lot better. It also means claiming your housing vouchers or any food coupons you're entitled to and using them without any stigma attached to doing so. You know, some people pass on them rather than damage their pride…so I've been working hard to make sure organisations help people get what's due to them. Others here see it differently."

He gave his opponents a moment's stare and nodded in their direction.

"Above all, your vote means that your money, what the City takes in local taxes goes and is spent on services, not on the heavy hand of bureaucracy. It's not, to me, money to be spent on keeping some people in jobs where they can seek to control every day lives and extract what they can from a distortion of an otherwise true, but under-represented democratic process.

"The Independence Party has had one simple message to give and that it has learnt during the few hard months of campaigning. It is getting the right treatment to as many people that need help as we can. It's an idea that has drawn many voters in…new voters and others that have changed sides. So, a vote for independent thought means a vote that you are all treated right, you get a helping hand…when you really need it."

John paused for a moment in his assured delivery; the notes off the flash cards were clearly recalled; he glanced occasionally at his opponents but reserved most of his attention for his audience.

"For those that don't need a helping hand I am standing to make the environment for business better, to allow self-reliance to flourish without the need to take away basic rights or benefits. There are many that still deserve them, and then, there are others that need to be encouraged to find a different way, citizens who don't work at making a life for themselves.

"I've seen a lot of pride on people's faces when they tell me what they've achieved. They ask me to spread the idea that most could take their lives in their own hands and make a better place of where they live and how they live their lives. And, to reassure them I have said that a basic premise of my candidacy is the right treatment for those that deserve it most. I tell folks that in those situations they're not alone…there's someone to look out for them if they really need it and local services are called upon. Otherwise, go on! Go on and make a life for yourself and I'll make the environment right for you to do that, or for others to come in and create work that you can take on so that lives can be lived the way the individuals want.

"And so, in conclusion…I say this…a vote for me and the Independence Party is seeing to a change in your lives and circumstances. It's time to see that there is a meaningful pay back on what is taken from you to make your District or Borough a better place. It's about putting you, the citizen in control."

He paused only to take a breath and to gather final thoughts.

"It's different," he said in a softer voice to reassure, "but it's not scary. It's like changing your job, or getting one for the first time…you know the outline and some of the detail. The fine points come out later…but the way ahead has been laid out for you to see. Enough of you have been persuaded to follow the Independence Party route. See to it, if you believe in our ways so strongly, that others do. Change, a real change in personnel and in the ways of delivering or performing a service outstandingly well, all of it for a changing population and ethnic mix…all of them are vital to the future of our city…our City of New York!"

He delayed for an instant.

"Yes, to achieve that a change is vital...vital to *everyone* in the City, not just to special interest groups."

49

Michelene had moved to her position, out of camera shot, and before John had finished. She spoke brightly once more.

"Thank you John Kahn. Before the next speaker...I'm asking that you keep questions until the debating process starts. However, there's nothing to prevent those who follow from making observations on what has been said so far. That's the advantage, or handicap, of the draw."

"Beejay?" she called out before correcting her over-familiar address; her reputation permitted such lapses. "William Newhouse...it's your call. John Kahn took a little over four minutes."

"I'll bear that in mind."

He looked up for a moment to see the studio clock a bright digital timepiece that could be made out beyond the studio lights. Beejay instinctively touched papers arranged before him in a moment of reflection. Observing him John noted the ordered mind of a man who had devoted much of his working life to finance and a comptroller's assignments. He was undoubtedly diligent but the brief touch to the papers and their perfect arrangement suggested a conformist nature; here was a man who abided by the rules.

"Hard as he may try to do so, John Kahn does not succeed in making me regret being the Republican candidate nor has he succeeded in persuading members of my party to cross the lines to join him." He looked to his side but did not catch John's eye. "Oh, a renegade joined his team...but we weren't uptight about that event for long."

"I'll make you retract that slur," John said to him, leaning away from his lectern and closer to Beejay, covering the microphone hidden under his jacket's lapel as he did so.

He was unconcerned for any intervention that Michelene might choose to make. But, she remained seated and John saw the nod of her head perhaps in response to instructions to let it go, to allow the heat to rise in any exchanges that might follow. The unpredictable nature of an event such as this could make for good television.

Beejay made out he was unconcerned by the intervention and waved him away.

"As the campaign has progressed, and this evening has just shown us, the Independence Party's role has been seen for what it is...opportunist and to many people a confection of ideas and policies. No one has endorsed them

323

except for those small groups on the fringes of main stream activity. The Republican and Democrat parties are the main stream political forces in the City, supported by a few special interest groups that are unafraid to ally their beliefs to ours.

"Long may that continue. The City needs certainty…not vanity."

"Another insult…of voters this time that you'll regret," John said a little louder but without turning his head.

Beejay felt compelled to pause but, again, only for an instant.

"My candidacy…and the Republican Party…we have the endorsements and the support of those who believe in sound governance of the City, in a well-funded and proportionate policing of our city against any external threat or the misdeeds of some citizens. The Republican Party continues to recognise the consistent, valuable and determined contribution of minority and ethnic groups to the city's growth and continuing vitality. So, there's nothing new in that either…John Kahn suggested in his *brief* statement that the recognition of other social groupings in our city was somehow his adopted party's sole preserve.

"We can and will do more. We aim to do more than simply promote the belief that the school system needs reform. We're goin' to take that on! Our present system doesn't work…it's poorly managed…and thanks to Democratic Party policies it leaves many school leavers ill equipped, under educated and unprepared for work in the modern world.

"With that legacy how can they hope to meet the day-to-day problems or the challenges of the future, for home-grown industry and from foreign endeavours? It's the only thing that I can bring myself to agree with John Kahn about."

It was clear that he felt passionately about this part of the statement as he tapped the lectern to make a point; he was light on his feet and moved as if in time with each point that he had to make in the few minutes allotted to him.

"I'll resist the temptation to speak about the Independence Party for longer than it deserves. It doesn't merit such consideration. It is, after all, a party that has in the past fused its registered votes to those of another. Now, rather than ride on the coat tails of a main party it mixes up the tenets of both and proclaims that a new dawn is about to break." He drew breath then cried out, "Baloney! Don't believe a word of it.

"The General Election is still, during the last few days of the final run in, going to be between the Republican and Democratic parties, between controlled spending and the *'tax 'em till it hurts'* mentality of my real political opponent. There was even talk…but it's gone quiet, on a *'shares traded tax'*. No, nothing has changed too drastically in the final days of this election. It is between a fit for purpose city government service of the Republicans and that of a party in debt to self-interest groups like the service unions.

"The choice remains sharply defined, between the Republican and Democratic Party candidates. The Independence Party is not the answer to the city's problems neither are the policies espoused by the Democrats.

"I have the experience, with the Republican party, to manage the affairs of this great City as all taxpayers would wish them to be governed and that is what I am calling on all viewers and listeners to vote for."

"That's two statements! Let's see now what Steve Cruz has to say for the Democratic Party. You can pick over what you've heard," Michelene smiled at him. "Beejay took just under four minutes."

"You see?" Beejay exclaimed. "You get more for less with me and the Republican Party."

"Including gratuitous and inflammatory remarks about my staff…and not a darn thing about real policy." In spite of Jacqueline's advice not to interrupt the proceedings John had to make the point. "There's nothing there to make the blood flow a little faster."

"You're in a new environment, John," Beejay retorted haughtily. "There are rules to a night like this."

"And you've broken some already…what an example." John made light of it.

"Ease up, gentlemen," Michelene spoke up at last. "We can all share in the repartee later! So save it! Before then…we're going to hear the story according to the Democratic Party candidate. What have you got to say that will ignite the discussion between you all, Steve Cruz?"

"Simply this, ladies and gentlemen viewers, first time voters on the register, or you long lived citizens of our great City. Many of you have seen these debates and elections come and go. But…there's a consistent thread running through them…a Democratic Party that stands for all the people…and this General Election will be no different. Why? It's because the Democratic Party is one of only two contenders in what Beejay has correctly called a two-horse race. Only, I'll correct him on one thing. My opponent's horse has two riders!"

Steve Cruz paused with great effect as he allowed his remark to settle on the mind and be thought through.

"From what I have seen over the last few weeks of an interesting campaign and who I am debating with tonight I am certain that my opponents blur into one…they are Republicans, but of dissimilar styles, that's all. The rightist attitude is conveyed in the double speak of my opponents, to my right…so very appropriate is the setting here.

"By 'double-speak' I mean nothing more than that it is right wing politics of the kind we expect from the Republican Party but the story of one, spoken loud and clear by Beejay Woodhouse, comes back as a distorted echo from the other, from a certain John Kahn.

"The one has done service for the city. The other has used the city to serve his own ends, be it on Wall Street and trades in his company's shares or on the streets where he has persuaded members of another party, the real Independence Party, to follow him on a political adventure.

"From both of my opponents here tonight, and elsewhere, I have heard the arguments of a well heeled elite rehearsed. They are the proposals for lower taxes and budgets squeezed so tight that the city's neediest citizens and young folk, the city's future, are to be the ones to suffer and who are denied their rightful place."

"Not so. You haven't been listening at all." John interrupted.

Steve made as if he hadn't heard him.

"Over the last few weeks, and again tonight…from John Kahn, we've heard the anti service union mantra. But who, exactly, without those hard working women and men, will serve our community? Who's goin' to do that and serve the people that John Kahn and Beejay Woodhouse claim to be speaking up for?

"I'll tell you…no one is, cos folks will go short, or turn to other ways to survive."

"Again, not true."

"You've had your say for now, John." Michelene cut in. "Let Steve Cruz speak for his party."

"Thank you." Steve paused.

The delivery of his statement was assured and displayed his own deep convictions, but, whereas Beejay noted what was said and he would respond to in time, John listened and watched.

He could see his image on a monitor nearby and took in now the disposition of the cameras; they captured the eloquently spoken tirade and every reaction that he or Beejay might offer. So far it had been him alone who reacted to things being said.

Jacqueline's words of caution still registered with him but he also felt the compulsion to show an audience that he was a man of his word. Conventional ways would be taken on and overturned in this election; he'd progressed this far and would make something of a very public opportunity if the chance arose.

"This Election, and it can not come soon enough for me, is between Republican ideology and Democratic…and Democratic…uhm…"

To everyone's surprise Steve paused and John seized the moment.

"Theology…Democratic Party theology, is that it, the word you're looking for?" There was a hard edge to John's voice and he looked at Steve directly. "There will be no other god but one of a Democratic Party persuasion?"

John heard a gasp of astonishment from Beejay and noted the instant that Steve's face set in fury.

"You're nothing but a filler," he growled, "you're caught between two real political parties."

"And, I'm giving you indigestion."

John spoke calmly and made no attempt to look at either opponent. Tactical initiative came from split second timing; he'd learnt it well, in the swamp and jungle as well as in the boardroom.

"And these companies that you'll soon return to, the pharmaceutical cartel you're a member of? They have the cure, do they?"

John's reply was interrupted.

"Gentlemen! Debate this after the statement! Steve Cruz…please continue."

"Time's almost up," John quipped.

"And that'll do!"

Michelene called out but she could not keep herself from looking at John. He was so calm and assured; there was a restrained politeness in how he spoke to interrupt a train of thought or to latch onto a moment's weakness in his opponent. She was told to wait by the producer. Michelene had made her point. It was for the candidates to abide by the rules, but as with so much else in this election, conventional debating practice was under the threat of change; plans for the evening's programme seemed to be unravelling but it made for spontaneous and different coverage of the event. Anything could now happen; John Kahn had needled the man.

"I'll ask him straight out. How can John Kahn dare to look people in the eyes here and talk about 'right treatment'? You have the medicines…take HIV/Aids medicines as an example? How can you speak of *'right treatment'* when people in the third world can't afford what you make and have stored up? Tell me! Tell everyone tuned in to this debate how you, with that background, as a candidate for mayor can dare to speak of right treatment!"

"Have you finished?" John asked him with a quizzical tilt of his head.

"No. You're an opportunist, an interloper! Politics is about real people… real policy and argument. It's not about money."

"And the election board has passed my budget…I've campaigned within the same limits as you. I've walked the streets and met folks…mine are open books."

"You still don't do drugs for those that need them most…at a price they can afford! What example is that?" It was no longer a debate but a personal attack, candidate on candidate, only John was not rising to the challenge by resorting to hot words.

"All I ask is that both of you…you can include Beejay in this…that both of you check the facts. When you're through doin' that ask me again, or, you can send one of your union supporters to find out what the companies I'm associated with really do."

He waited.

"Exploit illness…for financial gain."

"We're off the tracks, Michelene," Beejay spoke out now and with ill-concealed irritation.

"It's a debate…we've moved on. You can join in!" Steve laughed in derision. "We've moved on to fitness for office. The image doesn't match up to reality!"

"Outside interests don't figure in this," Steve was told.

"Oh don't they?" he answered sarcastically.

"No…party policy does," Beejay persisted undeterred. "Besides, he's been voted onto the Boards of his companies year after year."

He looked to John inviting him to say something but he gave the appearance of someone content for an opponent to do the talking in his defence. He would bide his time and wait.

The momentary silence that fell between the candidates provoked Steve to speak.

"It's like I said when I started this statement…the Democratic Party is riding one horse in the race, you Beejay, and the Independence Party, are on the other. You'll either get tired carrying all that baggage around that you call policy or you'll fall. I don't care which it is, but the Democratic Party will gain control of the city once more."

"And I'll offer this to get the debate back on the tracks as Beejay wishes it to be," John chipped in with obvious enjoyment at how the 'debate' had unfolded. He could take some credit for that. "Let's compare? I've been voted onto a company Board many times, which is more than many of your service union colleagues have achieved or gone through…no matter how important those organisations are. It's not as though each Borough has seen the same percentage of turnout, but…I'm pleased with the results. I simply made a case for a wider electorate to vote and many listened. A wider constituency that's looking for change, political change came out onto the streets. It looks like people are taking to the idea of being a part of this."

"And your policies? A debate of those?" Steve asked. "Did they hear that from you...the detail? Will we do so tonight, here...where there's no way to go but face up to the issues?"

Michelene suggested a break in proceedings, to allow a sponsor's interval. It might help to restore calm and a consideration of how the time remaining to them could be devoted to less personal engagements between what many took to be combatants.

Only...only one man had brought about the need for the interruption, a man advocating change, a man who seemed unafraid to break one or two cherished rules if differences between ideas and their protagonists had to be pointed out. The 'phone lines were jammed, with well wishers for a great show; people were engaged by the 'debate' and the forthcoming election. Something, the need for as many people to vote as possible, had caught the imagination. John Kahn had told anyone who cared to listen that generating an interest in how the governing of the City might affect everyone had been an important element in his decision to stand for Mayor.

If you're not involved, how can you effect a change? John Kahn's message had caught on.

50
The Reckoning

The New York Times referred to the debate as a dogfight with a political mongrel almost getting the better of pedigree acts. They repeated no more than an expression used by Steve Cruz during the proceedings to describe John Kahn's candidacy.

To his credit, the paper went on, he had let that comment go; the remarks passed him by for he regarded them as no more than a part of the exchanges that had often seen him besting his opponents. Only one adjective would count in his book, that of "winner" on conclusion of the General Election.

The show's presenter, the TV station, and the sponsors who saw the viewing figures, all were overjoyed; the word was appropriate and described perfectly the outcome of their decision to hold the debate before an audience and to have callers express their views over the telephone. The station's exchange was jammed; it was a story in itself, and all because of a parochial event, the pre-election debate of candidates for Mayor of New York City.

Other newspapers, journals, TV and radio stations, they all carried reports of the event, its tone and the transition from open discussion to furious exchanges. The night had shown the viewers how deeply held the participant's beliefs really were. Tellingly, web blogs concluded that the contest in just a few days was too close to call given that a wider constituency had been drawn into the process.

Even the most partisan Republican and Democrat viewers had to agree with John Kahn that a change in the political environment had taken place; the show had made for compulsive viewing. Convention and its ally, condescension, had given way to invention – the making of a new way in seeing a Mayor elected.

Sure, the placing of a vote by a mark or tug on a voting machine's lever was nothing new. What took them was the obvious draw of a new man with other ideas and the challenge to orthodoxy. At least, everyone was getting to hear that an Election seemed to be taking place and thinking, *'there may be something in it, for us, after all.'*

The newspaper that had been collected before boarding the flight from Schiphol to JFK, New York was stuffed into the seat pocket in front of him.

"We'll be part of it, the Election soon," Gerard told her.

"To the New World…to New Amsterdam…to new money made up from the old," Edith said in reply. They sat arm in arm, polite yet oblivious of their immediate neighbours on the flight and talked of the things that now came to mind. "Money, a family's inheritance…it opened up a new life for them and far away from us."

"We've been through this, lievert, too many times. Put emotion aside, please? Try?" Gerard kissed her wrinkled brow. "Away with those; we're on a mission and personal feelings come second for now."

"Easy for you to say," she said without rancour and nestled against him.

"Not so, we've been together for over a year and found each other. Your quest for closure, for resolution?" he continued, "it's not easy at all. My family's involved…the perpetrators…if you want to call them that, they may yet become the victims even if the moment of reckoning takes place over a century later."

"Yes," she whispered and reached up to touch his cheek. "It's been a trial for you…thanks for being with me."

"Life may soon be different," he smiled, "and you've found ways to distract me."

"With your help." Edith clung to him for an instant to make her point. "I can't bear the waiting, we're so close."

"Let's see him elected first or achieve a moment's glory."

Gerard saw another meaning to her words of closeness, the impassioned moments they often shared. A Kahn had stolen the inheritance from his deceased sister's family, from his own niece and her twin brothers. He could not fathom how a distant relative could perpetrate such a crime upon his grieving relatives.

"To mess up a saying of theirs, '*it's one strike or we're out*'. We won't get a second chance."

They lapsed into silence and he watched as the stewardess answered the calls of passenger's. Edith seemed to doze against him, the gentle rise and fall of the aircraft on the air had its own soothing rhythm. Finally, they had begun their journey, set off on the trail to *"resolution"* as she often called her quest. She made it sound like a definable destination; with an almost childlike innocence she wished a wrong to be righted; she could play her part in a judgement day. Edith believed in everyone's right to a new beginning, only the means to achieve that had been at the expense quite literally of a woman she regarded as her distant relation. That a new life could have blossomed into the bounty the Kahn's of New York enjoyed compounded her sense of grievance. That the descendants of an accomplice from those days long ago were still being paid off was absurd; it had all the appearances of an obscene acknowledgement of guilt, a lode that ran very deep, to the core of the family. Few, no, none spoke openly of it.

Edith, the young woman, the girl with a simple belief in right and wrong had astutely read his character; when he had least expected it but with exquisite timing she had entered his life and enlisted his help. Edith had fallen in love with him and he looked at no one else; the relationship with Monique was a memory that now belonged to another part of his life.

"Ger?" Edith asked dreamily.

"Hm?" he rested with eyes closed.

"Do you know what passes between us when my mother and I speak of those earlier times?"

"No, and I thought you were trying to get some sleep."

"No," she whispered in his ear with a warm breath that made him bend to her lips. "I can't...there's too much at work in me again."

"So...tell me."

"We look at the pictures, I read the poems and the words of long-forgotten songs...forgotten by some anyway...songs that filled the tall houses, places full of the children of our family, or lodgers higher up. Music filled the passageways...and all of it echoing to laughter. The sounds all came back after that awful day, after the dawning realisation of all that had happened. The sounds brought restoration and brightness to the house after initial disbelief and then the gnawing loss of trust."

331

"And the dishonour," Gerard whispered; she had described scenes in the house on Crooked Tree Water that he could readily imagine; the photos she had shown him at their reunion had now come to life as she spoke to him.

"No, not that...although it seems that's been passed on with time." Edith squeezed his fingers. "Soon...there may be no more regrets or anger at what happened. We can work to settle it one way or another. I know that of you. We can get on with our lives and...I can even think whether to obsess about you."

She looked directly at him now and he took his cue, kissing her lips with the wet slide of his tongue tip to her parted lips in a gentle caress.

"Better?" he smiled. Edith nodded.

She wanted to let go of her thoughts.

"When we get back I'll re-trace all the routes the family walked, where the horses were led to get to the stables after the bales of tobacco, or cloth, and the spices were stacked away in the warehouses by the wharf on Crooked Tree Water. We can imagine the silent quayside, the barges like sullen hulks, with their crews at home or asleep with their dogs curled up against them under the awning."

"A part of you will fly away when the story's last chapter is closed." He'd fallen in with her lyrical mood of speech.

"Yes, I'll have you to fill the emptiness. Another woman's loss has been my ecstatic gain." Her fingers, that had until then clenched his own, relaxed and she lifted his hand to kiss it. "Lovely man...my darling man." She stopped from adding 'cousin'. It had fallen from usage; she regarded him as a partner, in both a physical and emotional sense, although intrusive thoughts of impropriety between members of a 'family' could not be dispelled.

He stared at her in the dim light of the cabin. Edith was beautiful, as radiant in that fair skinned loveliness as he had ever seen her. She had brought rapture to him. Over the passing months her laughter had deepened, it seemed to swell in concert with her assurance that she had found a man to be happy with, a man in whom she could place her trust. He dispelled with a shudder the notion that any woman could place their trust in any man, but of himself with her he was now certain. With Monique the intensity of their relationship had been the product of times spent out of each other's company, the result of absence. Her seduction from him had been compared to the taking of a possession; and yet they had always told each other that they sought to 'belong' to each other.

A true companion had been discovered. Edith's laughter and lightness of spirit, the music and songs that made her live brought a dimension to his own existence that he came to realise had been absent with other female companions. Glamour had been usurped by beauty.

"I'm madly in love with you," he whispered, keeping the note of surprise from his tone, he hoped. Confessions of this sort had never fallen from his lips, until now.

Edith's eyes grew very still, her features settled and she met his gaze as if in resignation, the look of one who knew the moment had arrived when two people acknowledged a physical and spiritual union.

"Is that allowed," she asked him, "and for me to say 'I'm madly in love with you?'"

"It happened," Gerard smiled.

John Kahn was not to be the only one in the family who could break with tradition or conventional ways.

51

Would You Believe It?
Kahn The Unknown – He Wins It!

He's done it! The pictures tell their own story! It would only happen against all the odds everyone said but that's how he seems to like it. John Kahn, decorated 'Nam Vet, rich and powerful businessman that he is has been out on the streets of the city's neighbourhoods and seemingly overcome polarised views. He's sold his message and constituents – enough of them – have bought into the idea of a middle way. He's achieved a true consensus that has exceeded the simple majority that a first past the post election result would be expected to deliver. A majority under that system pulls in your own party supporters. You can't help but admire him, even if you hate his political opportunism or mix-and-match portfolio of policy announcements.

All he's gone and done is overturn cosy conventions; he's converted voters from all sides, the returns show that John Kahn's taken from everyone who thought they had their political allegiances all buttoned up – for years! Sorry Mom and Dad! Sorry everyone who didn't look too closely at what he had to say but the vote's been for change from the usual two party contest. For all we really know a walk on the wild side now beckons; no one can really foretell how the new Mayor will shape up. Wall Street and City Hall may be close, geographically, but that's about all you can say about the change from businessman to a man of the people (of New York).

Still, you can't help but respect a man who in spite of his wealth still has the will and ambition to put himself through four years of infighting, balancing budgets and persuading folks that don't want to budge from a cherished opinion that they should reconsider. In spite of the moneyed background a hands-on philanthropic streak runs through the man and yet he's modest about that work. He's shown a genuine concern for his fellow man and in particular the disadvantaged – they're the folks that to him are unemployed, have had poor schooling, are tenants in low grade housing or they suffer from poor health. He seems to have a well-developed sense of conscience about others. He's run a pharmaceutical company after all, so others…his fellow man seems to matter.

As an Independent, and a winning one he can now say, he's championed variety and a new approach, not the safety of prevailing ideas that pass for the status quo. He did not support untested theories the result of which meant, over time, the worsening of circumstances for long-standing citizens of some metropolitan neighbourhoods. Gentrification to him slammed the door in the face of those who had, until now, kept alive those neighbourhoods and who managed on small handouts or meagre help from the State government or City Hall.

CBI's, or Community Based Initiatives was one idea that hooked people; you pay taxes but why not see that some of the proceeds from that take are used in your own neighbourhood and by you, the citizen? Independence has taken on a whole new meaning; you make your own way, with help if you need it.

John Kahn's had experience of assisting co-ownership schemes get started, he's brought the ideas onto the streets and given them a wider context. Through his own property company interests (you may know it is not the only business he gets involved with), and by firing the imaginations of charities, he helped to create employment zones and homes. He was part of a team that stopped many neighbourhoods becoming vacant lots and condemning its citizens to a life of little hope. He was not unique in seeing that high crime rates would be a consequence of doing nothing. And that's where some of the man's political creed seemed to resonate or click with those that heard and voted for him.

You may have heard the slogan, "Doing not Being in Politics". They were the words of a man, a candidate like so many others in the beginning, who came out of a political wilderness. He stepped out of the (golden) bush to take the biggest prize – the Mayoralty of New York. Too often during the campaign the media, and we were as guilty as many others, said that he was too Establishment and nothing more than a political fraudster. 'Just what does he think he's doing?' so many of us said. Underneath the tight outer skin we'd be sure to find a flabby centre – great wealth, gold-plated connections and a different game to play for a while to ease the boredom of present day living.

How wrong we were when we first wrote those comments. Now it all sounds like a gushing accolade that we're bestowing on the man but we, like many others, seem to have underestimated him. We thought the tilt at establishment windmills was just a clever media gimmick to get some attention; it was nothing more than a gambler's *trick dreamt up by his small campaign team. Oh, but size wasn't everything he joked and we soon learnt what he meant. It was not, after all, a salacious aside but an astute observation by a man who had just persuaded Jacqueline Purcell to come onto his team. By this one act he gained credibility. If she was by his side on the campaign trail, or working at his party's small offices in just the kind of neighbourhood he intended to help, then others had to take notice. The political establishment had to think again, about the man and his message.*

We all know, now, how much notice many people took of him. The margin of victory was not large but who cares about the numbers? Think about it! He won when no one gave him any chance. The numbers don't count when you set them against the triumph of ideas over establishment doctrine – or Divine Right, as he once called it on a breakthrough cable TV programme. Remember that show?

The papers were full of it the next day. No one realised (or some might say 'saw the danger') that the dripping tap could become a flood.

Although congratulating John Kahn on his achievement, our words are not to be seen as an endorsement of him and his ideas. Everyone in business strives to do away with the middleman, if possible, and cut to the quick of a deal…profit maximisation. By electing him constituents seem to have accepted a middleman so now it is for John Kahn to show us all how it is really going to work.

In time we'll get to see if like so many that have gone before he was a 'being' in politics figure rather than a man 'doing' politics – getting things done radically, maybe, but oh so effectively! That was the underlying message.

Show us it was more than just words. Go and do it! Okay, John Kahn?

52
A Press Conference Is Attended

The lead car, carrying Elbee and the campaign aides stopped short. Delroy cursed but eased the company's limousine close to the kerb and a few feet from the rear fender of the vehicle before them. A cordon held back a crowd of well-wishers, onlookers and tourists. Some fencing, funnel shaped and leading to the steps of City Hall had been deployed to guide them.

John stepped from the car as Delroy unlocked the doors. He was premature but used the moment to scan the faces under the harsh lights of the street and cast from temporary light standards above him. Skills at seeing what you had to face had never quite left him and being in the public's gaze had sharpened the senses further. Most appeared to be benign, some waved in greeting either out of commiseration at what he had embarked upon and won or wishing him good fortune. Others expressed opposition in spite of the plurality he had achieved in the ballot. That was now history, the future beckoned but none of that was of immediate concern.

No, his eyes focused on a noisy group . Amongst them others held him in a sullen stare that posed a threat; the look induced the feeling he remembered vividly, now, of the hollowed shell he had so often become before action. Placards were being waved.

'John Kahn's Message in a Bottle,
Pay my Price – OR DIE!'

'From Drugs Baron – RICH'
To City Mayor – POOR?

WATCH OUT – FOR YOURSELF!'

JOHN KAHN?
New York's Happy Pill
HE AIN'T!

He took them all in with one scan of his eyes but concentrated all of his attention on a man with a facemask who had been shielded by companions. Now the exuberant waving of banners failed to offer any of them cover, nor did they hide the one man he was concerned with from view.

The group's chanting failed to break his concentration; he had become a grunt once more, a man in a different uniform, a suit, but his deeply ingrained training was instantly recalled.

"Delroy! Check! My two o'clock!" he barked.

Delroy knew instantly of the meaning. He took a step back and turned. "Echelon!"

"Get the women away!" John ordered loudly as he broke free from the tug on his sleeve.

"John?" Marie cried out in fright.

"Go…get inside!"

"Do as your told!" Dayle screamed and tugged on Marie's arm forcing her to move. "Dad's in charge!"

He could not understand why he was so possessed by an impending sense of danger. Instinct had taken over from the cool analysis of a situation. Events unfolded with bewildering speed.

John sensed that Marie and Dayle were behind him but still he faced a section of the crowd and waved meaninglessly; his attention was entirely fixed upon the placard-waving group. A canister, then two more were thrown at him with one striking him a glancing blow on the arm as he raised it to protect his face.

"Come away sir!" a guard bellowed coming to meet him.

"Take the women John!" Delroy called out as he too stepped in front of him but his boss had taken an offensive posture; he crouched and began to run…away from them, towards the group.

Against his instincts but in a moment's regression to military training Delroy once more deferred to rank. He pulled at the two women and began to move them on.

"Come with me! Marie…Dayle!"

This was no time for politeness.

"John!" Marie screamed out over her shoulder but it was out of sheer fright. Another side to her man's character had taken hold and she saw him run bent low, away from her, and towards a man now wielding a weapon pointed in their direction.

"John! Come back! Don't go!" she screamed and tried to resist Delroy's tug on her arm.

'Sheer lunacy' was how Elbee often described his actions in combat to her; it was no different now. He moved very fast, sideways on to their assailant, and presenting the smallest possible target.

The slime-ball with the cap and dark glasses that had first attracted John's attention was the one to go for only he had time to loose off one shot. John felt the stinging cut on his arm and was compelled to act through some primeval force of self-preservation. Only, it was not the impulse of flight but to confront as he had learnt so many years ago.

"John! Dad!" He heard the calls, from another detached place, then nothing else.

He felt cold, bloodless with intent and also surprised at the speed and agility he had re-discovered. His left hand swatted at the weapon as his right hand pushed the assailant's head up then gripped his throat. There was a stifled gurgle before his left hand took hold too and combined they delivered a single twisting, snapping and immobilising motion.

The man fell and before any one of his objectionable companions about him could react to John's counter-attack he had moved away, pulled clear also by security men. Their reactions had been slow and John felt his legs move as if they were controlled remotely, or had become unnerved. He stumbled now towards Delroy. The women had gone and his fallen man could only raise an arm feebly in greeting. He lay in cold isolation, screened from any further threat by security staff enclosing him with John.

"Delroy my man," he bent down to him and looked at the wound on his chest.

"Safe...they're safe." Delroy's paled lips quivered in a weak smile. "Go to them, man."

"Gotta check you out first, buddy." John knelt on the pavement, indifferent to his safety or his appearance. "Can't leave you, not now. These are our streets, and our home turf, man. How could they? We've been through all that...long ago, in another place."

He mumbled the words but his eyes studied his companion, not his employee. They had been through so much and money, rank, or social status had in recent moments been abandoned. It was as if instant recall brought them back to the field, to another time and a fetid distant hell on earth.

"I'm not going anywhere...not with this...it's not like other times, but we're still together." They gazed at each other in acknowledgement of the finality a few minutes had brought to them. Delroy groaned and twisted in reflex at the pain. His grasp on John's hand lessened.

"Medic!" he called.

"Make it right John…"

"I will…Semper Fi old buddy," John whispered as he cradled him, the bulk of the man was insignificant or he found the strength to make it so. "You're the best." He spoke into Delroy's ear shrugging off the clasping hands that sought to drag him away to what was taken to be safety.

"Sir!"

"Help my man!" he barked, "and do it now!"

"Semper Fi," Delroy croaked. "Had to be this way for me too…jus' a few years in between…so many buddies went before, so long ago." John saw the eyelids flutter and the eyes stare upwards. He doubted if Delroy could see him but he crouched by him on the hard pavement and under the watchful eye of the security cordon and the stunned gaze of the strangely silent crowd.

"Yeah," he said softly. "You're the best…I owe it all to you again, man, just like before. Always true."

"Always true…you and me both, man." Delroy gave a small quiver, the words on his dying breath, before his head slumped to one side.

The nearest security officer gave him no further consideration. "Now sir! You'll have to come with me."

John felt a hand grip then jerk him unceremoniously to his feet. "This way please, sir! No discussion, sir!"

He was being led towards a waiting car but resisted the tugging hands and took one last lingering look at his friend's lifeless form sprawled on the sidewalk. Paramedics were already wheeling a trolley towards them.

"No!" John regained a moment's lucid thought. "We're…I'm going that way!" he pointed to City Hall's entrance. "That's where the answers lie! That's where I need to be, not in a car driving away from events." He freed himself in a single twist of his arm and ran up the steps loosening his tie as he went and casting it aside. He tore at the buttons of his bloodstained shirt.

"John!" He heard the wail of Marie's voice and ran towards the sound, by the large heavily ornate timber doors of the Civic Hall.

"Dad! Dad!" Dayle quivered against him and looked up ashen faced, a tremble crossing her lips as she met her father's distracted look. Then she became tearful from the shock endured. "You're so pale…so hurt!"

"I'm here now darlin'," was all he could then find in answer.

"Safe! You're safe!" she cried and clung to him. "You're safe with us!"

"We all are sweetheart…only, my man has gone. Delroy's gone."

"The poor man…so true."

"Yes, girl," he answered holding her face in his hands for an instant that drew attention to them. "It's what I told him...just a few moments ago...before he was taken from me."

The noise inside was deafening with calls at him to turn and face the ranks of cameramen and reporters, to utter some reaction to events but he ignored them all after looking up, long enough, for any pictures that were needed to be taken. He breathed slowly. "Gather my thoughts...gather them up...I've gotta go on." His voice trailed off.

"You've never looked so mean!" Marie said in a small incredulous voice seeing her husband as never before. She stared at him over a hand that was pressed to her mouth, barely in control of herself and finally conceding to her tears. "You...you...you may have killed someone," she stammered.

"Yes! To save you both! I had no choice. You weren't meant and I never imagined you would ever have to witness anything like that...or how I did it. It...it belongs to my past."

"A past I helped you get through." Marie's shoulders shook as she wept against him, overcome by shock.

They moved closer to the crowd of photographers that had been gathered as a follow up to his arrival. "Say nothing...*absolutely* nothing," he told them as hand mikes were held out.

He had been to the pistol ranges, punched the bags and done the weights until he thought he'd bust. Delroy had been his mentor; the master had become the pupil. But even after thirty years the military training from so long ago returned instinctively; without it seemed a potentially fatal second thought he'd used his hands in one disabling twist. It had been enough. Delroy saved his women while he had faced the fire; he'd become point like on so many patrols in the jungle and swamp. If you went, you went...but here, on the streets of their home city? The event bust you open.

"You're not going in there are you?" Dayle asked gripping him with a strength he did not believe she could possess; yet his girl kept surprising him.

"Yes...there's no getting out of it, not for me."

"Your arm...what about your arm, your wound? You'll pass out...from the heat and loss of blood."

"I'll get patched up...before I go in. Make and mend in every way I know."

"Forget it John, forget it! Cancel the Goddamn thing...we can do it all another day." Elbee's voice carried over the din. "It's meaningless now."

"Like hell I will! Like hell it's *meaningless!*" John said staring at his friend. "Give me the bag! I'm getting cleaned up and I plan to carry on! Our man is down...*my* man went down. I'm dealing with this first...I'll face anything else later!" He pointed to his wounded arm. A bullet had grazed him but taken Delroy's life. "My people were in the front line tonight! Forget? Hell no!"

"There's the other business to deal with...the guy you took out."

"That's what I pay you for, to handle the problems from time-to-time." He looked evenly then put his hand to his friend's shoulder. "Help me through this," he said in a soft voice. "I can't be seen to leave anything unanswered right now, do you get me?"

"But John!"

"No but's...none!"

"Darling! Listen to him, please listen to us! Please!" Marie hugged him; they were a family in crisis and the lights were on them.

"Sorry...no. I'm not walking away from this."

"In case some wise ass makes use of it?" Dayle asked him with a disbelieving shake of her head.

"You just never know." One man had been killed. Another was probably dead if he'd done his work right. "What a fucking mess, way off the mark!" he said softly before tendering an apology to the women. He felt the gentle stroke of Dayle's fingers on his face as he hugged Marie. Another woman nearby in their apartment, a woman he cared for deeply, must be in shock at how lucky he had been to escape, and she could say nothing to him or offer her own caress of restoration.

"I love you Dad. You're the best and will do what's right, like you always have." Dayle met the kisses of relief that John planted on her face.

"Darling...darling," he repeated out of thanks, once more, that she had been spared any physical hurt.

"I'll stay with Mom...I'll bring her later. Go on, show 'em we're in shape and will be there for them, even now."

"Yeah...I love you." Shame you couldn't have been my son. "I love you all. Thank God you're alive." Tears welled in his eyes. "My buddy's down...killed on our own city's streets...after all...after all we've been through."

"We're alive because of both of you, because of Delroy." Marie wept against his shoulder with large heaving sobs. But, he felt detached; he had entered his own little world where he began to rehearse the words to be used in the Hall.

"I've got to make ready, get myself cleaned up...then I go in there, and talk my way out of this. It's nothing new, getting shot at...only it had to happen right here in my own city."

John pulled away from clutching hands, hearing the pleas to come home and make good shattered nerves.

He was taking a leak, shut away alone in an echoing bathroom when the call came. He struggled to grab the mobile 'phone wedged deep down in his trouser pocket.

"Wait one!" he said, "please?"

"John! John!" a voice called out breathlessly. "Thank God…you're safe! I had to call…I had to! I saw it all on the TV here in our apartment! Speak…speak to me!"

"Joey! I'm here…I went through my past once again, but out there on our own streets! My man…Delroy, he's gone…he's dead!" What a 'waste', literally, of a good man."

"Oh God! Oh my God! It…it…" she spoke out her deepest thoughts

"It could've been me?"

"Yes," she said in a whisper, "Yes John, are…are you hurt bad?"

"No…I've known worse, darling. Losing Delroy, it's not with me yet, not completely."

"And I'm here, on my own…when I could've been near you!"

"I'm not alone…"

"I know that!" she said waspishly in response then relented. "Sorry…I'm sorry. You're a part of me and of my life. I wanted to hear your voice…I need to see you and know you're okay."

"I will be…I have to be, and soon." There will be another scar on my body for you to touch, John thought, but not tonight as we had promised to each other, somehow. "Things have changed, for the moment…for tonight, they've changed."

"Good evening ladies and gentlemen. I would like to begin by thanking you for attending this evening. The Election was a close call and I would like to take the opportunity to pay tribute to my political opponents, Steve Cruz and William Newhouse. We had our differences, none more so than the final outcome, but…the citizens and voters of New York have decided. My opponents debated all the issues and I hope that when the need arises we may be able to work together for the good of all citizens."

He took some sips of water and shrugged off his jacket.

"Something happened tonight and the notes I have here in my hand are of no use to me now." He paused and stood for a moment with eyes closed.

"Semper Fi, Ladies and Gentlemen, always true…keep the faith. That's what one man, a special man called Delroy, who died tonight believed in. It bound us together…and now I salute a fallen comrade in arms from the Marines…we were deployed in the same unit overseas but he died here…on the streets of the biggest and arguably the most important city in the world. I brought a spare shirt…I couldn't change the outcome for one man's life. I came from a privileged

background, he didn't. But, one thing united us, some thirty years ago and out there on our streets tonight - it was a unity of purpose, selflessness for the sake of another. Colour, money and family made no difference; for a few heart-stopping seconds we were together dealing with what we had to face. There was no hiding place. I'll have to face what's coming at me after the events of this sad night.

My conscience speaks to me now…about what had to be done out there. To me the bullet doesn't overcome the word, I learnt that once…the hard way. People should talk and work through their differences.

Delroy worked for me, he taught me and he looked out for me; in the end he died for my family and me. We were all to be here to share an important moment, too bad it will be remembered for all the wrong reasons…and then, may be not. The people who planned tonight's demonstration and the individual who perpetrated a heinous crime failed to truly appreciate the work that is undertaken quietly behind the scenes, in companies that I have been associated with and by others in government, to change things on a global scale. The balance between self-interest and altruism is one I have to think of…day in and day out. I'll think on it even harder after losing a good buddy tonight.

The election was the beginning. I will try to do my part - no! - I will do my part for the City. I will look, and keep on looking, to those less fortunate, less privileged or downright disadvantaged. Change isn't going to happen overnight and we have battles ahead with Federal Government and maybe with the folks up in Albany. They've shown little time for independent thought but I hope we can work for a change in that…that's my aim. That is for later…tonight was to be a celebration and it is. But now it is, for me, the recognition of one life and of one person whom I came to know and grew to care for as a fellow human being.

One man, with a pistol, tried to bring a change in what others in the community he was supposed to be a part of had voted for. I said in the campaign I would work for all, and that's what I intend to do from the New Year when I take office.

Finally, I want to thank and recognise here, publicly, the help and support that I have received from Jacqueline Purcell, she with her bright intelligence and happy laugh. We both worked through the tough times of the election campaign. In the coming days I will be seeing to her appointment as head of a city agency that will bring help to those in the community I said needed to be helped and encouraged, for the good of all citizens.

Once more, he gulped at the water from the glass placed before him on the lectern.

"I've nothing more to say for now on this or the significance of tonight."

A carefully prepared speech had been laid on the polished sloping surface but he had ignored it. What he had spoken of came from the heart, unrehearsed and delivered with spontaneity that he usually reserved for his closest family and friends. Events had overtaken his plans just as he had imagined during his tenure of office they would do. Only, he had not expected the immediacy of such an adjustment.

The media took great interest in him. He had won the election as an Independent, supported by disaffected elements who wanted nothing more than real change and the opportunity to shake up convention that had reinforced the divides that he had spoken off during the campaign. His actions on the stoop outside City Hall had shown those that cared to really see what the true character had been of the man they had elected as Mayor.

He blinked under the glare of the lights. "Now, ladies and gentlemen I'll take some questions."

Hands went up, notebooks were waved at him but John asked them to be patient.

"But, before I do I want to reserve a slot of time for someone in particular, a journalist that I know will be here. He has followed my progress in his articles...for a foreign newspaper." One hand was now raised to shield his sight. "Is the "Owl" in the room? Forgive me, I should know better but I can't pronounce the name in Dutch?"

The assembled hacks and television commentators looked around at their neighbours in the cramped room and shrugged.

"If he's not here...I've a question for you," one said loudly as he stood up waving his pass.

"Later," John smiled. "I know you're here Owl...or Gerard Kahn. I saw your name on the list of accredited press...come on man...show yourself?"

The assembled pressmen looked about them and finally fingers pointed as there was a movement of figures against the back wall.

"I'm here Mr Mayor. Gerard Kahn, 'The owl" he pronounced firmly in Dutch. "I'm with De Telegraaf newspaper, of Amsterdam."

They stared at each other though what the mayor could see of him was debatable in the harsh glare of the lights. Gerard could make him out quite clearly.

"Want to go first...out of all these ladies and gentlemen of the press?" The voice was friendly and open.

"Thank you. It seems discourteous to be given preferential treatment over your city's and country's assembled press."

It was out of character to be deferential, especially in the circumstances, or to be accorded so much time to ask a question.

"Oooh...so polite," a hidden voice said loudly. Many laughed, but others were less understanding of the delay.

"I don't hear any protests...so, want to try?" John encouraged him now.

"Sure...I'll come a little closer so that you can see me."

"Polite...and considerate."

"Yes," Gerard turned smiling into space. "Those are attributes Mr Mayor...*cousin,* that you will learn run in *our* family! I'm not so brave as you have shown yourself to be tonight!" The smile had gone and he stared up at John. "But then, what bravery do I need to speak to a cousin, even if he's a distant one?

"What did you say? 'Cousin'?"

"Yes...I said *cousin*...my name's Kahn just like yours, only in Virginia others go by the name of Koehler; it sounds more homely as you will know. In Amsterdam the Kahn family has interests, interests your ancestors were once a part of."

John's eyes narrowed to focus intently on his questioner. He heard the caution from Elbee but turned only slightly to acknowledge the warning.

"What's your question pal?" a fellow journalist spoke up to him. "We're kind of short on patience here."

He gave the questioner a curt nod. "Ja!" he turned to face John once more. "In my hand I have a piece of paper...a receipt for money. It is dated 1876...signed by one Frederick Albert Kahn...your great grandfather and my great uncle."

"Someone else waved a piece of paper once..."

"There'll be no war this time," Gerard answered his questioner curtly.

The room fell silent following a low buzz of anticipation; pictures were taken and the moment recorded for later use. The election contest had been too close to call and now the finale had been marked by bloody mayhem out in the street. Doing the correct thing had given way to instinct and yet, now, John felt a visceral acknowledgement that the situation remained unpredictable. Others would judge whether the event required that he conform to a conventional set of rules and less on instinct. There was no time to consider the moment as a real test of his independence.

"What's your question Gerard?"

John gave not the faintest flicker of a response to the situation that faced him; tonight history had come knocking at his door in a seemingly vengeful and now, perhaps, costly personal revue but he wasn't going to let anyone see the effects any new assault might have upon him.

"Mr Mayor...cousin...when can the family in Holland expect to get their money back? As I believe you know...the seed corn our American cousins grew up on...it wasn't *entirely* theirs."

There was but a moment's silence from the assembled hacks.

"What took you and your family so long, pal?" one asked adding sarcastically, "you're out of time with your claims."

Another dismissed the question. "Let's get to the real business of the night, Mr Mayor…Mayor elect!"

"Yeah, I've got one," was the rejoinder from another. "Gerard Kahn's through!"

"We'll soon see," he answered them all and stood patiently, his notebook to hand, waiting.

All the while John had given no sign that he had considered the question put to him. Instead, he watched the faces of those gathered before him as the cameras flashed. He bought some more time and asked for his jacket and draped it, clumsily, over his shoulders.

"You've done us all a favour, Gerard," he spoke out loudly and without warning. "You may have done us all a favour, us that is who are a family on both sides of the ocean between us. We may find a way…in time, to acknowledge a legacy that had to be lived with." He waved away Elbee's interruptions. "From tonight that's all over with…I'm through with it."

"So, what's your answer, Mr Mayor?"

"It'll be dealt with, Mister!" He shouted out the words in the first sign of real anger that some of the journalists who had followed his progress on the campaign for Mayor had seen. "First I'm shot at on my own city streets. I lose a valued friend and colleague…now I've been mugged! You can count on it…I'm goin' to make a few changes around here and deal with you…and your question too!"

Silence fell for only a moment before a smile broke out on his drawn face to ease the tension. Someone began to clap and soon the room was filled with the sound; seemingly, they all acknowledged his strength of character.

"Thank you. Everything will be dealt with…in it's own time. Hear me Gerard Kahn?"

He nodded his own reply but felt compelled to speak. "Yes…Mr Mayor."

"Right." John met Gerard's look for only an instant. "Now, it's been a long night…so, let's move on while I have any blood left in me to do so. I came here to talk to all of you…let's do it. Next question?" He pointed to a friendly face. "Yeah?"

The 'phone vibrated in the small leather clutch bag that lay on her lap.

"Turn that goddamn thing off!" Marie hissed. "I can't take any kind of noise right now."

Dayle loosened her mother's grip and looked down at the screen for the text message icon. Their driver was taking his time and she welcomed Nico's interruption.

'Dayle…the beautiful, you're a 'lievert' to me - you're busy, frightened by what has happened …and angry by what has been said tonight, but, call me if you can and if you want to? Yell at me and call me names…I work for a newspaper, but was unprepared for one particular event tonight. Believe me, if you can.' – Nico.

'Nico…Tell me, better still, show me what 'lievert' means to you?' – Dayle

'Nico…Why should I yell at you? What's been said?' – Dayle

'Dayle…A story from the past…it concerns the Kahn family…here and in my country' – Nico

'Nico…and?' - Dayle

"That would be nice…but, ask John then see if it's still meant to be.' - Nico

"Shit!" She made a show of switching the thing off.

"What now?"

"Nothing, mother. It'll be dealt with…somehow. We'll wait for Dad."

"Mr Kahn?" A smartly dressed aide had found him and Gerard listened to her as he sought Edith's face in the crowd.

"Ah!" he turned to speak then moved away. "I have to meet someone."

"Yes, sir," was the carefully polite reply he received. "You have. Mr John Kahn would like to meet you, here…if you're interested?"

"And the attention to his wounds? What about that?"

"That's being dealt with…again. Will you follow me, please?"

"In a moment." He moved further away. "Edith?" Gerard beckoned to her.

She was permitted to pass through a gap in the railings that had at the start of the evening held back a crowd.

"I saw the pictures, on the screen! I could only guess what was being said…or at you."

"Yes…good. We'll talk about it later. Something interesting has come up." He pointed over his shoulder. "We've been asked to follow that woman and to meet John Kahn. Now's your moment. Cousin John Kahn asks for us to meet him."

"Ger!"

"It's okay. We're together…so, come? Destiny, of some sort…it may await you."

53

The setting was a panelled committee room, its high ceiling adorned by a chandelier that cast light over the centre of the table but left the corners in a softened darkness. Here, table lamps shone a narrow shaft of light up against the walls; portraits of city council officials hung upon them.

The introductions were soon dispensed with.

"Thank you, Julia," he spoke kindly to the aide. "See you get home safely, now."

"Yes, Mr John. You too, sir."

His guests, complete strangers to him until that evening, waited. He felt Gerard's stare upon him and he met it briefly before taking in once more his companion. Her bright inquisitive eyes regarded him and the deft handiwork of the medic for a moment.

"It's nothing I haven't been through before," he told Edith, "but...it's been a while since I was last shot at."

A new bandage had been applied to his left arm; the sleeve of his shirt hung in tatters as the dressing was tidied. Now, the medic fastened it with bandage clips to lend some order to John's appearance.

"You don't need this now sir...another meeting, if I may say so," Julia persisted in a touching display of devotion to his cause and the man.

"I'm fine enough...you go on home now. Give my thanks to the team for everything, again."

"And you, sir? What of Mrs Kahn and...Dayle?"

"They've gone home too. Take care how you go, Julia."

"Sir."

She waited then followed the medic from the room, accompanied all the while by the irritating tap of Elbee's pen as it slid through his fingers to beat an impatient rhythm on the table.

"I'm not surprised you're here," John said calmly, "not at all. Part of me...deep down, simply says *'what took you so long'*?"

"Admit nothing John! Take care of all that you say," Elbee intervened brusquely. "You've got nothing to apologise for or take any heat for... nothing."

"The time had to be right," Edith said after she had seen John's nodded acknowledgement of Elbee's advice.

"To take me on in my own back yard?"

"John," Elbee cautioned.

"Yes...to make a case and fight for it." Edith spoke with childish simplicity but she was surprised this time to see John acknowledge her remarks with a nod.

"Don't see it as a 'fight', either of you," he replied. "I've had enough of that...for one night anyway."

"Some other time? We can talk then," Gerard offered.

"Good idea," Elbee told them. "My client needs a break from all that's happened…all the incoming of today." He had assessed the meeting as potentially confrontational but John confounded him and the idea of preparing properly.

"I want these few moments," John said turning to Elbee. "It's not a fight to be won or lost…it's merely putting right a past wrong. Others might call it right over might, but I simply look at anything that we settle on as a family matter."

"Are we going to agree, on something?" Edith asked unable to keep a note of surprise from her voice.

"Sure," he smiled and gave a shrug, "on something…we can at least agree that you picked a good tactical moment, the Press conference, to launch an attack on me. As an ex-soldier I also know about tactical withdrawals."

"To fight on another day?"

"Sure, you've got it! Only, it's not in any way that brings harm to anyone, quite the opposite."

"Oh?" Edith stared at him unable to deny that he was charismatic; she also had no doubts that he was clever and very resourceful; John would draw you in and gain your trust and confidence before the counter bid or proposal set you back once more. His willingness to talk and easy manner was beguiling.

"Yes, I think we can settle things between us."

"Pay up on the IOU from eighteen seventy six?"

"Kind of…in a manner of speaking," he dissembled.

"Gerard!" Edith cried out but in response he only held a finger to his lips.

John smiled at them on seeing the gesture.

"Yeah…he's right. Wait for the detail…line up the numbers as my father used to say. He said look at the tally from both sides and see which one weighs the heavier, yours or the other side's."

"Ours does!" Edith cried out but Gerard silenced her with a call of 'Lievert!' She pouted in annoyance at his remark.

"The paper is all you have…and not on me."

"But John Kahn has a shining reputation," Gerard added, "that could be tarnished."

"I'll tell you this much…you picked your moment well, Gerard…only my reputation is undamaged. I, and my people, we can handle this."

"Fairly?" Edith asked with only a moment's glance at Gerard. He winked in response.

"Put a number to it, both of you…or one of you. Tell me what's fair by your reckoning…to make good, in some way, what Frederick Albert Kahn did…what he did so many years ago!" John's voice hardened and the easy set of his features changed. "My family, those of us over here have earned every nickel!"

"After an unfair start…dishonest even, according to some. There's over one hundred years of incremental value attaching to the stake."

"Easy to say, Gerard…not so easy to figure out."

"Says who?"

"I do…and a few nickels of common sense, Gerard. Frederick came here with his own money too…"

Edith thumped the arm of her chair. "Substantially increased by someone else's money! Family money…his own family, his own relative's money! How can you be so calm about it?"

"Frederick and all who followed him…you can count me in on that, we worked real hard to make what we have now." John tilted his head as if to enforce the stare that he gave her then Gerard. "We can talk calmly about all this…or, we can argue and call out to each other. What's it to be? Make it quick!"

"We'll hear what you've got to say." Gerard spoke up for Edith.

"Okay…fine." John was prepared to simply talk. "This, for me, is how it goes…like it or not. The Kahn family, all of us here in New York, achieved everything in our own way and with our own money. Sure, the initial stake may have helped…I'm not going to deny that to you, but I can't say what difference it made. It's legacy, it's history, in anybody's book. The Kahn family used their brains, their muscle sometimes and worked hard to make a dream come true; their perseverance paid off. A bit of luck along the way came into it too…during the Depression."

"I'd call it good fortune that no-one came over the horizon looking for what was rightfully theirs. Whichever way you dress it up…another's inheritance was taken and a family's trust shattered!"

"They made a choice…to do nothin'!" Elbee said, pointing his pen at Edith to reinforce his observation of an undeniable truth and to intimidate her.

"And the Kahn family and business have you and your law firm to protect them!"

"Right! You're right there, mister!"

"Wrong!" Edith yelled at both of them, then sat back in her chair for an instant. Gerard gave her time. At last she could let go of all that had possessed her thoughts on the matter of Anna Elisabeth's stolen bequest from her mother.

"Is that what you really mean? Your ancestors got away with it...or so they thought?" Edith went on, her gaze never for a moment leaving John as she spoke to him once more.

"No, that's not quite what I meant, and besides...it all happened *way* before my time. If you'll let me say it...I meant good fortune, luck if you like... during the Depression when a good eye for an opportunity was important to survival and retaining some hold on what the family had worked on so hard."

"Neither of you can put any figure to it. As John said...you're muggers," Elbee cut in, "and you're way out of line...and out of your depths in this."

"Easy, pal."

"Frederick had broken with his wife long before the Depression...we saw the outcome of the rift perpetuated by you yourself!" Edith went on quickly, pointing at John as she spoke, her thoughts expressed as they came to mind. "We got the pictures of your school visit to Virginia. You gave us a lead on where we needed to look...you publicised the event and we picked up on it, Gerard did."

Gerard smiled at her as he saw John nod again in acknowledgement of the fact.

"And I knew you were looking..."

"Oh?"

"Rest easy, Gerard...I've been prepared for a reckoning for quite a while. I have my ways too, and people who care about me and the Kahn family over here to keep me informed...and protected."

"How's that?"

"It's legacy, all of it. What you and Edith are trawling around for...it's Kahn family legacy, nothing more or less. Mary Beth does good work and I can support that. I don't feel guilt, none at all. I simply call it more of an obligation to those less well-off than me or my family."

"Which you'd have no need to be bothered with..."

"That's so, Edith...only, in spite of the cold heart that you think beats in me and my father...and his father before him...we all felt a bond, strained though it may have been. In my line of work I can also associate with what Mary Beth's school does to help less fortunate kids."

"Right Treatment?" Edith felt obliged to say.

"Something like that," John smiled, "yes. So, you do understand? The family's money did good along the way." John turned to Elbee. "We can agree on something...you'd better note that down. So...what now?"

John looked to each of them in turn.

Gerard could not help but admire the man for carrying on a family tradition, for concealing the origins of their wealth and new beginnings by means of charitable deeds. It was cover for a secret well kept but one that he, with Edith's encouragement, had opened up to public scrutiny. He also recognised that the pleasure of creating a scene at a press conference could so quickly turn against him. John was right, the story was a family legacy but one that he and Edith might yet be able to exploit although justifying their actions to others might take all the courage and strength of character that they possessed.

"So, the simple request is, pay up!" Gerard said it with a laugh. "Then, we can be reasonable and familial about it all."

"Yeah...we can reason it out...familial can mean between the parties involved. Get me? No one else knows the package or the detail, they stay ignorant of the make up of any settlement we may reach so that we lay to rest that episode...my family's legacy, my family over here!" He placed great emphasis on the last words. "I don't know that anyone else, apart from a few of your folks care two bits for all this. And here?" John spread out his hands as if to show the plan was already made out. "Why, it comes out on the street when we've agreed that the settlement of a family business matter was delayed by illness, and death."

"By putting an Ocean and a century between us," Edith said quietly. "It's not quite the truth though, is it? We found a piece of paper...Gerard and I, just to prove what had happened."

"The truth mattered...only to those long dead, Edith." John had remained seated during their conversation but he stood up now and yawned. "I'm sorry for that. Excuse me. It's been something of a busy day." He took sips of the water that had been placed before him in a tall glass. "You found a receipt...so, it looks like we've got to find a way to settle things and move on."

"When?"

"Tomorrow," he smiled at Edith. "Come to the house...to the apartment," John corrected. "You can meet my wife...maybe meet Dayle. You may get to see the paintings I have of great uncles to you both."

"And then?" Edith persisted.

"Why, we talk some more of course. Now, I'm sorry...but you'll have to excuse me. I've had my share of things to deal with, more than enough for one day. And, the saddest thing is that I've lost a buddy from many years back and a helper. I lost him right here on the city's streets. I have to think on what I can do for his family too."

John looked towards Elbee.

"He was a colleague to both of us...in 'Nam," Elbee averred.

"Your campaign sold the idea of family...all the citizens together," Gerard told John now.

"Yeah, and I meant it Gerard." He said the name in his own peculiar American way. "I'm goin'. I've had more than enough to chew on for one day. I'm goin' home to my wife and daughter. You can meet them...I'll send a car over tomorrow night...eight thirty sharp. Suit you? We can talk some more, then."

"Okay. Thank you...take care cousin," Edith said to him.

"I will...I always have, Edith."

"You have a pleasant evening," Elbee offered before the two men left the room.

53

"Huh...huh?" Gerard groaned on being woken by the trill of a mobile 'phone. "Yours...or mine?"

"Mine." Edith stirred from beneath the duvet and Gerard's warm embrace. "Only one person calls me at odd hours." The handset scraped on the bed side cabinet. "Hello?"

"Edith!" was her mother's happy greeting. "Hallo!"

"Ma," she said needlessly.

"Yes!"

"Do you know what time it is?"

"Breakfast time, dear!"

"Yes, Ma...where you are!" She was wide-awake now and sat up in the bed, drawing the covers to her naked body.

"Don't do that," Gerard murmured, "let me see your beautiful skin."

"Ger! Don't!" Edith giggled as he nuzzled her breasts. "Wait...wait a moment, Ma?" She slid from the bed. "You're impossible!" she laughed.

"Not to love?"

"That's true."

Edith came to sit by his side of the bed, on the floor, coaxing an embrace of one arm as he lay near her, face down. She felt his breath on her neck.

"Edi?" her mother quizzed once again.

"Ja, I'm here."

Questions rushed out. "What have you two done? Who have you met? It's made the news...Gerard has! Family tales, our family...it's on the TV! Not just there...it's here too now!"

"We've met them...met John Kahn!"

"It wasn't meant to go so far, Edi!"

"Well, it has...and I'm not the least bit sorry."

"Edi, listen to me?"

"No, Ma. It mattered to you and others for long enough. I'm going to try and settle it, now…with Gerard's help."

"How girl? He's big business…can squash both of you with the power he's got."

"He's human…flesh and blood, Ma. We're going to meet him, tonight. Nothing's settled," she went on slowly as the thought came to her. "Everything's been stirred up…"

"As if I didn't know! Hope Ger doesn't lose his job over it?"

"I don't think so, Ma. Journalists like him…persistent, investigative and sensitive to the real issues that lie under the surface…they're hard to find." She took in the time. "What a moment to talk of these things, Ma."

"I hope you're both okay?"

"Yes…do you want to speak to Ger?"

"Is he with you?"

Edith laughed and turned to see him smiling at her. "I'll make sure! Yes…yes he's here with me…of course he is."

She met his kisses.

"Oh!…Oh!" The penny dropped. "Yes…yes of course."

"No, Ma…it wasn't a matter of course. Gerard's special, we both knew that some time ago…way back when there was a reunion."

"As a man, as your cousin, Edi…but, as your…as your lover?"

"Yes Ma…that's how it is. None of this, the Kahn family thing, would have been possible without him."

"I know that, but still…?"

"Yes, let's not talk about all that…not now, maybe never. I've become the person I really am again, because of that man…Gerard Kahn."

There was a sigh but Edith took it to mean her mother had accepted a truth, or finally come to terms with the relationship.

"Mind out then, both of you. Look after yourself, Edi? Don't upset our American cousins any more…"

"Than I have to?" Edith couldn't help laughing once more. Just what would they in their swank apartment be going through?

"Yes girl. See what can be made of it. Should I tell Gerard's mother?" There was the hint of a mischievous chuckle on her voice.

"Wait…I'll ask him." She held the 'phone away and bent to nuzzle Gerard's cheek. "Does your mother know of this…or your father? Have you told them anything of what you're taking up with our cousin John?"

"No," he said in a voice muffled by the pillow. "Come back to bed."

"In a minute…what do I tell my mother."

"That you're being a naughty girl…but making me very happy."

"I think she's got that message." Edith clung to him for an instant. "Well, what do I say?"

"I haven't told my side of the family anything…they didn't make much of it the last time we spoke of it, over a year ago. So…let your mother make their day. The secret's finally out."

"And there's work to do."

"My thoughts exactly. Now, come back to me."

"Go on, tell them Ma! Sorry…but, I've got to go!"

54

"Good evening, mister Kahn," Manuel nodded politely, "good evening, maam."

The chauffeur was immaculately dressed and the call announcing his arrival had been precise and on time.

"Thank you," Edith smiled as the door was held open for her and she slid across the leather seat making room for Gerard to join her.

"Okay?"

"Ja…it's not quite what I had in mind when our cousin John told us he'd send a car," she said quietly and took hold of Gerard's hand as the door was closed on them.

Manuel took his place behind the wheel. They had no way of knowing. The darkened glass to the passenger compartment hid him from view.

"Very orderly," Gerard said now as they set off through light traffic. "We have a drink at his place, we talk some more and follow up yesterday's opening bids…talk for a while…then, we leave. It'll be all over in less than two hours. We'll be back by ten thirty." He made light of it.

"Done this before, have you?"

"Yes…you don't get the full story, or the deal, first time. In his case, he wanted to check us out…to use their parlance *'pitch us a few straight ones'* before tonight just to see what we had on him. His lawyer, that Elbee guy… he'll be telling John to make it harder…there's another phrase for that."

"Go on, tell me," she smiled and squeezed his hand.

"A few *curve balls* will be pitched."

"It's all a game, is that what you're telling me? We're going to the apartment in a plush limo just to put us at a disadvantage?"

"Sure," Gerard replied easily. "Now that you know we'll both be prepared for it. The whole thing will be played out once more, he'll no doubt remember what we said and throw it back at us if it doesn't tally with what he remembers us saying."

"We want some money…financial recognition for what happened."

"So long ago, Edith. He said as much yesterday…as if to make the point, 'why bother me with it all?'"

"Yes, so long ago. But, he has a conscience…I saw that much in John Kahn yesterday."

"So, let's see just how big that conscience really is when we meet him, en famille. His wife will be there…at least to begin with. First the pictures, now the reality."

"Yes…yes!" Edith gave a little shiver. "I'm glad I'm not alone in this."

"No," Gerard laughed. "We saw to it that a few people now know of it."

"Tease."

"Yes, I know." He kissed her hand. " But you like me, just a little."

"More, much more."

The car swept up gracefully under a canopy and slowed to a stop. They had scarcely looked at their surroundings until Manuel guided them into the foyer of the building to be greeted by another member of the Kahn family's staff.

"The elevator will take you to Mr and Mrs Kahn's home. Miss Dayle is also here to meet you," Manuel smiled and took his leave.

"Thank you," Gerard called out to him as the doors closed and they set off smoothly and without a sound.

"The past and the present really meet, at last, Gerard." Edith spoke softly, in Dutch, as she watched the floor numbers count their progress. "Yesterday was on neutral ground…this is different."

They were ushered into a small room and had to wait for only a moment before the door was emphatically opened. A maid carrying a tray with glasses and an ice bucket followed John and Elbee into the room. She placed it on one of the side tables that separated each of the leather settees that lined the walls. It felt like the protagonists would face each other across a square.

"It's quiet, private and out of the way," John observed. "I'll introduce you to my family…some of my girls later. What can I offer you to drink? Wine maybe, or a beer for you Gerard?"

He seemed at ease and naturally hospitable and his guests were caught of guard.

"Wine…please," Edith said.

"Mine's a beer."

"I'll join Edith. So, Encarna…a bottle of white wine, from the cooler in the snug. And two Buds, please."

"Si, mister John."

"All you had to do was knock on my door," John said in good humour when they were alone. There was even the hint of a smile on his lips.

"I don't think so," Edith bridled at his command of the situation. "You said much the same yesterday."

John shrugged and gave her another smile. The lady's easily provoked he thought.

"We could have called your office I guess, and made an appointment about it all," Gerard added in support of her.

"Yeah, that too, I guess."

There was that smile again. He had a way of disarming you that Gerard had noticed before, in film clips of interviews given. He couldn't find an explanation for the success of John Kahn's winning ways that Edith would be comfortable in acknowledging. The easy way out would be to look no further than that the man had seen it all and experienced extremes in the human condition that few others could lay claim to. On top of all that he had won through commercial tussles to expand the reach of the Kahn business interests. Compared to all that had passed before, a meeting with distant, very distant or remote, relations was not an event to excite him into a reaction that betrayed a loss of self-control.

"You never came looking for us Kahn's, back in Amsterdam, and the Dekkers were complete unknowns." This is what he felt like saying but instead Gerard spoke what lay at the centre of his own tactic to expose John Kahn and his ways.

"I guess we came up with a better plan to draw attention to ourselves… with you and those interested in a story."

"Yes." John looked at each of them in turn with steady unblinking eyes. He waited.

"Well?" Edith said at length. For her, the skirmish, if it came, was taking a long time.

John sighed, more for effect than for being at a loss for words.

"Well?"

"Well, at last we've met!" Gerard volunteered without any intention of moving the conversation forward or to break, for Edith's sake at least, an awkward silence. Her plan of confronting John had not included it seemed the circling of the protagonists, like the hunter and its prey. His role was supportive, breaking the ring of silence that the Kahn's had worked to maintain and oblivious to the possibility that any record of events so long ago still remained. Edith's strategy was to address John Kahn and to put forward her own reasoned arguments for pursuing him and seeking some form of redress. He had formed his own ideas of a "price" to be levied, but it was for Edith to decide.

He had noticed the softening of her tone; it was no longer as strident or sure-footed as before; the theft had happened, there was no doubt of that and they carried the "proof" with them. Circumstantial stories abounded but even an embroidered story of past events could cause loss of face or credibility; the act of concealment up to the present day would tell against him and the family.

"Yeah, we've met…and after such a long time. It's taken quite a while for any expression of what you saw as a "break" between the two sides of the family."

"It was a fact!" Edith answered shrilly.

"Yes."

"And nothing was ever done about it."

"No…whatever "*it*" was."

"Well?"

"Well," John smiled again, "no-one came looking. So we all got on with our lives."

"Until you two butted in!" It was Elbee's first contribution.

"Well, quite!" Gerard riposted. "Far off family coming over…how inconvenient for you, I'm sure. Inconsiderate even, having them come over uninvited and interrupting a big day."

"Not so…," Elbee began but John cut him off in mid-sentence.

"No, not at all…it's temporarily embarrassing, nothing more. But unwelcome? I'm not so sure…and I've already told you, it's not unexpected."

"John, hold up there." Elbee glanced over to him.

"It's okay, buddy. We've been there," he said before turning to Gerard and Edith once more. "See? You plan a campaign and build in possible pinch points that you may expect along the way. In the follow up…the clean up phase where you consolidate your position, let's say, you expect the occasional booby traps."

"Like us?" Edith smiled for the first time.

"Kind of…only there are others that try to maim or kill you." John's voice trailed off as he thought of Delroy. They'd been together for so long it would take a while to get used to not hearing his voice or penetrating deep laugh.

"Or they disarm you?" Gerard's voice brought him back.

"Oh no, never that! There's plenty of fight left and we can sort this out."

"Finesse it you mean, for the media?" Gerard volunteered, "try to make it work in their eyes?"

"Make you look good in spite of it all?" Edith added.

John looked at her for a moment then turned to Elbee and spoke in a hardened tone. "What do you think? Fight it out and make a mess of the peace we've got to work in for a while until the Mayorship takes hold and delivers?"

"No."

"That's what I reckoned. I'll make it work and without these side-shows to distract me!"

"Right," Elbee answered in the clipped tone that he often resorted to in mimicking John's blunt assessment of where they were headed.

"There's important work to do," John said to Gerard before giving Edith an affirmative nod. "It's what I was voted in for, to get down and do it for the City."

"More important than family, even remote family? A non-existent crowd until we came along to wreck your party?" Edith had found her true combative voice at last. Gerard gave her a soft smile.

"Steady girl…Edith," John said and he held out his hand to her, palm up.

Edith looked at him in puzzlement. "What?"

"Shake my hand…believe we'll work it through."

"Lawyers and all?" she said in a disbelieving tone.

"Heck no!" John laughed and winked at Elbee. "I think I can do this on my own. It'll be the three of us, that's if you, Edith, don't mind reckoning with two Kahn's?"

"It's not a Kahn versus Dekker issue."

"Dekker versus Kahn, isn't that what you mean, Edith?" John asked.

"Right against wrong in all of its many meanings, or interpretations…" Gerard began.

"We've read some of your work. What you know of us are simply remote interpretations or views, conditioned by where you're coming from," Elbee cut him short.

"It's putting one record straight. So, it's the Kahn and Dekker family from the old country meeting up with the Kahn family in the new."

"Hardly a meeting, more a face off!" Elbee waved his hand dismissing Gerard's comments as if they were irritating flies buzzing around him.

"It's not a contest, more of putting the record straight…I told you. Then, we move on."

"Really? It's as simple as that, Gerard? You just walk in off the street and take up with us…with John Kahn and his family? John Kahn, recently elected Mayor of New York! The night was difficult enough to carry on with…after being shot and losing a buddy."

359

"Yeah, it sounds inconsiderate, even inconvenient when you put it like that." Gerard was surprised how quickly his English had improved in the few days they had been in the US.

"You come in and kick up dust on something you *say* happened...only the trail's gone cold on something you *claim* happened over a hundred years ago!"

"Yeah," Gerard shrugged with a mockingly apologetic smile on his face. He glanced only briefly at Edith but she seemed to indicate for him to have his say. "Yeah, I know how you Americans love history, at least when it suits your case...or your interests."

John Kahn had taken the weight off his feet; he lounged in his seat and simply listened. And, he watched. The weeks and months of working towards the goal of the City's Mayoralty had become a memory, or so it now seemed. His action in the street to disarm an assailant had been adjudged to be an act of self-defence. There had been too much TV coverage to show that his behaviour had been anything other than protecting his own. Premeditation lay elsewhere; his assailant would live, but in gaol for many years, that much the Attorney General had told him was the sentence the guy could expect, if he was convicted. Due process had still to be followed. The man had killed a buddy and wounded him; all that training with Delroy and this to show for it. He rubbed at the bulge on his arm as he reflected on the past few hours; it was some start to a new job.

Elbee could play out the role he liked best; the dog at the gate warning off all that sought to intrude into John Kahn's life. It was not a description of his friend that came to mind so often, but the business he had until recently been CEO of owed him and Joey, the firm as a unit, one heck of a lot. Sure, the fees could be eye-popping but paled to 'an incidental expense' when they were set against the commercial security afforded by patent rights and ring-fenced copyrights to drugs and medicines that only those in a well-off western country could afford not to challenge. And why? Most of all, the citizens of those countries could pay for them, directly or through taxes that shortened to the blink of an eye relief from suffering. He made the comparisons in circumstances just as quickly.

There had been so little time to really reflect on the success he had achieved but he knew that touching peoples conscience, showing others that in spite of his own wealth he could still see another's way of life, that insight had counted for him. Others saw that his military service had made him part of the normal human crowd; he chose the ranks rather than the officer's role in the military. The decision, made so many years earlier, had struck a chord and Joey's charity, 'Right Treatment' had only confirmed his credibility and what he had to say about helping others.

He didn't spell his views out quite so simply, but people could see John Kahn for what he was.

And now, here he was looking at a distant cousin with the same name, a hack with a large following and a smooth flowing pen of reasoned argument that could change the cosy corner he called home. To almost lose your life on the streets was one thing; to throw away a hard won reputation was something quite new to him and not to be conceded to. The family legacy could so easily become the rope to choke off any life in his ambitions to become an effective and credible Mayor. Against all odds, he had won a fair fight for office, confounded his critics and detractors; he had even managed to win a place in people's hearts by his instinctive reactions out there in the streets of his City. He had projected his goals and vision, won his place in the media spotlight without which he had no hope of any kind of political career. It had all come to matter one hell of a lot. Why have it screwed up now?

The appearance of Gerard and that doll, she was a pretty woman, no mistake, and the heightened media interest would now be on matters way out of field, way off the track he was headed out on. He'd have to hold Elbee back, rein him in and see how they would settle this family skirmish, for that was all it was; it should not be a big deal and they'd handle it, early and permanently. The trick was how? Family they may be, but whatever it was that lay between them now was not going to be settled in private, not the main thing. Oh no! Each would have to see a win:win outcome that satisfied each of them in turn.

John shook himself free of the thoughts crowding in.

"It's not hearsay, family gossip handed down with mother's milk; it's fact and it's documented. Your actions in Virginia, at a school for children...Mary Beth...the donations, all of it we know of...we've even got the pictures...all of it a cover for a guilty conscience."

Edith had found her voice and felt less inhibited by the luxurious surroundings of John Kahn's apartment. She walked over to the large window nearest to her and shivered, expressing a soft cry.

"Oh!"

"Come away, lievert" Gerard said as he moved to offer her support.

She took only one step back. "No. Without that *oh so distant* stake none of this would have been possible...no far off views from a lofty vantage point. The swollen purse containing a young family's inheritance gave a new beginning to another...*in the family*...that many could only dream of then. They were dreams that some held to their own dying day."

"Hard work helped," John Kahn observed flatly, moved at last to speak.

The pair of them had been cunning, clever and stealthy. They had picked their moment, perfectly. He had lost count of the times he'd been told to prepare for the unexpected; what was the bull-shit term? *"Expect the un-expected"*…yeah, that was it. He'd gotten the drift years ago and applied it to maximum effect, only these two had found a weakness in the defences; just like the gooks on bikes over in 'Nam all those years ago, you couldn't always figure them out. They'd killed plenty, through honest mistakes. That's what they told any inquisitor; but family blood then ran cold and the military's words of justification only served to recruit former allies away from the cause they had been sent to 'Nam to uphold.

Gerard again brought him out of his daydream.

"Sure, we're not here to deny any of that or to minimise the credit where it's due. But, please listen carefully…*credit*. The definition may be a sign of someone's probity, their good intentions…a sign that they had the money to repay a debt. Edith and I have not found the reason why the money was taken, but we know it was and have the receipt to prove it. The two sides of the family have never regained the closeness that existed before the events of so many years ago."

"There's nothing new in that…it happens all the time."

"What? Stealing from one side of the family?" Gerard stared at John. "Is Elbee talking for you, by the way?"

"Say what you have to say first, then we'll see what I have to tell."

"Credit is a debt…the money's still due." Gerard felt Edith shaking as she put into words what he had been thinking. "The passing of the years doesn't make the act, between one side of the family and another and in the circumstances of the time, one of extreme pain and loss, any less evil!"

"You're way outta line!" Elbee yelled. "You're waaay out of time even if there was anything to the story."

"You know there is Elbee," Gerard answered for them both and before Edith could reply. "Where we're coming from on this, the Statute of Limitations or whatever your legal mind wants to label it…all of that is meaningless. The story has immediacy, it's out there and it's running."

He had spoken for them both; Gerard knew that Edith's voice would be full of emotion having finally entered into the circle of a cousin that had perpetuated a wrong that she felt had been done to her side of the family.

"Yes, and there's only so many ways to put an end to it," Edith said firmly.

"Sounds like a threat coming our way, John."

"Heck no, Elbee," Gerard tried to sound reasonable. "We're just putting cards on the table, we're sure that's what you'd rather have." He looked from John to Elbee but saw no reaction on their faces to what he had to say. "We could lay them out for you…soon. Then, we talk some more."

Gerard moved to Edith's side and held her elbow, tight.

"Ger?"

"Come with me…no questions," he whispered through barely parted lips. She resisted only for a second the tug on her arm then followed him to the door. The handle did not move.

"Now what?" she said in Dutch. They turned as one.

John stood closeby. "I have it locked when I don't want a meeting disturbed."

'Handy, when I'm not quite in control of events,' Gerard could have added.

"We'd like to go, please. You have our hotel and contact details. We'll think it all over and wait for your call. Maybe we'll meet again, before we leave."

"When's that?" John said in a growl and without moving to open the door.

"Soon, in a day or two. We've got jobs to return to…at least I can file mine over the net."

"And the European Commission's Internal Affairs department won't let me stay away much longer, will they Ger? I've asked them."

There was a soft knock at the door and John pressed a button on the wall to release the catch.

"Come in!" he said, then went on, "stay a while longer? Have a drink at least for your trouble."

The drinks were set out on the table between them and John played the host and used the moment to let the heat go out of their dealings.

"Thank you," Edith felt inclined to say and looked at him.

"What interests you in all this?" she was asked in such a matter of fact tone of voice that Edith hesitated to collect her thoughts.

"Are we staying?" she asked Gerard.

"We'll have to see."

"What interests me is also of interest to your business…medicines. Only, the profit motive is missing, the sale at a high price to maintain a share value doesn't figure in my take on things, not one bit. The only gain, and it's more valuable than money…is life itself! For me any settlement we reach concerns the making available of medicines through an acceptable dispensing organisation in areas of the world where there's little or no money to break the hold of companies like PulcriMed."

John did not interrupt. He only turned to see what his lawyer man made of the scenario being so eloquently described. Elbee made notes, he scribbled quickly on a pad in an effort to take down almost verbatim what Edith had to say.

"We're talking Elbee. Let's simply listen up and leave the recording of things until we're settled on something." He took a few sips of wine and topped up his glass; he seemed at ease, disconcertingly so.

"What we're hearing of, John, is in effect a step towards undercutting a known and regulated market in medicines."

"Run for the benefit of big companies!" Edith interrupted.

"For a very good reason. Quality of the product so that the end-user, the patients, don't go dripping something into their bodies that'll hasten their end not bring them the life you...and PulcriMed, and others, want for them."

"I didn't see the people out on the pavement a few nights ago believing any of that."

"Easy Edith," Gerard asked her with a weak smile.

"No! I came here to say my piece."

"You're my guest," John observed quietly but with his gaze stilled upon her.

"I'm being honest...just honest, with you. I was asked for my opinion on how we might resolve the little difference between us, so here it is. We find a way to release medicines to the market, in chosen and the most needy areas...and its done with a hidden subsidy that Kahn money, your money, makes possible."

"Until other pharmaceutical companies object to the distortion of the market. It'll bring renewed regulation down on us, John." Elbee shook his head in an attempt to persuade him not to go down that route.

"It may have a totally different effect," Gerard told them, "it might shame others into joining with you. You'd be seen as a pioneer in breaking the hold of certain patent rights on medicines that can be produced locally and at a lesser costs because you, the patent holder, don't make a few easy bucks from it."

"It's never been easy!" John reacted. "You see it from the outside...I'm dealing with it, or I did until a few days ago...from the inside."

"Protecting shareholder and company asset values," Edith reminded him once more. "You can't escape that little weight on your shoulders, can you?"

"And what do you expect out of this, both of you...for you alone?"

"Nothing," Edith said quickly.

"Ha!"

"Yes Elbee, ha! Took you by surprise didn't it?" Edith gave a small smile. "It's not about what I get out of it...not one bit."

"What then? A moment of feeling good at shaking up a family you've never met before?"

"But I've known all about you for two or so years...followed every move that I could, I've collected the pictures...and I set them against the album of photos I have here." Edith opened her bag and held out the family pictures, collected in a small album for easy reference.

John took the folio and studied the pages quickly.

"Recognise any of them, John?" Gerard asked.

He could only nod.

"Yeah." They fell silent. "Come with me, please?" he said finally.

They all followed him through the echoing hallway with its sweeping staircase to the upper level and into the snug that also served as his office. A woman's voice called out to him, asking if they were done, but John answered he'd soon be with them.

"There," Edith cried out as they were shown three portraits. "There he is, Frederick Albert Kahn, just as I've seen him...in my grainy photo."

"Yeah, that's him Edith...the others are my grandfather and my father. You may not have seen them," he said without rancour. "The pictures tie up the bond...of a few years back...we can agree on that at least."

"Yes."

Edith stood by him and after looking at the portraits once more sighed deeply.

"Speak, tell me what's on your mind, Edith? Do that for all of us. Gerard's a help to you...I can see that, but this is between you and me."

"Yes." It was all she could say and Edith bit her lip. "I don't ask for much...I can't expect anything, much..." she managed to say at last. The first tears welled up in her eyes. Looking round she held a hand out to Gerard. "Ja!" she whispered on a sigh, lost it seemed for the right words to express all that she had felt over recent years.

"Want me to help?"

"No, John." She shook her head to clear defeatist thoughts. "I would like to receive the initial family stake, for my self...for my side of the family. That's all. It matters to me now...it won't quite undo what others did so long ago, but it will help heal a rift. That's what I hope for."

She stared at John Kahn for a moment.

"And?" he asked. Her moment's lapse of control left him unmoved.

"A cross subsidy...of the medicines you and your company decide can be eased from patent right controls. Putting a price on that...say two hundred million dollars?"

"Fantasy! Quadrupling the sum won't come even close to what you're asking John...PulcriMed...KPM to do!" Elbee clapped his hands together noisily to make his point. "The Kahn's don't owe you...you, in particular a cent, Edith!"

"Just a debt of honour...let's bring it down to more human levels. It's what John Kahn's candidacy in the elections for Mayor told everyone he stood for. I took some of the words I read of his speeches as referring to a sense of *'conscience'* to others...and to do the right thing."

"Did he?" Edith grasped Gerard's arm. "When was that? I never heard you speak of it."

"I had to keep something in reserve for the night of the press conference, lievert."

"He's right, Edith. Your cousin's right on that, keep something in reserve... I've done the same myself." John shook his head in a rueful admission of his own ways of doing things when the need really arose.

"Come in!" There had been a knock on the door. "Dayle!"

"Yes, I heard you had visitors..."

"Cousins...distant ones," John smiled at her.

His inflection on 'distant' did not escape Gerard's notice or the brief exchange of looks between father and a lovely young woman. The photographs he had seen had done full justice to her.

"We meet at last," Edith began in a friendly tone and held out her hand in a formal greeting.

"Yes...the circumstances could've been different. That's what I would have hoped for." Dayle looked at John as a forced smile faded quickly and her hand loosened its fleeting grasp. "Goin' to settle this quickly?"

"We're just talking, Dayle. Meet the other side of the family...Gerard, the Kahn's first visitor from the homeland."

"This is home, our home...it always has been."

She turned to look for Marie whom she thought had agreed to come in to be introduced to their visitors; evidently, her anger with Gerard's opportunism, and Edith's by association, had not fully subsided. Her mother's furious comments that they shouldn't even have been permitted to cross their threshold still rang in her ears.

"You've picked the wrong man...the wrong family to pick your fight with, Gerard." She could only nod in her perfunctory and dismissive greeting.

"It's not going anywhere near that far, Dayle...ease up."

"That's what you should be doin! Almost killed by that creep on the steps of the hall and then you have to face his attack!" She pointed angrily at Gerard.

John held a finger to his lips to quieten her fiery outburst but there was also the hint of a suppressed smile at his girl's all too predictable take on the situation and her own assessment of what the revelations meant for them, as the New York Kahn's.

"We talk and move on, Dayle."

"Sure...Gerard, sure! Where I come from...we talk things through quiet, before we go out and loud mouth the details...and on a very public night too!"

"Everyone seizes their moment..."

"Jeez...you pick the words! You don't really care what you say to us now, do you?"

"Dayle...Dayle?"

"No Pops! I'm no politician...I can tell them how it damn well is!"

"Go on...tell it." Gerard beat her father to making the same remark.

"It's a mean thing that you did! And, from what I know of it now I guess that man Nico...Nico Brant had something to do with it too! Fed you the information while he talked to us...talked to me!"

"Not so. Keep him out of this...for your own sake. Anyway, isn't this all supposed to be about your father?" Gerard said it all far too smoothly.

"Sure it is! Only we are family involved in this too! We all worked on his election, in his campaign to beat the Establishment in this place! And when we do...what? So called *family*, people like you two show up...or a man with a pistol that almost kills our man, our family's only man!"

She had moved to John's side as she yelled out her opinions and now clutched his arm.

"Don't say anymore girl...please?"

John whispered it, moved by the few words she had just spoken so lovingly and without reflecting on the deeper significance they might hold for him. It was her natural and deeply felt belief in her father that had found a voice. But, for him the reminder of being the only male in the Kahn line touched deeper.

Dayle would not desist and he held her tight as she railed against Gerard then Edith.

"Whatever it is you're both after...it's no deal! We've said our piece...I have. My mother's too upset about all that's gone on; she was all shook up before you arrived on the scene. Right now I don't feel like a member of any Kahn family than my own...I don't recognise what you've done to my father! Not a goddamn thing!"

"I love you," she whispered and gave John a kiss, clinging to his neck for a moment as she did so, then she left the room without a glance at either of the guests.

They all waited until the door was emphatically closed.

"Fiery! She's put the whole thing rather well, John," Elbee told him with a satisfied grin on his chubby face. "Don't you think so?"

John took his time and swilled his drink round in the glass he held in a tight grip. Gerard noticed for the first time the pallor of John Kahn's face; for the moment the vigour and willingness to argue the finer points of any case brought had deserted him.

"Let me think on it some more, that's all I'm goin' to say to you both right now." He stood up. "I'm feelin' a little weary...tell you the truth, but I've heard all you've had to say. It's not something that's goin' to gather dust, believe me if you can."

"And...and...?" Edith stammered.

"And we'll hear from them...that's the best way to tell of it. Right?" Gerard tried to explain.

"We've agreed nothing!"

"No Edith," John told her, "but we've spoken and you've made a case. A few days out of a hundred years or so isn't going to make it any harder for you to wait."

"We leave..."

"Yes, you do," John smiled. "But, we've seen each other and tossed the dice. We'll both have to think on it and see what the result finally is. I've heard your bid for closure...you'll have to wait on mine."

Mayoral Election
Postscript by Gerard Kahn© De Telegraaf : in New York

Over the past few days I've met, talked with and grown to know an exceptional man, a politician not to be underestimated. That he happens to be a namesake, a distant cousin, is an accident of birth. That over one hundred years separates the last contacts our side of the family had with what became our distant relations, in New York, is also an episode in history.

What everyone here has learnt is that he has made history; he won new friends and the grudging acceptance of political opponents that he is a man of his time, he found a place for his ideas in the hearts and minds of those that voted for him. He may also be seen as a reminder of how it once was in life, morals and politics. He won by force of argument and man, was he polite! He said things that made you think but there was usually a smile on his face, not as the outward sign of arrogant self-belief but founded upon what his team of helpers and office found to be the message out on the street.

Others will say he was the consummate opportunist; he saw a chance to make a vital difference in the City of New York and he took it. Ruthless advantage was taken of his opponent's weaknesses; he exploited old failings and the disillusionment with the political status quo. He broke the Republican and Democrat hold over the City, he said I'm brave enough to take you all on; I won't avoid the need for change and instead seek a comfortable political billet with one of the main political parties.

In short, it was a political mugging that will make everyone of all political persuasions look at cherished beliefs and practices and see how they can make a comeback. The margin of votes cast for him may not have been large but the shift in people's thinking and by local government has been seismic.

He took some personal hits along the way, and John Kahn almost ended his life on the streets he has grown up on and knows so well. John Kahn showed supreme depth of character and bravery on the night that an idiot with another political agenda took some shots at him. John Kahn showed true character, true grit if you like, in facing a problem. He also sought to protect a fellow citizen.

Whatever else was said on that night, and I was guilty of one personal revelation, he thought of others first. Whatever the millions of words spoken and written may have told everyone during the campaign, the guy's actions outdid all of them. He set an example; it's what true leaders are made of.

So – I, for one, hope that the burghers of New York, whoever they are and whatever their political persuasions may be, will give the man a chance to see what his achievement in winning office can truly deliver.

55

"You've caused something of a stir…helped to make a big night memorable for other reasons. Was it worth the wait, one side getting even with another side of the family?"

Edith looked at Gerard; her smile seemed to say, 'I told you so, our time to speak would soon be upon us'.

And all that he spoke in reply was, "I love you, lievert…I'm crazy about you."

He had spoken in Dutch but to the audience and interviewer his meaning was unmistakable.

"What did you say to her?" Michelene asked needlessly after the provocative opening to the interview; Gerard and Edith could only laugh.

"There was never any argument between our two sides of the family," Gerard told her instead of answering the whole question put to them. "There may have been anger and disbelief…in equal measure, but no arguments. People…"

"They just mellowed over the years, and got on with their lives," Edith finished for him as if on cue. "They weren't a party to it…not in Holland, not directly after so many years. But, families have their shared memories."

Gerard smiled at Edith and winked.

"You can guess the rest," he said turning once again to face Michelene. The interview held its own risks but they had already achieved so much on a deeply personal level from this '*family*' matter. "Do we have to spell it out for you, Michelene?"

"Our two sides of the family can, hopefully, be reconciled at last," Edith's voice now held a heavier Dutch intonation as she spoke; to make her point she took hold of Gerard's hand as it rested on her arm.

"Not so long ago," Michelene observed, "we had John Kahn in this studio for the mayoral debate. He was an assured, utterly committed and cool customer."

"We know...we saw the programme and we've seen all that you say of him demonstrated again...but in different circumstances," Gerard remarked coolly.

"Why bring all this up now? What is your objective, now? What do you get out of it all? You've exposed a wrong," the questions were quickly asked, to unsettle them, "so what? Many who may be watching this programme will say what's the deal? It's interesting but ancient history...let's move on!"

"For some, maybe," Edith observed calmly. She gave no sign of being intimidated by the direct line of questioning. "To me...to us both, it's never too late to right a wrong...never."

"And nobody died because of that particular wrong done."

"Whereas, the other night?" Michelene prompted.

"Ja!" Gerard delayed in giving his reply and stared back at Michelene for an instant. "Thank God, and his bravery, John Kahn was only wounded... people saw the inner man a little more clearly a few nights ago." Gerard continued under Edith's attentive gaze. "He also saw to it that a companion was cared for...until he was lost to him."

"You saw that, Gerard, and you still went on, to cause some embarrassment?"

"Yeah...my cousin's a man of many parts. I've learnt that over the time I've followed his progress and written what I've found out about him."

"Is that it? That's all you're telling us?"

"Yes...the events, past and present are only too distinct."

"I see," Michelene said doubtfully. "You've caused embarrassment, intruded on a moment of some civic importance to people here in the city... but real hurt? Have you hurt him in any way that counts? What do you say to that, Edith?"

"No, but we touched his pride, Michelene...and his vanity. All of it was built, to my reading of the story, on shifting sands."

"We pointed out a few moral principles that got lost along the way, or some hoped would go away over the years..."

"That all sounds very pious, Edith. But what do you realistically expect to get out of all this? Is it financial recompense in some way? First of all the man's shot at…a colleague on his staff is killed. Then Gerard, here, mugs him…they're John Kahn's words no less, said at the press conference! How many times are you going to take him on?"

"Not many. Whatever happens…the outcome is family business."

"But," and Michelene paused to make her point, "there's no harm in telling some of it, here…in this studio…just to bring some kind of pressure on the decision making process?"

Edith was held in view and Michelene directed all attention upon her as she spoke.

"A financial settlement was not the primary motive," Edith answered, "it was simply, if I can put it like that, 'simply'…it was simply obtaining some recognition of what happened. Gerard and I did not know if my initial hunch…that John Kahn was a relation and that it was true…we couldn't believe in it, at first. Nor did we hold on too tight to the hope, or idea, that the outcome might be the two *'estranged'* sides of the family getting together."

"I'd hardly say it was a *'welcome back'* that many here would expect from well-meaning people or they'd cross the street for, let alone an ocean."

"That's your take on it, Michelene," Gerard spoke out.

"Right," Edith nodded.

"And you're a journalist, Gerard…there's a story in it for you."

"If you're so touchy about it why ask us here?" Gerard met Michelene's look without a blink. "It just could be the same rationale as you asking us here to explain…only the story's in pictures. It beats the word…sometimes."

Edith intervened. She saw their purpose, appearing on TV, as giving a reasoned justification for their pursuit…her pursuit, of closure to a family rift.

"We didn't know if my hunch would have any supporting evidence. But, luckily for us and not others, historical records remained. They were hidden," she smiled, in spite of the tension the interview had created, "but we found them. It's amazing what our family lawyer found in an old Deed box. Lawyers keep old papers, and," she said still smiling happily, "are we glad for that! Dusty papers led us onto the path that finally ended here…in New York, a few nights ago!"

Edith sat back and turning to Gerard raised her eyebrows as if to tell him to carry on for her.

"We found confirmation of a simple truth that has haunted one side of the family more than the other…in Holland. And, over here…just over here the Kahn's came to arrangements with other family members.…in spite of the passage of time between events."

"Where?" Michelene interrupted.

"Here…right here in your country." Gerard too fell silent.

"Some would say, and I'm goin' to remind you of it Gerard…that whatever the difficulties, the two sides of the family dealt with all that came between them…at the time."

"Up to a point and for what suited them…suited them alone!" Edith told her in a shouted emotive exclamation. "The side of the family over here dealt with their own problem…over here! There were to be no reparations to the grieving family left behind…and who suffered the real loss!"

Gerard sat in silence and observed the two women exchange their opinions. He came to wondering how far should they go with this line of question and answers for nothing was really settled with John Kahn, nothing at all. They had talked of the issues brought out into the open, nothing more; there was no settlement, no closure to anything now laid open to public scrutiny. Go too far and the whole project, Edith's need for an end to this episode, would fail.

Michelene persisted. "It's naïve and plain wishful thinking to believe anything really positive can come out of this…isn't that so?"

"No…no!" Edith shook her head.

"All you will get, have got…are a few headlines, a TV interview or two…then what…so what?" she finished harshly.

Her guests looked at one another and Gerard touched Edith's arm in encouragement as he nodded in Michelene's direction. 'Go on, you answer that' his look seemed to encourage from her.

"If the family here and ours in Holland draw closer after all that has been said and done…then that's one result to be thankful for. What happened over a hundred years ago died with those immediately affected, but," she hesitated, "but principles endure, family blood ties persist in whatever weakened state they have been allowed to fall into."

"Beautifully put, lievert," Gerard smiled as Edith fell silent. "The man in high office is human…he has to sleep at night."

"It doesn't show…that he's lost much sleep over this," Michelene quipped.

"Maybe…but, he has a family and he has to look them all in the eyes," Gerard went on, continuing Edith's theme and performing a supporting role in their 'double act'. They both knew what had to be told, they had rehearsed it so many times as the papers and photos collected over the years were consulted. They acted as the spur in the charge at an important and well-known society figure, but someone who could, so easily, make them look small and of no consequence.

But, in the circumstances he had been pitched into so suddenly and to John Kahn's credit they had seen another side of the man.

"So," Michelene began in a tone of voice that betrayed her lack of continuing interest in them, "where's this all heading for?"

"Many could gain from a small humane gesture. Mayor Kahn, the company he keeps and the businesses he will continue to control...even from the fringe, can make a difference, he can still win something from this situation."

"I'm sorry," Michelene interrupted, "that's plain naïve."

"Is it?" Edith couldn't help smiling. Without too much effort and the even replies that she had given, with Gerard, they had both succeeded in frustrating this woman. "Tell me then what's so wrong in proportionate gains for each side?"

"Meaning what, exactly?"

"A selected group of needy people are helped by John Kahn's companies... they take another look at a few patent rights they guard so jealously...they help people in Third World countries get a few basic medicines at an affordable price. He gains by acknowledging in his own very distinct way that they have a right to life, or the chance of it. As for us, we, Gerard's family and mine? We get to heal a wound, to close the gap and work at making the bond closer again...it's hung by a thread, for years and years."

Edith's lips trembled. In spite of the cameras capturing every word, and expression on her face, as she confessed to all that had moved her in the quest for righting an ancient wrong she could not sustain her calm.

The monitors held images of them both, Edith and Gerard, in frame; they seemed an unlikely couple to have brought such repercussions to the hours following the press conference.

"Gerard?" Michelene pointed at him but it was a softer gesture than those she had used to make earlier intrusive questions tell upon her guests.

"I began the project thinking of it as a collaborative venture. I met once more a beautiful woman...she was a member of a distant family, our paths rarely...ever crossed. It has ended now with me falling in love with her...with Edith. She kept the flickering flame of family...or of unity between two sides, Edith kept that going."

They sat close to each other and Gerard now held his open hand out to Edith. She clasped it with a whispered call of his name, and lievert. Gerard felt it tremble and he shook it gently, in a sign of encouragement and belief in all that they experienced since their meeting so many months ago, in a canal-side restaurant, so far away.

"Will you lose your jobs over this?"

"Bernstein didn't, for exposing something far more serious, and immediate," Gerard laughed, but he also gave a shrug. "Who knows? How much can I know?" He said the last in his native tongue and Edith answered him.

"It won't matter a bit, Ger." She too spoke in Dutch and, as if alone with him, she leant over to kiss his cheek.

"Come for a coffee, Mr Mayor?" Gerard said looking directly at the camera held upon him. "Better still, come for a few Dutch beers...walk along Crooked Tree Water and see where it all started. Will you do that?"

"Yes, or exceed all expectations...come to our wedding."

Gerard looked surprised but laughed out. "Are you proposing to me... here?"

"And now?" Edith laughed back. " What do you think of it, Ger?"

"Ja!"

"Bring some good news to us, Mayor Kahn...or cousin John. Think about it, then do it. Release some of our family's money to help those far less fortunate than any of us are? Win your country some new friends or start a reconciliation process that goes far...far wider than the Kahns. Only," and Edith paused for a moment to control the renewed tremble on her lips, "only leave it to local people to dispense the charity you can bring. Let others do the good you talked of...and John? Help others to bring the gift of life or the chance for a new and better, healthier life."

The End

Printed in the United States
85488LV00003B/16-27/A

9 781434 311788